THE ODDITIES OF SOUTH COUNTY D. 1

RIA VON

TABLE OF CONTENTS

CHAPTER ONE

She sits on the sand. Immobile. Watchful. Alert.

Radiant moonlight blankets the sandy coast, casting deep pools of intense, stark shadows.

The continuous crash of the waves reverberates through the deep, vivid night.

Propped on her arms, she rests back, her dark dress tents her bent knees, an unnatural pool of darkness on the open sand.

A movement out in the black water catches her breathless attention.

She watches.

The full moon hangs low across the ethereal ocean. Ribbons of wispy clouds stream across the horizon.

The dark sea ruptures from the waves before her. Shedding liquid silver, a large shadow of a man emerges from the mysterious waters like a god. Racing towards her.

For a heart's beat, she notes her sea god's beautiful form. Her eyes rove up, gasping as their eyes connect. His sharp awareness pierces her soul.

A maelstrom of charged emotions explodes within, launching her into action.

Run! With a pivot, she shoots off in fear flight. Struggling against the loose sands, she races towards the dark houses, feeling unrelenting danger stalk her trail.

The dark, shadowy god races by seizing her hand.

Jolting with warp speed, she almost falls, scrambling to keep her feet. Then she's flying, strobing through dark voids and luminous moonlight.

He stops in a sea of black.

Jerking her back around, she slams into him.

His arms lock around her as they collide. Drinking the gasp from her lips, his tongue strikes to conquer, igniting a firestorm of desire.

Possessed, her arms snake up his wet back, latching on to his corded shoulders. Wild in her need, she jumps up, wrapping her legs around his hips, overbalancing him.

With his wicked, knowing laugh trapped between them, the world violently spins and slams to a halt.

Jolting up in bed, Jillian gasps in shock. Her eyes search the darkness, panting. Realization hits her hard. *A dream; that same damn taunting, maddening dream, again!*

With a haunting moan of thwarted raw desire, Jillian falls back into her pillows, her body humming in fiery need. The heavy lust fires a fever in her blood. The wanting driving her insane, mindless.

Oh, God! What is happening to me?

This is the third time she's had this dream. Always waking at the same point. Her body's reaction gets worse each time. She can feel the sheets and nightgown against her hyper-sensitive skin, drawing another moan from her. Flinging back the blankets, Jillian climbs out of bed. The swirling air from the ceiling fan ripples across her skin, followed by shudders of lust.

Her sea god haunts her mind.

Growling in helplessness, she snatches up her dark silk robe from the end of her big bed. She looks at the bedside clock: 4:27.

Same time!

She slips the robe on and ties the belt tight in irritation, tight like those hard arms. With a whimper, Jillian turns to the bathroom. Slapping on the light, the pink and green tile bathroom blooms from the darkness.

Flinching in distaste at the dated bathroom, Jillian moves to the shower, untying her belt. Dropping her robe, she steps into the stall, closing the glass door. The cold water hits her head. With a loud squeak, she quivers as sheets of icy cold water cascade across her fevered flesh, heating it more.

She moans on a whimper. Her hand glides to her thatch of dark curls, her fingers slipping between her lips, plunging into a sea of swirling desire. Her other hand braces on the wall as her sea god rises up from the waves. She strokes the tempo of the waves, crashing over and quickening to flight, bursting on collision, conflagration at accord.

Jillian hears her cries echo as she rests her head on the tile wall. The icy sheets frosting her back, she pushes herself back into the shower spray and stands until her teeth chatter. Her feverish blood barely cooling, the spears of ice bombard her rigid nipples and pimpled skin. Helplessly, instead of shielding them from the zaps to her nerves, her hands move to her nipples. Her fingers pinch hard, pulling in frustration, she cries out. Her turgid lips spasm as hot need aches deep in her womb, throbbing with the beat of the sea.

Shaking her head in defeat, Jillian wrenches off the water. Her pants turn to sobs as she crumples to the floor. Lust thunders through her veins, unquenched.

Sitting back on her heels, giving her button a few flicks, her orgasm hits her hard. Beating out her need for the only remedy for this insane fever: her sea god.

With a bitter laugh, she gets to her feet, grabs a towel for her hair, and climbs back in bed. Her teeth shill chattering, she wraps the towel around her head and falls back. Drawing the covers over her head, fearful of replaying the dream again.

Exhaustion and lethargy drag her back to sleep.

CHAPTER TWO

"Can you meet me for lunch?" Jillian Mathews inquired hopefully. Lost and frazzled, she was standing on the street corner, juggling papers and her purse and clutching her cell phone in one hand.

"Well, hello to you too." Amethyst James says smartly to her longtime friend. "Are you okay?" She asks curiously. "You don't sound so good."

"With one sentence, you decide that? Please." Jillian bumps into someone, jumbling the phone back to her ear. "The answer is no! Can you? I think I'm losing my mind if I haven't lost it already." She says desperately, walking down the sidewalk.

"Oh, in that case ... sure, where are you?" Amethyst asks carefully. "How about in an hour?"

"Yes! I'm downtown working on that permit." Scanning the corner, she sees the crossing light is about to change. She picks up speed, dodging around slower-moving pedestrians. "O'Malley's? Okay, I'll see..." Jillian collides with a man. Her papers fly up on impact, arms windmilling as the ground rushes up.

Strong hands reach out and grip her ribcage, drawing her back up quickly, and squashing her against the hard wall of flesh. Her heart echoes the rapid tempo deep in his chest.

Panting, desire slithers up her spine, quivering her skin. Jillian slowly raises her head to see who she ran into. The sun hangs over his shoulder, blinding her. His dark silhouette, that of her sea god, numbing her mind.

"Are you all right?" A grating nasal voice asks from above. "You're everywhere...your papers are everywhere." The grating nasal voice continues and turns to look down.

"Huh?" Shaking her head in shock, she sees the hunched-shouldered, sallow-skinned man.

4

He looks back at her, pushing up bulky black oversized glasses that magnify his eyes, then points down. "Look," the horrible, grating nasal voice snapped her out of her daze.

Her eyes follow his finger. Her papers settled on the sidewalk and street like used confetti. "Oh!" She lunges away to collect her papers, diving between two cars parked at the curb to rescue a couple of papers that dance onto the street of oncoming traffic.

The oncoming truck blows its horn, slamming on the brakes, screeching in protest as a hand yanks her back on the sidewalk.

"What is wrong with you? You could have been hit!" A deep, dark, masculine voice yells at her. "Here are your damn papers. Watch where you're going." A strong, powerful hand thrusts a stack of papers at her hands commandingly.

Slowly, she takes them, her eyes locked on that hand.

The gratingly nasal voice by her ear says. "Be careful, pretty lady." The beautiful hand pulls away, brushing lightly across her arm.

In slow motion, Jillian turns to follow that hand as desire thunders just below the surface, building pressure.

That hand is attached to the grating nasal voice. He slumps away, turning to lift that hand, then pushes up his huge glasses. With a snorting laugh and a big goofy grin, he trips as he moves on his way.

Jillian shakes her head in disbelief at the ache of longing that grows the further away he gets. "Oh My Everlasting Life! I want him badly. There is something seriously wrong with me." She says breathless. Frozen at the corner, the foot traffic flows around her fearfully. She looks at a passing man who is fairly good-looking for a suit. Nothing. Her eyes snap to the next man to step within her radar. Nothing. Sighing in relief, she finally hears Amethyst shouting through the phone. "Jillian, damn it!"

"What?" Jillian answers calmly in a fog, clearly lost even to herself, as she pulls her forgotten phone in her hand to her ear.

"O'Malley's, Now!" Amethyst's voice cracks across the air. "Jillian!"

5

"What?" Walking unaware, Jillian calmly asks.

"Where are you?" Amethyst demands. "Look around and tell me where you are."

Jillian turns around, looking for hints, a strange sensation, recognizing everything but unable to access it. Her eyes snag on the green street signs. Softly she says, "Main St. and 7th."

"Good. Walk to it. I'll meet you there." Amethyst breathes deeply.

"Okay, see you." Jillian closes her phone and slips it back into her purse. Haltingly, she walks down the sidewalk, stopping and starting erratically. Her fevered mind clashes between her sea god and the office geek; both crank up the heat on her fevered lust.

CHAPTER THREE

Noah Skylar Robinson slips down the alley and ducks behind the old downtown store. He leans back against the red bricks, breathing heavily. He takes off his glasses and closes his eyes, pinching the bridge of his nose. Banging his head back softly, he says to himself quietly. "Get a grip. Get a grip, man." He turns, bowing his head, one arm supporting against the wall with his glasses in his hand, and rubs the back of his neck.

What the hell was going on? Why was his reaction to that woman shockingly intense? He laughs, remembering her clothes today. It seems she's having very strong reactions to him as well. When he least expects it, he runs into her. It all started three weeks ago, the dream…

Swimming in the deep night the brilliant moon hovers, trailing him, lighting the shore.

He sees her sitting on the beach and heads for her, wanting, needing, and lusting. He feels the danger close, threatening her. He has to get to her before it does. It drives him, not just the insane desire but the need to protect. The knowledge that only he can keep her safe.

She sees him and watches, entranced as he comes out of the water, moving at full speed. Her gaze was a physical caress feeding his desire, giving him more power and speed to reach her. His eyes were hungry for her, wild need prowling within.

Her eyes widen in shock and fear, hops up and runs away from him.

Her flight angers him, fueling more speed. The hunter captures his prey, grabbing her hand he drags her along behind him. They race through the dark shadows and bright moonlight.

He stops suddenly in the deep sea of darkness. She flies by, and he jerks her back to him. She slams into him, his arms snap around

7

her, locked. His lips capture her gasp of surprise devouring her. Unable to stop, urgent wild need floods his mind and body.

She latches onto him, arms around his neck, her legs climb up to wrap his hips, just as wild and out of control.

Exuberant at her matching passion, he laughs. He spins, the world tilts and slams to a halt…

He wakes up at 4:27 a.m. at the brink of orgasm, covered in sweat, muscles quivering, charged for battle, gun in hand, with a knife in the other. The residue of danger triggered his survival instincts.

The first time, he had to patrol his entire apartment complex before he could let down his guard and put down his weapons. Now, after this third time, he flops back on his pillow and sighs. He puts his gun back on the nightstand, his knife back in its sheath between the headboard and mattress above his pillow.

After the dream, the need rides him hard.

He climbs out of bed and heads for a cold shower. Even with the icy spray frosting his body, his blood boils with desire for this woman. He works his rod, looking for relief, only it gets worse when he finds release. With each dream, the intensity increases the feeling of danger, the need for her protection, the lust. The entire business was very distracting. Add to that, physically running into her while working and being unable to do anything about it.

He was heading towards disaster.

He slipped character with her, not that she noticed, but anyone watching would have seen. He had to take action before he had another slip.

He tips his head back, looking up blindly at the cloudless sky, searching for control, tamping down the need to go to her. He had a job to do, and today, it was temp work at the permit office. He hoped he didn't run into her again today. Like attracting magnets, drawn to each other whenever near.

Just thinking about her brought the desire back in full force, riding him hard.

Unable to stop himself, he recalls their most recent collision. Shuffling along with the crowd she appears before him suddenly.

Her head down, dodging pedestrians, talking on the phone, she enters the crosswalk and slams into him. Clutched to her chest, her papers fly up out of the folder and flutter down around them. She bounces off him, falling backward, arms flapping.

In that flash, before he grabs her back, he notices her insane outfit: a weird pink and white top covered with an ugly green blazer, gold leggings wrapping her lower half, and her feet shod in black heels. Her hair was shocking with wild curls and a curious flat section.

Somehow, her appearance reflected his internal chaos.

They were both a total mess.

As soon as his hands touched her back, the desire flashed hot and strong. Unable to stop, he drew her fast to his body, clutching her snugly, contact of their bodies weakening his resolve.

Looking down at her plastered to his chest, he instantly recognized the danger. If he wasn't careful, he would mount her here on the street. He held onto his slipping control, Not confident of her will to stop him, and asked. "Are you okay?" In the most obnoxious nasal whine he could manage. "You're everywhere…your papers are everywhere." He gave himself a mental slap but was satisfied with his recovery.

She looked up at him, her stunning grey eyes smoky, masking the raging fires within. He starts to sweat, his heart slamming into his chest.

Confusion fogged her mind. "Huh?"

He had to separate them before it was too late. With an iron will, he peeled his hand off her body and, with a shaky hand, pointed down at the papers littering the street and sidewalk. "Look!"

When she finally broke eye contact and looked down, he closed his eyes and took a deep breath.

"Oh!" She realized what she was looking at and lunged into traffic to grab the two papers.

The horn and screeching tires whipped him around from collecting her papers off the sidewalk. He grabbed her out of the way of the oncoming truck. His heart nearly stopped, he yelled. "What is wrong with you? You could have been hit." He slapped his stack of papers into her hands. "Here are your damn papers. Watch where you're going!"

He didn't know why he did it, but for whatever reason, he was pleased he did it. He slipped the emerald ring onto her finger. Maybe it was a declaration or staking his claim.

She didn't even notice when he did it. That would give her something to puzzle about as if she needed anything else.

It was really getting ridiculous. Was she questioning her taste in men?

Next to her ear, he whined, "Be careful, pretty lady." With a monumental will, he forced his hand away, brushing her arm in his passing.

It was a close call when she followed the connection of his hand up to his face. If she had been quicker, she would have caught him.

The need for her pulled at his body. He slumps away, fighting the physical attraction. His hand burns from contact with her. To distract his hand, he pushes up his glasses and snorts at his state of mind. Looking back at her, he waves with a big goofy grin at her state. At least he wasn't the only one, and trips.

She stood there shell-shocked, staring at him aghast. Slowly, she brings her phone up to her ear. She starts moving in his direction, then stops, unsure. Looking around, confused. She looks up at the street signs.

He turns away when she continues moving down the sidewalk away from him.

He had to get a grip on himself. He didn't have the luxury to pursue her right now. He had to do the job, though it might kill him. He straightens up, shakes his body, and puts his glasses back on. Smooths down his hair and takes a big deep breath.

Closing his eyes, he steps back into character and slumps down the alley towards the permit office. He stops by the deli and gets a bag of lunch. He passes a window and catches his reflection.

The big short sleeved white dress shirt and cheap clip-on tie complete with bulging pocket protect dragging it down. The baggy shirt cinched in with his extra-large polyester pants gathered under his cheap belt. The whites of his socks flashed bright between his high waters and ugly shoes. He pulls out his black comb from his shirt pocket and tidies his hair on the center part. Longer in the front, he combs it behind his ears. He adjusts his glasses, his eyes huge behind the magnification. With a shudder, he returns his comb and walks away.

Poor girl, she wants this. What must she think?

Chapter Four

"Jillian!" Amethyst jogs up, hardly winded. She slips her arm through Jillian's and escorts her to the pub a block away on the main square of the historic downtown area that surrounds the large, beautiful wooded park.

As soon as they cross into the gloom of the pub, they hear O'Malley. "Me bonny lasses, what ya have? We're celebrating my nephew's arrival from across the pond." He beams at them proudly.

"Give us a couple of shots and pints." Amethyst smiles sweetly. "Welcome to your nephew. We look forward to meeting him."

"Go sit yourselves down then. They'll be right up."

"Thanks, O'Malley." Amethyst steers Jillian to a back booth tucked out of the way. Pushing her in on one side, she slides in on the other. "Okay, what happened when we were on the phone?" Amethyst's golden amber eyes hone in on Jillian's cloudy grey eyes.

Jillian quivers on the bench, trying to pull herself together. After a deep inhale, she says, "I ran into a man."

"What, an old flame? An enemy?" Confused, Amethyst shakes her head. "What did he do; hurt you, frighten you?"

"No!" Jillian shakes her head, shrugging her shoulders as lost as her friend. "Nobody, nothing, not exactly."

"What do you mean not exactly?" Amethyst pounces on that answer. "Who was it?"

"I don't know who he was, just some random office geek with stooped shoulders, sallow skin, nasal voice, snorting laugh, and big eyeglasses. And I want him so bad." Jillian says calmly. "I'm going insane."

O'Malley delivers their drinks and slips away.

Jillian picks up her shot and taps it against Amethyst's, then lifts it up and says, "To my god of the sea." She shoots it back and slams the glass down. Shuddering, the raw alcohol feeds her fire. "I hope to find soon." She whispers, "Before I lose my mind." Big tears fall rapidly, splashing on the table.

Amethyst watches her silently, picks up her shot lifting it high. "To a wanted sea god and sanity." She flips her glass back and slams the glass down on the table with a sharp crack. Heads around the dark wood-paneled pub glance over. Amethyst holds up two fingers and looks over at O'Malley, who nods. "An admirable toast, but why a sea god? We all strive for sanity, though it seems to become more elusive the harder we chase it."

Jillian waits with her head bowed.

O'Malley puts the pair of shot glasses on the table, pauses a moment, and then places his big, meaty paw on Jillian's shoulder.

She nods in thanks but remains silent as large tears rain down.

He tosses his dry bar towel on the table before her and walks away.

Amethyst says, "You may want to bring us the bottle, O'Malley, if you don't want to keep pacing back and forth." She turns to Jillian, "Am I right?"

Jillian nods, her tears puddle the cloth before her while tremors wrack her body.

"Right, ya are, lass." O'Malley agrees and returns with the bottle of amber liquid.

"Thanks," Amethyst says as he walks back to the bar. She pushes the full shot towards Jillian. "What about the office geek?"

Jillian shudders violently and picks up her shot. "To random paths colliding." She tips back her head, emptying her glass, and slams it on the table. She stares up at the ceiling.

Silently, Amethyst knocks back her shot, watching Jillian's tears run across her temples and into the wild confusion of her dark brown curly hair. Clearing her throat, Amethyst asks, "Is this a new look for you?"

"What?" Jillian tips her head down to look at her friend; confusion stamps her eyes. "What?"

"I said, is this a new look?" Amethyst smirks waving her hand at Jillian overall. "Did you dress yourself this morning?"

"Of course, I dressed myself." Jillian wipes her face. "But I overslept and had to rush." She remembers throwing on what was close to her hand, her heavy hair blocking her sight.

"Ahh…I understand, late and lost in the dark." Amethyst gives a throaty laugh. "Have you looked in the mirror at all?"

Jillian swallows a healthy gulp of her pint, looking at Amethyst in fearful surprise. Her hand goes up to her head, feeling her large, lumpy cloud of dark curls. Her eyes bug out, and her hand stops at a flat patch on the side of her head. Jillian closes her eyes, lowering her hand. Her head drops, her eyes open to inspect her clothes fearfully. Over her hot pink pig pajama top, she wears an olive-green blazer, below shiny gold leggings hug her tight. Jillian closes her eyes and whispers, "It was dark, and I pulled from my castoff pile." She shakes her head. "How bad is it really?"

Amethyst belts out a bawdy laugh, suppressing it quickly. "You really don't want to know." She picks up the bottle and fills all four shot glasses, pushing one across the table.

Jillian nods. "It's probably best if I don't." She picks up her glass. "Here's to fashion. I hope I haven't angered any of the fashion gods." She flings her whiskey down her throat.

Amethyst laughs and follows suit. "Okay, tell me."

Jillian sighs deeply, shaking her head. "I've had the dream again, and it's getting worse. Goddess, I really feel like a wild beast in heat." She rakes her fingers across her head, halting abruptly halfway. She tries to pull her hands out, but her curls lock on her fingers.

"No wonder the office geek caught your eye." Amethyst eyes Jillian's head curiously. "Have you noticed that you are running into a lot of men, and you want them all, too?"

Jillian tugs, trying to release her fingers. "Yes, this makes the third." She tries to push her hands deeper. The curls tighten around her fingers, locking them to her head. Snorting, she rests her elbows on the table as if holding her head in her hands.

"Who were they again?" Amethyst tilts her head, keeping firm control of herself while watching her friend. Unconsciously, she brushes through her tawny golden locks. They settle back into place perfectly, brushing her shoulders.

Jillian slides over on her booth seat to get closer to a full shot. "Carpenter and an exterminator." She leans across the table for the shot glass, her lips reaching around, gripping it. She throws her head back, shot glass wrapped in her lips.

"Party tricks this early?" Jackson Andrews says as he slides in beside Jillian, sliding his hand along the back of the booth behind her. "Where's my invite?" His arm glides across the back of the booth, moving in close to her.

Jillian scowls at him and spreads her elbows wide setting her territory, her fingers still locked to her scalp. Leaning down, she drops the shot glass from her mouth. "We didn't send one."

"Good thing I saw you two on the street then," Jackson says cheerfully, smiling over at Amethyst. "Is that one for me?" His hand reaches for the full shot glass.

Amethyst lifts the last full shot glass to her lips and tips it in tauntingly. "No, sugar, and it's a private party. Leave your gifts by the door." Her eyes gleam with suppressed laughter. "Maybe next time." She says doubtfully.

Jackson turns to Jillian, hopefully, his eyes imploring.

Jillian sits up straight, spreading her arms wide, staring silently, waiting for this physical retreat, her demand quite clear for all her stillness.

"All right, I will gracefully retreat for now," Jackson says, amused as he withdraws from the booth. "Look for me, ladies. We shall engage again."

Jillian flaps her winged arms. "Whatever."

Amethyst bursts out laughing, gasping for breath, holding her sides, wheezing.

Jillian stares at her strangely. "What?"

Amethyst falls over sideways on her bench, choking on her laughter.

"I really don't know what you're going on about," Jillian says, waving her elbows for emphasis.

Amethyst catches the gestures as she pulls herself upright. Peals of laughter ripples around them. Gasping for breath, she says accusingly, "Your fingers are caught." She wipes the tears from her eyes.

I don't know what you are talking about." Jillian says innocently.

Snorting, Amethyst says, "I want to see you sashay across the pub with your fingers tangled in your hair; Va-Va-Voom, Big Boy." She laughs harder.

Jillian cracks, howling with laughter, laying her head down on the table, her arms winged out, "Help!" Laughing so hard she can barely get out of the desperate plea.

Amethyst taps her own head on the table a few times, fighting her quaking laughter. Gasping for air, she looks up at Jillian's dilemma. It snaps her control, bursting out giggles. "Okay, okay. We'll get this. Breathe."

They both take a deep breath and then let it out, slow and controlled.

Jillian moans, "What have I become? How can this happen? Look at me. How did I come to this!?" She shakes her head in wonder, giggles, peals out, and grows strength.

Amethyst is just as confounded and amused. Laughing while she pours out the next four shots. "I must fortify myself before battling your wild hair to retrieve your fair hands." Attempting to control her laughter, she scans the pub.

Everyone watches them.

Amusing her beyond silence, she lifts her glass to the pub at large and cries, "To Valiant Quests."

The pub patrons, nearly a half dozen, all cheer, raising a glass.

Laughing harder, she slams back her shot. Amethyst reaches out and grabs one hand, assessing the problem. "You've caught your rings. Let's see if we can get those off your fingers." She works quickly, releasing one hand and then moving onto the other.

Jillian feels her hair with her newly freed hand, buried deep in a nest of tangles, the hand shape of her rings taunt.

Amethyst frees her other hand, then sits back and laughs, wiping at her eyes.

Jillian shakes her head, her rings tinkle together. Then shakes her head harder. Nothing flies free. She picks up her beer and chugs it down her throat. She sways on the bench.

"Jillian, you need food." Amethyst states, grabbing the menu to scan quickly. "How about a meat pie?"

Wiping her mouth up her arm, Jillian nods, picking up her shot glass and tossing her drink down her throat, uncaring.

Amethyst moves the bottle out of her reach and calls out. "O'Malley, two meat pies, please." She turns back to Jillian. "Okay, what's going on with you?"

Nodding drunkenly, Jillian starts quietly. "I've already told you about my dream. I've already told you what happens after the dream. The thing that worries me is that it's getting worse, more intense…raw." She shudders and lowers her voice. "I can't find release from it; no surcease." She takes a sip of her ale. "We tried to find me a man, and they all repulsed me, yet the fever is thrumming in my veins. The only ones that didn't, I collided with at random. And have no way to find them again.

Amethyst holds up her finger wisely. "We can scope out the location of these accidents. Maybe get lucky…or at least you will." Chuckling, she flips her hair back, which swings back in perfect order. "Are you eating? Sleeping regularly?"

"No, to both." Jillian pokes at a ring dangling by her ear. "I'm afraid to sleep." With a vicious yank, she pulls the ring out with a sizable hairball knotted around a large emerald. She stares at it, confused. "Did you lose this when you were in there?"

"What? No, it was on your left ring finger." Amethyst points at her left hand.

"Huh? I've never seen it before. It's pretty." She slides it on her left ring finger and pulls off the hair.

Amethyst squeaks wide-eyed, pointing at the ring. "That's an engagement ring!" She accuses.

"Well, I don't know how I got it." Jillian stares at it, pulling the last of the snarl from her ring.

Amethyst laughs. "Wouldn't it be funny if your snorting geek placed it?"

"Yeah, funny." Jillian pants softly, thinking about this morning's collision. Fanning herself, she looks over at Amethyst. "So when can we start casing those scenes? I'm desperate, here." She pokes at another dangling ring, batting it around. "This just can't go on. I'm mindless, forgetful, edgy, and maintaining a painful arousal."

"I didn't think women could suffer like that. Can't you just take care of it yourself?"

"Oh, we can, and I do!" She looks off in the distance. "Carnal thoughts ruling your mind, a deep ache untouched by therapy. A wild, hungry beast was restless to be free. Oh, goddess, you've got to help me." Jillian implores her best friend.

"Sure, Sugar. Let's eat first." Amethyst says as O'Malley delivers their food. He also places two tall glasses of water. "Thanks, Sugar."

After they finish eating, Amethyst gets up and moves to the bar with the bottle of whiskey. "O'Malley, hold on to this for us. I'm sure we'll be back to finish it off later."

"Is Jillian okay? She's not looking so good today." O'Malley rubs his chin, concerned.

"She's had better days." Amethyst looks over at Jillian. "I'm not sure what's really going on, but I'm working on it."

In the booth, Jillian shakes her head. Her long ringlets fly out around her head flashes of gold and silver twinkle in the dim light.

Amethyst chuckles softly. "She's such a mess. Did you notice she got her hands caught in her hair, both of them? Flapping her elbows around just about did me in."

They watch Jillian climb out of the booth. She teeters drunkenly to her feet, clutching the table to find her balance. Slowly, she straightens up, pausing to find her composure, adjusts her green blazer, and then heads to the restroom.

"She is a character, our lassie." O'Malley chuckles. "Let me know if I can help."

"Will do, Sugar. You know you're our go-to guy." Amethyst heads over to the booth, collects Jillian's purse and papers, then follows her to the restroom. She opens the door and finds Jillian staring in shock at the mirror. "I told you it was better not to know." She chuckles at her friend's reaction.

"Oh, Gulping Guppies! I went out in public like this?" Jillian gasps, horrified. "No wonder I was getting those strange looks. I'm glad I didn't make it to the permit office. Who could take me seriously dressed like this?" She pokes at a clump of hair that sparkles.

Amethyst steps over, placing Jillian's purse and papers on the counter. She opens her purse and pulls out a large, toothed comb. "Well, we can do something about this mess, but we'll have to hit the store to fix your outfit." She looks down at Jillian's feet. "At least you put on the same shoes. That's a bonus. Though those heels with the gold leggings are a bit much."

Jillian looks down at her feet encased in fancy black patent pumps and moans. "You know my life was so normal not that long ago. What happened?"

"That's a good point. Let's start at the beginning. When did the dreams start?" Amethyst extracts a ring from a nest of curls and places it on the counter. "Which came first: the dream or the first collision with the carpenter?" She continues to work the comb through the tangled curls.

Jillian sways back and forth, eyes focused on the past. "It's been almost three weeks, I think. The dream came first. The next morning, I went for a run to work off some tension. I took my usual path around my neighborhood. I was near the end when I ran into him. I looked back for some reason, and when I turned around, he was rounding a tall hedge. You know, the one just across the street from my place, that old three-story." Jillian unconsciously combs her fingers through her tangles.

Amethyst nods. "I love that house. Did it finally sell? It's a shame it got into such bad shape."

Jillian nods. "I think about a month ago. I'm not sure if anyone lives there yet. It still looks empty."

"We can stop by and see if the carpenter is still working. Or maybe get his info." Amethyst drops another ring on the counter. Runs the comb smoothly through Jillian's hair and steps behind to work on the back. Watching her friend's face, she asks softly. "What happened after you ran into the guy? He came around the hedge..."

Jillian's eyes glaze over, staring into the mirror, her cheeks glow rosy. "...and slam full body into him. He drops everything on impact. I bounce off. His hot, hard arms catch me as I start to fall and pull me back hard and fast. I grab his shoulders, broad, thick, strong..." she starts to pant and whispers. "He's hot and sweaty...smells of sawdust and fresh cut grass. My nose is against his massive chest. His hands sear my back...fire burns every inch of my skin where we touch."

Amethyst watches Jillian in the mirror, her eyes passion fogged, her skin glowing with desire.

"I look up at him. The sun hangs just over his shoulder. He's in shadow. I can't see his face. He looks down at me and chuckles. "Are you okay?" He asks, his voice warm, deep velvet stroking along..." Jillian sways, closing her eyes, and a shiver wracks her frame. Panting faster, she continues. "My mind is mush. Weird sounds slip past my lips as if parts of each word are missing. I don't even know what I was trying to say. I give up and nod stupidly. He steps away, picks up what he dropped, and says, "It was nice running into you." Chuckling, he climbs into his truck at the curb and drives off. I don't know how long I stood there staring after him, but finally, I stumbled home, walking along like I was drunk." Jillian shakes her head and opens her dilated eyes, swaying on her feet, and looks directly at Amethyst.

"Holy Cats, girl!" Amethyst starts combing again. "I'm getting hot just hearing about it." After a moment, she asks, "That bad?"

Jillian laughs dryly. "Not even close. Multiply that by ten, and you're getting close. But that was only the first time. Every time I have that dream, it gets stronger, a lot stronger." Jillian shudders. "The second dream happens a week later. I wake up at the same point, at the same time. My need is twice as bad, and my climax is twice as quick and twice as unfulfilling. I just want more. I feel like it's like drinking salt water in the desert." Jillian starts to quiver. "That morning, I ran into the exterminator at the permit office. I slip into the archives, searching for information on that request from Pembleton, and fall over the exterminator crouched down on the floor. Somehow, he caught me inches from the ground, like a deep dip. He straightens up, dragging me up with him until I'm on my feet. I look up at him and stare in shock. His greasy, lanky hair hangs in his face. All I can really see is that he hasn't shaved in a couple of days. All I can smell are the fumes of pesticides. But his strong hands burn my arms, pouring fire in my blood. All I want to do is rip open his dirty coveralls and climb in. He had narrow shoulders, a sunken chest, all arms and legs skinny. But he was tall." Jillian rubs her face in confusion. "I just don't understand. This is driving me insane."

Amethyst runs the comb smoothly through Jillian's hair, entranced. "Does he say anything?" She asks breathlessly.

Jillian snorts. "Looky what Ize caught me. Might I keep ya fer a pet?" Then he brays, I swear it sounded just like a donkey. There I am, frozen in place, staring. He leans in close and says, "I'll stroke ya real nice and gentle like." My mouth starts to water, my body clenches as his minty breath caresses my lips. I can almost taste it. My body aches empty, but suddenly I'm so wet. He leans back and says, "Naw, I'll let ya go fer now. Ize likes me sum huntin', so I'lls just catch ya again." He brays again and almost makes me come. He picks up his spray tank and wand, brushing by me whistling. His hand strokes down my hair and then along my spine as he ambles away."

21

The comb hangs suspended above Jillian's hair. Amethyst stares in shock. "What?"

"I know, right?" Jillian nods, then shakes her head. "I've got a serious problem." She turns to her friend and notices her highly aroused state, and chuckles. "I hope whatever I have isn't contagious."

Amethyst snaps out of her daze and looks in the mirror. Laughing, she says, "Wouldn't that be something, the CDC called in and quarantine for rabid desire." She shakes her head. "No, no reoccurring dreams here. I think the rest of us are safe." Amethyst draws a deep breath and lets it go. "Next, we need to fix your outfit. Collect your rings." She reaches over for the stack of messy papers. Finding a folder in the middle of the stack, she pulls it out, opens it, and sticks the papers inside.

Jillian slowly turns back to the counter, adroitly putting her rings back on her fingers. The beautiful emerald winking at her. She stares at it in wonder. "It wasn't there this morning." Blindly, she reaches for her purse with her other hand.

Amethyst gently nudges Jillian towards the door to get her moving. "Maybe we better have one more for the road." She suggests noticing Jillian's quaking body and high sheen. "it might just calm you down some or just deaden the nerves."

Still panting, Jillian nods, her eyes still glued to her new ring. "Yes, I think that might be best."

They make their way to the bar. Amethyst calls out. "O'Malley set us up with one for the road. We need to fortify."

O'Malley raises his brows in question as he fills two tumblers with two fingers each and slides them over. "It's pretty early in the day for this much support. What are you lasses planning?"

Amethyst smiles over at Jillian. "First, a fashion redo. Then we're going hunting."

Jillian closes her eyes and laughs, shaking her head. "We're out to catch us, a rare breed." Laughs harder, picks up her glass, and shoots it back.

CHAPTER FIVE

He enters the county office building and approaches the main desk.

The two guards snicker at each other, watching his arrival. Choking back a laugh, the heavier guard asks, "Can I help you?"

In his grating nasal voice, Toby says, "Ah, yes, ah hem…" Pulling up his pants, he continues, "I'm here to work. They need some help, so they called me in." He nods with importance.

"Really, they called you in." Holding back a laugh, the bulky guard nods encouragingly.

"Yes, the lady on the phone was quite adamant. She seems to need me. Who can refuse a lady in need?" Suave is difficult in this persona, but by the reaction of the guards, he pulls it off.

Their eyes grow huge like they swallowed their tongues, nodding.

The smaller of the pair steps up, coughing, and pats him on the hump of his spine. "Yeah, man, always got to meet the needs of the ladies."

Toby Robins nods and snorts in manly agreement.

The heavy guard moans, holding his side, his face ruddy. "Well, you don't want to keep the ladies waiting when they are in need." He gasps. "Just follow the signs on the left corridor until you find H.R. They can tell you where your services are needed most."

The other guard warned. "Go gentle on them. Don't want to overwhelm; otherwise, they'll be dropping at your feet."

Toby nods sagely, pushing up his glasses. "Yes, I should tone it down. You know how distracting a stud is with the fillies." He adjusts his clip-on, his tight collar accenting his bobbing Adam's apple. "Thanks for the warning." He gives them his goofy grin, slaps the counter, and slumps away. As soon as he rounds the corner, the guards break down. Their laughter follows him down the hall. He slows his pace, looking around as if lost. H.R. is just ahead. He hears a phone ring in the office. He turns around slowly, looking around, waiting for his cue. He listens closely.

From the office, he hears "H.R.," a woman answers. A pause, and then she says, "Seriously? No, not yet…"

Noah, as Toby, turns and slumps into the office.

The woman at the front desk looks up and squeaks, the phone suspended in her hand. Silently, eyes huge, she nods.

Noah wheezes in a breath and grins. "I heard you want me."

The phone drops loudly to the desk, and the woman sucks in a breath and starts to choke.

"Oh, my, pretty lady, are you alright?" Toby slumps around the desk quickly. Pats her on the back, briskly holding her arm to keep her from collapsing. The rapid tattoo on her back barely made contact.

Like a rapidly spreading virus, the rest of the office fills with the sounds of a coughing outbreak. "Please, pretty lady, sit down. My goodness, no wonder you need me."

From the desk, the phone emits gasping laughter, faintly heard echoing down the hall.

A door opens in the back of the office. "What's the meaning of this?" A neutral, monotone voice cuts through the coughing.

Noah, as Toby ignores the voice, remains focused on the woman. His grating nasal voice beseeches. "Please, dear, please breath." Her color starts to worry him, turning from deep purple to blue. "Please, dear, don't fall at my feet," Toby whines, an agitated slumping flutter around her, dipping down to check the condition of her bowed body. Inspiration strikes, and his body straightens a bit. Looking around, he asks desperately, "Water?"

At the closest desk, a pretty woman sits, her hand covering her mouth, eyes huge. Her quivering arm raises up and points to the far wall.

24

Toby turns in that direction in a slumping run that looks slow motion. He reaches the water cooler. Deliberately, he pulls a cone cup from the dispenser, carefully positions it under the spigot, and presses the button. Chilled water flows out into the cup and out the bottom, along his pant leg, into his shoe. He bends to the side, shakes his head releasing the button. He whispers to himself. "Oh, come on, really?" He twists around, holding the paper cone up, looking through the hole in the bottom at the convulsing women, reassuring them. "Hold on dear, don't know my own strength." He turns back towards the water cooler, tossing the paper cone over his shoulder. It floats into a trashcan by the closest desk.

A whisper of surprised awe swirls in the air.

Out of the corner of his eye, he sees a more masculine, fastidious reflection of his current character, pocket protector and all. His twin is wearing a bemused expression, watching him closely as he retrieves another cone. With the support of the depressed spigot, Toby lifts his soggy leg and shakes it vigorously, reminiscent of a dog.

Once the cup is full, he returns to the poor woman in his slumping slow-motion run, his squishing shoe every other step without spilling a drop until he catches the corner of her desk, spinning him around to land sitting in front of her. She cowers back, gasping in surprise. Her color is getting better, but not great. His hand snaps out, catching the water that escaped the cup. He hands her the paper cone.

Automatically, she accepts it. Frozen in shock, she just stares.

Toby dips his fingers into his cupped palm and flicks the water into her face. In a grating nasal whine, Toby implores. "Breathe." The gentle droplets of water make contact.

The woman snaps out of her daze. Her body slams back into her chair. Air loudly fills her lungs. Then exits too quickly. Almost panting now, the woman continues to stare at him in wonder.

Toby leans forward, guiding the cup to her lips. "Dear, please drink. Calm yourself."

She gulps down the water.

Toby takes the paper cup from her nerveless fingers and tosses it behind him. It arrows into the can by the entrance.

Echoes of awe whisper around them.

Watching the woman carefully, Toby notices her foggy eyes losing focus. He shakes his head sadly, grips her neck, and pushes it down between her knees. He slides off the desk, hunching down next to her, his head bobs, resembling a vulture. "Dear lady, you must calm your raging heart." Still cupping water in his palm, he rubs his hands together and places one on her neck and the other pats her face gently. "I'm so sorry...I often forget how potent I am. I will try to tone down my impact on others." Toby shakes his head sadly. "We can only hope you build up some resistance to my charms. Until then, I will step lightly around you." Toby's grating nasal whine suggests. "Alright?"

The woman, now breathing if only panting, nods and sits up, eyes tightly closed, tears streaming.

Toby turns to the pretty woman who helped earlier. "Maybe you could help her to the lavatory for a breather...well, maybe not there..." Toby pats the woman on the shoulder gently. "This nice lady will help you calm down, dear. Please take care." Silence throbs as Toby straightens up to hunch back and lightly tip-toes away over to his bewildered twin, squishing every other step.

Another round of violent coughing overtakes the office.

In a carrying whisper, Toby asks his twin. "Is it terribly contagious? It sounds like it's spreading."

His manly twin coughs in surprise, his eyes flashing with humor, shaking his head.

Toby steps back carefully. "Better safe than snotty. Maybe I should have a separate work area just in case."

Nodding in agreement, his twin asks. "Who are you again?" His voice was gruff, suppressing great emotion.

"Oh, we never got to that, did we?" He extends his hand limply. "I'm Toby Robins. I'm here to fill your needs. I'm well versed in all forms of services you may require." Toby limply shakes his hand at an awkward distance. Then, from a pocket pulls out hand sanitizer and squirts out a glob, working it in vigorously.

His twin clears his throat and hoarsely says, "I'm the H.R. Manager, Phillip Constantine. Why don't you step into my office, and we will get you situated." He coughs, and his hand indicates the open door behind him.

Toby, giving a wide berth, passes into the office, squishing along gently.

Taking a deep breath, Phillip reaches up, strips off his tie, and unbuttons the top two buttons of his short-sleeved white dress shirt. He turns towards his office, yanking the full pocket protector and tossing both into the trash before stepping into his office. When his door latches shut, the outer office explodes in cheering and laughter.

Phillip coughs.

Toby turns at the ruckus. "Quite the excitable bunch out there. You may want to work on some calming exercises for them. Proper balance elicits productivity."

CHAPTER SIX

Jillian and Amethyst turn away from the door and walk back towards downtown. Once on the sidewalk, Jillian turns back to the house. The feeling of someone watching was strong, but no one answered the door. Shrugging her shoulders follows Amethyst down the street.

Amethyst looks over at Jillian. "That dress really looks great on you. Why did you fight me on it?"

Jillian looks down at the flirty wraparound dress. "This red is not me, it's kind of weird the two tones. The black is okay, it makes me dizzy to look at. It's comfy, though. I just won't look unless I'm standing still." She shrugs. "It really looks good?"

Amethyst laughs. "Yeah, the black shades in all the right places. Super nova hot, babe. Your little geek will love it." She laughs. "So will the other two if we can find them."

"We can ask at the county office for the exterminator's contact information." Jillian waves her folder. "I also need to drop this off."

Amethyst nods and looks at her watch. "Hey, it's 4:15 already. Where did the day go?"

Jillian walks on, lost in thought, panting lightly, wondering what kind of reaction she would get. Especially if she revealed what was underneath, one simple pull of the tie and her dress would be open, exposing her red and black lace bra and panties and her black lace bands on her silk thigh-high stockings. Her imagination fills in her shadowed sea god, crouching down in front of her spread legs, devouring with his eyes.

Amethyst looks over at Jillian, noting her high color, smoky eyes, and heavy panting. "Let's stop by O'Malley's for a quickie."

Jillian shudders at the suggestion.

Amethyst laughs. "I mean a drink."

Nodding, Jillian fans her face.

Amethyst opens the door and turns Jillian into the dim pub. "Set us up another, O'Malley. We have one more stop, so we're only in and out this time."

Jillian shivers. "Quick, man, before I lose it." Heavy panting disrupts her words.

O'Malley looks concerned, filling two tumblers with amber whiskey.

Jillian rushes to the bar, grabs both, and shoots one back, panting to catch her breath, gripping the other to her chest. She puts the empty back on the bar.

O'Malley's curious gaze slides to Amethyst.

Amethyst holds out the empty tumbler to him.

He splashes in two fingers, looking back at Jillian. "Are you sure this here, lassie, is okay?"

Amethyst looks over at Jillian clasping her glass with both hands shaking. "Honestly, not really. But you seem to have the only cure for what ails her. We're hunting for better medicine. Remember that rare breed we're hunting, the two-legged kind."

O'Malley nods wisely. "The fever's got her. Good hunting, those rare breeds are hard to find and harder to catch."

Amethyst chuckles.

Jillian takes a deep breath, steadies her hands, and pours the second glass of whiskey down her throat. She puts her head down on the bar, hands gripping the bar.

"Hey, babe, you okay?" Jackson Andrews puts his hand on Jillian's.

Amethyst stands up straight, sensing danger. "Jackson, you might not want to do that."

Jillian becomes very still. Her head slowly rises off the bar and looks down at the hand touching her.

Jackson, ignorant of the danger, squeezes Jillian's hand, looking at Amethyst. "And why not? I'm not afraid of Jillian."

Jillian's head slowly moves up to look at the smirking, over-confident man standing next to her.

Amethyst shakes her head, predicting his doom. "Don't say I didn't warn you. Foolish, Jackson, very foolish."

Jackson laughs, looking down at Jillian without truly seeing her. "Please…"

In a swirl of red and black, Jillian slams Jackson's head on the bar, wrenching his offensive hand up and back, kicking out one of his legs wide.

Jackson cries out in surprised pain, getting louder as his arm goes up and his leg goes out.

Artic winds blow through Jillian. "If you touch me again, I will rip it off and wear it to remind you; hands off!" She bangs his head for emphasis and steps away.

Jackson comes after her. "You bitch, what the hell is wrong with you?" His hand reaches out to grab her.

Jillian stops, looks down at his hand and slowly turns back to look him in the eyes. She steps forward, and he steps back. "Jackson, did I not get your attention?" She takes another step forward.

He retreats. "Yes, but don't you think that was excessive?"

She takes another step forward, her eyes chilling from frosty to dead. "Obviously not excessive enough if you didn't get my message."

Jackson steps back, and his back hits the bar. He looks to both sides and realizes he's hemmed in by barstools. "Jillian…Jillian, we can work this out. Maybe today isn't a good day." He cajoles.

Jillian steps closer. "Everything will be fine for you if you keep your hands off." She smiles up at him from below her lashes. "Do you want to test me, Jackson?" She steps closer, menace rolls off her. "Do you?" She whispers.

Pushing against the bar stool, Jackson leaves quickly. "I got to go, Jillian."

She tracks him and whispers. "Just remember what I said, Jackson."

"Yeah...yeah...see you..." Jackson slams out the doors at a full run.

Jillian shakes her head sadly and turns calmly to O'Malley and Amethyst. "Some people just never learn." Taking a big breath, she nods and smiles. "I feel pretty good."

O'Malley and Amethyst turn shocked faces, face each other, and break out in hoots of laughter.

The tension now broken, the entire pub convulses with cheers and laughter from its patrons.

Jillian looks around at the crowd, then back at Amethyst. "What? What's so funny?"

Amethyst slaps the bar, gasping for breath and control.

Jillian turns to O'Malley, confused. "O'Malley?"

O'Malley falls over behind the bar, laughing so hard his face is purple.

"Are you okay?" She steps on the kick bar and leans over the bar to see O'Malley better.

"He's fine." A handsome man looking like a younger version of O'Malley walks up behind the bar.

Jillian smiles brightly, open and friendly. Guessing his identity, he says. "O'Malley's nephew!"

He nods and holds out his hand. "Fin O'Malley."

She takes his hand. "Nice to meet you, Fin."

"You too." He chuckles, looking around the bar.

"Can you tell me what's so funny? I think I missed something."

"You were just too close to the action to fully understand." Fin smiles deeply at her. "Give me about an hour, and I may have a good explanation." He already feels connected to her, like they fit together in some way.

Jillian smiles, shrugging her shoulders. "Alright, Amethyst and I need to make one more stop then we will be back. Will that work?" She asks sweetly, completely comfortable with him, like an old friend.

Fin chuckles. "Works for me."

"Great. Did you meet my friend, Amethyst?"

"Nope, haven't had the pleasure yet." Fin smiles at the laughing golden beauty.

"Amethyst!" Jillian yells over the noisy laughter, which catches everyone's attention. She smiles at the room at large, her hand up and nodding. Then, waves over Amethyst.

Tears course down Amethyst's cheeks, her eyes wide and attentive, suppressing her laughter, shaking with it.

Jillian shakes her head at Fin. "Fin, this is my friend Amethyst James." Turning to Amethyst. "This is O'Malley's nephew, Fin O'Malley."

Amethyst reaches over the bar and shakes hands with Fin. "Great to finally meet you. O'Malley's been bragging about you for some time."

"Ditto, he's always talking about you two. I must say today was a surprise. He never prepared me for this." He chuckles, looking over at Jillian.

"For you and the rest of us." Amethyst flings her arm around Jillian's shoulders. "Jillian is having a trying day. Normally, she is as quiet as a mouse and just as dainty. But today, you saw what few will witness…when the timid mouse turns into the ferocious tigress, stripes and all." Looking at Jillian, she says. "I love that dress."

Fin laughs. "I'm glad I'm here."

O'Malley slaps the bar.

Amused, Fin reaches down and helps his uncle to his feet.

O'Malley holds up his hand as he catches his breath. When the room quiets, he shouts. "A round on the house. All hail Jillian, our own Tigress!"

Jillian stares, stunned, looking around.

Everyone in the pub raises their glasses and cheers. "Jillian!"

A little embarrassed, she gracefully curtsies, flaring her skirts. She rises up to silence and looks around.

The pub ruptures with cheers and laughter.

Jillian looks over her shoulder and asks, "What now?"

Fin laughs, holding the bar. "Give me that hour."

Jillian looks over at Amethyst with a raised brow.

Amethyst shakes her head laughing, grabs the glass O'Malley filled, and knocks it back.

Jillian turns to O'Malley.

He shakes his head and hands her a glass. "Best to wait, lass."

"Oh, Gobbler! We've got to go. It's 25 'til. We'll be back." Amethyst grabs both purses and the folder off the bar. "Come on, Jillian." She grabs Jillian's hand just as her glass hits her lips and is dragged to the door.

She barely drains it and hands it off before she crosses the threshold. Her hand comes up instantly as the sunlight hits her eyes. Off balance, she stumbles behind Amethyst blindly. Collecting her composure, she pulls Amethyst back. Her eyes clear, and they step off boldly, hurrying to the county offices a couple of blocks away.

Amethyst hands Jillian her purse and the folder. "Feel better?"

Jillian takes a moment to assess. "Yes, actually."

Amethyst laughs. "Not surprised, not at all."

Jillian looks over curiously. "Really, why?"

"Because sex and violence are closely related."

"Huh?"

"You'll understand in an hour."

33

"Okay." She shakes her head, confused, prowling down the street. Her dress flashes red and black stripes as she moves gracefully, unaware of her visual impact as she

CHAPTER SEVEN

They climb the steps to the county offices.

A well-dressed man in a nice suit steps out and holds the door for them.

They both thank him.

After Jillian steps past, he responds with an eyebrow wiggle and a flirty growl. "Rawr!"

That stops Jillian, and she turns back to him.

He winks and bows respectfully with a broad smile.

Amethyst snorts, nodding. "I'm always amazed at how fast words travel."

"What?" Jillian rubs her forehead.

"Come along. We don't have much time."

They step up to the reception security desk.

"Hello, boys." Amethyst greets the guards.

"Hello, Ladies." Jeff, the burly guard, smiles warmly at the women.

Jillian smiles at both guards. "Jeff, Steve, How are you doing?"

"Great." Jeff chuckles. "It's been lively around here today. We got a new temp working in permits, and he's making quite an impression."

"Well, I guess we'll get lucky. We're heading there now. Oh, by the way, do you have the name of your last exterminator? We need one. He was here last week, I believe." Amethyst inquires, keeping an eye on Jillian as she sniffs the air, strangely focused.

Jeff, not paying attention, looks down at the book on the desk. "Sure, give me a moment. Let me jot this down for you."

Steve, on the other hand, only had eyes for Jillian as she sniffed around the foyer.

Jillian closes her eyes and breathes in long and deep through her nose. Her head turns to the left, and her body follows, drifting lightly off following the scent.

Jeff hands off the paper to Amethyst when Steve taps him insistently. He turns to Steve, who is pointing at Jillian, and barks a laugh. "Ah, Amethyst, Jillian looks like she's floating away."

Amethyst snaps around, grabs the forgotten folder, and chases after Jillian. "How is it possible she can float faster than I can walk? Jillian!"

The guards laugh hearing her.

Jillian turns back and opens her eyes, all smoky and dark.

Amethyst catches up and holds her arm.

Leashed, Jillian drags Amethyst down the hall, following her nose, eyes closed once again. She pauses just before the H.R. office.

People walking down the hall watch curiously, passing them quickly up against the wall.

Amethyst smiles and nods, trying to reduce the charged atmosphere.

Jillian slinks towards the office and enters.

Mary, sitting behind the desk, is on the phone. She looks up, eyes wide in surprise.

Feeling the danger mounting, Amethyst tightens her hold on Jillian.

Jillian moves beyond the desk, passing from the water cooler to the reception desk, back and forth.

Mary says into the phone, "Yes, they just walked in..." She nervously pulls up the back of her hair.

Jillian's head snaps around. Her eyes pop open, and she lunges towards the woman, her clawing hand just inches away from ripping her to shreds.

36

Mary stumbles away fearfully, falling out of her chair and dragging the phone with her.

Amethyst digs in her heels and drags Jillian away from the terrified woman.

Jillian screams in frustration.

Mary squeaks and collapses to the floor, the receiver still in her hand.

Jillian breaks away and leaps to the fallen woman. Bending down, she sniffs her face and neck.

Amethyst carefully approaches. "Jillian, we don't have time. Remember the permit forms we need to drop off."

Behind her, a door opens, and a very frustrated male voice asks. "What is the meaning of this?"

Amethyst turns towards Phillip.

Jillian's head comes up, scenting the air. Rising from beside the prone woman, Jillian prowls over to Phillip, circling him. Her nose twitches delicately and stops by his suspended right hand.

Frozen in shock, Phillip's eyes follow Jillian's strange movements.

She breaks away and prowls into his office.

Amethyst rushes to the office. "Jillian, really, we have to get to the permit office before it closes." She walks over to Jillian, sniffing a chair, and drags her out by her arm. "So sorry for the inconvenience. I think Mary will be fine in a moment. She just had a fright. Tell her to call me." She continues through the office and down the hall, turning left to go to the permit office at the end.

Jillian reluctantly follows and then takes the lead.

"Not again, Jillian. What's gotten into you?" Amethyst holds on for dear life. "Well, we're going in the right direction, at least."

Jillian drags Amethyst into the permit office and stops. Panting, her head scans the room.

Amethyst scans the room also, wondering who her friend is going to terrify next. Slapping the folder in the submit bin, she watches Jillian closely and notices when her eyes lock onto a man in a white short-sleeved dress shirt engrossed in his work. She was a moment too late tightening her grip on Jillian, who broke away, slinking over to the man.

Just as Amethyst cries out in surprise, Jillian launches herself at the man.

CHAPTER EIGHT

His head pops up in danger and shrieks as Jillian lands on his lap, covered in black and red silky fabric.

Her nose runs along his neck and chest, up into his hair, pawing and petting. She moans softly.

His hands latch onto the armrests, quivering, he whines. "Get her off. Get her off." His huge green eyes are stark with fear; panting, sweat breaks out, running down his temples.

A golden-haired beautiful woman rushes forward to pause a foot away, tilts her head to the side. "Is she purring?" She looks closer at the man. "Did you run into Jillian this morning on the street?"

Toby pants, every muscle-locked taunt whines. "Please, lady, get her off!"

Jillian licks his temple, moaning in delight.

Toby jerks at the electric contact of her tongue on his skin. The charge building between them, weakening his resolve. He had to get away from her. His head tilts away, trying to avoid Jillian's tongue.

Jillian's friend laughs and reaches for her arm, peeling it away from his head as she crawls up. "Jillian!"

Jillian looks over at her friend, her eyes dark grey and dilated.

"Come on, Jillian, climb off the nice man. I know you want to gobble him up, but not here and not now." Her friend gives a hard yank.

Jillian stumbles to her feet.

Toby quickly kicks his chair back, rolling as far away as possible. The chair slams into the shelves behind him. He springs out of the chair and crouches down, ready for his chance to run.

Phillip walks in, stopping between Toby and Jillian, blocking her view. "Toby? What is the meaning of this?"

Jillian hisses behind Phillip's back. Her friend tries to control her.

Whining, Toby states nasally. "I'm sorry, Phillip, but I can't work here anymore. It's much too dangerous." He launches into a fast, slumping run towards the doorway, dragging the door closed behind him.

Phillip yelps in surprise.

Jillian screams her frustration.

Her friend laughs hysterically.

The door bangs in the frame a couple of times behind him. The rush of air is his only warning. He ducks into the H.R. office with a wave and a silencing finger to his lips. He slips behind the propped-open door. His heart thunders in his chest. No fucking way! Keep it together, man. You can escape. He looks down at the door handle and twists the lock. That might buy him some time.

Shifting red and black stripes catches his eye as she enters the office. Her friend close on her heels, slowing her down. She reaches the other side of the front desk when she stops.

Toby swings around the door, pulling it with him until it stops halfway closed. Jammed; panic fuddles his brain.

Jillian turns and moves towards him deliberately.

Jerking desperately at the door, he whines in fear, then finally pops off the door wedge at the bottom and kicks it away, slamming the door closed with Jillian steps away.

On the other side of the door Jillian pounds the door and screams again.

The sound, wild and desperate, sends excited chills up his spine. He turns and lopes down the hall, dodging through all the motionless witnesses. His accordion gait moved him quickly toward the exit.

Laughter rolls from the closed office.

Toby reaches the main foyer when a door slams open. He lengthens his stride, heading for the front doors.

The two wide-eyed guards watch on with open mouths as he lopes by.

Out of nowhere, with no warning footsteps, a red and black body streaks through the air and lands on his back.

He stumbles just ten feet from the door. He shrieks again.

Jillian latches on, nuzzling his neck.

He hops around, trying to shake her off.

She's latched on like a tic.

He whines, feeling his control slipping.

Jillian's friend moves as fast as she can, with convulsive laughter wracking her body.

The two guards behind the desk hold each other, crying with laughter.

Toby's voice reedy in panic, beseeches. "Lady, please, get her off me."

"Name's Amethyst." She gasps, bending over at the waist, hands on her knees, sucking air. "I'm trying my best to control her, but you see how that's going." She laughs at the sight of Toby trying to dislodge Jillian from his back, nervously hopping from foot to foot, leaning dangerously to each side.

"Lady Amethyst, I don't know if I can take much more," Toby whines, warning.

Amethyst laughs harder and chokes out. "O'Malley said she has the fever and only one cure." She shakes her head in wonder. "It seems to be you."

Toby stops. An unholy light shines out of his magnified eyes. He reaches across his body for Jillian's arm. In a lightning-quick move, he pulls her around and latches his lips to hers in a deep, hungry, devouring kiss.

Jillian moans and falls limp in his arms, pulling away from his lips.

He closes his eyes, gasping for breath, grasping for control, while his heart races like wild horses on the plain. His body quakes from the power of the kiss. In the absolute silence, he Slowly raises his

41

head to look at her friend in absolute silence. His vision is foggy, and trying to clear his sight, he blinks repeatedly.

He gets the hazy impression of her standing straight in shock. He blows out a hearty sigh, and his vision clears some. He snorts as he realizes his glasses are fogged. He snorts at the golden woman's expression; her face flushed with passion, her mouth hanging open as a bead of drool escapes her lips, her eyes dreamy and dilated.

Toby looks past her at the two guards, both wearing similar shocked expressions.

He glances over his shoulder at the audience that followed the action. He looks back down at Jillian laid out across his arms in a deep dip, crouching over her. He could only imagine the picture they made, the Hunchback of South County and his maiden. Carefully, he changes his position and scoops Jillian's limp body up. Slumping over to Amethyst, hunched over Jillian's limp body draped over his arms. "Here, Lady Amethyst, I think she just fainted." He looks over at the two guards. "I guess I need to work on toning it down. I think I overwhelmed her." He shrugs his humped back.

Amethyst choked on a laugh.

Toby turns back to her, concerned. "You're not going to faint at my feet, too, are you?"

Amethyst howls with laughter, shaking her head. "Since you tamed my friend for a while, let me buy you a drink. And another for watching a master at work." She turns Toby to the door. "Can you carry her a couple of blocks, Toby?"

Toby nods, his grating nasal voice carries. "A lady in need is my good deed."

They pass through the doorway, stepping out into a warm summer late afternoon and dead down the steps, drawing startled and amused attention from everyone around.

42

CHAPTER NINE

"You know, Toby, I think I like you."

"Thank you, Lady Amethyst. I like you too. It's always good to make new friends." Toby whines at her.

"Isn't that a fact? Especially if they are true friends." Amethyst watches Toby slumping along beside her. "Are you a true friend, Toby?"

"Yes, Lady Amethyst, I imagine I am."

Amethyst nods in acceptance.

Toby nods down at Jillian draped over his arms, clutched to his chest. "What about this little lady?" He whines carefully.

"Ah, Jillian, poor girl. She's having a tough time these last three weeks. A recurring dream haunts her fiercely. And with only me as her close, true friend. She could use another."

Toby trips and stumbles on hearing about Jillian's recurring dream. Coincident? Doubtful, especially since she's in his dream. He wonders if it's the same dream. "Yes." He whispers, knowing it's the same.

Amethyst glances over at that odd declaration and squints at him. She shakes her head and opens the door to O'Malley's.

Toby steps in with his lovely burden. Cheers and whistles greet him, stopping him in his tracks a few steps into the pub. He looks around curiously.

Amethyst follows him in. "I see news proceeds us. Don't be shy, Toby. Go lay your burden in that reserved booth." She points to an empty booth on the wall across the room. "I'll be right with you."

He slumps off to the booth with back slaps and greetings all along the way. He nods along, grinning at all the attention and well wishes. Over his shoulder, he sees Amethyst fighting her way through the crowd to the bar.

She yells out. "Set 'em up, O'Malley, and pass the bottle, too." She looks over at the other bartender, a younger version. "Hey, Fin, come here for a minute."

Smiling, Fin nods, moving down the bar. "What do you need?"

"You." She grabs his shirt and drags him over the bar, meeting him halfway, sealing her lips to his for a deep, hungry kiss.

He grabs the back of her neck and returns the favor.

The crowd cheers in approval.

Toby snorts and looks down at Jillian. He whispers in her ear. "Look what we started."

She moans and snuggles up in his arms.

"Please don't wake up yet." He whispers.

She relaxes into deeper sleep with her arms locked across his back.

Toby stands at the table, testing his theory that his tic is back. He releases her upper body. He tests the table and slides it over a bit. He scratches his head and notices the silence around him. He turns to his audience. He snorts in his grating nasal voice says. "Ta-Da!" and holds out his free arm.

Jillian doesn't move.

The crowd cheers.

Amethyst comes over. "It doesn't take much to amuse this crowd today. They have been primed and flocking in droves." She tries to unlock Jillian's arms. "I'm sorry, but I think you must wear her for now." She laughs at his expression.

He shakes his head at his predicament.

"Sit," Amethyst says, amused.

Noah's back was killing him, hunched all day, then toting around Jillian. It wouldn't be so bad if he could stand up straight. He slides to the corner and rests Jillian's back against the wall, trailing her legs across the bench. Her arms across his back make relaxing impossible. He leans forward, bracing his arms on the table to ease the tension and discomfort.

Amethyst laughs at his situation. "Not very comfortable, hun? Here, have a drink first." She slides over a tumbler half full of whiskey.

Toby looks up at her with brows raised. "Really?" He whines carefully. "Is this what you ladies usually consume at cocktail hour?"

"No," Amethyst laughs, "only today, all day…off and on. It's been a tough day for Jillian. Just before we got to the permit office, we stopped here, and she downed three like that in about twenty minutes. I think that's probably what saved you, my friend." She laughs. "We are going to have a movie premier here tonight." She chuckles, taking a sip of her whiskey. "It's called A Not So Very Good Day in the Life of Jillian."

Toby takes in a healthy sip of the whiskey, sucks in some fumes with a gasp, and proceeds to choke violently.

Jillian pats his back in her sleep.

Amethyst chuckles sheepishly. "Sorry about that. My bad. I should have waited until you swallowed."

Toby nods, holding up a hand, trying to catch his breath.

Jillian rubs his back soothingly, still deep asleep.

Toby looks over at her, shaking his head in wonder. He turns back and catches Amethyst staring at him. He grins, goofy. "Nothing like this has ever happened to me." He whines. "I'm still in shock."

Amethyst nods. "Me either, and me too." She looks at Jillian. "So, Toby, I'm guessing you were the new temp today."

"Yes, that's pretty much my job, professional Temp. I go where I'm needed."

"Really? Is the money good?"

"Depends on the job. My reputation is very good. I can usually take my pick." Toby gingerly takes another sip, wheezing for effect. It fits the character. He shudders as Jillian's hand roams down his back. He pulls down her arm hanging on his neck, placing it in her lap. He shrugs and bobs his head, relieving some of the tension. He leans back a little and traps her hand. "What do you do, Lady Amethyst?"

She smiles at him. "I own a boutique. Just a couple of doors down. I also design. A.M. Designs is my label."

"Wow, that's wonderful. You must be pleased." Toby says, impressed.

"Yes, I am. I recently discovered that a department store chain is interested in my line. Nothing is decided for them or me, but it is exciting."

"Congratulations." He toasts her with his raised glass.

"Thank you." She picks up her glass and taps it with his.

After a sip, Toby puts it down on the table. "What about sleeping beauty here?"

"Research analyst, freelance. She gets calls from all over the country. She only takes the jobs she's interested in for the right pay. Normally, she's as docile as a lamb, not that you witnessed. Today, she was wild and fierce at the other end of the spectrum." She chuckles. "When we got into the building, Jillian smelled you. She was like a bloodhound, tracking you down. She was nearly floating down the hall to the H.R. office. I don't know what you were up to or why you were touching Mary at the front desk, but when Jillian entered, she nearly took out Mary. The poor girl fainted dead away, the phone still clutched in her hand."

Toby nods and whines nasally. "Poor Mary, she had a trying morning, dear lady." He takes a fortifying swallow, holding in the chuckle and the facts.

Brows furrowed, Jillian tugs weakly on her trapped arm.

Toby leans forward enough for her to pull her arm out. He grips her upper arms, lifts her up, sliding over, and sets her on the padded bench, propping her up in the corner. Her legs draped over his lap. He looks down and notices black lace and bare skin. His mouth starts to water, fists clenched on the table. He can't look away. That patch of bare skin, a siren song, drawing him ever closer to disaster.

Fidgeting in the corner, a frown mars her face.

Amethyst watches them silently, dips her head under the table, and sees what's caught his attention.

Sweat beads on his forehead, his hands slowly moving to the table's edge.

Suddenly, Jillian sits up, grabs his upper arm, hugs it tightly to her chest, and falls back to the corner with a sweet smile.

Tilted sideways, his arm snuggled to her breasts, his hand right where he wanted it on that patch of bare skin. Her lips temptingly close. Toby pants, fighting for control.

Amethyst takes pity on him moving his glass in reach of his quivering fist. "Toby, have a drink, then we will try to get you out of her clutches."

Toby nods and moans piteously, closing his eyes and taking a deep breath. His nostrils flare drawing in Jillian's scent, swirling in his brain.

"Toby, open your hand, drink."

Noah fights to open his fist. He feels the cool glass in his grip and Amethyst's hand holding his, moving it to his mouth. Nodding, he gulps it all down. Gasping for breath as the fire hits his belly.

Amethyst takes the glass and pours more in, then leans over the table, holding it to Jillian's lips. "Jillian, your turn to drink. Come on, that's a girl." She holds it tenuously to get a reaction from her.

Jillian releases Toby's arm to steady the glass.

He quickly sits up, snatching his hand away from her leg. Carefully, he covers it again, not that he can erase the taunting memory seared into his brain.

Amethyst slaps the filled glass back into his hand and lifts both.

He knocks back the three fingers in one go. A shudder wracks his frame. Looking up, breathing deeply, his control settles firmly back into his iron grip. He looks at Amethyst and grins goofy.

47

She laughs with a nod. "I'm starting to worry this fever might be contagious. First Jillian, now you. I'm feeling a little warm."

"Jillian is throwing off so much heat it's affecting us," Toby whines doubtfully.

She laughs. "Yeah, right, except I can see it in your eyes. I've been seeing it all day with Jillian. I'm sorry, my friend, it's the fever." She chuckles. "Have you eaten?"

"Not since lunch."

She slides a menu over. "Everything is pretty good. We need to feed Jillian, too. Are you up for that? I figure if we keep the booze flowing and maybe separate you, we might keep things in hand."

Toby looks at her doubtfully. "Only if you sit between us, and she stays confined in the corner."

Amethyst laughs. "I'll even get you some backup."

"Deal, but if I have to, I'm running."

CHAPTER TEN

Amethyst laughs. "Like you did last time? Maybe you could use the same tactic to defend yourself and kiss her unconscious. Just overwhelm her." She says innocently.

"I'm not positive of the same results."

"Oh, I don't know about that, Toby. I have a sneaking suspicion you're made of stronger stuff." She raises her brow.

Toby tips his head respectfully. "You do me great honor, Lady Amethyst. Let's hope you are right." He whines unconvinced.

"I'm not overly worried."

Toby snorts, reviewing the menu. "I'll take the roast beef and a water."

"Sounds good. Jillian, roast beef, Jillian?"

Jillian tips her head forward.

"Good enough for me." She raises her hand and waves it.

The older bartender ambles up, a warm smile on his face. "Is this the medicine?" He asks Amethyst.

She laughs. "Yes, O'Malley, meet Toby, the cure-all. Toby, our champion, O'Malley."

Toby charmingly whines. "Oh, it's good to meet you, Mr. O'Malley. You have a great establishment. Everyone is so friendly. I felt like an honored family member as soon as I walked in."

O'Malley coughs and clears his throat. "It's just O'Malley, me boy. Thank you, it is pretty great. I've been wanting to meet you. Heard a tale or two tonight. You've been busy, lad." He says, amused.

Toby clears his throat. "Yes, like I told Lady Amethyst, leaving the county offices, a lady in need is my good deed. A motto to live by."

O'Malley chuckles. "The rewards can be limitless. If only more young men lived by that motto."

Toby raises a finger. "Ah, but that would lessen the demand for my services. Not all are as skilled as I am. Only the best for the ladies." He whines confidently.

Amethyst snorts, then breaks out in laughter.

Toby raises his brow at her seriously. "Am I wrong, lady Amethyst?"

Gasping for breath, Amethyst squeaks. "Spot on, Mr. Toby."

Jillian echoes. "Spot on." Smiling sweetly.

Noah snorts in surprise.

O'Malley and Amethyst, not so restrained, loose it.

Noticing the lower volume of the crowd, Toby looks around. They seem to be the center of attention again. A familiar face passed by. "Phillip, I'm truly sorry for running out like that. That's never happened before."

Phillip stops by the table. "Don't worry about it. You completed your work. If you'd like to return, I can set you up."

Toby shudders, as does Noah internally. "Oh, my heavens, no. Much too dangerous. Not just the wilting ladies but the virulent coughing spreading through the offices. It seemed like it was following me. Not to mention getting attacked at my desk by the clients." Toby wipes his forehead. "Too much excitement for me. But thank you for the offer."

"Let me know if you change your mind." Helplessly amused, Phillip coughs.

Toby leans away towards Jillian thoughtlessly.

Her arms snap out to capture his neck.

He dodges back the other way, barely escaping. "Phew, that was close." Toby shudders.

All three roar with laughter, along with those close enough to hear the conversation.

Amethyst turns to Phillip. "Looking good, Phillip. You seem relaxed and happy. What gives?"

Phillip smiles easily. "Took a good look in the mirror and had an epiphany." He smiles over at Toby.

Toby grins back. "That's wonderful, Phillip. That proves we always grow, especially when we catch our image when we least expect it. Clarity through surprise." Toby nods wisely, comfortable in himself.

The pub cheers in agreement.

Toby looks around, eyes wide in surprise. He whispers out of the side of his mouth to the other three, keeping his eyes on the crowd. "Are we the entertainment tonight? I don't believe I was notified." He looks over to Amethyst and winks a huge eye at her.

She chokes back a laugh. "Toby, I think you're entertaining wherever you go. Why should tonight be any different?"

"Oh, it isn't, though they're usually not obvious." He whispers to her with a grin, picking up his glass and draining half. "O'Malley, my good man, would you please feed us? We're a might puckish. We all agreed on the roast beef with water, please."

"Have no fear, my boy. We will extinguish one burning hunger." O'Malley chuckles, walking back to the bar.

Amethyst snickers.

Jillian echoes her.

Noah coughs, picks up his drink, and drains half in one swallow. Looking into the swirling amber, Noah's mind whirls. Unable to latch onto any subject to distract him from Jillian, shifting restlessly next to him. His eyes scan out to the crowd seeing most of their eyes. The whole situation was just ridiculous. He chuckles out of character.

Beside him, Jillian snaps up straight, her eyes pop open, staring at him, hungry, her eyes dark and smoky.

Toby squeaks, launching out of the booth and backing away in a slumping gait. "Lady Amethyst, contain her before she attacks." His eyes, huge and fearful, never leave Jillian.

51

Amethyst smirks. "Jillian, do you see what I brought with us."

Jillian nods, her eyes never leaving Toby, hurrying along the bench towards him, slow and deliberate.

Amethyst soothes. "Jillian, do you want him to come back over here?"

Jillian's eyes gleam, fire flashes through the smoke, and she nods, licking her chops.

Noah wipes his sweaty brow, gasping for breath. A shiver ripples his body.

Amethyst looks over at Toby and nods to someone next to him.

A drink materializes in his hand. He chugs it down like water and hands it back.

She turns her surprised eyes on Jillian and says, amused. "Drink this and hurry back to your corner, Jillian. If I sit between you, he will come back. Do you want him to come back?"

Jillian nods, takes the glass, pours it in her mouth then slams it down on the table. It cracks like a shot.

Noah jolts at the sound.

Jillian slides back to her corner and curls her finger at Noah.

He still stands deer in the headlights until Amethyst sits in the booth, blocking Jillian from an easy exit. Timidly, he takes a mincing step closer, one halting step at a time.

Amethyst smiles at Toby. "It's okay, Toby, come sit down. Jillian will be good. Won't you, Jillian?"

Jillian smiles sweetly, nods, and chuckles darkly.

The sound ripples along his skin, similar to his earlier chuckle. Moaning in distress, Noah stops.

At Amethyst's nod, another glass appears in his hand. His mouth dry, he pours it in, breathes deeply and hands the glass back, eye contact with Jillian unbroken. Slowly, he inches forward, her eyes drawing him closer. He slides into the booth, moving closer and closer.

Amethyst laughs. "Toby, you're squishing me. Jillian, close your eyes."

Jillian closes her eyes and breaks the connection.

Noah whips his head around and sees most of the bench open. "So sorry, Lady Amethyst." He hurries back to the end. "I quite lost my mind there," Toby whines nasally.

Jillian whines.

Noah starts to turn his head then stops just before he sees her. "Tsk-tsk, Lady Jillian, you almost caught me in your trap again."

Jillian snaps her fingers in regret.

Noah snorts helplessly, amused.

Jillian asks. "What's your name?"

Her voice was just as dark and dangerous to his senses as her eyes, and his muscles lock and quiver making him unable to respond.

Amethyst answers for him. "Toby, he's a professional Temp. He goes where he's needed."

"Toby." Trying out his name, she knows it's not right. "I need you, Toby."

Wow! Her words stroke down his body like a full caress. His fists clenched on the table, his muscles locked, his skin rippling, his eyes on the table. He shakes his head, too dangerous to stay. "No, Amethyst, I can't stay, too dangerous," Noah whines to Toby piteously.

"Please, Toby, please." Jillian desperately pleads.

Every syllable shudders his frame. He closes his eyes, breathing deeply, searching for control.

Plates hit the table.

His eyes pop open, and he dives at the food like a starved man. Before either could raise a chip to their mouths, Noah finishes.

Jillian whispers to Amethyst. "What happened to his food? Did he throw it on the floor?" She asks in wonder.

Amethyst whispers back. "No, I think he ate it."

"Did he chew or just hoover it up whole?"

"I'm not sure. Was there time for chewing?"

"Toby, my sweet, are you still hungry?"

Noah slowly turns his head, his green eyes glowing with raw, wild hunger, "Ravenous." He growls in his true voice.

The girls jump back, slamming into the walls of the booth.

In a dark whisper, Noah asks. "Are you going to feed me, Jillian?" His tongue flicks out the corner of his mouth, and his half grin exposes his sharp eye teeth. "I want to eat you all up."

Amethyst jumps over closer to Jillian with a faint, "Eep!"

Her smoky laugh is an invitation. Jillian slides her plate over to him. "I'll feed you this for now."

Noah tips his head respectfully, slipping back into Toby; he says nasally. "Thank you, Lady Jillian. I seem to be quite famished." He turns back forward, sliding the plate in front of him, takes a breath, and digs in.

Both women watch avidly.

"Do you suppose he's a wolf in sheep's clothing?" Jillian whispers.

Amethyst whispers back. "I wouldn't be surprised. You better watch yourself, little piggy, or he'll gobble you right up."

Jillian giggles. "Alright."

Her infectious childlike giggles delight filled. The tone is clean and pure.

The sound makes Noah smile from his heart. He pops the last bite from his second plate into his mouth, reaches over, takes Jillian's water, and pours it in. he gently places the glass on the table, takes his napkin from his lap, pats his lips, folds it neatly, places it on the center of the plate.

"Done." A yell came from the crowd.

"9.4," A man calls out.

"9.2" Another yells.

"9.5," A woman yells from the back.

"9.8," A deep booming voice calls out.

"Are they scoring my technique?" Toby asks the girls, then turns to Phillip across the table. "Or the speed in which I consumed my food?" Toby whines curiously.

Jillian snickers. "I'm betting your technique is better than a 10, and speed is more than 10 seconds."

Amethyst hoots. "I believe they are timing you on your speed. The betting book is on the back of the bar. The ones that called out were armature timekeepers. If anyone gets it right they win the A.T.K. kitty and special notice on the back wall. O'Malley is the official timekeeper and judge of any betting dispute." She points to the bar.

O'Malley steps up behind the bar and rings the bell. "The first meal was 5.2 seconds. The second meal was 9.1 seconds. Both consisted of The Roast Beef, chips, and a glass of water."

The room erupts in noise.

Jillian nudges Amethyst's plate over. "Bottomless pit or hollow leg?"

Toby slides the plate in front of himself. "Feeding the leashed wild beast within so it doesn't feed on what it truly wants." He snaps out his napkin.

It cracks in the silence.

He places it in his lap. Picks up half of the roast beef sandwich. In three bites, it's gone, munching on chips between each bite. He picks up the other half. The amazing sight, he wasn't rushed. He picks up Amethyst's water and drains it gently on the table. Takes up his napkin, blots his mouth, refolds it, and places it on his clean, empty plate.

"Done!"

They "Oooh" in amazement.

"I believe that was faster than the first. I wouldn't believe it if I hadn't watched this time." Amethyst says in wonder.

"5.5," A man calls out from the crowd.

"4.9," A man yells from the other side of the pub.

"4.6," A woman calls out loudly.

"5.2," A man yells out.

"5.0," Toby whines.

Jillian turns to Amethyst, amused. "Can he do that? I don't think he looked at a watch."

Both women look at Toby's left arm.

"Look, nothing up my sleeves." Toby pulls back the short sleeves on his shirt.

The crowd laughs.

They look at Phillip across the table, his hands clasped on the table, a watch rests on his left arm but is worn on the inner wrist, watch faces towards the table.

Amethyst leans towards Jillian. "He didn't move while Toby inhaled that meal. I think he's in shock."

Jillian reaches over and pats his hand. "Phillip, are you alright?"

Phillip chuckles. "Yes, I'm doing great. Our friend is just an enigma. Remember how much I enjoy puzzles. Even if I only have one piece, I enjoy turning it over and over." He looks at Toby, his expression open and friendly but an open warning, working on the puzzle before him.

Noah tips his head minutely, eyes crinkling in the open, friendly challenge, a respectful invitation.

Phillip smirks and picks up his glass, offering it to the table. "To tease the mysteries of nature."

Noah clinks his glass to Phillip's and snorts, appreciating the pun. "To the nature of teasing the mysteries."

Jillian pipes in tapping her glass to both. "To mysteries, nature tease."

Amethyst chokes out. "To the fever that is a mystery, of nature and a tease." She lifts her glass.

Their audience cheers with many "Here, here." Shouted out.

Noah snorts. "Is O'Malley's always like this?"

"No." Phillip and Amethyst say in unison.

"Not to this degree." Jillian laughs. "This is a prime time. You must have the right mix of characters and events conjoining at the right time. But these days live forever within the walls of O'Malley's."

Amethyst nods. "Next to the betting book is the running history log of O'Malley's. At the beginning of each log day is a captain's accounting of the day. Then the witness statements."

Phillip tips his head towards the side. "Some days only have the captain's accounting. Others have as many as a hundred. Today may be the most noteworthy." He looks around the crowd. "Not only do witness accounts mention action within these walls, they can wander further afield, as long as it's an event that happened today. From sunrise until the next sunrise."

Amethyst laughs at Toby's expression of trepidation and nods. "Yes, you may accept that every breath you took today will find mention in the book from one witness or all." She laughs. "We have an amazing tool at our disposal in this town; no malicious rumors can survive, only the ugly truth."

Jillian agrees. "Our citizens understand that in this day and age, there are no real secrets, only the hidden truths. And that truth is. Many try to color it to suit their purpose, but it reveals itself once stripped of influence by others."

Phillip nods. "The three of us went to school here. It was different than when O'Malley opened his doors and started the book. The people changed how they treated each other. The beginning of the book is fascinating. Well, it's more than one book. O'Malley has his archive."

Amethyst smiles. "The middle school kids descend O'Malley's when studying local history. O'Malley has in his library many genealogy books on the area's families. Even historical accounting of the past events in history from those families."

Noah shakes his head, amazed. "How long has O'Malley's been here?"

"It was O'Malley, the elder, who opened the doors in the mid-70s with the help of his son. The O'Malley you met, and I think Fin is his successor; O'Malley, the younger."

Phillip nods towards Fin, wending his way through the crowd towards them, a large tray over his head.

Jillian flips her coaster over in front of Noah.

He looks down. It's a circle with O'Malley's printed in green, and at the bottom of the framing circle sits "since 1974" on the framing border in tiny script. "Run by Rory O'Malley from 1974 until 1998, then Ian O'Malley took control in 1998 to present. His successor is Fin O'Malley." At the bottom three words bold in the same faint script; truth, love, joy.

Noah smiles over at Jillian and nods.

Soft and gentle, Jillian smiles, her eyes warm and welcoming.

Her trap is soft and appealing; he falls in deeper and deeper, surrendering gladly. The surroundings, the people, and the noise all fade away. There is only Jillian and Noah merging minds and souls seamlessly, without resistance or fear.

A large tray appears before Noah's eyes. He blinks, confused, shakes his head, and rubs his forehead.

Fin slaps him on the hump of his spine. "We may need to put blinders on you two. Amethyst nearly burst into flames from the sparks flying between you."

Noah nods, heartily happy that Fin showed up and rescued him again. "I did warn her of the danger. I must heartily thank you for the rescue again. Your timing is impeccable." He whines gratefully.

Fin chuckles. "They never understand the dangers around them, they boldly taunt. When danger has them in its grip, they call, "Save me!" Fin laughs. "Even though I met them today, they are family. I'm here for you, man. I can tell you remember their safety when giving the warnings." Fin holds out his hand. "Fin's the name or O'Malley, the younger, as I'm finding out."

Noah extends his hand in a normal shake, surprising Fin and giving him a closer look. "It's a pleasure to meet you, Fin. I hear we will be watching a creation of yours tonight."

Fin nods, speculation flashing in his eyes. "Yes, I put something together for Jillian. It has grown by leaps from my original idea." Watching Toby, Fin says. "Jillian, that's a beautiful ring. Are you engaged?"

Noah looks over at Jillian, curious about her reaction.

"Thank you. It is very beautiful." She gazes at it. "It appeared on my finger today. Well, Amethyst says it was on my finger. I pulled it out of my hair the first I saw it."

Noah's brows shoot up with repressed humor.

Jillian chuckles darkly.

The sound ripples along Noah's nerves. Goosebumps pimple his arms. He rubs his arms vigorously, picks up his glass, and slugs it back. Looking for a distraction, he looks around. Out of the corner of his eye, he watches Phillip surreptitiously exchange his glass for a full one.

Jillian sighs. "I'm guessing the one who placed it is marking his territory. I've been wracking my brain trying to figure out who could have placed it on my finger without my notice. Very strange."

Amethyst looks at him.

He can feel her speculation.

"Another mystery in a day full of them." She says dryly, amused.

Noah looks at Fin, watching the group. He looks at Jillian's ring and then directly into Noah's eyes. His brows raise slightly, his eyes knowing.

Noah expressionless Toby basks. "What other mystery have you had today?" He picks up his glass for a sip.

"Jillian keeps running into men, collisions, body striking body. You are the only one we tracked down today, though we're hunting for all of you."

Noah closes his eyes, fighting a cough, sucks down more whiskey, and clears his throat. "So, I will have competition for the fair, Lady Jillian?" A laugh perches in his nose at this preposterous situation. In competition with himself for the same woman. How true was that last statement, "hunting for all of you," since Jillian has only experienced pieces of him? And the rest only one. Sometimes, it was a challenge to be himself, complexity upon complexity. No time now for introspection. He was Toby Robins right now. He was a whiney, scared ladies' man with a pocket protector, bad posture, pronounced features, and a slumping gait. Don't forget the hunched back. Pleasant and amusing, or timid and scared. That's who Toby Robins is: very intelligent, well versed in all topics, a working knowledge, the professional Temp. "Who is my competition?" He whines, worried.

Amethyst pats his arm comfortingly.

Jillian hisses at her.

Amethyst snatches back her hand with a nervous laugh. "Toby, I think I more understand your concern."

Fin laughs. "Not even scratching the surface, lass."

Noah tips his glass to Fin in acknowledgment of the truth.

Phillip laughs. "Who else did you run into?"

Amethyst watches Phillip. "Maybe you met one of them. He was at the county offices last week, the exterminator, Jarvis."

Phillip tilts his head back and closes his eyes for a moment.

Amethyst continues. "You know the reaction Jillian has for Toby here? Not as strong with Jarvis, but Toby's had more exposure, so who knows."

Phillip raises his glass, taking a thoughtful sip. His eyes pop open. His head snaps down. A look of horror on his face. "The exterminator from last week?"

"Yeah, that bad?" Amethyst turns to look at Jillian, eating peacefully beside her.

"Oh, god! I don't know if I can explain." He chokes out a horrified laugh. "Where did you run into him?"

Jillian looks up thoughtfully. "I fell over him in archives. He caught me before I hit the ground. Very gallant, not refined like Toby. I'd say more crude country folk, hillbilly redneck sort." She nods, pleased with her description, her eyes a little dreamy.

Noah coughs delicately, fighting the laugh at her accurate description. "You found him appealing?" He asks doubtfully.

Phillip nods. "That's it exactly, though emphasize the crude. I had so many complaints about him, I don't know if I will use him again. He was a big disruption."

Everyone heard the unspoken, not as big as you, Toby.

Jillian clears her throat. "He wasn't as appealing as you are, Toby. It was just the feelings I got from him. He needs a lot of work."

Noah pushes. "Would you go out with him?"

Jillian laughs. "Only to the forest, no. I would only consider it if he meets a barber, a wardrobe, and a bath. The fumes of pesticide hung around him like a cloud." She thoughtfully scratches her head. "I honestly don't know how I didn't notice him there next to me. The fumes alone must radiate ten feet." She shakes her head in wonder, going back to her meal, only half gone.

Fin perches on the opposite bench. "What feeling did you get from him?"

Jillian shrugs. "Hot sex."

Taking a drink, Noah chokes.

Phillip yells in shock. "With that?"

Jillian looks around and leans forward. "I didn't say I was going to, just the feelings I got."

Fin leans over, slamming Noah on the back.

Jillian slides her glass of water over to him.

He nods as tears leak out of his eyes, gasping for breath.

Phillip stutters. "But…but, him?"

Amethyst lays her hand on Phillip's. "Remember, she's got the fever. She's been dealing with it for the past three weeks." She looks over at Toby and then turns to Jillian. "It's not like we can dictate our feelings for someone. We can only dictate our actions."

Conceding, Phillip nods. "But still, him and sex? The consensus I got was closer to the landfill and him."

Noah snorts. "So, does that mean I'm in the lead?"

Amethyst bumps his shoulder with hers. "Right now, you are the only one."

Jillian hisses her disapproval at their physical contact.

Amethyst scoots an inch away from him. "Besides, she hunted you down and caught you. So your position is superior. She said it herself; she wants you, Toby." She chuckles at the reaction she gets.

Noah whines, fidgeting, wiping his brow.

Jillian moans, her breathing increases.

Phillip and Fin both watch a tennis match, and the tension builds.

Amethyst stacks the empty plates and moves the tumblers closer to their hands. "Okay, time out! Drink."

Noah and Jillian's synchronized actions appear as if one person controls them both, down to the minute details of a drop of liquid on the lip, the wipe with the finger, and the resigned sigh. They look across the table at Fin and then Phillip with the same dumbfounded, confused expression. "What?" They say in unison. When they get no response turn to each other. "What?" they say in unison.

Amethyst laughs. "That was the strangest experience of stereo I have ever had." She looks at Toby. "Left input." She turns to Jillian. "Right, input." She shakes her head and looks across the table. "Am I right?"

Fin and Phillip wear similar expressions of amazement and nod mutely. They look at each other and laugh hysterically, triggering the rest of the people around them who witnessed the event.

Noah knows by the reaction around him that this event "was noteworthy in the book." "Since we are on a time-out, I will take this opportunity for my nature's call and excuse myself. Ladies." Noah gets to a hunched stance and bows elegantly, turning to Fin and Phillip. "Gentlemen." He snaps his bows and then turns to the room at large. "Friendly masses." He elegantly executes an elaborate bow with an imagined cape, cane, and top hat. With a flourish, he slumps towards the restroom. Hat on, cane tucked under his arm, and full cape swirling at his heels.

The air ruptures with applause.

CHAPTER ELEVEN

The rest of them at the table, noticing their cues, rise to the challenge.

Fin holds out his hand for Amethyst's.

She takes his hand.

They rise with a bow and curtsey, then follow Toby.

The applause continues.

Phillip stands holding his hand out for Jillian.

She takes it and stands. Her red and black dress flows with her graceful movements. Regally, she curtsies, bowing her head and flaring her skirt. She rises, and Phillip spins her to his other side, where she repeats. Upon rising Phillip grips his imagined formal jacket, settling it with a sharp tug, adjusts his bow tie, and picks off an offending bit of lint from the arm he offers Jillian.

Jillian sweeps her imagined skirts, adjusts her bodice, touches the jewels around her neck, checks her hair, and adjusts her full-length gloves before smiling gently at Phillip. Then daintily placed her hand lightly on his offered arm. She opens her imagined fan with her other hand, and they sweep from the room.

The crowd loves it. The house rocks with appreciation, feet stomping, clapping, laughing, hooting and hollering.

Once Jillian and Phillip enter the hall for the restrooms, the pub buzzes with the life within.

Phillip drops his arm, bowing to Jillian, laughing. "Thank you, Jillian."

She laughs and curtsies back. "You're most welcome, Phillip. But may I ask what you thank me for?"

Phillip smiles. "For being you, for your acceptance, for always seeing me, and for being a true friend all these years."

Jillian grabs his hand earnestly. "Phillip, you are a wonderful man, and as a boy too. I don't understand why you hide behind a pocket protector and bad clothes."

Phillip opens his mouth.

Jillian raises her hand. "Spare me the merits of the pocket protector, Phillip. We've all heard them repeatedly. But come on, how often does a pen bleed? It's a disguise. It's time to remove it so you can shine."

Phillip nods. "I agree with you."

Jillian looks stunned. "You do?"

"Yes." Phillip laughs easily. "I realized it's time. This morning I threw my full pocket protector and tie away. To the great pleasure of my employees, "Good riddance," they said."

"What happened all of a sudden?"

"Toby."

"Huh? You just met him. How can Toby do it in hours when Amethyst and I have been working on you for decades?"

"You probably don't want to know this, but it only took a few minutes."

"What, minutes?" She asks in disbelief.

"Yeah, hard to believe, I know. When you were sleeping, he said something that explains what happened."

"What?"

"Clarity through surprise."

Jillian shakes her head. "What? I still don't understand. What does that mean?"

"Let me see if I can explain. This morning I was in my office with the door closed. A ruckus was going on in the outer office. I step out, and there's Toby in all his special glory. Valiantly trying to calm Mary from the fit she was having. It was so funny that I can't even describe what happened. What was even funnier was everyone's reaction to Toby. He was just so sweet and respectful. Nobody

65

wanted to hurt his feelings, so everyone was coughing, humming, and holding their breath. You name it, they were doing it. Looking at him was so eerie like I was looking in the mirror or a vision of the future if nothing changed. Clarity through surprise."

"Phillip, that's great. Please ask Amethyst to help you find your style. She knows clothes, and she will love them. Don't allow anyone else to influence your decisions."

"Yes, I was planning on talking to Amethyst about that. I just haven't had the time."

"Talk to me about what?" Amethyst walks towards them from the ladies' restroom.

Jillian turns towards Amethyst. "I'm making a pit stop. Phillip wants personalized fashion advice."

Amethyst dry washes her hands. "Oh, goody. I love raw material. Come, Phillip, unless you need a minute. Let's put our heads together and see what ideas we come up with."

"Sounds good, Amethyst. I do need a minute, though. I'll meet you at the table."

Amethyst follows Jillian back into the restroom. "So, Jillian, what do you think of Toby? Are you glad I brought him along?"

Jillian flushes, stepping out of the stall and heading for the sink. She stares at her reflection. "I like him a lot. He's funny, sweet, respectful, charming, a lovely man. And yes, I'm glad you brought him along."

Amethyst checks her hair in the mirror, perfect as usual. "But..."

Jillian sighs, turning off the tap after washing her hands, and grabs some paper towels. "But he needs work too, more from the medical field."

Amethyst wipes under her eyes. "And..."

Jillian tosses the used towel in the trash and steps back, checking herself in the mirror. Adjusting her bra, the line of the dress, then her hair. The emerald flashes with green fire on her finger. She brings her hand down and looks at it. "And I get the feeling of hot, wild sex." She shakes her head. "When I ran into him this morning, I had the same impression. When I finally got a look at him. I was seriously questioning my sanity, especially when I had no feelings for every other man on the street."

"So…" Amethyst watches Jillian hold her hand with the emerald, staring at it.

"So…so, I want my sea god." She shakes her head. "Where I will find him, I don't know. But with the intensity of the dream getting stronger, I don't know what will happen." She sighs, stands up straight, and puts her shoulders back. "It's not something I'm going to worry about now."

Amethyst smiles. "Good girl. We're here to unwind and have fun. We are having fun, aren't we?"

Jillian laughs. "Oh, yeah, I'll say one thing: Toby certainly livens up the place."

"He sure does. One in a million, our Toby."

"Yes, all good. I think I made a lifetime friend today. He's special."

They step out into the hall, walking out into the pub.

A few feet away stands Jackson Andrews, loud and obnoxious. He watches for them and moves in quickly. "Hello, Jillian. Are you in a better mood now?" He moves in closer to her.

"I was until you showed up, Jackson." She gives him an exasperated, dead-eye stare. "What do you want?"

"You, baby." He puffs up his chest, moving in closer.

"Well, that's never going to happen." Amethyst leans over to Jillian. "Dumber than a stump, this one."

Jillian leans towards Amethyst. "I know. You would think he'd catch a clue this afternoon. Obviously, we are not that lucky."

The alcohol makes him bold. "Listen, bitch, I decided to go easy on you today. But watch what you say to me."

Jillian asks Amethyst calmly. "Did he just call me a bitch?"

Amethyst nods. "Yes, he did. You know that stump is top of the class."

From behind them, Toby whines. "Excuse me, Ladies. I couldn't help but overhear this creature insult you, Lady Jillian."

Jillian smirks. "Yes, Toby, he did. He won't stop bothering me. It's been going on for years. I keep telling him no. He keeps ignoring me and returns like I changed my mind."

"Apologize, sir. No gentleman behaves in this manner. When a lady declines, a gentleman cuts his losses and moves on. If he does not, he will only experience the further reaches of Hell. Not only do the ladies possess the power of life, Heaven, and Hell."

Their audience cheered.

"Get lost, man. It's not your business."

"I disagree. It is my duty as a gentleman to come to the aid of any lady in need."

From the crowd, a group yells out. "A lady in need is his good deed."

Toby nods earnestly. "Quite right, but these particular ladies are friends of mine. I take extra special care with my friends and family. There is only one person who gets supreme care. That is Lady Jillian, who was in both arms when I stepped foot in this establishment. She is mine to defend by right. So, apologize, sir. I cannot abide such treatment of a lady."

"Are you for real, Jack?" Jackson stares at Toby like he's a joke.

"Yes, I am real. My name is Toby Robins. If you are questioning my sincerity, don't. I am very serious." Toby states firmly in his grating nasal whine, pulling up his pants.

"Whatever." He turns his eyes on Jillian. "Come on, Jillian," Jackson grabs her arm and tries to drag her away.

Toby's loud, horrified gasp stops him. In his distinctive slumping gait runs up to step in front of her. He reaches around and grabs Jackson's thumb like a repulsive bit of trash and throws it away from her.

Jillian looks at Amethyst, her eyes glowing with laughter. She turns back and peeks around Toby's hump on his back.

Jackson stares in amazement and shock, rubbing his thumb.

Toby pulls up his pants. "I demand you apologize for insulting Lady Jillian and fowling her person by laying a hand on her."

Jackson steps closer, a few inches taller than Toby, his feeling of superiority apparent. "Listen, bub, I've had enough of your yapping. Let's take it to the ring."

The crowd roils with surprised displeasure.

Toby turns to her behind him. "Does this mean he challenges me to a fight?"

Jillian looks over at Toby worriedly. "Yes, but Toby, you don't have to accept. This is nothing new. Jackson is always an ass. And I've dealt with him for years. I don't want you to get hurt because of me."

Toby takes her hand gently and pats it. "Don't fret, Lady Jillian. We will stop his pestering tonight; have no fear." He turns back to Jackson. "I accept your challenge, sir. If I win, do you agree to apologize for all your abhorrent behavior to Lady Jillian, then after never speaking to her, stay at least ten feet away forever?"

"Sure, whatever."

"And if you win?"

Jackson laughs confidently. "That you won't bother me anymore."

"Agreed." Toby holds out his limp hand. "We must shake on it to seal the deal."

Jackson rolls his eyes and grabs Toby's hand, tries to crush it and lets go when he fails.

The crowd yells. "The Ring!"

At the bar, O'Malley rings the brass bell twice. "A challenge has been offered and accepted. The match will be between Jackson Andrews and Toby Robins. Man, the tables and set the ring. The match will begin in thirty minutes. May the best man win."

69

Jillian takes Toby's arm and steers him to the booth.

Amethyst follows.

He bows, offering for her to proceed with him.

She smiles at him and tips her head, sliding to the corner.

He repeats the action for Amethyst.

She responds with. "Thank you, kind sir."

"You're welcome." He sits at the end of the bench, watching the swarm of activity at the center of the pub.

In short order, the tables and chairs were repositioned, leaving a large open area in the front of the bar. The whine of a winch precedes the arrival of a boxing ring from the ceiling.

Toby looks up, intrigued. "Interesting."

Jillian and Amethyst laugh.

Amethyst leans closer to Toby. "Jackson has never lost a challenge."

Unconcerned, Toby shrugs. "The odds are in my favor then, he's due." He looks back at the girls. "If I were a betting man, I would lay down serious money in the defeat of Mr. Andrews. He's over proud. That's a sure sign of coming defeat." He turns back around.

Jillian nods to Amethyst and grabs her purse. She digs around and collects all her cash, three hundred twenty-seven dollars.

Fin walks up with papers and a book in hand. "Are we betting tonight, ladies?"

Jillian nods at Toby and hands over her cash.

Fin quickly counts the stack of bills and tucks them in the apron at his waist. He makes a notation in the book, writes a paper, and hands it to her. He repeats the actions for Amethyst. "Thank you, ladies. Toby. My money's on you."

"Thank you. Fin. This should be an entertaining exhibition. I must say the boxing ring was a surprise." Toby watches the four corner posts fit into the floor. The floor of the ring is three feet thick. "Is that a regulation floor?"

Fin laughs. "Yes, O'Malley says if we're doing it, it better be right. We wrestled with having it come up from the floor or down from the ceiling. Too many problems were coming up, but coming down was a challenge. The key to our success is the supports in the basement below."

"Very impressive. I would love to see that sometime."

"Sure, no problem. I have more money to collect if you'll excuse me. Ladies." He moves on to the next table.

"Quite the operation they have here." Toby nods.

Amethyst places a drink at his elbow and passes one to Jillian. Toby picks it up and sips, watching the industrious workers change the pub into a boxing club. "Will they go over the rules of engagement?"

Jillian sips her drink. "Yes, O'Malley will be calling you up shortly. He has three Judges, a timekeeper (A.T.K., to be correct), an announcer, the bell, the stools, the bucket, and the ring girls. O'Malley is the referee in the ring. He has a doctor on hand and EMS on call. He is licensed, is completely legal, and is a friend of the police. The only real difference is that the fighters go in just as they are; no gloves or trunks. It would be allowed if you got into a dispute in your swim trunks while wearing boxing gloves." She laughs. "That happened once."

"Any special rules?" Toby asks as the previously mentioned stools appear in each corner.

Amethyst answers. "I know for sure; no groin, no biting, no gouging. Otherwise, I think anything goes. Oh, try not killing your opponent. He has no fault waivers, so you are the only responsible party for your injuries. If you don't sign, you don't fight."

"I like it. Not restricted to straight boxing?" Toby whines excitedly.

Jillian sips again. "Nope, more like street fighting. Oh, and no hair-pulling. You forgot that one, Amethyst. He'll go over the scoring. Most matches are decided by your total score. Very few TKO."

71

Phillip walks up. "Did you know O'Malley has a contract with WMMO radio for live coverage? They break into their broadcast for the fight. Their van just pulled up."

Amethyst laughs. "A new development."

Jillian laughs. "It's only right. Toby will be fighting for my honor for the first broadcast."

Toby snorts. "It seems Mr. Andrew's apology will be much more public than anyone expected. I will rest easier knowing everyone in the area will help protect you against Mr. Andrews."

Phillip chuckles. "You know Toby, you will be our local celebrity after today."

Amethyst laughs. "Just that scene with Jillian at the county offices marked you for that title. You're a shooting star, my friend."

Toby snorts. "Good Heavens." He shakes his head, bewildered. "This place is truly unique, in my entire life, I have never experienced a place like this. It's truly wonderful."

Amethyst nods. "Yes, we think so too. That's why we all live here. Each of us left only for school and returned as soon as we were done. I probably leave the most, but not for long, mostly for business."

O'Malley rings the bell once, looking at Toby, waving his hand, and waving at Jackson.

Jillian leans on the table. "That's the ten-minute warning. O'Malley is ready for you now, Toby."

Toby stands. "Does each contestant get three in their corner?"

Phillip nods, smiling. "Yes, of your choosing."

He nods. "Would you three do me the honor of standing in my corner?"

They nod, smiling. "We'll be waiting for you."

Toby looks relieved. "Phew! That's great since I only know three: the O'Malley's working the event and the challenger. But I wouldn't want him in my corner."

72

They laugh as he moves away.

Phillip watches Toby slump away. "Where did he come from?"

Jillian looks at Amethyst dryly. "His mother?"

Phillip shakes his head. "Do you think he will win?"

Amethyst answers first. "Without a doubt. He's fighting for a lady's honor."

Jillian nods. "He was confident of Jackson's defeat. No worries."

"Good, 'cause I got forty bucks on Toby."

Both girls laugh hysterically.

Jillian gasps. "Three hundred twenty-seven, how about you?"

"Four hundred seventeen." Amethyst laughs at Phillip's expression of shock. "Hey, if Toby wins, let's pool the money and split it three ways. Let's see, seven hundred eighty-four in the bet, which means we would each put in two hundred sixty-one and thirty-three cents. Phillip, you would owe me one hundred fifty-six and Jillian sixty-six."

Jillian nods. "Works for me. We are on the same team. It's only right."

"I accept," Phillip smirks. "I should have got more money today."

"I know what you mean. If I had more money, I would have put it on Toby." Jillian watches Toby.

His head is bowed in concentration to what O'Malley is saying.

Jackson props back against the bar, watching the crowd, unconcerned. He scans the crowd, sees her watching, and kisses her.

Amethyst leans close. "Did he just blow you a kiss?"

Jillian makes a repulsed face. "Yeah, can you believe it?"

Standing next to him, Toby shifts closer.

Jackson's face shows pain.

Toby turns to him and says something with a slight bow, then turns back to O'Malley.

73

Amethyst laughs. "Did Toby just step on his foot for blowing you a kiss? And then apologize?"

Jillian nods. "That's what it looked like."

Phillip leans in. "I think he positioned Jackson to fight."

Amethyst nods. "I agree. He kept pushing, looking for this outcome. Even in a better position for not throwing out the challenge. So even if he loses, he wins the people's hearts for only fighting for the honor and reputation of a lady."

Jillian smiles. "He is something special."

Amethyst hands her a glass. "Take a drink, Jillian."

Jillian empties it and hands it back obediently. Thoughtfully, she says, "I don't think any man has fought for my honor before."

Phillip chuckles. "I think he's my new role model. Indeed, his fashion sense is worse than mine."

Toby turns and slumps back.

O'Malley rings the bell twice. "Contestants, to your corners, please. The match will start in five minutes."

Amethyst hands Toby a glass. "To hold you over until this business is done."

"Thank you, my dear lady." He drains the glass, hands it back, and holds out his arm for them to proceed. "Ladies, if you are ready."

CHAPTER TWELVE

Their small parade doesn't take long. Phillip in the lead, Amethyst next, followed by Jillian and ending with Toby.

Phillip hops up on the skirt and opens the ropes for Toby. Amethyst climbs the steps next to the ring and walks to the other side of the corner. Jillian takes the corner. Toby steps up and hunches through the ropes. He gets his foot caught between the bottom two, hopping around and shaking his leg, trying to untangle his foot.

Suddenly, released and overbalanced, he hops in the ring, his leg still extended, his arms out fighting for balance. Coming to a stop, he straightens as much as he can and grins at the crowd.

They cheer for him.

He pulls up his pants and turns to his corner, full of purpose.

Amethyst pat the stool with a smile.

Already sitting in his corner, Jackson shakes his head and shrugs his shoulders. He lounges with his arms hanging on the ropes, legs spread, at ease.

Toby sits down, crossing his legs. One starts to swing, puts an elbow on his knee and rests his chin in his palm. "So, Ladies and Gent, how did you like my little act? Was I believable?" He whines nasally.

The three sputter.

Toby nods. "Ah, good. The first thing I'd like to teach you about fighting is…the ego. Their ego is your best weapon, and your ego is your biggest weakness. When fighting, leave your ego with your wallet and keys. If you can't, such as tonight's match, tuck it in your pocket."

They can't help but chuckle.

Amethyst asks. "Would you like some water, Toby?"

"Ooh, yes, please."

She hands him a large water bottle with a thick straw extending through the lid.

He sips daintily, leg still swinging, elbow on knee, and chin in hand. "Now, two key areas of smart fighting are surprise and misdirection. My motto in fighting, as well as in other areas, is "Smart, not hard." Surprise; do the unexpected. Misdirection; move one way strike from the opposite. Do you understand so far?"

The three, barely suppressed in their mirth, answer in unison like rapt pupils. "Yes, Toby."

"Excellent. Defense and Offense. The reason for defense is to protect all the tender, soft, squishy bits in the body. We were born with armor, the skeletal system. For instance, a punch to the mouth or eye hurts a great deal, but a blow to the skull not so much, with the added benefit of serious pain and possible broken bones of the hand of your assailant. They don't have the same impact when a hand is broken."

Phillip coughs. "Ah, Toby, where did you learn this?"

"Here and there. I collect knowledge like children collect stones. Each one is unique and priceless; when polished, it is beautiful in its simplicity." Without spilling a drop, he squirts a stream of water into his mouth from a foot away. "Oh, I did Temp at a sports medicine clinic once. Where was that…Philly or Detroit…I'll have to think about that." He looks off into the distance, then shakes his head.

"Where were we…Ah, yes, defense. Another example would be a punch to the gut. It can be smart, that big target, hard to miss, that tender, soft, squishy area. An area of no armor. If you swing your arm in the path of that blow, you can deflect it. The arm is a smaller target with two features: the back of the forearm is mostly bone from wrist to elbow, and the top has muscle padding. To make your armor stronger, tighten the muscles surrounding it." He looks back.

All three of them hang on his every word.

Toby nods, turns back, squirts from two feet without spilling a drop and hands the bottle back to Amethyst. "Offense. The goal of any physical confrontations is to walk away safely with no worry of getting jumped from behind, so we must work within the range of incapacitated to death. Death is not an option here, so there won't be an example."

They look at each other in amazed disbelief.

"Offense is striking your opponent, period. Gaining control and keeping it. Don't rush. Better to protect your tender, soft, squishy bits than let your ego lie to you, putting you in the path of pain. Remember: Pain and fear are the mind killers. Smart, not hard. Pulling yourself off the floor is hard when your bones are broken, and your opponent is still strong. We are in the land of survival of the fittest, not strongest, not smartest, and not fastest. It helps, but to me, fittest means balanced. Proper balance elicits productivity. Right, Phillip?"

Phillip coughs and clears his throat. "Right."

"Wonderful. Tender, soft, squishy bits are the key to controlling your offense, thus your opponent, and finally, the fight. We now have general targets. But what tool will we use to strike? One you always have on hand is your hand." Toby snorts repeatedly. He lifts his head from his hand. "Please note hand positions."

He stretches his hand back, curling his fingers upon themselves, leaving his palm exposed. "Strike area is the palm heel, the support, and the forearm. As it is for most hand positions." His hand curls into a fist. "Remember to keep that thumb on the outside, holding down those fingers curled up tight. It's not hard to break digits. Keep the knuckles lined up with the forearm. A straight line is stronger than a curved one. You see evidence of that in the majority of cubed buildings, their supports being straight lines. If the lines are not straight, the foundation is weak, and the building falls. The Japanese are known for the support structures in their traditional building practices. Their main support is a living tree. Round, you say, but you would be wrong. A tree is made up of fibers, line fibers; because it is alive and is flexible, stiffness is always bad…well, maybe not always."

An outbreak of coughing occurs behind him.

He turns his head.

All eyes he sees are watching him, sparkling.

He snorts and turns back around. "Rigor mortis is always bad."

More coughing.

He shakes his head.

Jillian asks sweetly. "Ah, Toby, this is fascinating, but what do traditional Japanese building practices have to do with striking positions of the hand in the offensive?"

"Getting a little too deep, am I? If you're interested in that line of thought, we will visit again. Or, more to the point, the mixture of physics and physiology. Fascinating, really; it's my hobby."

More coughs from the crowd.

Toby leans over towards Phillip. "Are there county office employees here besides yourself?"

Phillip laughs. "Probably."

"Ah, that explains the outbreak. You must look into strengthening their constitution."

Phillip chuckles. "I'll look into it, though I think you have done more for their constitution in one day than they have over the past year."

"Excellent, improvement. We're headed in the right direction, Phillip. Ah, but I digress. Let me say this about the closed fist: if your structure is wrong, you will know and wish we had spent more time with the traditional Japanese building structures. By the way, they are superb fighters. Connection? Hmm."

Choking and coughing disrupt the silence.

Toby positions his hand flat, fingers extended. "The flat hand must be muscular and tight. If not, your house will fall, and the Japanese will laugh. You can use all five sides. The most well-known are the slap palm side. The backhand, self-explanatory and the karate chop, the edge of the hand with the pinkie. The two are not as well known but infinitely more dangerous when done properly. The first is the fingers' ends, used together or in combination. It depends on their strength. The other edge of the hand is the last. To utilize either edge, your wrist must have the strength to endure the impact trauma. The most effective position for the

78

thumb is braced on the first knuckle of the pointer finger. And look what? We have two straight lines connecting at a sixty-degree angle, if I'm not mistaken. Good support and a pointy object for those tender, soft, squishy bits. The last I will discuss tonight. Good for self-defense, Ladies, against unwanted male attention. Similar to a normal closed fist, except the thumb is extended, its last knuckle sits on the second of the pointer fingertip of your thumb on that second knuckle, and keep it tight.

The other tools we have are elbows, knees, and feet. We won't go into those now. It depends more on how long I can use that fighting dummy. So you can get the most out of the first round, I will highlight a few debilitating tender, soft, squishy spots. These I will indicate nerve clusters. On these spots, you can strike to pain, stun, numb, unconscious, or death by the force you use. I will start with the lightest and work my way up, stopping short of death. Probably only one unconscious strike, cause you don't get the effect when your opponent is unconscious."

Toby looks around. "I know it's been more than five minutes." He looks across the ring.

Jackson sits facing the audience, beer in hand, laughing it up with his buddies.

Toby shakes his head, looking around and spots a familiar cone. Facing forward, he says softly. "This place has great acoustics."

Jillian says just as softly. "Yes, it does."

He snorts as full understanding hits him. "O'Malley is quite the man, genius. Did he install the directional sound speakers in the ceiling? That looks a lot like a directional parabolic microphone." He nods at the cone facing him.

"Good eye, and yes to both. If you wish, he can give silence, not tonight, you understand." Jillian whispers softly into his ear.

Her breath baths his ear in a sultry caress. He shivers, his breathing increases. He clears his throat. "None of that now, Lady Jillian. I must retain my mind." He holds out his hand to Amethyst.

She places a full glass of whiskey in his grip.

He nods, slurping it down and hands it back. Then he takes a deep breath and releases it.

A door on the back wall opens, and multiple men and two women file out.

Fin behind the bar rings the bell. "All betting is closed. Thank you for your patience. Our delay is due to the accident on I-95. Our good doctor, a judge, and EMS were caught in a traffic jam. Happy to report, there were no serious injuries due to the wreck, just a lot of rubber necks."

The audience laughs.

"We need the doctor to check the fighters, the judges to find their seats, and the referee in the ring. Then we can begin."

The audience claps, ready for the fight to start.

The doctor approaches, and two young men open the ropes for the doctor to enter. He steps over to Jackson first, a look of concern on his face. In his late forties, the doctor is in good health and is still fit. "Hello, Toby, I'm Dr. Paulson."

"Good evening, Doctor," Toby whines nasally, a welcoming smile of the goofy strain. "How are you?"

"Good." The doctor squeezes up Toby's arms. "How are you?" He moves down his legs.

"Great. Thank you for asking."

"Do you have any health issues, Toby?"

"No, healthy as a horse."

"Any restriction or mobility?"

"No, limber and quick."

"Any back problems?"

"Not really, just a little tight from working all day. Nothing to be concerned about. I'm fit and healthy." Toby nods at Jackson. "I just won't get hit. With exercise, the tightness will evaporate."

The doctor nods, gripping Toby's shoulders and looking at Toby in the eyes, accessing. He runs his hands down his chest to his rib cage and abs. His eyebrow raises, holding eye contact. He reaches around, grabbing his hips, then letting his fingers walk up his spine, testing the ribs as he goes. He moves his hands back up to Toby's shoulders moving down.

Toby tips his head back, keeping eye contact.

When the doctor reaches the hump, his other brow joins its neighbor. A slight smile and his sparkling eye betray his somber mask. He nods and pats his shoulders. "You'll do."

"Thank you."

"You can never judge a man from his outer appearance alone."

"You are a wise man, good doctor. That is an internal attribute that can only be measured by actions." Toby's nasal voice grates.

"Yes, you'll do fine." He turns away.

"Ah, doctor, you may want a few things for Mr. Andrews."

"Do you have any suggestions?"

"Well, since you asked, the backboard and neck brace are required for a ride with EMS. Plus, hand splint and nose splint. I think those will need immediate care."

Dr. Paulson smirks. "Left or right?"

Toby looks up thoughtfully. "I believe it was the right. Oh, plenty of gauze. He looks like a bleeder."

"Is that all?"

"I certainly hope so. Isn't that enough? Though I'm sure he'll do something stupid. He didn't seem too bright. But I'll try to keep him from hurting himself."

Dr. Paulson nods. "Just do your best." He left the ring.

Another man enters, this one in his early twenties.

A mic comes down from the ceiling in a controlled descent as the lights dim and a bright spotlight snaps on in the ring.

Toby snorts.

CHAPTER THIRTEEN

"Ladies...and gentlemen, tonight a challenge was offered and accepted to be decided here in the ring. The dispute is over the honor and respect of Lady Jillian Marlowe. Jackson Andrews challenges his right to be a free-range ass. And Toby Robins defends the lady's right to an apology, silence forever, and ten feet distance from Jackson Andrews, a.k.a. an ass. May the best man win." The young announcer's voice is prime for radio, rich and smooth. "The judges for tonight's match are Mike Johnson, David Sharp, and Nathan Parsons. Our residing doctor, Frank Paulson. Our A.T.K., Patrick Victor. South County Hospital provides EMS. South County Police Department provides crowd control. Please respect the boys in blue, and you don't get out of hand. They won't take you in hand...cuffs to the pokey. Our referee for tonight's event is our own O'Malley. Give it up!"

The audience cheers.

O'Malley steps into the ring and takes the mic, holding up his hand for silence. "You forgot one, Pete. Our commentators are announcers from WMMO, Rick and Wesley. Good job, Pete. Let's hear it for Pete Simpson, his first time announcing. Real good, lad. Now, onto business. This match is three rounds, five minutes each. Scoring: one point for contact, two points for a stun (down, not out by ten counts), and automatic loss for a knockout of a ten count. No biting, gouging, hits to the groin, or pulling hair. Don't kill too much paperwork. No sharp objects, i.e., keys, knives, and pencils." He looks at Toby on that one. "Keep it clean. Shake hands, return to your corners, and come out fighting at the bell." He releases the mic. It retracts a few feet above their heads.

Toby extends his hand.

Jackson slaps it.

Toby slumps back to his corner.

The ring girls holding up the Round One cards, circle the ring.

Toby scrapes his hair behind his ears and pulls up his pants.

The bell rings.

Toby flinches, steps forward, and pauses to fumble out a thick marker from his pocket protector.

"Wesley, it seems Andrews imitates Robins."

Toby carefully selects a big bright blue marker.

"Robins stopped to get...is that a maker from his pocket protector, Rick?"

Jackson holds his sides, laughing, standing in the center of the ring, waiting for Toby to reach him.

"Yes, Wesley and Andrews seem to think this is a joke. I believe that pocket holds a white vinyl pocket protector. We can tell Robins is a safety man. Bleeding pens are frightful."

He timidly slumps forward, holding the capped marker out in front of him like a knife.

Jackson howls with laughter. "What are you going to do? Color me into submission?"

"Rick, I believe Robins chose a bright blue marker for his weapon."

"Andrews is having a fit, Wesley, no defense at all."

Toby slumps down. His hands come together. He removes the cap and slumps up. Then he lunges low with his maker extended. He taps it firmly at the front of each ankle. He moves up fast below both knees, leaving bright blue ink behind.

Jackson wobbles on contact.

Toby's marker flies two-thirds up from the knee to the inside center of the thigh on both legs. Moving up fast, he taps the solar plexus.

Jackson expels air.

Toby doesn't slow down. He marks in the v at the base of the throat, a cup of the shoulder, the base of the neck on the side, under the ear beside the jaw, temple. He takes a diagonal slumping step to the side and now stands at Jackson's shoulder: temple, under the ear, the base of the neck, cup of the shoulder, back of the arm, above the elbow and inside wrist. He takes another diagonal slumping step, now directly at him. He dots him; back of the neck, both sides of the spine halfway up. Another diagonal step is to dot the back of his arm above the elbow and under the wrist. Another diagonal step gives a quick scan. He shakes his head, then jabs it between Jackson's eyes at the top of the nose.

Jackson's head tips back pretty far, and starts to lose his balance, his arms come up.

Toby slams two-thirds from the elbow inside the center on both arms into the underside fast. He calmly slumps back, taking the cover and snapping it on. Tilting his head from side to side, appraising his artistry.

The crowd in O'Malley's cheers wildly. "Encore! Encore!"

Enraged, Jackson screams.

"Rick, I can tell we have our work cut out for us tonight. Sorry, folks, Super Geek Robins dotted Andrews from head to toe with his mighty blue marker."

"Yes, Wesley, Andrews looks ill and not just from all the blue spots that cover him. Super Geek Robins has a unique accordion gait. His entire body springs up and down. Andrews the Ass is on the move, rushing forward."

"Super Geek Robins dropped his pen cap, bends low and scoops it up. The man has no fear or isn't paying any attention to Andrews the Ass."

"Look, Super Geek Robins is inside his defense. There goes the mighty marker, up under the chin."

"Wow, look at that technique. He caught him with his mouth open."

"Is that blood? Andrews the Ass seems to have bit his tongue. Super Geek added two new dots, just in front of each ear."

"Hold on, Wesley, two more, back of the hands. Watch out, Super Geek Robins is circling again."

"Just above the backs of the knees. Andrew the Ass is turning. Super Geek Robins dropped his cover again, Rick."

Toby jams the cap on his left middle finger. Dots the tops of both feet since he was down there.

Jackson grabs the material of Toby's shirt and hauls him up, only he's going faster than expected. Jackson's arms fly up, followed closely by Toby's flat hands, thumb knuckle out, hitting the blue dots.

Jackson cries out, shaking his arms.

Still off balance, Toby tips back at the last minute. The impact sounds, a crack of the whip. Toby plants a foot and gains control, looks around, amazed he still stands.

Jackson screams, shaking his arms. "Get off my foot!" His face was purple on one side more than the other.

"Oops, sorry." Toby gingerly retracts his foot. "Have you seen my marker? I must have dropped it." He looks around, searching. "Seriously, Jackson, we could slip...oh, good, you found it."

Jackson hops on one foot, lands on the marker and crashes to the canvas, screaming in rage and pain.

Toby tiptoes to the marker and picks it up, looking around for the cap. "Did you need some help getting up, Jackson?"

Jackson screams and rolls over onto his face, his arms useless flesh hanging from his shoulders. He gets his knees under him.

"Ah, no wonder I couldn't find it. You were sitting on it. I'll take this." Toby grips the cap embedded in Jackson's butt and yanks.

Jackson screams in pain.

"Ah, hell, why not?" Toby dots two more at the base of the spine on either side, snaps on the cap, and then notices the blood. He removes it again, whips a handkerchief and wipes the cap and marker. "Pardon me, Ladies, a slip of the tongue." Toby pulls out hand sanitizer from his front pocket, squirts some in his hand, snapping it closed and drops it back into his pocket. He dips his finger in the glob, then wipes everywhere the blood touches. "Dr. Paulson, he is a bleeder. But that was a total accident. I warned him there was a foot hazard. Who knew a plastic marker cap could cut through two layers of denim and flesh?" With a clean section of cloth, wipe the sanitizer off. Snaps the cap on and puts it into his pocket protector. He looks up and around.

Jackson rests with his ass in the air, a red dot blooming on his back pocket with a dime-sized hole.

In shock, O'Malley stares, unmoving and speechless.

Toby walks over to him and snaps his fingers before his eyes. "O'Malley, it's been more than a count of ten." He points to Jackson. "He's still technically down. I'll take care of it." He slumps over to Jackson, scratches his head, and nods decisively. Gripping Jackson's upper arms, he lifts him back so he sits on his feet. He gives Jackson a gentle shake. "Are you awake?" He leans over his shoulder and looks at his face. "Ah, very awake, I think that's so mad I'm speechless. Oh, I forgot one." Toby whips out his marker and dots Jackson's Adam's apple. Snaps the cap on and slips it into his pocket. "Right, where were we? Yes, standing." He leans back, grips his upper arms and pulls up. "A little help, if you would, please. Thank you." Whines Toby. "How's the foot, Jackson? Will it hold you up?"

Jackson growls, steps away trying to shake Toby off, and starts to tip over.

"Careful," Toby uses a finger to push him up straight and notices the red spot has grown to the size of a dinner plate. "Ah, Jackson, I better shove my hankie down your pants for that wound. It's not dirty for you. I mean, it already has your blood on it and all. Hey, the sanitizer might keep the wound clean. I'll fold it that way." He stops to fold.

Jackson teeters away, shaking his head violently.

"Hey, come back, Jackson. If you're that opposed, I can at least put it in your pocket. Better than nothing." Toby slumps after him in his weird slow-motion run and stops behind Jackson. He pulls the pocket out with one finger, and his other hand dips down with the hanky.

Jackson spins around, his deadened arms fly out and knocks Toby's hands away.

The hanky floats down in front of Jackson's face.

Toby leans way over and snaps it away, regaining his balance.

Jackson squawks.

Toby turns to him. "Jackson, what happened to your lip? You have blood leaking out. That's not good. Do you want my hanky?"

Jackson growls and steps forward.

"I'll take that as a no. It's still in the condition it was before. It never actually touched your bottom." Toby looks around. "Did we go through a dimensional shift? Those people out there seem to be caught. In time, perhaps? Maybe we were going so fast we vanished before their very eyes. And that's the reason for everyone to share the same expression." Toby looks over at Jackson, who stands still, watching the frozen crowd.

Timidly, Toby steps forward, a slumping step at a time. "Jackson, can you still see me?" He bobs to the side and bobs the other way. "His eyes are tracking me, so I'm guessing his vision is okay. You know, Jackson, you have that Flesh Eating Zombie look." Toby mimics Jackson, arms limp at his sides swinging, gait stiff on both sides. "Just imagine the blood here, dripping down the chin and chest." Toby tries again, only growling without the slumping. He turns to his corner, shuffling and growling. He looks directly into Jillian's eyes and growls and shuffles, arms dead at his sides, swinging free. He growls again.

Helplessly, Jillian giggles wildly.

Rippling around the room, her sweet laughter breaks the weird spell trapping everyone.

Sound ruptures the silence.

Jackson snaps, charging Toby.

Toby drops the hanky and bends down to pick it up.

Jackson goes flying over.

Toby grabs his trailing right hand and holds on tight.

87

Jackson heads to take a header on the corner post. Instead, he whips around at the shoulder with his momentum and body mechanics. Both legs are now in danger.

Toby leaps back, still holding Jackson's hand. He stays on his feet, but Jackson rolls on. Then loses his grip and leaps six feet to land in front of the ropes and the drop-off beyond.

Jackson comes to an abrupt stop against Toby's legs.

Toby carefully steps sideways, slumping along until he clears Jackson's body and moves to O'Malley, snapping his fingers again.

O'Malley's eyes focus on Toby.

"O'Malley, I know it's not my place to say, but could you please count? I'm starting to feel trapped in an alternate reality where time doesn't exist. If that's true, then all science crumbles. If science crumbles, then reality as we know it will cease to exist. Then where will we be? Nothing but clouds of energy co-mingling. Honestly, I don't want to co-mingle with Jackson. I wouldn't mind with Lady Jillian, but in this reality, we can co-mingle without rupturing reality." Toby sighs big. "Let's go back to basics. We must have time. To begin time, we need a number. Let's call it one." Toby shakes his head sadly. "Maybe I should restart time myself. A friend in need is a friend indeed. Okay." He turns smartly and slumps over to Jackson. "If you had said anything, we could have stopped this long ago. Such useless suffering. Have you any idea the fear I have of ruptured reality? I could be drinking right now in time. Now I must restart it. At least I'm not alone." He leans over and inspects Jackson, opens an eye and sees the pain and dilation. "Hold on, Jackson, as soon as I start time again, you will get medical aid. Let me reassure you: if you feel pain, you are alive. And since you probably won't get up alone, you owe Lady Jillian an apology. Have you lost your voice, Jackson? I think we can give you some time to find it. Maybe you left it with time." He adjusts his pants and takes a deep breath. Closes his eyes and prays. "One." One finger points down   at   Jackson. "Two...Three...four...five...six...seven...eight...nine...ten." Toby flings both arms out.

He opens his eyes. Nothing changed. He shakes his head, staring down, and notices blood on his shoe and white sock. "Eek, Zombie blood!" he snaps out his hanky, wipes it off his shoe, and tries to blot it off his sock without much success. Toby clears his throat. "Dr. Paulson, Dr. Frank Paulson. Paging Dr. Paulson, Dr. Frank Paulson. Paging Dr. Paulson, Dr. Frank Pau…"

CHAPTER FOURTEEN

Dr. Paulson steps into the ring.

"Oh, my heavens, thank you for answering your page." Toby points at Jackson. "Man down, man down." He leans into the doctor, whispering. "I have this weird feeling I'm in an alternate reality. I don't think time works here."

Dr. Paulson nods. "You're not alone."

"Well, of course not. I now have you and Jackson. You're better, you talk. I think he may have lost his voice with time." Toby shakes his head. "How is he, doc? I tried real hard to keep him from hurting himself, but he really challenged me there at the end when he was heading straight for the corner post. I guess the flesh-eating zombie was too much for him."

"Yes, Toby, I guess it was."

"Did I get it close? He really did look like a zombie."

"We will talk about it later."

"Oh, sorry, here I am going on about me. How rude of me. How can I help? I have some medical knowledge."

"I wouldn't be surprised. We need the EMS personnel and equipment."

"Are they inside or outside?"

"Inside, I'm afraid. They are over by the bar."

"Okay, I'll get the equipment first." Toby slumps by O'Malley. Stops. Tips his head and steps back in front of him. "I'm sorry, my good man, but we need your help." He flicks him between the eyes.

O'Malley gives a soft "Ooff." His eyes start watering, rapidly blinking he takes in a deep breath. He shakes his head, trying to clear it.

"Okay...O'Malley, are you here? Can...you...hear...me?" Toby waves his hand in front of his eyes.

O'Malley clears his throat and nods. "Yes."

"I'm really not sure what's going on here, but help me get EMS moving and working. You can move, can't you? Jackson lost his voice when we lost time. Very disturbing."

O'Malley chuckles. "Yes, I can move."

Toby slumps at a rapid pace, leaving O'Malley to catch up. He collects everything and pauses long enough to flick EMS Techs between the eyes. He passes O'Malley on the way back. "Help them snap out of it. I flicked them between the eyes, flick them again, hard, if you don't get results." He slumps back into the ring. "I'm telling you, doc, this has been a very strange day, unlike any other." Toby lays out the backboard and agilely slips on the neck brace, then adeptly transfers Jackson to the backboard, strapping him down. "Hand splint? Sling?" He grasps Jackson's upper arm and shoulder, gives it a twist, and pops it back into joint. "I flicked O'Malley between the eyes pretty hard. I think he will have a bruise, and so will those two EMS."

Toby slips the sling over Jackson's head and around his arm, shoving it up and away from his hand. He looks around and pulls over the cases, pops them open, searching. "Hand splint?"

Dr. Paulson passes it to Toby.

"Thank you." He places it on Jackson's thigh. Then pulls out a syringe and alcohol swab and rubs the center of the blue spot on his arm. "For swelling." He bites the cap, inserts the needle and presses the plunger. He spits the cap out, places the syringe on the floor, and takes out another. He bites the cap, inserts the needle, presses the plunger, spits the cap to the pile, and places the empty syringe on the floor next to the other one. "For pain, though he will." Toby takes out gauze and wipes Jackson's chin and neck, opens a couple of alcohol swabs and cleans him up better. The cut on his lower lip was just oozing. Noah takes clean gauze, tucks half between his teeth and lip, and takes out an antibacterial cream and a swab. Puts a nice dollop on the swab and spreads it around. He drops the swab on the gauze wrappers. Rips off two inches of tape, folds down the gauze tapes it across his chin. "Did you check his right foot?"

Dr. Paulson remains silent.

Toby's eyes slowly track up, and he looks around. He shakes his head sadly.

It's creepy. Eyes following his movements, but frozen in place. Unresponsive.

Toby looks at Jackson and sees the pain, but no sound comes out of him. "Well, Jackson, it's just us again. Look at them." He watches Jackson's eyes track over, get a little bigger and look back at him quickly. "Creepy, right? Look, we have to communicate. With your eyes; up and down means yes, side to side means no. Do you understand?"

Jackson's eyes go up and down.

"Good. Now, do you know what happened to your voice?"

Side to side.

"Was it when you got really mad?"

They roll in an arc.

"Before?"

Up and down, yes.

"Was it when I was spotting you?"

An arc, before.

"Between your laughing and my spotting."

Yes.

"Nothing happened, did it?"

No.

"Let's move on. Do you have pain other than your lip?"

Yes.

"Hold on." Toby slumps over Jackson and moves Dr. Paulson. "Sorry, doc. You're still residing. I'm just helping. I'm the temp, remember." He pulls the medical cases over to him on the other side of Jackson. He pulls out an I.V. kit and gets to work rehydrating Jackson. "Now, let's see, are both your arms still numb?"

Yes.

"Don't worry, I just numbed them temporarily. It's like they are asleep." He puts the tourniquet on and slaps his arm. Just below the elbow, he inserts the needle for the I.V., tapes it down and connects the hose. He hangs the saline bag off the open case lid and then adjusts the flow. "You are wearing a neck brace and are strapped to a backboard. I put your shoulder back in the joint. Now I splint your hand." Toby picks up a roll of gauze and wraps the splint to his hand. Searching the case he finds an inflatable hand and arm cast. He gets that on and slips the sling down in place. Finds another strap and ties it all down on his chest. "I know your butt hurts."

Yes

"It will have to wait. Is it your foot?"

Yes.

"Can you wiggle your toes on the left?"

Yes.

"Now the right."

No.

"Do you want me to look at it? Or wait for the hospital."

Yes, look.

"Okay, but once the shoe comes off, we can't get it back on. And it's going to hurt, and I may have to cut it off."

Yes.

"Okay." Toby moves down to Jackson's right foot, unlaces the boot, pulls back the tongue and looks at the top of his foot purpling. "Well, I can give to relief from the pain, but I need to touch it first." He scoots up by Jackson's head.

Yes.

"As soon as I can, I will numb the pain."

93

Yes.

He moves back to Jackson's foot and pulls the boot off his foot in one quick motion.

He gently probes the area but can't feel the break. "I think I need a second option. Watch the doc. Paging Dr. Paulson, paging Dr. Paulson, Dr. Frank Paulson, Paging Dr. Paulson, Dr. Frank Paulson. Wouldn't you know it, that trick only works once."

Toby stands and walks over to the doctor. "If you don't want a bruise between your eyes like everyone else is going to have, snap out of it, Dr. I need your services." Toby raises up his hand slowly. "Paging Dr. Paulson, Dr. Frank Paulson. Paging Dr. Paulson, Dr. Frank Paulson. Last chance. Paging Dr. Paulson, Dr. Frank Paulson."

Dr. Frank Paulson's eyes blink, he shakes his head.

"Doctor, would you please look at this patient's foot? I need a second opinion."

The doctor nods and crawls down to the exposed foot. He gently probes with his fingers. "Can the patient move his toes?"

"No."

"Let's wait for X-rays before doing anything else. We need to get him to the hospital." He starts to look up.

"Stop!" Toby whines desperately. "Don't look at me, doc. Can I give him a shot for the pain and swelling on his foot?" He gets up and retrieves the two shots."

Dr. Paulson watches the foot before him. "Yes, Toby. I'm sorry I froze up on you."

Toby nods. "I understand. No, I don't really." He opens the alcohol swab, wipes Jackson's foot, and drops the swab in the wrapper. Bites the cap off a syringe, inserts the needle, presses the plunger, pulls it out and, puts it next to the others in the trash, spits out the cap. "You have to admit, doctor, if you look around, this is not normal. This is an entranced captive audience." He puts the empty syringe down next to the trash. Bites the cap, inserts the needle, presses the plunger, pulls it out and places it next to the other

94

empties on the pile. "The fact that I "woke" you four up, you fell back into your…what state were you in? I wonder…"

Toby stands up and slumps over to one of the EMS Techs. "Please, don't take offense. I'm going to test a theory, all in the name of science." He hunches over and looks into the guy's eyes. "Can you hear me? What's your name?" Toby looks over the guy for a name. "Zack!"

He watches Zack's eyes and takes the penlight from Zack's jacket. Clicks it on and flashes each eye. They respond properly to light, if just a little slow. "Zack, can you walk?" Toby places one hand on his lower back, the other on his chest, and pushes Zack a little towards their patient.

Zack moves mechanically.

Toby stops him with a slight pressure on his chest. Toby moves his arm up. Let's go. It stays. He picks up the I.V. and hangs it on Zack's finger, pulling his hands away quickly.

Zack and the I.V. stay.

Toby snorts and looks down at Jackson, watching him. "You still with me?"

Jackson's eyes move up and down, yes.

"I think it's Doll Daze, and this reality must be the night of the living dolls." Toby tips his head at Zack. "The lights are on by nobody's home?"

Jackson's eyes crinkle with a sparkle.

"Are you laughing?"

Yes.

Toby snorts. "How's your pain? Did I miss anything? Besides your butt."

No.

"Ah, well, that's something." Toby looks around. "Hopefully, we will find your voice when we find time."

Yes. Laughing.

"Well, at least I have my trusty sidekick, the flesh-eating zombie Andrews."

Yes. Laughing.

Toby spots the clipboard, picks it up, and takes out a pen from his pocket protector. Clicks it with commanding intent and starts filling out what he can. "You nearly scared the life out of me, diving for that corner post."

Yes.

"I'm sorry I wrenched your arm out of your shoulder. It was that or shorten your legs. I figured you like your height, so your shoulder took all the abuse. You need to know after the first dislocation, you will be prone to it. Seriously, let it heal, don't use it at all until your hand is better, six to eight weeks, the physical therapy for hand and shoulder together."

Yes.

"Good. Dr. Paulson?"

"Yes, Toby?"

"Are you still not looking?"

"Yes, Toby."

"Excellent. We are getting somewhere. Have you been listening?"

"Yes, Doll Daze. It certainly feels like a daze. I think that you're such an unusual, amazing person that this is an extreme form of awe."

"So what you're saying is that I'm so awesome, I have entranced these people?"

"Yes."

"Well, thank you, doctor, you are pretty great yourself. You aren't affected to the same degree as the rest."

"Thank you, Toby."

"Do you think they will thaw back to themselves on their own? Or take measures? I hypnotize that exposure to me keeps them like this." Toby reviews the form, slumps over to Dr. Paulson, and hands him the clipboard and pen.

He turns to clean up the medical mess. Puts the covers back on the syringes, grabs a hazardous waste bag, dropping the trash. Tucks it back into the case. Snaps it closed and puts it aside. Moves to the other case to pack it back up. Snapping it closed, he sets it next to the other one.

"Well, they should thaw, as you call it, but we don't know how long that will take." He looks down at his watch. "And since we still have time, they are going to need it. I have to get Jackson to the Hospital. So, I can't help you here right now. After I get him settled, I will call here; if you still need me, I will come back."

"Thank you. I'm sure I can manage for now. But let's get you, Jackson, Zack, and his partner on the move."

"How do you propose to pull them from the daze?"

"A hard flick woke them up once, maybe an ice bath wash to the face will shock them to reality. I'll be right back." Toby slumps over to the ropes and slips through gracefully, flowing down to the floor. Then slumps across the pub, moving through the motionless, watchful crowd of people. He moves behind the bar, searching for a bucket. Finding the ice bucket, goes to the back room for the ice machine, with on quick, strong shovel fills it with ice. Goes back to the bar with the filled bucket and fills it with water, a pitcher at a time from the faucet and the water button on the fountain hose. He grabs a clean bar rag and tosses it into the ice water.

He turns to Fin standing next to him. "I'm sorry, my new friend, but I have to test it on someone."

CHAPTER FIFTEEN

Toby flicks Fin hard between the eyes. Grabs the wet cloth, barely squeezing any of the water out, and sloshes it across his face and neck.

Fin jerks his shaking head back with a gasp, blinking his eyes repeatedly.

Toby steps behind him. "Fin, can you hear me?"

Fin laughs shakily. "Yes, Toby."

Toby gives a big sigh. "Phew, it sounds like you haven't lost your marbles."

Fin laughs stronger. "I'm glad to hear that, though I wasn't too sure." He starts to turn.

Toby stops him. "We have a big problem, Fin."

"What's that?"

"Well, I'm calling it Doll Daze. And tonight is the Night of the Living Dolls. I know it's corny, but we do what we must to keep our spirits up during trying times."

"Yes, I'm with you so far."

"That's just the thing: if you see me, you may fall back into the daze. The only one who doesn't seem to be affected is Jackson, and he lost his voice somewhere between laughing at me after the bell rang and when I dotted him." Toby snorts. "I need to wake up the EMS fellows and have them drive Jackson to the hospital. Do you have all your faculties? Could you drive safely?"

Fin holds his sides, laughing hard. "Yes, if I had to." Fin gasps for breath. "I'm sorry, Toby, but look around you. You weren't kidding about the night of the living dolls."

"Yes, I do know. It is beyond funny." Toby snorts. "To the point of scary, almost. After we get the doctor, patient, and crew going, I'll show you something I discovered."

Fin nods, gasping for air around his laughter.

"I either have to get you blinders, stay behind you, or you have to promise not to look directly at me." Toby shudders. "You don't understand the fright I had after waking up the doctor, your uncle, and those two EMS techs. I look up, and they're surrounding me, staring again."

Fin wheezes. "Does this sort of thing happen to you often, Toby?"

"Good Heavens, no! Nothing has ever happened to me like this. I seriously questioned if Jackson and I slipped into another reality or something. Just wait until you get in the ring and see if you don't question it yourself."

Fin stumbles out from behind the bar, moving around all the frozen people, looking this way and that, laughing at each one. His laughter echoes weirdly through the pub. "This is unreal."

Toby nods, following with the bucket of icy water. "Yes, you are starting to understand." They climb into the ring. "Do you know which one drove tonight?"

Fin walks over to Dr. Paulson and Jackson. He puts his hand on the doctor's shoulder.

Dr. Paulson looks up at Fin and smiles. Sees Toby and snaps his head back around. "I see Toby succeeded in waking you up."

Fin crumbles into hysterical laughter, eyes tearing. "Does not looking help keep you out of the doll daze?" He chokes out.

Dr. Paulson laughs. "Yes, actually. I stupidly watched him expertly patch up Jackson. You know he temped at a hospital once." He laughs. "I believe that is part of our problem, the dazed dolls. We have never seen anything like him."

"I agree. But he is awesome. And hilarious. Maybe we are overdosing on exposure to him."

Dr. Paulson nods, laughing. "You may have something there." He snorts. "Maybe we should put a warning label on him. Warning: Overexposure causes excessive drooling and fits of laughter. Temporary side effects: loss of voice, mind, and motor function."

Fin falls over laughing. "Doll Daze."

99

Toby steps behind the doctor after putting the bucket by O'Malley and the EMS techs. "Turn around, Fin. Look at those two."

Fin turns, choking on his laughter, holding his sides, wiping his eyes. "What's that purple spot between their eyes?" He gasps out.

Dr. Paulson laughs. "The Mark of the Dolls in the Daze. You have one, too."

Fin's fingers automatically touch the tender spot on his face. "A bruise?" Snorting, laughing.

"It was the only thing I could think to do, a little shock to the system; eyes water, blinking starts. It worked on all three, but they got sucked back into the daze before I knew it." Toby whines sadly.

Fin laughs. "Don't worry, Toby. It will be a trophy to everyone here. Especially since I remember everything." Fin crawls up to Jackson's head. "How is the Flesh-eating zombie?"

Jackson's eyes move up and down.

Fin turns to Toby, standing behind the doctor, looking worried. "Toby?"

Toby looks at him, concerned, then looks around guiltily. "Don't look at me, Fin. You could slip back into the daze." He whines piteously.

"If I do, you'll bring me back. I'm not too worried. Talking helps. The interaction is what kept Jackson from falling into the daze."

Toby nods his head. "That makes sense. The doctor was fine for a while, then stopped talking, and I found out the doll daze got him." Toby brightens up. "Okay, you are now my interacting sidekick since the flesh-eating zombie is out of commission."

Fin laughs. "Do I get a good sidekick name like Jackson's?"

Dr. Paulson chuckles. "He went through a lot of pain and suffering for that. Are you prepared?"

Toby snorts. "We'll have to wait and see, Fin. Find one that fits you. It's not something to rush." He adjusts his pants. "All right,

100

now, how are we to get the two techs, the doc, and Jackson out to the ambulance and drive away?"

Dr. Paulson clears his throat. "I'll wait here with Jackson. You get those two out to the ambulance, then wake them up. Toby, you come back, and you and I will get Jackson out to the ambulance while Fin is restarting their minds. I'll ride along to make sure the conversation continues to the hospital." He nods. "You two will work on the crowd here. I'll catch a cab back for my car and possibly a bottle." He laughs. "The Night of the Living Dolls will live on forever."

Toby nods, looking a little concerned. "Do either of you know or care to guess if we are still on air? Those radio guys fell into the daze. Do you suppose people in radio land listening in at their homes are in the doll daze, too?"

Fin laughs helplessly. "That's a horrifying thought. Makes me a little leery stepping outside.

Toby snorts. "We interrupt our regularly scheduled programming for this live update. Doll Daze is sweeping the nation. If you see this man, please call your local authorities. Warning: he is a charming gentleman and dangerously funny. Please use extreme caution with limited exposure. Update at eleven."

Fin and Paulson choke on their laughter.

Toby shakes his head. "I don't think I can say this enough today. It has been seriously strange. I feel like I stepped into The Twilight Zone." He moves over to the EMS tech and checks his name tag. "Hello, Charles. We're going for a stroll. Nothing to fear, my good man. We'll get you out of the daze soon enough. I don't mean to be forward, but I need your keys. I will be putting my hand in your pocket."

Toby pats down the man and finds the keys and pulls them out of his jacket pocket. "Aren't we all happy I didn't have to get in your pants?" Keys in hand.

Paulson and Fin howl with laughter.

"Now, Charles, we are walking to the ropes and lie down. But no naps for you. No, you are on the clock. We need to get the hamster back on the wheel." Toby nudges him forward on his back. Turning him with a touch on his shoulder. Stops him with a hand on his chest. "Stop. Good. You're going to bend your knees and lower to the floor." Toby pushes down on both shoulders.

Charles' legs fold to a squat.

"Not bad. How to get you to lay down?" Toby steps behind, grips his shoulders and moves him back and down. Now sitting, he backs up and lowers Charles's shoulders to the floor of the ring, supporting his head. "Now, your legs." Toby steps over and gently pushes down on both knees.

Charles's legs straighten.

Nodding, Toby turns and sees both Fin and the doctor staring. "Why aren't you talking?"

Dr. Paulson shakes his head and clears his throat. "Sorry about that, but that was surreal. Doll Daze is such a fitting name."

Fin blinks and falls over, laughing. "Doll Daze...Doll Days!" Struggling back up. "Toby "The Dazer" Robins."

Toby snorts. Climbs between the ropes and hops down. "Are you going to assist or just wallow in your mirth?"

Paulson and Fin laugh.

Fin crawls to the bucket. Pats his uncle's leg. "How are you doing, O'Malley? We'll be back to rescue you from the daze." He climbs to his feet and picks up the bucket, moving towards Toby.

Toby grabs Charles' arm and waistband and slides him over onto the skirt around the ring. Takes Charles by the shoulders and sits him up, takes his legs and pivots him around. Pulling his butt to the edge, lowers his legs to dangle over the edge. "Here we go, Charles. One little hop. Then, a short walk to the ambulance, where we will pull you from the daze with a sharp pain and a cold dousing. Fin will stay with you for some conversation and rev up your mind."

Toby stands in front of Charles, takes his shoulders and pulls him forward and up.

Charles stands.

Toby steps to the side and pushes gently on his back, heading towards the door. "Fin, can you get the door?"

Fin hoops down, grabs the bucket, and jogs to the door. "Sure, Toby." He chuckles. "You control your doll very well."

"Yes, well, I was never one of those children that popped the heads off their dolls and flung them around by the hair."

I'm sure everyone here is eternally grateful." Fin laughs, holding the door open.

Charles steps out into the quiet night, followed by Toby. "Do you know where they parked?" Reaching the sidewalk, Toby stops him.

"I think in the back." Fin puts the bucket down and trots off around the corner of the building to the lot for O'Malley's customer parking. He reappears and stops next to Charles. "It's in the alley. Let's wake him now. I'll stay and get his marbles rolling. You go get the ambulance. Pull it up close."

Toby nods, looking up and down the street. Not a soul in sight. "Is it usually this quiet?"

"Not on a Friday night. Let's not worry about it yet, it could just be a coincidence."

"I'll be right back." Toby looks a Charles. "Time to pull you out." He flicks him hard between the eyes, grabs the bar rag out of the ice water and sloshes it over his face and neck. Dropping it back into the bucket, he turns and, in a slumping run, is gone from their sight.

Charles blinks repeatedly. His hand comes up and rubs between his eyes and then down his wet face. Looking around, surprised.

"Charles, I'm Fin O'Malley. Dr. Paulson will answer what questions you may have in detail. We don't have time for it now. Do you understand me?" Fin puts his hand on Charles' shoulder and turns him so they are face to face.

Charles nods. "Yes."

"Good. We need you to drive a man, Jackson Andrews, to the hospital. He's seriously injured and requires more aid. Can you drive safely?" Fin looks into Charles' eyes, watching him.

"Yes." Charles bends down, stands up, squats, stands, lifts one leg, then the other. He extends his arms and brings one finger to his nose, then the other. Turns his head left and right, up and down. "Yes, definitely. Where's Zack?"

"Inside being an I.V. stand. Don't worry, you will take him with you. Awake as you are now. I hear the ambulance coming. Whatever you do, do not look at Toby. It seems that once you fall into the Doll Daze, you are susceptible. You cannot fall into the Daze and get your patient help. Cover your eyes if you have to when Toby pulls up. We have found that talking helps keep you out of the Daze."

"Doll Daze?" Charles asks, confused.

"That's what Toby calls it, and it's a fitting name. Give it time, and you will remember. Go take a quick look if you want, but get back and keep your eyes down around Toby. We woke you up the second time first since you have to drive. Keep moving at keep talking. Don't look at Toby." Fin turns towards the parking lot. "By the way, everyone we wake has a dark purple bruise between their eyes." He turns back to Charles and points to his bruise. "The mark of the Doll Dazed, on the night of the living dolls." He turns back and walks to the approaching ambulance, light flashing only.

Toby stops and hops out. Walks to the back, opens the doors, unlocks the gurney and pulls it out. All seamless actions of a veteran. He looks at Fin curiously. "Where's Charles?"

Fin laughs. "Don't worry, he's functioning. Just taking a quick look." Fin looks over his shoulder. "Here he comes now." He turns to the approaching man. "Remember, Charles, keep your eyes down."

Toby wheels the gurney up the sidewalk, passing Charles. "Charles, wait out here. I'm bringing out Zack next. Then, Dr. Paulson and Jackson. I filled out as much as I could on the paperwork. Review it before you leave, and I'll answer what I can. Jackson, on the other hand, lost his voice somewhere tonight. He is aware and conscious of all faculties. Eyes up and down means yes, side to side means no." Toby moves to the door. "Ask Fin while you have him. His job is to ensure your mental clarity."

Charles looks at Fin. "What?"

"A good start. It seems Toby has some medical training. He did all the work on Jackson. Because you three fell into the daze a second time. Dr. Paulson will ride along and keep the conversation going. I would like you to call the pub when you get there so Toby won't worry. He feels responsible for the Doll Daze and its victims. A concern we both have is that it was a live radio broadcast, and we don't know if those listening were affected. We did notice that the downtown traffic is nonexistent." Fin rubs the back of his neck. "So if you notice anything strange on the way back or at the hospital, let us know. Our job may get bigger than it already is."

Charles nods. "Okay, I'll let you know one way or the other."

Fin smiles. "Thanks. So what did you think in there?"

Charles chuckles nervously. "Creepy."

CHAPTER SIXTEEN

Fin laughs. "It's much worse up in the ring. All eyes are focused there."

"I've never heard of something like this happening before."

"Our Toby is awesome and amazing. With a little time, it gets really funny. And for me, laughing helps a lot. So laugh it up on the drive." Fin looks at the door, walks over and opens it. "If you can keep talking or laugh, watch why Toby calls it Doll Daze. Remember the wake-up process, though I don't know how hard he flicks. Watch."

Zack walks out stiffly, only his legs moving.

Toby follows closely.

"If I start talking to Zack, nothing happens?" Charles asks.

Toby smirks. "Did you wake up when I was talking to you?" He puts his hand out to stop Zack.

Zack stops.

"Try it, it at least helps you from falling into the Daze. But watch this. Zack bends over." Toby places his hands, and Zack bends at the waist, arms swinging. Toby reverses his hands, and Zack stands.

Charles laughs, holding his sides. "Is everyone like this?"

Fin chuckles. "You were standing in the ring, and with a touch here and there, he had you walk, squat, sit, lay down, straighten your legs, hop down, and walk out."

"I understand the name better." Charles chuckles, wiping his face.

Toby pulls the clipboard out from under his arm, takes the pen puts it into his pocket protector and hands the clipboard to Charles. "Our flesh-eating zombie will be out presently with the doctor. Prepare your questions. I will run down his injuries and what actions were taken." Toby turns to Zack. "Here we go, Zack, again."

Toby flicks Zack hard between the eyes, bends down, grabs the icy rag and sloshes it on Zack's face and neck. Drops the rag back into the bucket and turns to the door. "You're up, gentlemen."

"Zack, can you hear me?" Fin asks.

Zack reaches up and rubs between his eyes and down his face, eyes watering and blinking furiously. "Yes."

"Good, now move around and start talking. You have a patient on his way out. His name is Jackson Andrews." Fin pats him on the shoulder.

"One of the fighters," Zack says slowly.

"Yes, good." Fin looks over at Charles. "Keep him talking. Let's move to the ambulance."

Toby steps into the eerily quiet bar. The gurney sits just inside the door, off to the side. The area between the door and bar was clogged with tables, chairs, and dazed people.

The TVs around the pub all show the action in the ring.

Toby starts moving the people out of the path to the ring. It's too congested to get the gurney closer. "Hey, doc, how's Jackson?"

Dr. Paulson lifts his head. "As well as can be expected. Zack and Charles are awake?"

Toby nudges a large man aside, stopping him before he runs into a young woman. "Yes, Charles was before I came to get Zack. They have Zack moving around out there." Toby moves a woman a few feet away. "I have some concerns about the nonexistent traffic on a Friday night in the downtown area. Keep your ears open when you get to the hospital, and if there is a need, let them know what you experienced here." Toby guides a young man over. "I wouldn't like it if panic runs across the countryside. As it stands, I'm considering moving on."

"Do you really feel you have to leave?" Dr. Paulson looks concerned. He stands next to Jackson, holding up the I.V. bag.

"I'm not really a social person. My books and hobbies have always been my companions. With what's happened here tonight, I think it best. There are at least one hundred and fifty people here tonight. What if something bad happens to one of them because their minds are befuddled? I somehow caused their current state. It's my responsibility to return them to normal. One way to ensure no repeat of their Daze would be to take out the cause of the ailment, me." He moves the last two people out of the way. He climbs up on the skirt of the ring and slips through the ropes.

"Maybe you should give it a few days before you leave. I'm sure there are a lot of people here who would really miss you. You are a very fascinating man. I, for one, would love to sit and talk with you. And we both know I'm not as susceptible to the Daze."

Toby hunches over Jackson. "We're on the home stretch. I'm sorry, but you're going to get jostled around some. I can't get the gurney over here. I have to carry you to it." He moves to the head of the backboard. "Ready?"

Jackson moves his eyes up and down.

Dr. Paulson puts a hand on Toby's shoulder. "Please, Toby, wait a few days before you make your decision."

Toby nods. "Fine, I need to make sure everyone is okay beforehand anyway." He leans down and picks the backboard up about a foot and drags it over towards the door.

"Thank you." Dr. Paulson follows, holding the I.V. bag.

Gently, he puts Jackson down. "Have you noticed any signs of life in here while I was gone?"

"No, that is a bit worrisome. I was hoping that without you as a stimulus, they would thaw back to normal. They may need more time." Dr. Paulson rubs his chin.

Toby slips through the ropes and hops down from the skirt. "I think I'll put one person somewhere and see what happens. If the Daze wears off after a couple of hours, I will feel better. I would hate to think it was permanent if untreated."

"That's a good idea. We are in unchartered territories." Dr. Paulson feeds the I.V. through the ropes.

"There are a lot of firsts for me today." Toby slides Jackson under the ropes and angles him up, sliding the edge along his shoulder.

Dr. Paulson slips through the ropes and hops off the skirt. "Hold on, Toby, I'll help carry him."

Toby positions himself under the board, in the middle and lifts, making a slight adjustment to find the balance point. "That's alright, doc, I got him. No sharp movements, Jackson. Otherwise you'll end up on the floor, butter side down. Nobody wants that." Toby glances towards the silent doctor. "Doc, are you with me still? We'll have a serious problem if I've lost you again in this position."

The doctor doesn't respond.

Toby slumps forward slowly, hoping that the dazed doctor will follow on his tether. "Jackson, you may have some pulling on your I.V. line. Make some noise if it pulls the tape off. You know, zombie sounds. Can you do that?"

Jackson growls.

Toby snorts. "Thank you, Jackson." He takes another step forward and feels resistance. He moves forward again, and the resistance is gone. Toby listens carefully. Light steps follow. "Dr. Paulson?"

Silence.

Halfway to the gurney, Toby says. "Paging Dr. Paulson, Dr. Frank Paulson. Paging Dr. Paulson, Dr. Frank Paulson. Crap!" He continues to move to the gurney. "You shouldn't have watched that, doc. You know better. It looks like you're getting the doll daze mark. We can't take any chances." Toby continues the last few feet to the gurney, worried.

The door opens.

"Don't look!" Toby whines. "I've lost the doctor, and he's following. Fin?"

"Yes, I'm here, Toby." Fin chuckles. "Are you serving Flesh-eating zombies for dinner, Toby?"

Jackson growls.

Toby snorts. "Fin, can you tell if Dr. Paulson is pulling the I.V. hose?"

Fin laughs. "Your little doggy is right on your heels. There's slack in the hose."

"I didn't lock the gurney wheels. Could you dash over here and lock them for me, please?"

"On my way." Fin turns his head. "Don't look in. I'll be right back." Fin rushes in and locks the wheels.

Toby stops by the side of the gurney.

Dr. Paulson stops at the end.

Fin stands on the other side. "What do you want me to do?" Fin asks, amused.

Toby squats down and slides the backboard onto the gurney. "Unlock your wheels. When we get outside, take the I.V. and get the guys to load Jackson. I'll give Dr. Paulson the treatment. Then we load him in, answer questions and send them on their way." Toby straps Jackson to the gurney. "Then come back and have a large drink. Wake a few. Have a large drink."

Fin laughs. "Sounds like a good plan." He opens the doors.

Zack and Charles take them, looking down.

"We lost the doctor again. Toby was being awesome, and the doctor watched. Keep your eyes down, boys. Here they come."

Toby snorts, unlocking his wheels, wraps the I.V. hose around his hand, gives a gentle tug and rolls Jackson out of the pub. On the sidewalk, he stops by the bucket. "Zack, Charles, please come and get the I.V. and Jackson. I need to see the doctor. Fin, put a hand on the doctor's chest and stop him, please. He got away from me."

Fin laughs. "You could just reel him in."

"You're my sidekick, and I have to keep you in action to keep the Daze at bay." Toby steps away when Zack takes control of the gurney.

Charles steps over to Dr. Paulson, takes the I.V. bag and moves over to the other side of the gurney. "Toby, would you run down Jackson's injuries real quick?"

Toby nods. "Of course. He has a split lower lip that might require a stitch or two. He probably has whiplash or strained muscles in his neck, no serious damage. He will require the neck brace for a time, though." Toby points to each area. "Dislocated shoulder that's been reset needs sling and immobility for one and a half to two months. Broken hands, broken bones under the blue dot, possible nerve damage. He twisted out of my grip. But I think (the middle two bones) broke clean. His hand is in a splint after setting the bones and cushioned by the inflatable cast. Six to eight weeks in a cast." Toby looks at the techs.

They look at each other, amazed. Their heads start to turn to Toby.

"Don't look at me, please. Are you still with me?"

"Yes, Toby." They both say in a monotone voice, then laugh freely.

"I was worried there for a second of a different stage of the doll daze, the talking doll." Fin laughs.

"Gave me the goosebumps." Toby rubs his arms. "Are you two really here?"

"I was feeling a little fuzzy around the edges, but laughing and talking works. I'm more focused now." Charles chuckles.

"I'm right here with you, Charles. We're fine, Toby. Continue, please." Zack marches in place.

"During the exhibition, I hit Jackson's nerve clusters underside of his arms, the blue dots. Both arms are numb or asleep. You still have a couple of hours before they wake up. I really didn't want him to hit me. It hurts."

They all laugh.

Toby points at Jackson's hip. "He has a wound on his butt that I didn't treat, pen cap circle cut." Toby points at the other foot. "I think it's just bruised with nerve trauma. I stepped on it. I didn't think any permanent damage. I gave two shots to his hand, one for inflammation and one for pain. Even though it's deadened right now, I wanted to keep ahead of the pain for him. I gave two shots to his foot, the same combination." Toby scratches his head. "Oh, yes, he

111

lost his voice somewhere between me extracting my marker from my pocket and when I dotted him. If we find it, we'll bring it over. Watch his eyes; up and down, yes, side to side, no." Toby steps away, moving to the doctor. "Anything else, gentlemen?" Toby flicks the doctor between the eyes hard. Grabs the rag and sloshes it on his face and neck. Drops the rag in the bucket and turns to Fin. "Get his gerbil on its wheel."

Everyone chuckles.

Charles clears his throat. "No questions right now. But if we do, will you be here for a while?"

Toby snorts. "Indefinitely, yes. I have at least one hundred and fifty people to wake and leave safely."

"Our shift is over at eleven, so if you would like help, we'll come back. Even if it's dealing with the newly awake." Zack looks over at Charles. "I think we might need a drink, too."

Charles nods, smiling big.

"Thank you, gentlemen. I will gladly accept any and all help. Go get Jackson settled. Keep each other laughing and talking on your drive. We'll see you later. Find Fin when you get back." Toby turns to Fin and Dr. Paulson. "Doc, I think you just wanted the treatment for the distinctive mark of attendance."

Dr. Paulson sheepishly rubs between his eyes, then wipes down his wet face. "It's hard to look away when you are in action, Toby. But when you started carrying Jackson like a suckling pig on a silver platter, poof! It was too late. You don't do the expected, so we pay attention to see what happens next. Hence, the doll daze." Dr. Paulson laughs. "I will not say I'm displeased for carrying this badge."

Toby snorts. "You may change your mind when you have two black eyes tomorrow." Toby snickers behind his hand at the doctor's surprised expression.

"Do you mean that everyone will have a raccoon mask tomorrow?" Dr. Paulson sputters.

Fin bends over laughing. "Even your treatment is funny days later."

"Probably lasts about a week, green and yellow near the end." Toby grins, goofy.

"And laughing at each other when paths cross." Dr. Paulson laughs. "You really bring the community together with humor."

"It's better than any other way." Toby pats the doctor's shoulder. "Your ride is ready and waiting. Please give us a call when you get there." Toby picks up the bucket and turns, waves, and slumps into the pub.

CHAPTER SEVENTEEN

He moves through the frozen crowd. "Excuse me. Hello. How are you doing?" Their eyes follow him as he walks through the masses. "Nice time we're having." He works his way to their booth. Sets the bucket down and looks over at the womenn.

Jillian and Amethyst stand on the ground by the corner of the ring.

"Jillian, my dear, I really don't want to give you a raccoon mask. I hope you don't think I'm taking liberties." Toby turns her to face him. He looks into her eyes, watching her, leans in and gently brushes his lips against hers. Lightly kissing her with reverence and sweetness. He pulls back a little to see what effect it has on her.

Her eyes darkened a little, but otherwise nothing.

Noah whispers. "Jillian, please wake up. I need you." He leans in and kisses her with need, drawing her to him, keeping a chokehold on his desire. He kisses her deeper. Letting this loneliness and desperate need call to her. Beckon her closer. Calling to her. Asking for a response. Just when he thinks it's not working, she kisses him back.

He's so happy. He hugs her tight draws back, and looks at her, grinning big.

Jillian's eyes flutter open, warm and smoky. She blinks repeatedly, rubs her eyes and looks at him.

His grin is pure joy.

She smiles back. "Toby?" Her voice is warm and smoky, a bit confused.

He hugs her again, quick and tight, then releases her. "Oh, thank you, lady Jillian, for waking up so nicely."

Her confusion increases. "What do you mean?" She realizes the pub is eerily quiet and looks around. She looks back at Toby, concerned. Walks over to Amethyst. "Amethyst?" She says concerned.

No response.

"Amethyst, wake up!" She pokes her in the side.

Amethyst takes a step to the side and stops.

Jillian hops back and looks over at Toby. Then looks around at all the people with the strange expression, eyes wide, watching. "Toby, what's wrong with everybody?"

Toby snorts. "I'm calling it Doll Daze." He looks around at all the people. "Creepy, isn't it? It's worse up there. I get people to wake up, and then when I'm not looking, they fall back into it. Dr. Paulson was dazed three times. I'm getting a little nervous. Fin is outside making sure the EMS techs and doc are functioning well enough to get Jackson to the hospital and fix him up. I did all I could for him here." Toby rubs his neck, turns around, and heads to the booth. Sits down and pours whiskey into the glass almost to the brim.

He picks it up, closes his eyes and knocks it back. Gently places the glass on the table. Takes a deep breath, holds it and lets it go.

Jillian walks over and sits down across from him, placing her hand on his. "Are you okay, Toby?"

Toby looks at her. Sees earnest concern. He shakes his head. "No, not really. Today has been trying. Tonight, surreal and worrisome. Possibly dangerous and not just for those here. But anyone who might have been listening on the radio." He shakes his head. "Maybe I'm being paranoid. Nothing like this has happened before, and it's disturbing."

"What exactly happened, Toby?" Jillian asks softly, holding his hand.

"I wish I knew. I was busy in the ring with Jackson. Who did not fall into the Daze but lost his voice early on, though I found out about it much later." He shakes his head. "The first time I noticed something was when Jackson was face down, his bottom up in the air. I walked over and asked O'Malley why he wasn't counting. He had that expression on his face and didn't say anything. So I went

115

over and picked Jackson up. We were way past five minutes, but no bell sounded. Jackson was mad, and I ended up making it worse. Especially that whole flesh-eating zombie bit."

Jillian giggles, slapping a hand over her mouth in surprise.

"Please laugh, it helps. You're giggle seemed to break the spell for about a second, and then Jackson fell over me, and I had to act. It seems that when I do anything, people fall into the Daze." He hangs his head, shaking it sadly. "I was really having a nice time tonight, and somehow I stepped into the ring and out of reality."

Fin walks up. "I see you got one awake."

Jillian looks up at Fin. "What's that purple spot between your brows?"

Toby snorts.

Fin laughs. "That's the mark of the Dazed."

Her fingers test the spot on her head.

Fin laughs. "You don't have one, so that means he did something else to wake you." His brows rise in question."

Toby snorts. "Yes, I kissed her. There's Amethyst. See if you can get a response from her. I warn you. You have to draw a response. I almost didn't succeed. You know what happens if you can't get one." Toby pours a glass and slides it over to the end of the table. "On your way back, with or without Amethyst, we will form our plan on how to deal with these nice folks."

Fin picks up the glass and shoots it back. Puts the glass down, picks up the money and pats Toby on the shoulder. "Don't fret, my friend, I've been thinking about it. I'll bring the bottle and Amethyst, even if she's still dazed, and Phillip, too. But could you go up and get Ian? I don't have the confidence to bring him here. Go show Jillian why you call it Doll Daze." He walks off.

"Okay, come on, Jillian. You'll probably get a kick out of this." Noah pours out the last from the bottle into two glasses. "To the Night of the Living Doll Daze." He taps it into her glass and pours it down his throat.

116

She snickers. "To the Daze and the night of living dolls." She drinks. "Let's go." She holds out her hand to him.

He smiles and takes her hand. "A little advice: interact with me, laugh, yell, I don't care. I don't want to see you fall back into the daze. I liked how I woke you up, but down that path is dangerous all on its own. Besides, each time I woke up the doctor, it was harder. I woke him up three times. The EMS techs felt the slide and described it as feeling fuzzy around the edges. If you start feeling fuzzy, jump, laugh, or do something, talking works, too. But I imagine it's hard to think of a question when feeling fuzzy." He assists her on the steps up to the ring, hops over and holds the ropes wide.

She almost doesn't have to bend. She snickers. "My, how strong you are."

"The better to carry you off with, my dear."

She hoots. "You are a wolf in sheep's gear."

"So the ladies tell me."

She giggles. "A man of hidden abilities."

"As you wish." He snickers behind his hand. "Take a look around. I seriously questioned my reality, the loss of time, or if I had completely lost it."

Jillian turns around, looking everywhere, at everybody frozen in place, an awestruck expression, the eyes following them. She moves closer to Toby and grabs his arm. "Okay, I'm officially weirded out. Wow! No wonder you questioned your reality. I'm doing it now."

They walk to O'Malley. "I first really noticed something was wrong after the zombie bit and dislocated Jackson's shoulder to save his legs and stop his uncontrolled roll. O'Malley stands in the same spot as when we began and didn't, wouldn't, couldn't do the ten count. I got a little frustrated and counted it out. Questioning time in this reality, then wondering if I was moving so fast you couldn't see me, and those expressions were because I blinked out. I woke up the doctor by paging him the first time. He walks up into the ring like nothing is out of the ordinary. I left Jackson in his care, saw O'Malley and woke him up, took him with me to get the EMS techs, and grabbed their gear. I was moving faster than O'Malley but think

117

anything was wrong. Woke, the two techs grabbed their gear and hoofed it back to Dr. Paulson because Jackson was in bad shape.

I passed O'Malley on my way back and told him to bring the other two back. So I get back to Dr. Paulson, and he's moving slowly, looking over Jackson. I just started helping out. I did some temp work at a hospital for a time or two. It wasn't long before I got this crawly feeling. I look up. There is O'Malley..." He points to O'Malley and looks at Jillian.

She smiles and squeezes his arm.

"...and the two techs with Dr. Paulson on the other side of Jackson. They were spread out in a half circle." He points to where they arced. "Jackson was badly injured directly and indirectly because of me. Not a body was moving except mine. So, I repositioned the doctor and kept working. The only one not afflicted was a mute, Jackson. This is really starting to bug me." He looks down and rubs his forehead.

Jillian wraps her arms around him, patting his back. "Don't worry, Toby. We'll work it out, wake everyone up, and get them safely home. Okay?" She hugs him tight, breathing his scent in deeply.

He wraps his arms around her and rests his head next to hers. "Thank you, Jillian. I need your help, and I'm glad I could wake you in a pleasant way." He absorbs her scent, every pore opening to draw her in. "I think we are playing with high explosives and better step away. I don't want to put on an X-rated show for the doll dazed. Can you imagine them watching?" Toby snorts and steps away from Jillian.

She laughs. "That thought makes my skin crawl, and not in a good way." She nervously rubs her arms.

"Then let's have some fun and play with my dolls. Watch." Toby pushes lightly on O'Malley's lower back and starts him walking. He puts a hand on one shoulder, and he turns. Then the other shoulder, he turns that way. Turns him again, heading towards Toby's corner. He puts a hand on his chest at the ropes.

O'Malley stops.

118

Music fills the pub, happy up beat music, not too loud, but not soft.

Toby nods. The quiet was getting to him. He pushes down on both of O'Malley's shoulders. He sits. Lays him down, touches both knees, and his legs extend. He opens the ropes for Jillian to step through and follows her through. He holds her hand, descending the stairs.

He walks over to O'Malley, grips his upper arm and waistband, and slides him under the ropes to the skirt. Grabs his shoulders, pulls up, pivots his body around by his legs and pulls his butt to the edge. Let his legs dangle. "Okay, O'Malley, hop down." He clutches his shoulders and pulls forward and up.

O'Malley hops down and stands.

"Good, let's go to the table." With slight pressure to his lower back, O'Malley stiffly walks towards the booth.

Fin coming from the other side with Amethyst and Phillip. They walk stiffly, arms limp at their sides, swinging free, barely moving.

Phillip's angle is a little off. The gap between Phillip and the other two grows with each step.

Jillian sees disaster on the horizon. But too far away to do anything. "Toby, Phillip is about to run into someone."

Toby puts his hand on O'Malley's chest and stops him. He turns just in time to see Phillip run into the woman, bounce, and walk backward at a slightly different angle.

The plump woman starts moving away from Phillip in a sidestep. She bumps into a man with a cap. She reverses direction, heading for a clustered group of nearly a dozen. The man in the cap moves towards the wall. He backs up when he can't go forward.

Toby snorts, gasps, and then laughs a real belly laugh. Laughing so hard he doesn't notice everyone around him turns and starts moving towards him.

The people on the other side of the room were bumping into each other, setting off a chain reaction of movement.

119

Jillian laughs deeply, looks at Toby, and stops abruptly. Runs over, plastering her lips on his, and wraps her body around him.

Toby finds breathing suddenly difficult. He tries to pull away from Jillian, but she grabs his head and kisses him deeply. His control slipping, holding on by a thread, he feels someone press up against his back. Then another on his side. He opens his eyes.

People surrounded them, coming closer.

He rips his lips away from Jillian and snorts, calling out. "Fin! I'm surrounded, man, and Phillip runs loose, creating chaos. Help, Fin! Jillian is attacking me."

"Toby, what did you do?" Fin laughs standing on a booth to see them. "They haven't moved on their own before."

"Me? You let Phillip run loose; now look what he's done." He points to the other side of the pub.

Everyone standing moves. One man backs up and sits on a woman sitting in a chair and stops.

"Is that Phillip who just sat on that woman?" Toby starts laughing again; deep, rich belly laughs roll out of him, and tears stream from his eyes.

Jillian clings tighter, diving for his lips to kiss.

Toby dodges her every move she makes.

She ends up kissing him everywhere but his lips.

Uncontrolled laughter boils out of him, and the press of people gets tighter.

Fin laughs so hard that he falls off the bench. Climbs back up, wheezing. "Get out of there, Toby, or get them to stop."

Gasping, dodging, laughing, squeaks out. "How?" "I don't know, but I think they are attracted to your laughter, as is Jillian."

"That's what I'm worried about when she catches her target. She's latched on again." He looks around and sees the heavy pipe overhead. "Will that hold our weight?" He points to the pipe.

Fin looks up and nods. "Yes, I think it will. O'Malley had it installed for an event he had years ago, but I don't remember the event. I only heard about it. It was such a pain because it had to hold 400 lbs. O'Malley was having fits, but the event was paying for it, so he installed it. What are you going to do?"

"Hopefully, not kill me or Lady Jillian." He squeezes Jillian tight, resting her head on his shoulder. "If you hold on really tight, I will give you a kiss."

She nods, nuzzling his neck.

He takes a deep breath. "Laugh, Fin, laugh and jump. I don't want you to fall into the daze." Takes another deep breath and jumps hard straight up, catches the pipe and hangs about two feet above the heads of the people.

Fin laughs in amazement, running in place. "You are so awesome, Toby. And you're doing something amazing and Daze worthy."

"Good heavens, I hope so." Toby swings his legs forward and back, forward and back. He keeps going until he has a good pendulum at the apex, lets go, and soars up into the rafters, flipping over to land on his feet lightly with Jillian clutching to his chest.

Her head pops up, she looks around, and then looks at Toby. Grabs his ears and plants one on him.

He can feel the steam rising off them. He starts slipping into the sea of desire.

Fin yells. "Ten, perfect landing and form." He walks over and tries to pull Jillian off.

Jillian tries to push him away with one hand, but her other hand slips around Toby's neck, wrapping her arm securely.

Fin wraps his arm around her waist and pulls hard. He moves them both forward. "You have to help, Toby. She's superglued to you." He knocks Toby's head. "Help me!" It's hard to sound fierce when laughing so hard.

Toby surfaces from the sea of desire. Gasping for sanity, he ducks his head under her arm at the same time Fin pulls hard.

Jillian pops off.

Overbalanced, Fin starts to fall back.

Jillian screams in frustration at losing her prey and goes wild in Fin's arms.

Toby leaps over, catching Fin and Jillian.

She sees Toby behind Fin and tries to get to him.

Fin holds on for dear life. "Jillian! Please, Jillian! I don't know how much longer I can hold her."

Laughing, Toby stands Fin on his feet. "Just a little longer. Did you bring a bottle?"

Fin laughs. "Yes, on the table. And stop laughing. They are headed this way."

Noah valiantly tries to stop laughing, but the situation is too much. He grabs the bottle and dashes back to Fin and Jillian. Twisting off the cap clears the bottle just as it reaches her mouth.

Her hand grabs it like a baby bottle, pulling deep draws into her mouth and gulping them down. Her eyes, dark smoky grey, sparkling with fire, watching him to devour.

When her eyes start to mellow, he pulls the bottle away. He offers her his hand.

She takes it.

Fin puts her down gently, and they all move to the booth.

Fin was correct, and the crowd was moving slowly toward him. He puts Jillian in the booth, flicks Amethyst between the eyes, grabs the icy rag, presses it to her face and sloshes her neck. Toby turns away to Fin. "Bring her out and have her guard Jillian from Jillian. I have to do something." Toby slumps away, placing a stopping hand on every chest he passes. Standing those who were sitting on others or straighten those bent over chairs, booths, or each other. He works his way around the room.

CHAPTER EIGHTEEN

Amethyst rubs between her brows, eyes watering, blinking furiously, and wipes her hand down her face. She looks around, confused. She sees Fin watching her. "What happened?"

Fin smiles. "Doll Daze."

She smiles back, confused. "What?"

Fin chuckles. "Toby."

She nods. "When?"

He laughs. "In the first round, my guess would be within the first minute. I don't know for sure. I was dazed, also. As is everyone here except Jillian." He points to her sitting in her corner, eyes dreamy, hugging herself. "The fever spiked."

She laughs, shakes her head, and looks out at the room, watching Toby slumping along, placing his hands on everyone until they are still, then moves on to the next moving person, leaving frozen bodies in his wake. "How?"

Fin laughs harder. "Toby being Toby." She turns to Fin, chuckling. "Why?"

Fin shrugs. "We really don't know." He looks over at Toby, creating order out of chaos. "You need to be warned. Don't look at Toby when he does something new. We are susceptible to slipping back into the daze. Doc slid back three times. It's understandable by the stuff he witnessed, but each time, it's harder to awaken you."

Amethyst looks out at the room. "Who won the match? Let me guess, Toby. Where's Jackson?"

"Hopefully, arriving at the hospital. We sent the doctor, two EMS guys, and Jackson in the ambulance. The two guys were awakened twice, the doctor three times. Jackson is so damaged and lost his voice around the time the Daze struck the masses. Though he never got the daze." Fin shrugs. "Toby thinks it's because Jackson was participating with him. It could be because he was so mad. I remember that. How mad Jackson was after being dotted in bright blue." He looks over at Amethyst. "With time, you will recall everything clearly. Weird how you can't remember anything when you first awaken, then slowly events clarify."

"I remember a flesh eating zombie, Jackson, and Toby was mimicking him, coming for us. Jillian laughed, and everyone laughed then it got hazy. Wait…I remember…beautiful, rich, deep laughter. It swirled around me like a warm hug. It was incredible. I wanted more…it seeped in bone-deep…cold without it…wanted to be that warmth, that pure joy." Her eyes open dream, and she blinks and focuses on Fin.

"That just happened. That was Toby laughing. I was moving you and Phillip, and Phillip got away from me and it was hilarious, all the bodies bumping into each other and got those frozen ones moving. It was the perfect example of chaos." Fin laughs and points across the room. "See Phillip sitting on that woman's lap? After he worked around the room he just sat down. It looked like he was watching what he had done. It was so funny, Toby lost it. He needed that laugh." He looks over at Toby and notices that his avid followers have spotted him and are closing in. "He feels all of this is his fault, and responsibility sits heavy on Toby." The hordes were getting closer. "You better look away. I've a feeling Toby is about to be amazing."

Amethyst turns and hears Fin call out to Toby.

"They're closing in, Toby."

Toby nods. "Yes, plug your ears."

Amethyst leans over and says. "Jillian, plug your ears!" She sticks her fingers in her ears.

Jillian obediently puts her fingers in her ears, just in time.

Toby bellows. "Halt!"

Everyone stops and turns to face Toby.

Fin bursts out laughing.

Amethyst collapses in the booth, howling.

Jillian giggles.

Everyone turns to face Toby, even the three awake with their fingers in their ears.

No one moves.

Toby shakes his head walks away exasperated. He stops by Phillip, placing a finger in each armpit and pulls up.

Phillip stands.

He puts a hand on Phillip's back and gets him walking stiffly, his arms unmoving. Through a series of shoulder touches expertly navigates Phillip across the room. They stop close to the table next to the bucket.

"No more mischief, Phillip. I need your help, not create more problems, though it was very funny." He flicks Phillip between the eyes hard. Takes the rag and sloshes it over his face and neck. "See to him." He turns and walks to O'Malley. Drives him back to the booth while Phillip wakens. He repeats the process on O'Malley. Then walks towards the restrooms. He drives a man closest to the hall ahead of him into the hall.

Fin looks worried and turns to Amethyst. "Get them talking, moving, laughing, thinking. I need to check on Toby." He turns and jogs after Toby.

Entering the men's room, the silence is ominous. He looks under the stall doors. The first stall had a pair of legs. He opens the door slowly. Sees it's the guy Toby drove back here. Closed the door softly. Moves down the row, checking under each stall until he finds Toby's ugly shoes and bright white socks. One with a blood stain.

Slowly, he opens the door.

Toby sits on the toilet, fully clothed. His elbows are on his knees, and his head hangs forward.

"Do you need anything, Fin?" Toby asks, exhausted.

"No, do you?" Fin asks gently.

"My sanity would really be great about now. Normalcy would help tremendously. A vacation that would let me wake from this nightmare." He shakes his head. "I thought I was experienced in everything, but this?" He snorts derisively. "I don't think anyone, anywhere, has experienced this. How did this happen? That keeps running through my head. Every last person was affected except me, so I must be the cause. How did I do it? If I know how I did it, then maybe I can undo it." He rubs his face.

Fin noticed his glasses hanging from his pocket protector. He represses the laugh. "Toby, you were just being you. You're an amazing, awesome man."

Toby snorts. "Yes, I was Toby being Toby. The problem is that Toby isn't awesome. Amazing, yes. Awesome, no."

Fin shakes his head. "What?"

Noah shakes his head. He's said too much. But this situation was a serious problem. He may have to retire Toby indefinitely. Word would spread. Who knew Toby had it in him? The problem stems from Noah leaking out through Toby. Way more than he thought. He needs to clean this mess up tonight, and Toby needs to disappear. He can monitor the situation as someone else. Maybe Chip, that dummy, should be able to ask all kinds of questions with no one the wiser. A big problem was Jillian. Maybe "the fever" can explain her jumping a new guy when Toby disappears. She will be the one to figure him out. Every moment with her is touch and go. Very dangerous. Need to stay away from her until the jobs are done. It couldn't end fast enough. He got what he needed today, so he can check the site tomorrow. Was that today? God, will this day ever end?

"Toby?" Fin asks carefully.

"Yes, Fin." Noah rubs his temples. His back hurt from being hunched forever. On top of that, dangerously horny and unable to do anything about it.

"Why did you put that guy in the stall?" Fin asks curiously.

"A practical experiment; deprived of exposure to me, how long it takes him to wake," Toby answers.

"Ah, okay." Fin sighed. "Toby, we will get through this. I'm sorry to lose Phillip and that whole chain reaction. But who could predict anything in this situation, let alone control it? We know how to wake them up. We can limit their exposure to you after you wake them. The more we wake the more help we have to get all these people home and hopefully to bed, to sleep it off." Fin places his hands on Toby's shoulders and grips them. "I know you carry all the responsibility for this, but how were you to know this weird Doll Daze would strike one and all? I think Jackson was affected. That's why his voice left him trapped. There's always a first time, and your number was up for Life's Phenomenon Lottery. You drew this; for months and years, we will be laughing about ping-pong Phillip and Flesh-Eating Zombie Jackson."

Toby snorts. "You have a way of putting things into perspective. Thank you. You could tell I was spiraling down, couldn't you? "Toby puts his glasses on and looks at Fin.

Fin laughs. "Listen, man, if it were me in the ring and this happened, I would lose my mind trying to get someone to talk to me. All those things you mentioned probably would have cracked me. Then where would we all be? Lost." He tips his head towards the pub. "They are lost, but there is hope for them, Toby. You. Only you have to pull the lost back. If you're ready, let's get our plan in order to help them come back." Fin looks unsure. "Amethyst said that your laughter warmed her, that it was relief from the cold."

Toby stands to a slouch. "I had no idea. I never even thought about their physical state. Some of those people have been standing for hours."

"I didn't tell you that to stress you, just pointing out that we can help them. Come back from that and get warm. Amethyst said your laughter was warm, bone deep. That's probably why they mobbed you. Survival instincts were kicking into some extent."

Toby nods. "Yes, makes sense. I need a drink and a plan, then another drink. I'm not really a social person, Fin, and this situation is not refuting my habits." They walk out of the men's room. Toby stops, turns around retraces his steps. He pulls out his blue marker and writes on the door of the first stall.

Out of Order

Conducting Practical Experiment

Duration of Doll Daze Untreated

Stimulant: Toby

Stimulant Free: 10:45 pm

Friday, June 23

Contact Management

If signs of life are detected

Fin laughs and leaves, with Toby following.

"We need to change him to sitting soon. Not me. You are in charge of our Dazer."

Fin nods. "Don't worry, I'll take care of him."

"Okay, every thirty to forty-five minutes, change from sit to stand."

"I got it, Toby. Relax, that drink is coming up. I left Amethyst with O'Malley and Phillip. I didn't get a chance to explain everything that's gone on. But hopefully enough to get those two in the here and now."

"Good. We can answer any pressing questions and not worry about the rest now. I want this day to end." Toby sighs deeply.

"I can understand that." Fin pats him on the shoulder, "Take your regular seat, and we'll get started." Fin slides in the booth opposite Toby. "Pour this man a big drink."

CHAPTER NINETEEN

Noah accepts it and empties it in one motion. He holds out his glass for a refill. He repeats the action once more before putting this glass down. He looks up, and everyone at the table watches him. He turned to the crowd, and they were watching also. He notices they now turn to always face him. He needs to hurry. The symptoms were getting worse. He can feel time ticking away. "What?" He snorts. "I'm just drinking."

Jillian answers. "It's not what you do this time, but how you do it, with skill and grace. You have taken a belligerent "I need a drink!" and turned it into a beautiful merging of art and passion." She looks around the table. "Am I right?"

They nod their heads.

Toby snorts and holds out his glass again. "I need a drink!" He states in his most belligerent tone with a whine.

Amethyst pours.

He drinks and slams the glass down.

Everyone jumps except Jillian who smirks and shakes her head. "Nope, didn't work, but very funny." She giggles.

The rest laugh.

Toby shakes his head and snorts again. He winks at her,

She winks back with an impish smile.

He sighs. "I think we need to work in stages. I need to be behind the newly awake so they don't slide back into the Daze. How was it for you, O'Malley?"

O'Malley chuckles. "It happened even before I was gone. Slippery slope, my boy."

Toby nods. "Just talking to the EMS techs started the slide, they said fuzzy around the edges. It's harder each time they slide into the daze to get them out. It might be how long in the daze also. I feel like time is running out, so we need to wake them."

Fin nods. "It worked well with Charles and Zack, but we should have outside for the awake completely separate from you. Keep me with you. I've lasted the longest without a slide back."

Toby nods. "Good. That also keeps a safe distance between Jillian and me." Toby snorts. It was too close the last time for his comfort.

Three heads turn to Jillian.

She looks around innocently.

Everybody chuckles except Toby.

"When we get enough awake and possible volunteers, let them replace you once you're comfortable, they ensure alertness and safety in driving for those who want to leave once you find your replacement, come back in and start herding the people to me. We will go quicker the faster we can get the people to me. Let's move as many towards the door. Two of you take the first two out the other two will follow. Any questions?"

Everyone shakes their head. "Good. Let's get to work." Toby stands and picks up the bucket. The ice was mostly gone. "We need more ice, Fin. Can you bring some?"

"Sure. Hey, if we need to, we can start another ping-pong Phillip and have them walk right to you."

Jillian smiles. "Or you could give a deep belly laugh. They will flock to you in herds." She snickers.

Toby snorts. "Amethyst, get her out of here." He walks towards the door, stops about six feet shy, and puts the bucket down next to him. "Okay, who's first? Yes, you, sir. Step right up." Toby reaches out and nudges the man closer. Stops him. "Jillian, I have your first Dazed."

"Right behind you. Ready, willing, and able." She says sweetly.

Toby snorts. "Why are you back there?"

"The better to see you, my dear."

Noah growls. "In front."

"Didn't get my tasty morsel today." She saunters around him, smiling.

Toby turns his head. Flicks the man hard, grabs the rag, reaches next to him and sloshes Jillian's neck.

She squeaks in surprise. "What was that for?" She laughs.

Toby sloshes the rag on the man's face and neck. "Just to help cool you down. You're just a little too hot for me to handle right now." He pushes the man forward. Then Noah whispers for her alone. "But not later."

Her head snaps around, and she stares at him hard.

He gives her a big, goofy Toby grin and nudges her forward.

They step out the door.

Toby snorts. Noah can hardly wait to get his hands on her. Toby sighs, shaking his head and pulls the next person over.

Amethyst steps up in front of him.

He smiles and flicks the guy, sloshes him and sends him off with her outside.

The next one goes with O'Malley. Good outside representative.

Then Phillip gets the next one.

Fin pours ice into the bucket.

Next, Toby flicks, sloshes, and pushes them to Fin. They get into a rhythm. Then, the people were too far away.

Toby whistles a little tune, and a few show up. Then he was humming more and moving towards him. Fin takes over sloshing. They were really picking up speed with the doors standing open.

Toby stops and looks out the door.

A group of people were watching him.

He nods to Fin.

Fin Looks, shakes his head and calls out. "O'Malley!"

O'Malley steps into view. "What?"

"We have gawkers with glassy eyes. Move them along, put them to work or send them home. Have Phillip herd the awakened down further. We're picking up speed, so I'll prop the door open."

"Okay, lad." O'Malley turns to the group of gawkers. "Right this way, ladies. I could really use your help."

Fin turns back to Toby, nods locks the door open.

On the other side, Phillip gives a wave.

Toby nods. And starts on the next dazed, humming getting back into the rhythm. Toby wasn't stopping them when they walked to him. He gives a flick and a nudge to send on to Fin.

Fin doesn't stop them either; just sloshes them on their way by with a nudge to Phillip.

Phillip gets into the rhythm and turns them with a nudge.

Fin starts laughing. "Do you know what you are humming?"

Toby stops humming and looks at Fin.

Phillip laughs. "If I only had a brain from the Wizard of Oz, Scarecrow."

Toby snorts and hums something else, another mindless song.

Fin laughs, and the rhythm continues.

Phillip chuckles, shaking his head.

O'Malley steps over to the door. "We are overrun. People don't want to leave. They want to go back to the pub."

Toby looks at everyone. "I didn't foresee this problem. All I want to do is go home. We still have two-thirds in here in the daze." Toby scratches his head. "Enlist their help; have each one that wants back in take a newly awakened. Let them know that they cannot gain admittance if they don't help and until everyone is treated." Toby shrugs. "That's my suggestion. This is your bar. You could send responsible ones in through the back and have them herd the dazed. But they can't look at me. I don't know what causes the slide but not looking has worked as far as we know." Toby shudders. "As soon as the last one is treated I'm out of here. It's just too dangerous."

"I understand, lad. I'll send over the lasses. They can herd the folks to you. I'm not trusting any others with you. It's a bloody circus out here."

"Do you want me to come out and juggle?" Toby offers.

O'Malley laughs. "It would serve them right. No, I'll deal with it."

Fin and Phillip laugh.

Toby snorts. "I almost started in the ring. I planned to use my hanky, my blue marker, and hand sanitizer. But things went downhill fast, so I didn't."

Fin and Phillip cry with laughter, streaming eyes and gasping for breath.

Toby snorts and starts to hum again. The treatment line speeds up, and almost a constant stream of people leaves the pub. Toby slows the song down, the line slows, then speeds it up, and the line moves faster. He snorts.

Amethyst comes up. "Ah, Toby? The radio guys won't get up."

Toby stops humming and turns to her. "What do you mean?"

She shakes her head. "I can't really explain it."

Toby looks over at the table where they sit. "Is there any immediate danger to them or others?"

She shrugs. "I got a real creepy feeling. Those two aren't like the others. Somethings wrong, different wrong, not Doll Daze. Something else."

Toby looks to Fin. "Have Phillip block the door. You come with me. He turns back to Amethyst. "Go herd the others to the front, leave a path open to the door, but pack them tight. Let Jillian know. If you find any other oddities, let us know." Toby and Fin walk over to the radio announcers at their own table, complete with a radio banner hanging across the front, tabletop mics sitting in front of each unmoving man.

Noah squats down in front of them, looking closely. Watching their eyes, he stands, moving far to the left and then right. He stops beside the blond-haired man and notices both men have their hands fisted around their mics, white-knuckled. Their other hand was pressed up to the ear of their headphones, muscles delineated on their arms. Their posture ridged, backs arched, chins up, head leaned back.

Noah pulls a penlight from his handy pocket protector and clicks it on. He leans over and looks the man in the eyes. "Hello, I'm Toby Robins. I'm going to check your eyes. We are in the middle of waking up a bar full of people who have fallen into a strange, mesmerized state. I'm calling it the Doll Daze. I am the only one completely not affected. Jackson just lost his voice. Everyone else was caught in the Daze. Now, we find you two in the crowd, different than the others. Those others can be brought back fairly easily since I stumbled on how to do it. With you two, we start from scratch." Noah flashes the light into his eyes. They dilate too fast, shrinking in pain.

Noah noticed his pale skin, washed out and gently touched his forehead, which was very hot. He guessed 104-105. He runs his hand down to his neck, cold. He touches the hand by his ear, then the hand on the mic, both very cold. He looks closer at the man's hands, tinged blue.

Noah crouches down slips his hand up his pant leg, and touches his skin, pulling his fingers back quickly. Looks under the table, pulls up his pan leg, and sees blue-tinged skin. He struggles to pull off the man's shoe and sock. He recoils, seeing the black tinging the tips of his toes.

"Frostbite?" Noah shakes his head. "Come on, really?" Noah looks up. Searching for answers in his mind. "Fin, how was that man in the stall?"

Fin looks confused and scratches his head. "Fine, the same as before." He thought about it. "No, harder to move."

Noah waves Fin over to his side of the table. "Take a look. Then, feel the skin on his leg, his hand, neck and head. Can you feel the temperature difference?"

Fin gets down and does as instructed. "This is serious, Toby." He gets up and steps back, worried.

Noah stares down thoughtfully. "Yes, it is." He rubs the back of his neck. "Go check the man in the John and see if he has similar discrepancies in temperature. On your way back, bring enough hot wet towels that we can wrap their feet." He looks at the two announcers concerned. "They are showing signs of acute frostbite, we need to raise their body temperatures, but they are showing dangerous signs of fever, and we have to lower it." He rubs his jaw. "Bring two ice bags, also. Maybe we can cool the top and heat the bottom. Could you send the girls over on your way to the john?"

"Sure, be right back." Fin dashes off.

Noah rubs his lower back, looking at the equipment under the table. He stares at an unusual piece of a moment before he really sees what it is. A specially designed amplifier is very rare. Hard to come by, except in certain circles of the very rich or the very secret. The danger with these amplifiers is the effect on the tech listening in. There were strict guidelines used with this machine. Exposure was limited to under an hour, anything past that was damaging to the mind, the synapsis of the brain become compromised.

These two are in serious danger. They had been present and hooked up during the onset of the Doll Daze. Had it amplified directly into their brains?

Noah wonders if these symptoms are the untreated Doll Daze, if it was exposure to that amplifier, or something worse, a merging of the two. He rubs his forehead, wondering when this day will end, but not soon enough.

"Toby? Are you okay?" Jillian gently places her hand on his shoulder.

"No, not really. Things just got a whole lot worse." Toby whines sadly. "I need you to..."Noah pauses to order his mind and his helping hands.

"What do you need us to do, Toby?" Amethyst places her hand on his other hunched shoulder.

Noah nods resolutely and stands to his hunched erectness, and turns to the women. "I need one of you to go out and get blankets or whatever from the people out there." He points to the front of the bar. "We need to contact Dr. Paulson, the two EMS techs, Charles and Zack, and get them back here. With as many thermal blankets as they can carry." He turns to look around the room at the people still filling it. "How many are still dazed?" He leans over and takes the pulse of the man he inspected. Weak and erratic; not good. "Tell them to get here on the double. This one doesn't have much time, so probably neither does the other."

Jillian finishes a quick count. "About forty-three still Dazed."

Noah nods. "I need the other to strip these two down to the shorts. No time for modesty. Then, fill as many containers full of hot water as hot as you can make it. We are going to wrap them then pack them with heat from the shoulders down, ice around the heads to cool the fever." Noah nods. "That's the best we can do for these two right now." Noah looks at both women. "It's serious, their condition. We can only do what we can." He turns to the group of dazed and approaches a woman in a skirt who bends down and touches her foot, calf, and thigh. He stands, touching her hand, upper arm, neck, and forehead. He turns back, looking worried.

Fin appears with a tub of steaming towels. "Yes, John's temperatures are off. I checked a man in the crowd, and he wasn't as bad. I'd say John's somewhere in the middle of extremes."

"Jillian, tell the doc that these two are showing signs of frostbite and fever and that the rest of the Dazed are headed that way. Tell O'Malley what's up and have him take Phillip's place herding the people newly awakened to the group. Have him find his own replacement. Phillip will take Fin's spot. Fin and Amethyst will tend to these two and get John out here. Bring him to the front of the line. We need him awake since his condition is worse." Noah sighs big. "And I'll wake as many as I can as fast as I can."

Amethyst looks at the announcers. "Why don't you try flicking them now?"

Noah shakes his head. "You were right that these two are different, off. They are hooked up to a special amplifier with known adverse effects when exposed for too long. I don't know what would happen, and their pulse is very erratic." Noah shakes his head. "After we wake all we can before they end up like this, I can call someone

I know and ask some questions. I won't attempt anything unless pushed, that being a step away from death. Unless we can control their temperature they are running there now. So control their temperature and give us some time. Go, Jillian. Fin, let's make some warming chambers. Sorry for the destruction." Noah walks over to the closest booth, picks up a full beer, chugs it, puts it back on the table, lifts the end up high, kicks the center leg out with a crack and slams the table down, bridging the two bench seats, leaving everything still standing on the table. "Amethyst, get their shoes and socks off and wrap the towels around them."

Fin, at the next booth, over with the table up, kicks repeatedly.

Noah snorts and steps over. "Go help Amethyst. I got this. We need to move them over here." Noah kicks the table, and with a sharp crack, it slams onto the benches. He goes back to the blond announcer and tries to move his hand away. He's locked in place. Tries to pull off the exposed ear cuff of the headphones, but it doesn't move. He bends for a closer look and sees the plastic cushion melted to his hair and skin. "Good God!" He whines in a whisper. He bends down between the two men and unplugs Blondie's headphones.

A whine starts and grows in pitch and intensity, like back feed, distressed.

Noah's head snaps around, and he looks at Blondie, he slowly plugs the headphone cord back in.

The sound stops immediately.

He looks at the other man and pulls his headphone jack from the amplifier. The same eerie back feed sound comes out of them. It too sounds distressed. He plugs it back in.

The sound stops.

He looks closer at the man's earphone muff and sees the melted plastic. He closes his eyes, breathing deeply.

CHAPTER TWENTY

"What's going on?" Phillip walks up, looking at all the action.

Fin and Amethyst work under the table, the banner flipped up.

"Hell for these two," Noah whines. "We can't unplug them. I'm afraid to pull the power. Are they still broadcasting?"

Phillip nods. "Yes, everyone was curious about what was going on in here. Someone turned on the radio and now everyone is listening in."

"Great. Just what we need, a possible relapse brought to you by way of radio land. Phillip, call the station and get them to cut the feed. I'm sorry to all listening, but these men's lives are worth more than your entertainment."

Fin and Amethyst crawl out from under the table. "Done."

"Okay, we have to move them together. Amethyst, you monitor the equipment on the table and move with us." Noah picks up the amplifier and a few other things and places them on the table. "This one is important. Hold onto this one."

She goes to grab it and squeaks, drawing back her hand. "It shocked me." Shaking her hand.

Both men twitch.

Noah straightens the plastic banner over the equipment and table. He touches the lump of the amplifier, but nothing. "Okay, Put your hand here and slide the table with us."

Amethyst gingerly places her hand where Toby indicates nothing happens. She nods, gripping the table on the other side, ready for action.

Fin gets behind one and grips his chair.

Noah behind the other.

They drag them over to the two modified booths.

Noah moves to the side and picks up Blondie, kicking the chair away. The man remains frozen in a sitting position.

Noah sits him on the lowered table top. Scratches his head and grips his shoulders, places a bent leg on the man's lap and pushes. He steps back.

Phillip comes back over. "No answer at the radio station."

Noah waves him over. "Put all your weight on his legs." Noah gripped the man's shoulders again and pushed until he started to tip back.

"Toby..."Phillip laughs.

Noah turns his head and sees Phillip teetering on the man's lap. He lets go, and the man shoots back upright. Phillip launches off and tips onto the table. "Oops, sorry."

Phillip laughs. "It's okay, Toby."

"Fin, can we get your help?" Noah adjusts the man to the edge of the table. Places his bent leg on his lap, gripping his shoulders, and waits until Phillip and Fin each take a leg. "Ready?"

"Yes." Says Fin.

Noah pushes hard, and finally the man starts to unbend slowly. Noah, sweating by the time he gets him flat, flops over on the bench, breathing heavily, his arm over his eyes. "Could someone out in radio land please get over to the station and see if you can get someone to call us here at O'Malley's pub? Please ask for Phillip." He sits up. "If you can't find anyone or if they are unresponsive, please call us here and let us know." He stands in his Toby posture and slides the man back on the table to his bent legs. Takes a deep breath, braces one hand above the knee grabs the ankle and pulls up.

Fin cups his heel with both hands and strains up.

Slowly, the leg straightens enough. "Stop."

They move to the other leg and mostly straighten it. They slide Blondie back until his heels rest on the table.

Noah pushes hard above the knee, and the leg straightens the rest of the way. Then pushes down on the other one. He steps back and wipes the sweat from his brow. "We should do the other one on a table out in the open and at a better height."

Buried under blankets, Jillian calls from the front door. "Help."

Phillip trots off to assist her.

Noah looks at Fin, sweating beside him. "Are you ready for the other one?"

Fin chuckles. "I'm getting a workout today, that's for sure." He wipes his brow. "After we straighten him out, I'm going to stand John back up."

Noah nods. "Good idea, no need to make work for us." He looks around the bar. "Have one of the girls stand up any that still sit."

Phillip and Jillian stumble over, loaded down with blankets and various clothes.

He sees a couple of silver emergency blankets. He nods. "We need him stripped and warmed. His head should be on the outside. His feet need to be monitored closely. Let's finish this one, then work on the other one." Noah pulls a folding knife out of his pocket. "Drop that stuff. Get more hot towels and rewrap his feet. Bring one thermal and a regular blanket. Get a lot of containers of hot water and something large to cover these two booths." He bends by the man's leg, pinching his pant leg, inserts the blade of his knife, running up his outer leg, slicing the material in two. "Oh, and that ice pack for his head." He pauses when he comes to a belt. He unbuckles it and, with a quick, decisive tug, whips the belt out of the loops. It cracks when free, releasing the energy of the motion. He drapes it over the back of the booth. Bending down and slicing through the waistband and starts on the shirt, up the side and down the long sleeve.

Jillian watches the controlled, precise movements. "The doc is on his way with the EMS guys and another team."

Noah nods and leapfrogs over to the other bench. Starts on the other leg, zipping his knife up the man's body, slicing his clothes in two.

140

"O'Malley is now guarding the door. Everyone out there is listening in. The car radios are blasting. There were a few people I noticed looking a little dazed, unmoving in the party that was going on out there. Told O'Malley to monitor them and get someone to talk to them. He has about ten responsible concerned patrons helping him. The rest are enjoying the entertainment." She says, a little disgusted.

"Let me tell those listening out in front of O'Malley's. Right now, we are dealing with the extreme cases of Doll Daze. They are approaching death's door and will be knocking soon if we can't stop them. Everyone who is dazed in here is following down that path. We need your help to keep the once-dazed from slipping back into it. Watch the people around you. Keep spirits up, laugh, interact, and move. Get the glassy-eyed to twinkle. If you find anyone unresponsive, take them to O'Malley. It's easy to fall back into the daze and harder to get back out again. Right now you are my helping hands out in the world. I am asking for your assistance so we can all enjoy another day tomorrow. Hopefully, utterly dull, unlike today."

Noah snaps his knife closed and crawls out of the booth.

Phillip walks up with the tub of hot towels.

Amethyst, on his heels, follows with a crate of liquor bottles.

Fin jogs up with another crate, and a bowl sits on top.

Phillip wraps the hot towels around the men's feet.

The toes look better.

"Okay, group effort. Jillian, stand by with that thermal blanket. When we pick him up, put that thick blanket on the table. Amethyst, take his clothes away. Fin, grab that side. Phillip, stand ready. We are going to rotate him around." He grabs either side of his torso. At Noah's nod, everybody lifts him.

Jillian slips under the man and flings the blanket out.

Amethyst snatches away his clothes as he rotates around,

Jillian flings out the emergency blanket onto the other one. Then climbs up onto the table, grabs the man's legs, and moves back. When her back hits the wall, she straddles the table and lowers the

141

man onto the blankets, folding them around him. She stands and moves to climb down.

Toby holds out his hand to assist her down.

She takes it, squeezes and steps down.

Toby releases her hand with a regretful smile and turns to the group. "Will the lovely ladies pack, blondie, with the hot bottles, then cover him with another blanket? Gentlemen, let's drag that table close and unbend him on that. You two on one side, me pulling on the other, yes?"

"Sounds like that might work better." Fin laughs. "Though we won't have you pushing down on his legs."

Toby snorts. "We'll figure it out."

The women get to work.

Fin and Phillip move chairs and drag the table over.

Noah picks up the other man, frozen in a sitting position kicks the chair away, and steps as far away as the headphone wire will allow. He tips him back so his leg clears the table.

Phillip and Fin slide the table under and gently sit him down.

"Now, on to the hard part," Toby whines. "Get into position, gentlemen."

Fin and Phillip each take a leg, pressing down on the knee while Noah pulls back and down on his shoulders, hanging with his weight.

The table starts tipping.

Fin starts laughing. "Grab hold, Amethyst."

The table evens out.

Slowly, the man straightens, with Toby sitting on the floor, his feet braced on the table.

Noah falls back and closes his eyes to catch his breath. After a moment, he opens his eyes and climbs to his feet. He nods at the two men and moves to a leg. "Phillip, can you keep the table steady?"

Phillip laughs. "Sure, Toby." He moves around to the other side, placing his hands on either side of the man's shoulders.

Fin cups his hands around the heel, ready to pull up.

Noah places his one hand above the knee and grips the man's ankle with a nod everybody does their part. They repeat the actions on the other leg. "Phillip, support his upper body so we can finish straightening his legs." He slides the body along the table like a plank. He pushes down on his thighs above the knee on both legs.

Noah pulls his knife out of his pocket, flicks it open and zips up the man's clothes, pausing at the belt blocking his way. With one hand unbuckles the man's belt and whips it from his pants. The belt cracks when free of the loops. He flings it over his shoulder and continues to slice the clothing. "Let's rewrap his feet before we move him." Noah turns and sees the other booth prepared with blankets and bottles lining the benches.

The men pick up the man and step over to the booth. Jillian takes his legs and backs up, straddling the table. She lowers him down.

She flicks the thermal blanket over him, then the other. Quickly, she places the bottles along his side and the valley of his legs, with two standing at the bottom of his feet.

Amethyst stood by with another blanket and handed Jillian the end. They drape it over the man and bottles.

Jillian walks along the bench and hops down.

Amethyst places an ice bag wrapped in a towel on the man's forehead and crown supported by folded material.

"Good job, my friends," Toby whines. "We need to keep checking on these two every five minutes or so. We can awaken more people and get them out." Noah turns to the door. "Phillip, you're with me. Fin, retrieve John and bring him to the head of the line."

"Wait," Amethyst says, stepping over with a bottle and a glass. "A little fortification and good spirits." She hands Toby the glass full to the brim.

Toby snorts. "Good spirits." Tips it in. Hands back the empty glass. "Thanks. When the towels on their feet cool replace them with

143

hot ones." He turns back and moves to the door with Phillip on his heels after slugging back a drink.

Noah knocks on the door and pushes it open. The crowd cheers and claps. Noah shakes his head and raises his hand, acknowledging their praise. To O'Malley, he says. "We are starting the line going again. We are doing what we can for those two. Get your people ready. We are starting now." He reaches up and locks the door open. He steps into the pub and takes his place. "Are you ready, Phillip?"

With a nod, Phillip takes Fin's place and dips the rag in the ice water.

Noah starts whistling a jaunty, quick tune.

The dazed move closer.

He pulls one near, flicks hard, and sends it on to Phillip.

One after another, they stream out of the pub, awake but confused.

Fin shows up driving John.

Noah stops whistling.

The dazed stop.

He shakes his head at the unreality of him being the pied piper.

Fin chuckles. "I just had this vision of you skipping through town whistling with a crowd following you."

Toby snorts. "I, too, had that vision, and it gives me the heebie-jeebies." Noah leans down and touches the man's shin. Stands, touching his arm, hand, neck, and finally, forehead.

His fever hovers around 101-102, and his body temperature is a little below average. Maybe 95-96. "Phillip, if we wake him, tell O'Malley he needs heat and aspirins to lower the fever and to watch him closely. Any change needs to be noted. When the doc gets here, check him first." He turns back to Fin. "We need ice and check on the two guys. What are their names?"

Fin nods. "Rick and Wesley. I think blondie is Wesley."

Noah turns to John. Flicks him hard. "Hey, sir, can you hear me?"

John blinks and stares.

Noah feels his body waken and then slide back into the Daze. He flicks him harder. "Phillip, soak his head."

Phillip brings the bucket over, grabs the back of the man's head and submerges it quickly.

John comes up sputtering. "Hey! What are you doing?"

Phillip smiles. "Soaking your head. Do you know your name?"

"Of course I do. It's John Smith."

Noah laughs. "It's great to meet you, John Smith. Could you please step out and see O'Malley? He will want to talk with you. I'm sure you have some questions. Go and ask him, please. Thank you." Noah gently pushes him towards the door. Then turns to Phillip. "I meant with the rag."

Phillip laughs. "I thought we would have better success with a dunking where all his cells would wake up and say, "Hey! "

Toby snorts. "They did, good call."

Fin jogs up with two pitchers of ice in hand. "The two are evening out, but the pulses are weaker and more erratic. Their breathing changed."

Noah nods in acknowledgment. "We still have about thirty people to work through. Let's go." Noah picks up his jaunty tune and gets the dazed moving towards him. Flicking them hard and sending them to Phillip to get a dousing.

About halfway through, the remaining dazed, a commotion starts outside.

Noah stops whistling and calls out. "Fin, go check outside." He resumes whistling and keeps the line moving.

Fin slips by and steps outside.

About seven dazed left when Fin calls out to him. "Toby, get out here."

Noah turns back to the seven and flicks them hard, two at a time. Then dashes out, slumping up and down with each step. "Soak everyone, Phillip."

CHAPTER TWENTY-ONE

John stands in the middle of the crowd, holding a knife to a pretty woman's neck, his eyes feverish and wild. Flushed, his color high, foam flies from his mouth due to his heavy breathing.

"Good evening, John. What seems to be the problem?" Toby slumps forward, calm and easy. He catches Fin's eye and tips his eyes down at his hand. He points at the crowd and circles his finger, pointing at his eye, and slightly shakes his head. He looks at O'Malley. Pointed to his eye again and slightly shakes his head.

"Sarah knows what she did. It's all her fault." Raging, John's spittle flies.

Toby looks at the woman. "Are you Sarah?"

Terrified, she whispers. "No, Becky."

"John, you have Becky, and she's scared. Why don't you let her go? Then you can tell me what Sarah did." Toby slumps closer. From the corner of his eyes, he sees Fin going one way through the crowd and O'Malley the other, turning people around, their backs to John and Toby, now in the circle with him. "Becky, would you do me a really big favor? I know you are scared, but would you please close your eyes and keep them closed no matter what until I tell you to open them? Dear lady, I swear nothing is going to happen to you."

Becky whispers fearfully. "Yes."

Toby wrings his hands. "I see a lady in need and I know my good deed, to protect her from harm. Close your eyes, dear lady, and we will have you out of this predicament before you know it." Toby focuses on John. "John, my friend," he slumps closer, "I know you don't feel well. A fever is clouding your mind." Noah notices Fin and O'Malley had almost met on the other side of the crowd. A few people see what's happening and turn voluntarily. Buying more time, Toby asks. "What has got you so upset, John? You can tell me. I'm here to help you in any way I can."

John mumbles to himself, then gets louder as he continues. "Alimint vitrolly whilt pie zat match crum."

"Are you sure about that, John?"

"Pleck fit sim oxtoy motrel tix."

Noah notices most everyone turned.

O'Malley and Fin nod.

O'Malley closes his eyes.

Fin does not.

Now is the time.

John continues. "Lipculp tem..."

Noah pulls the large marker and throws it hard.

It hits the back of John's hand. John drops the knife.

Noah steps up, reaching over the woman's head, and taps the side of John's neck hard.

John stops talking and goes boneless.

Noah catches him under the arm. He removes the arm around the woman.

Toby takes the woman's hand. "Dear lady, let me see your beautiful eyes."

Becky opens her eyes and looks around, stunned, but smiles at Toby. "Thank you."

"Oh, you're most welcome. Please know that John here is sick right now. I'm sure if he was in his right mind, nothing like this would happen." Squeezing her hand. "O'Malley, could you please assist the fair Becky and help settle her nerves after her fright?"

"Aye, lad." O'Malley steps up and takes her hand, leading her away.

Fin takes John's other shoulder, and they head for the pub. "I think a few watched."

Toby shrugs. "Couldn't be helped."

"What did you do with this?" He holds out Toby's Blue marker.

Toby snorts. "Stung his hand, so he lost his grip on the blade and dropped it."

"And how are we carrying him?"

"I knocked him out."

"You didn't punch him."

"No, I touched a spot hard enough to render him unconscious for a time."

"His neck?"

"Yes."

Phillip stands by the door with a group of seven milling around just inside the doors. "I kept them here until I knew they wouldn't see anything they shouldn't."

"Good. Please escort them to O'Malley and come back."

They move through the exiting group.

Jillian pushes a cart from behind the bar, two cases on the bottom and two cases on the top. "John's back?"

"He held a knife to a woman. Becky and Toby diffused the situation. And his fever is up." Fin supplies the answers.

Jillian nods. "The other two are getting a bottle change. The towels were just swapped. We noticed their eyes are twitchy, which is not a good description. Come take a look when you get him settled."

They move him to the next booth along the wall. They rest him against the booth, and Fin holds him up.

Noah crouches in front of John and feels his shin chill. He feels his forehead, about 102. "We need to know if O'Malley got aspirin in him."

Phillip walks over. "No, Becky was handing them when he freaked out. Word is Sarah always took care of him and just recently died, about two months ago, in a car accident."

149

Toby shakes his head sadly. "Ah, John, I'm real sorry, and now you are dealing with this and not much drive to go on. When you pull through, you will find someone else." Noah says Toby's words, not believing them, especially now having met Jillian.

A woman who affects him like no other. If he lost her even before real intimacy started, he would still be bereft. "Let's remove his shoes but leave him in his clothes. Wrap him in a blanket, and if the other two bottles swap still have some heat, let's use those cold cloth for his forehead and crush the aspirin and, mix a little water pour them in. Phillip, did you bring them?"

Phillip rattles the bottle, smiling.

"Good man, you prepare the aspirins, double dose. Call me when it's ready. Fin pulls his shoe's. I'll get a blanket if we still have any." Toby slumps away, moving towards the girls.

They both wear gloves on their hands. Jillian passes bottles to Amethyst. Amethyst passes bottles back.

Noah stops at the cart and takes a returning bottle, still very warm. He nods and places it in the crate. "Do we have any more blankets?"

Jillian nods behind her. "We have a few."

"Good, when you're done with these two. Pack John with these. He's not as bad just a chill. We are leaving his clothes on for now and about to give him aspirin to bring down his fever. He needs a cold compress instead of the ice pack. Let's put him in rotation with these two until we have a change."

Jillian nods. "We can do that."

Noah places his hand on her shoulder and squeezes gently. "Thank you." He looks over at a watching Amethyst. "Thank you, both."

"No problem, Toby, we'll get through this together. Right, Jillian?" Amethyst pulls Jillian's dreamy eyes away from Toby to focus on her.

Jillian chuckles. "Right, we can get through this together." She tips her head to her friend.

Toby squeezes her shoulder and slumps away to the blankets, then back to John. His fingers touch the man's neck, watching his watch.

Jillian shakes her head handing over another hot bottle to Amethyst. "There's something about him."

"He is something." Amethyst snickers. "A man of diverse talents."

"Yes..." Her eyes unfocused and think about those kisses they shared. "Supremely skilled talents." Her eyes focus on Toby. "But there are inconsistencies. I keep feeling he's a different person, hot and hunky."

"Could be the fever, or your seeing his repressed self, his true self hiding behind this camouflage." Amethyst nods. "Come to think of it, I think I've seen those flashes of a different man. But look at Phillip tonight. He's way hunkier than just earlier today."

Jillian frowns, watching Phillip striding over to the men a few booths away. A glass of cloudy liquid in his hand. "Huge change, but that's due to Toby. We both know he had it in him, but it only took Toby a few minutes to destroy all his excuses for not being himself."

"Yes, I see what you mean." Amethyst watches him.

Toby takes the glass and tips John's head back, pours in the liquid, cupping his chin, shutting it, anchoring that hand by pinching John's nose and with his other hand stroking his neck. When John swallows repeatedly, Toby opens his mouth and looks in with a nod.

"Yes, inconsistency. He bears watching." She steps over from the booth back to the next.

Jillian rolls the cart over. "Yes, I can't seem to take my eyes off him. Even in those clothes and hunched over most of the time. He's like eye candy. And those glasses just kill me, his beautiful eyes so huge it drives me crazy. All I can think about is falling into those great green pools. I even love that stupid pocket protector." Jillian shakes her head sadly. "I must really have an extreme case of the fever."

151

Amethyst looks over at her flushed face. "When was the last time you got laid? Oh, wait...was that seven years ago?"

"Eight." Jillian chuckles. "Yeah, I hear you, Amethyst. But those dreams have me hornier in the last three weeks than in all my years since puberty, times ten."

"You're due an excellent experience. It's all about the feelings you create in each other, not his financial status, family lineage, or proper employment." She hands over a warm bottle and takes a hot one. "And I have superior feelings about this one. Maybe he is repressing the hunk for stupid reasons like Phillip, or this could really be camouflage of the urban sort. I've noticed a few things that make me question, but as far as that man goes, he's been true to us more so than any other man we've ever met."

"What about Fin?" Jillian whispers and laughs. "We just met him before Toby."

Amethyst chuckles. "He's a hot one, and man, oh man, can he kiss. To me, yes, Toby has been truer because Fin wants me but hasn't come right out and said it, unlike Toby. And let me point out, he keeps ensuring your safety but doesn't trust himself or you to keep that danger away." She looks at Toby as they create another sick bed. "He knows that you have been drinking all day, and he has started after we arrived. Even now, with all this going on, he keeps watch over you from a distance." Amethyst replaces another bottle. "You have your work cut out to beat that strong will he has."

Toby steps over. "John's ready for you ladies." He watches Jillian.

The bar phone rings.

Fin runs off to answer it.

Phillip goes to the front.

After a moment, Toby steps around the cart and checks on Wesley.

Amethyst says. "See?" She steps over Rick's prone body and over into the next booth to John. "Hello, John, we are going to warm you up, sugar. You've had a tough time tonight. Let's get you on the mend."

Jillian hands over bottle after bottle, then the blanket hanging over the booth.

Phillip returns with the bucket of ice water, pulls out the rag, twists out the water and places it on John's head.

Fin runs back. "That was Doc. They are caught in another traffic jam, an accident, a bad one. They are working the scene and will be delayed. They aren't far from the hospital, so a fairly quick turnaround. I'm going to let O'Malley know and see if he needs a drink or a break."

"Thanks for the update." Toby has his fingers on Wesley's wrist with his eyes closed, and concentration lines his face.

Fin turns away. "He found out we're still on the air and confiscated someone's small radio and has been listening in. He says keep up the good work."

"Thanks, Doc. Be safe, but get here quick." Toby opens his eyes, pulls out his pen light, and clicks it on, flashing it into Wesley's eyes. He shakes his head, his brows furrow in concern. He touches Wesley's temple, his cheeks, the backs of his neck, and under the blanket to touch his chest. "His core temperature is up. That's good. His fever is down, that's good. His pulse is weak and more erratic. That's bad." He pulls the blanket down and places an ear on Wesley's chest. "Labored breathing and erratic, but lungs clear, bad and good." He covers Wesley's chest. "Hang in there, Wesley. We have help coming. I'm going to check on your partner, Rick, now."

Wesley's eyes twitched at the words.

Toby gets down close and whispers. "Can you hear me, Wesley?" He watches his eyes.

Wesley's eyes twitch again.

Still speaking softly. "Can you control your eyes?"

Wesley's eyes twitch.

Noah looks around for a basic question that could survive his trials. "Are you a man?"

Wesley's eyes twitch.

Sadly, Noah shakes his head. "I'm going to check Rick, then make a phone call."

He finds Rick in the same condition. He turns to the group. "Where's the phone?"

"There's one on the bar, far corner, next to the wall. There's another in the office, thru the door and to the left." Amethyst offers.

"Thanks. Keep an eye on them." He turns and slumps away. He sits down in the chair behind the desk in the office. Picks up the receiver, punches in the numbers, and hears it ring on the other end. After seven rings, he disconnects and redials. He lets it ring two times, disconnects and redials. He lets it ring ten times, disconnects and redials again.

Answered on the first ring, though the line remains silent.

"Ah, Hello?" Toby's grading nasal voice timidly asks. Noah is perversely amused. "Ah, hem, hello? Uhm...Noah told me ...ah...to call this number. Hel...Hello?"

"Yes." A sharp reply barrels through the line. "What?"

Noah can hear the aggravation in Stevens' voice, having to deal with this timid mouse. Noah gets Toby's voice to crack while suppressing his laughter. "DOAXT Receiver."

"What??" Stevens barks.

Noah laughs normally and drops Toby from his voice. "Thought that would get your attention."

"Shit, man, was that you?" Stevens howls. "One of them, wasn't it?"

Noah laughs, straightening his spine, tucking the phone on his shoulder and stretching his arms over his head. "Yeah, one of them."

With Stevens, tread lightly. Don't refer to anything he finds wrong or unpleasant. With Noah, it was his different disguises he honed and used repeatedly. It was a sore subject between them. Stevens worried Noah was having an identity crisis because he never showed himself his true self.

154

"He gave me the creeps, man. I wanted to reach through the phone and choke the little pussy."

"Now, that wouldn't be very nice, especially since he found you a lovely puzzle to figure out. He was also attacked by a smoking babe today, got into a fight and won, kissed the babe to unconsciousness, carried her away, defended her honor, made some friends, mesmerized an entire crowded pub into a horde of Doll Dazed mob that only had eyes for him, is still on the radio because the two yahoos with the amp were in the crowd and dazed with the rest and now are having weird reactions not like the rest, the newly awoken, Toby saved the day for about one hundred and seventy-five individuals."

"Wow, that little prick has been busy. Tell him to take a hike and let the real man out to clean up."

"I wish I could. I've been bleeding through tonight, which is part of the problem. Toby will disappear tomorrow. I don't think me or Toby can handle another day in this town. Surreal man, had a serious moment to question my sanity and reality. Scared the shit out of me, honestly."

"It had to happen." Stevens sounds pleased.

"Yeah, I know. The jobs are almost complete. I check the sight tomorrow and hopefully be done by the middle of next week."

"Get the job done, then take some R & R with the damsel. No need to run away."

"Who's running? Did I say anything about leaving? If I leave, I'm taking her with me." Noah finally admits aloud what he knew when he placed the ring on her finger. He noticed she kept looking longingly down at the ring, a dreamy look in her eyes.

"No, shit!? Hot damn, about time, too. What's the Mrs.'s name?"

Noah laughs. "How'd you make that leap?"

Stevens snorts disgusted. "How can I not? You have never singled out a woman and never has your voice gone all soft when referring to one. I can hear the preacher already. Does she know you yet?"

"No, and the job's not helping. She ran into me literally three different times while I was on the clock. She's a little confused. But I think we are sharing a dream. I've been having the same one since I got here. And if hers is the same one, she'll figure it out. The hormones are screaming as it is, hers and mine. All they want is to get together. Hell, I've been a blink away from mounting her a few times with the audience and all."

"Fuck me, man. You are so going down." He laughs harder when he realizes his pun.

Noah shakes his head. "Undoubtedly, but it won't happen tonight if I can't leave this nightmare. I need help."

"Okay, okay. I can hear your desperation. Take a moment and collect your thoughts and run it through for me. Let's start when the woman attacked. Don't leave a detail out. Remember, the small things trip us up. Give me your amazing total recall with thoughts and impressions. Don't even leave out your other. I want it all. By the way, what is her name?"

Noah sighs deeply. "Jillian Marlowe." He takes a deep breath and recalls his day for his friend.

CHAPTER TWENTY-TWO

Jillian looks at the back door. She leans forward in her chair, about to stand, then sighs and sits back. She looks away at the patients that Fin and Phillip monitor.

They were now working together in teams, alternating jobs. Every twenty minutes, they changed the hot towels and bottles. They check body temperatures and pulse every five minutes.

They had moved a table over close and brought the glasses and a bottle of whiskey. Everybody has a glass, and every time it empties, it gets refilled. Not that they were getting wasted, just putting the glow back on.

Fin brings out food; a cold platter filled with meats and cheese with fruit and crackers.

Amethyst reaches for a piece of cheese. "He'll be back, and he has his responsibilities. That man is the definition of the word."

Jillian nods. "I know." She gets a slice of summer sausage.

"Fin, I hope you have another one of these. Hoover Robins will suck this one up in two seconds. He's expended a lot of energy since his three dinners."

Everyone laughs.

Fin nods. "Already prepped and waiting. His is more substantial, a subs plater for twelve. Anyone want to bet he won't finish?"

Everyone shakes their heads, laughing.

"Why would we want to throw money at you?" Phillip chuckles, taking his seat at the table. "I've never seen food vanish so quickly at an unhurried pace." He reaches for a sample of a few items, stacking them, then pops it into his mouth.

Amethyst watches Jillian. "Yes, isn't it strange?" She looks over at Phillip. "Why would a great guy like Phillip here hide behind a look? Let's come right out and say it. Toby is no more a geek than I

157

am. It's more like he's wearing a coat. The coat is the geek Toby. The man wearing that coat doesn't become the coat, but it protects him from the adverse elements."

Fin walks up, shaking his head, pointing at the radio banner on the table between the two announcers' heads. "No! I think Toby is comfortable with who he is. How many men would admit to having a hobby of blending Physics and Physiology and enjoy it?" He points at the banner again, cups his ear, and points to the front of the pub.

Jillian catches on immediately. "Even though he's a geek, he's sweet and respectful. He even defended my honor. He was offended that Jackson called me a bitch. Only true geeks of today hold such high standards of conduct. He won't even get too close to me. I think he's worried he'll compromise me." Jillian watches Amethyst intently, cupping both ears and turning side to side.

Amethyst nods. "Well, Phillip, I guess you can give us your perspective on this matter."

Phillip notes all the signals. "It comes down to comfort with who you are. The difference between what I was and Toby is that Toby knows who he is. I, on the other hand, was denying some basic elements of me. What really broke my ridged mindset was Toby's confidence in himself. He knows people see the package, point and laugh. He's laughing, too. He has the right to dress any way he wants. I think it's lower on the list of priorities. We all agree he has a superb mind, and he knows his stuff. We didn't have to stand over him so he wouldn't create more work today. He caught up with several departments. So, on Monday, as we all sit around waiting for work to walk in, we will be praising the amazing Toby and his efficiency. I must say, Amethyst, you are a bit materialistic and focusing only on the outer package. I know from experience. You want to beautify the planet, one geek at a time. Leave Toby alone, and he's perfect the way he is." Phillip winks and laughs silently as the crowd cheers outside.

Amethyst winks back. "I find Toby exemplary. I'm just pointing out to Jillian that if she's got the hots for the man. That shouldn't stop her." She smirks at Jillian.

158

"Thank you, Amethyst, for being a broken record. And whether or not I have alone time with a man is not a subject to have constantly. I have always had high standards and strict control over myself, so I won't be hopping into bed with someone I just met today."

"A woman with the same personal code of conduct. A worthy Lady in deed." Toby whines, slumping towards the table.

Jillian blushes crimson, ducking her head a little. "Just finished your call, Toby?"

"Yes, I just talked to a fellow who enjoys puzzles and electronics. My, oh my, we could spend a month on the advantages of the semiconductors but we weren't able to get into that discussion. We spoke of Wesley and Rick specifically. Irving now listens in, say hello to my friend."

Amethyst nods. "Hello, Irving. You should come and join us. We would love to meet Toby's friend. He's our new friend."

Jillian smiles. "Hello, Irving. I'm Jillian. It will be lovely to meet you. Thank you for your help. Toby has been having a tough time tonight, but we're trying to shore him up. When he needs it, we can't help but see he's amazing when he's trying to divert disasters. I'm sure you are of the same caliber."

Fin laughs. "Hey, Irving, my man. Fin O'Malley of O'Malley's Pub in South County in the downtown area. Can't miss us. Come on in. I'll buy you a beer and show you something you'll want to see. Like nothing you've ever seen before. I guarantee it."

Phillip laughs. "There's no way to top that. I'm Phillip. Thanks for being a good friend to Toby, a great man that few really know or understand. Cheers, Irving! We're drinking to you, the man behind the man."

After a slight delay, the crowd cheers. Then chants.

O'Malley opens the front door, walks over to the bar, and reaches beneath it. Pulls out a radio and turns it on. Smirking he walks over and takes Fin's glass and shoots it back. Turns, and walks to the door, taking a chair with him.

159

"Toby. Toby, answer the damn radio." A husky, deep voice comes over the radio.

Everyone starts laughing.

Noah answers in Toby's grating nasal whine. "Hello, Irving." And snorts.

"I'm kicking your ass when I see you next."

"Why's that, Irving?" Toby gives his goofy grin.

"You know what happens when that name is spoken."

"Why you get so bent out of shape over a name your mother gave you, I'll never understand." Toby snickers with a snort.

"Just remember, I warned you."

"Yes, Irving."

"Now, boys, is that any way to treat each other?" Jillian asks

"Yes." They say in unison.

Jillian giggles.

"Ah, sweet Jesus, was that Jillian? I'm coming for a visit."

Jillian laughs sensually at Toby's look of exasperation. "We'll be pleased to meet you. When you get to town, stop at O'Malley's and see Fin. He'll contact us. I'm looking forward to meeting you, Irving."

"It will be my pleasure, my dear." Irving's voice comes over the radio, warm and rough. It was for the bedroom, hot and husky.

Toby's expression turns disgruntled. "Are you playing on the radio, Irving? Or were you testing your limits?" He whines hard.

Irving chuckles. "Oh, a little of both."

"Can you cut the feed broadcasting? These two are still hooked up, and no response at the station."

"Yeah, I'll call." His voice was serious. "Fin, I'll take you up on the drink and show and tell. Phillip, you are a wise and observant man, a worthy friend. Amethyst, you sound like a hot hand full. And Jillian, I'll see you in the future, sweetness."

Jillian giggles again.

"Ah, music to my ears. Toby, tell Noah to step out from behind and stand in the light." The radio goes dead.

"Who's Noah?" Jillian asks Toby softly, nearly breathless.

Her saying his name has a strong effect on him. Desire slams down to his groin, making him hard and shoots up into his head, making him dizzy.

She stares deep into his eyes.

"Who's Noah?" Her question comes from behind him, not from her lips this time.

"Are you all right?" She asks, her lips moving temptingly close, leaning towards him.

From behind him, echoes. "Who's Noah?" In her voice. "Are you all right, Noah?"

He quivers every time he hears her say his name. His control was slipping, coming unraveled. He was lost in her smoky, flashing grey eyes.

The radio continues to echo the two questions overlapping them. "Are you Noah, Noah? Who are you? Who are you, Noah? Noah? Noah. Alright, Noah. Noah." All in Jillian's soft, sweet voice.

He starts shaking, gripping the arms of his chair, squeezing tight to keep his hands off her. From stopping him from snatching her up out of her chair and running off with her.

Yes, his mind screams, I'm Noah! Look at me with those eyes. Want me? Please, take me and never let me go.

"Oh, God, Jillian. Help me!" He whispers desperately.

She leans closer and strokes his hand. "It's alright, I'm right here. I'm here for you. Calm down. We are here together." Her concern and sweet words soothe tender scars while her closeness and attention flame his fires of desire.

Her scent swirls around in his head, tangling with reason. Her touch coaxed his will to let go and take her. Her eyes were a siren song, pulling him happily to his doom. He floats adrift in his senses of Jillian.

He can feel her breath on his skin. The vibrations of her heart as it speeds up to match his. Her lips call to him, her taste still on his tongue, in his mouth, in his blood. He needs her. As important as air, water, and life.

He needs to protect her, even from himself. He can't get away and can't stay if he can't control himself. If he moves, his control will shatter.

The paradox twists him: He is Noah, Noah is Toby, Toby is Noah, and Noah is him. "Caught me, Jillian. Help me!" He beseeches gutturally.

A loud thunk sounds before him, and a wet, cold cloth sloshes across his face and neck. A platter appears before his eyes. The vision is gone, but he can still feel her close. He feels the loose of her touch immediately.

Someone turns his unresisting head until his eyes spy the platter of subs before him. He takes a deep breath. Her scent swirls around with the scent of food. He pries his fingers off the wood of his armrests.

Two solid thunks crash on either side of him as his fingers grab desperately at something he can do: eat. Starving, he eats quickly, like his life depends on it. And it does. Jillian's safety is now his life. Nothing else matters.

Not the job, not friends, not family, not that he had any. Nothing except Jillian and her happiness. His hand searches for food when his empty platter gets replaced with a cold platter comprised of cold meats, cheeses, crackers, and fruits. He mows through that with his hand still reaching for more.

A glass appears in one hand.

He moves it to his mouth.

One appears in his other hand.

He brings down one and up with the other. Up, down, up, down, his arms pump, pouring in whiskey. A tall glass of water replaces one of the tumblers and then the other, a few more rotations, up, down, up, down. Then he lifts an empty glass to his lips. He pulls it back and looks in, confused. He looks around. He sees Fin and Phillip watching him, smiling. Before them were a bottle and a pitcher, both empty.

The women were absent.

Noah relaxes with a deep sigh. He closes his eyes and breathes again. Letting all the tension drain away. He bends his head, his hair hangs forward, hiding him and removes his glasses, rubbing his face and eyes. He puts his glasses back on and peeks at them through the curtain of his hair. "How bad was it?" Somehow, he remembers to use Toby's voice.

They look at each other and lose their minds laughing hard.

All Noah could really understand was their actions, trading them back and forth. From what he could interpret, Toby was steaming in heat for Jillian, who apparently was crawling out of her skin to get to him. He sped through enough food for twelve in under three seconds, demolished a large cold platter and sucked down two pitchers of water and almost three-quarters of a bottle of whiskey.

Toby snorts. "So, what you are saying is it was bad but immensely funny."

They look at each other and nod, laughing again.

Toby takes the fullest bottle and pours out three glasses. "I commend you all. For quick actions and steadfast loyalty." He taps both glasses and shoots it back. "You saved me from myself once again. Thank you, gentlemen." He tips his head respectfully. "You are truly friends. I don't call many friends, and you are in an elite group. I look forward to assisting you in need."

Phillip tips his head, showing equal respect. "Thank you, Toby. I understand not calling many friends. I'm glad I was able to help you. A true friend is priceless."

Fin leans over with the other bottle and fills all three glasses. "A friend in need is a friend indeed." He raises his glass. "My first day here in town has been monumental. The highlight has been finding my crew. You four fit me perfectly. Each one comfortable with me, as if we've been lifelong friends."

"Good to have an understanding among friends, but if we keep this up, I may start weeping in my whiskey," Toby says, deeply touched. "How long did the episode last? For some reason, I've had time distortions today. And I find it disconcerting."

Fin and Phillip look at each other and laugh.

Fin clears his throat. "Ahem, maybe fifteen minutes." He looks at Phillip for confirmation.

Phillip nods. "Just under. We last checked on the hour." He gets up. "We were a little busy breaking the connection, then feeding and watering you, so I'll go check on them." He turns and walks over to the patients.

Fin leans in, watching him closely. "Are you okay now?"

Noah nods. "Yes, I was caught in an untenable position. You threw me a lifeline."

Fin chuckles. "Yeah, I got that when the chair broke and still you clutched the arms in your hands, crushing the wood." Fin laughs harder at his surprised expression. He points down. "I'm amazed the chair didn't collapse from all the stress it went through."

Toby looked down, bent and picked up the mangled chair arms. He places them on the table. He scratches his head. "Another first. How's Jillian?"

Fin chuckles. "Mad as all hell to be taken away from you. But otherwise, okay. She was sporting that "fever" flush, lush and alluring. We could practically see the flames sparking off you two. Amethyst was the general of this battle. She sent her troops scurrying to her orders and truly won the day for us." He chuckles. "She kept repeating. "Not the time, not the place." Over and over, between barking orders. She kept trying to get either of your attention. Failing that ordered a retreat."

"An amazing Lady." Toby smiles. "Remind me to reward her properly."

Fin nods. "Noted. I'll remind you in a few days."

164

The bar phone rings.

Fin runs off to answer it.

Phillip calls. "Toby, come see this."

Toby gets up and walks over to Wesley. He notices movement.

His eyes are twitching and moving around watching some action that wasn't happening on the ceiling.

Noah glances over at Rick. He exhibits the same actions. He looks back and forth between them and notices that they look like they are commentating back and forth. It seems that they share the same internal vision.

Toby steps back. "Whoa! Am I seeing this right? Are they interacting?"

Phillip turns to Rick, then back to Wesley. "It looks that way. I don't understand how that's possible, but many things happened today that I would have said were impossible yesterday."

Fin walks over with the cordless phone, holding it out to Toby. "It's for you. Irving."

Toby takes the phone. "Yes, Irving?"

"You know I'm obligated to beat you for this "Irving" bit."

Toby snorts. "I expected nothing less."

"Ah, looking for a fight to burn off some of that boiling passion. Yeah, Fin filled me in on what just happened." Stevens laughs, sounding very pleased.

"I would have seen your work if I wasn't distracted. Are you still connected?"

"Are you so drunk you have to ask?"

"Obviously, painless but too sober. The situation won't allow anything else. What have you got?"

"Well, did I hear right that those two connected are now active?"

"Yes, it appears they are commentating on a shared event, though they stare at the ceiling."

"Okay. I dug up some info and have a call into a psychologist who works with those affected by that amp. I found out that they go internal. The wiring gets snarled and can't make contact with the outside, though they can hear and understand. The isolation cracks the nut. They can hear themselves talking, but nobody responds. Bodies freeze in one position, and they no longer have the controls."

Toby nods. "I can understand to some extent what's going on with them. So if we can make contact and a way for them to communicate out of their trapped circumstances, it could possibly keep the nut whole."

Stevens chuckles. "Do I know my boy, or what? I've emailed you a program to translate the brain waves crashing off them. They've been that way awhile, they must be distressed. We need to run their signal through the translator program, but to do that, you have to identify their signals. Did they arrive with a satellite van by any chance?"

"I do believe so. I heard something to that effect."

"The only way I can figure it out is to send their signals through that amplifier so you can get a strong enough signal to latch on. Then, filter through the program and out through the speakers. We'll have to reconnect to the station. It would take too long for a closed loop. I'm on my way there now to take control. E.T.A., thirty minutes."

Toby nods. "Yes, that might work for the temporary. That specialist will take them?"

Stevens laughs. "Without a doubt. There hasn't been a duo trapped together, experiencing the same continuous event."

"Good. I wouldn't want anyone to experience that isolation; very nerve-wracking."

"Which is saying something when you are ruffled. It would bring the rest of us supreme males to our knees. Don't worry, my friend, we'll get them communicating with the outside world soon."

"Thank you. I don't need to tell you."

"Then don't. You've work to do. You know how to hook them up?"

"You need to ask? Are you drunk?"

"No, damn it." Stevens laughs. "I'll see you when I see you."

"Thank you, Irving."

"Oh, man, you're so getting your ass kicked. I'll even do it in front of that sweet honey, Jillian." He hangs up on a laugh.

Toby shakes his head. He looks forward to it. The only man he found who can give as good as he gets. They honed their skills on each other, though Stevens lost more than he won in their battles. He just claimed that Noah keeps him humble since he outshines him in so many other areas, especially how much more handsome he is.

He turns and comes face to face with Jillian.

She stands on the other side of the pub but rivets him in place. Her smoky eyes called to him. Her sweet lips smile in welcome.

Amethyst steps in front of Jillian, blocking his view and breaking the enchantment.

Toby bows respectfully. "Thank you, Lady Amethyst. You have once again earned my respect for your keen mind and quick actions. I'm in your debt, fair lady."

Amethyst bows her head regally, smiling sweetly. "A true friend looks out for them when they cannot themselves. But no debt between true friends, just an honest give and take as needed. If we keep score it would no longer be true, but a competition."

Toby bows again. "I am humbled by your wisdom, dear lady, and accept all as intended. Thank you."

"You're welcome. I ask that you refrain from looking directly at Jillian for the moment. We still have a way to go before we can call it a night."

"I shall endeavor to your wishes, wise that they are, and ask that we keep you between us. I think it may be safer for both parties, though you put yourself at risk."

"I can handle it for my two true friends."

167

Toby gives a quick bow and turns just as Jillian peeks around Amethyst's back and gives a sweet wave.

CHAPTER TWENTY-THREE

Toby snorts and clears his throat. "We have a plan now to help those two. Their situation is dire, any way you look at it, so we are going to try to save their sanity and give them some hope. How's John doing?"

Phillip and Fin were just turning from John.

Phillip looks back at John. "He's awake and suffering. I'm guessing the achy body from the fever but depression from grief. He remembers the episode outside and is very upset by it. He wants to talk to Becky, to apologize."

Toby nods. "I'll send her in. I have to get some supplies from the radio van. Can we find the keys?"

Jillian and Amethyst go to the pile of cut-away clothing, searching.

The phone in Toby's hand rings.

He clicks it on. "O'Malley's Pub, Toby speaking."

Dr. Paulson answers. "Hello, Toby. How are you guys doing?"

"Doc, great to hear from you. Better, are you on your way?"

"Yes, that accident was messy, but all survived."

"That's great. We are holding our own here as well. All the dazed are awake and interacting, probably still outside, wanting to get back in. We have a special situation with the two radio announcers. The only dazed we had a problem with was John, our control. I isolated him in the men's room after you left. I couldn't have picked worse if I tried. He's experiencing grief after losing a dear one two months ago, I believe. So he has a fever and depression. There was an incident outside that spiraled him down into self-loathing. You may need to take him back to the hospital."

"We're about twenty minutes out. Do we need to rush it?"

169

"No, I have someone else getting me help for the announcers. They need something different though we need to set them up with fluids and waste. I'll fill you in when you get here."

"Hang in there. We'll be there soon."

"Thanks, doc." Toby hangs up and places the phone on the table.

Amethyst holds out the keys. "Here they are. What do you want us to do?"

You and Jillian, go talk to Rick and Wesley. Let them know that I'm working on opening two-way communication between us. Tell them we are taking care of their bodies and more help is on the way, help that better understands what's really going on and can help them get control of their bodies."

"We're on it." Amethyst turns to Jillian at her back. "Did you get all that?"

"Yes." Jillian nods and reluctantly turns away from him.

Toby looks at Fin and Phillip. "Watch John, I'll send Becky if she's out there. Keep his spirits up and push fluids. I'll be out in the van. Doc is on his way." He turns at their nod.

Stepping out into the night is refreshing and freeing. The crowd hasn't thinned much. He spots O'Malley holding court facing the parking lot, keeping the masses away from the door. "Hello, my lad. How are things going?" O'Malley spots him and rises up to meet him.

"I can see the light at the end of the tunnel, O'Malley. Doc is about fifteen minutes out. Rick and Wesley are going to be broadcasting again soon though I have special help alerted to their situation and will probably arrive tonight to take them away. So, possibly within the hour you get your pub back. If it takes longer for Rick and Wesley's departure, I'm sure we can rig up something to keep them separate from the crowd.

O'Malley nods. "Good, these folks won't leave for nothing. They want back in and are starting to test my patience with them." He says the last loudly so everyone hears.

170

"John is awake now and would like to apologize to Becky. Is she still here? Fin and Phillip are both on hand."

O'Malley calls out. "Becky, lass, are you still here?"

"Yes, O'Malley." Becky steps through the crowd.

"Would you go talk to John? He's really upset about what happened and would like to apologize to you. Fin and Phillip are inside to protect you. Amethyst and Jillian are in there, too. John's really not feeling well. He's running a fever and is seriously depressed."

"Alright, I know John and he would never do what happened before normally. I knew Sarah. She was my best friend."

"You are probably the only one who can really help John right now. His depression is the most worrisome. Let him know he's not alone." Toby pats her shoulder. "Go right in, my dear, he's waiting."

"Thank you for taking us out of danger."

"You're welcome. I knew he was confused. A fever can do strange things with the mind. Don't keep him waiting any longer. Go talk with him. The doctor and EMS are on their way. Stay with him and keep him company."

She nods and timidly approaches the pub doors.

Toby turns back to O'Malley. "Do you know where the radio van is?"

O'Malley nods, pointing. "Right there, front and center." He chuckles. "It's been a trying night for you, my lad, hasn't it?"

Toby snorts. "You have no idea." He moves through the parting crowd. Many greet him. He acknowledges everyone but doesn't pause in purpose. He picks up a few followers that yammer on behind him. When he reaches the van, he turns and waits for silence. "If you can keep quiet, I could gladly use your help. If you insist on filling the silence, go back to the group. I have to concentrate on delicate exact science and can't do that if a lot of excessive words are flying around. Well?" Toby looks at each one.

One was bold enough to respond. "Yeah, man, I can keep quiet. Now I know…"

Toby just points at the group and stares at the man silently.

The man turns and walks back to the group, talking the entire way.

Toby looks at the other three men standing silent before him. He nods, turns, unlocks the van, and climbs in. He scans the contents of the van with a glance, then starts collecting the equipment and supplies he needs. He sits at the console, making some adjustments for optimal performance for the combined equipment and what they intend to do. He double-checks his settings.

He gets up and pulls out four large spools of cable. He turns and pulls out a few feet. "Run the cable into the pub, place it three feet from the booth with the middle man Rick. Then return. The next one will place their spool two feet away to the left. The third man was two feet away to the left. And the last man, two feet to the left. No gawking, get in, get out. Got it?"

All four nod.

"Good. One, go." Toby takes his end and plugs it into the transmitter. He uncoils a few feet from the second spool. "Two, go." He continues plugging in the cables and sending the men running. One shows up and sends him with the first load of equipment. Two arrive and carry off the second load. Three show up, and Toby turns to him. "Go ask O'Malley if he has a large tarp or extra walling. I'm looking for a way to partition off those three booths with some floor space out past the spools. Can you handle that? You can enlist one of you four. I need two to guard this van."

Three opens his mouth and waits, his eyes laughing.

Toby snorts. "Yes, tell me."

"I'll take four, and yes, give me about ten minutes. I've got plenty of tarping in the truck."

"Fantastic. Will you need any other muscle?"

"No, we've got this."

"Thank you. Please remember to respect these men's privacy."

"Don't worry, Mr. Toby, we respect you, sir, and do as you wish."

"Thank you. I'm pressed for time right now, but I look forward to speaking with you and the others later."

"Thank you, sir. I'll get to it. There's four." Three snickers.

"If you have any problems or need anything to complete your task, see Fin O'Malley. He looks like O'Malley."

"Right, sir."

One and two arrive at a run, slightly winded.

Toby picks up the last few items and steps down, closing one of the doors. The other has the cables snaking out. "One and Two, I need you to guard this van. No one except me, will enter. If someone gets pushy, start blaring the horn. Do you understand? Those two men's lives are in your hands. If anyone touches those controls, it could kill those two. You are a part of big science tonight. We are constructing a bridge to the internal mind where those two are trapped. Do you understand how important your jobs are?"

"Yes, sir, nobody would dare messing with you. We all know you are worried about those two and are trying real hard to bring them back as you did us." Two holds out his hand. "Thank you, sir, for rescuing us, pulling us out like you did. It sure was chilly and lonely, but you shined like warm sunshine."

One nod. "You started laughing and warmth just filled me up. It gave us hope. We couldn't ask for help, but you understood and got us out. We're here for you, whatever you need."

"Thank you, gentlemen. If something happens, get a message to Fin O'Malley, the younger. I'll leave you to it." Toby slumps quickly to the pub, acknowledging all greetings. Stepping through the doors brought him up short. A metal frame encases the three booths, extending out four feet. The cables snake across the floor tapped down in the low-traffic areas.

Jillian sits next to Wesley's head, talking softly.

Amethyst mirrors her actions.

It looks like they were the commentators for the activities around them.

173

John lies in the same position, but Becky sits curled up on the bench beside him. She looks up and smiles at Toby.

He nods and moves over to the cleaned-off table, placing his items there. The spools line up per his specifications. The two crated loads sit on One and Two's spools. He brings them to the cleared table.

Phillip walks over.

"Grab hold, need this in there," Toby says, indicating the table and metal frame.

Phillip lifts his side. They move it close to the radio table with a couple of feet separating them inside the structure.

"Good." Toby nods. "Do you know how to strip wire?"

Phillip snorts in disgust and holds out his hand. "Please, just tell me how many, how long."

"Good, I need another right hand." Toby pulls the taped banner from the table and hands it to Phillip.

Phillip puts it over a table outside the structure and brings back two chairs. He slides one up to Toby's legs, who sits and pulls it closer to the radio table.

Phillip takes the other chair to the work table. He unloads the crates and stacks them back under the table out of the way.

He lays out the equipment, tools, and supplies, transferring the amp/ohm meter, oscilloscope, screwdrivers, soldering iron, solder, and pliers to the radio table.

Noah straightens the radio table and moves one mic to the top of the bench between Rick and Wesley. He opens the radio station's laptop, quickly extracts the program Stevens sent him, and downloads it to the computer. Reads Stevens' note highlighting the amplifier and the program. He nods and wipes all existence of his activities from the computer. While the computer restarts and loads the program, Toby inspects the equipment.

He gets a screwdriver and removes the amplifier case. He looks it over carefully. "Can you find me more light, please?" He finds a legal pad in the computer case, pulls a pen from his pocket and gets to work, drawing diagram after diagram. Light blooms over his head. He looks up and sees spotlights shining on the two tables. "Thank you. Could we get cover for those two benches? They're extremely light sensitive."

A tarp floats down over the tree benches, with enough overhang to drape the seats.

Jillian and Amethyst laugh in surprise, chatting with their companions.

"Thank you." Toby doesn't stop working. "Phillip, clip a USB double-ended in two and strip it. Fin, when Doc gets here, have him check John first, then come see me with Charles and Zack with their full kits. They should be here soon."

Fin laughs. "The strobing lights just arrived."

USB cable halves appear at his elbow. He reaches for the USB cable, soldering iron, and solder. Before he touches anything, a grounding band snaps on his wrist. Without stopping, he attaches the USB cable to the output on the amplifier and then connects the other to the secondary output. "Thanks."

"Welcome," Phillip says quietly.

The Ethernet cable is next, cut in two. On the cut ends, I need two inches of stripped wire a foot stripped on the strand casing on each half. And see if you can get me the two I.V. kits from Zack or Charles, and sixteen electrode pads with conductive gel. If they have clippers, that would be good. Oh, and colostomy bags. Go." He turns to the computer, checking the program. Satisfied, he goes to the spools, grabs the ends and pulls them over. Closed the computer and pops the back off, finds the output for the sound card. He strips and solders in the four cables. The prepared Ethernet cables appear at his elbow. He separates the wires and solders them into their proper places on the two inputs. He checks each connection twice through the entire line until he assures that the electronics work flawlessly.

Two I.V. kits appear at his elbow, two colostomy kits, a box of electrode pads, a bottle of conductive gel, and the whine of the clippers.

"Excellent. Go play barber, take it all. Let him know what you are about to do and why. Fin, we are now in a cone of silence, correct?"

Fin laughs. "If you mean no mic, no speakers, then yes. This side of the pub is switched off."

"Great, keep the radio handy but not too close. I didn't work on backfeed and delay, but we will need it once we get these two up and running. I don't see why those avid patrons can't return, respecting the boundaries here, of course."

"I'm sure we won't have a problem." Fin laughs. "Dr. Paulson wants to take John. Becky's going to ride along. He wants to give a medical overview on these two before others pick them up, you know, the red tape of passing the buck."

"Yes, send him to Rick first. I will be along directly after I get fluids flowing with Wesley." He picks up the two kits with tape and alcohol swabs. "I need light and access to the back of the booth."

The canvas folds towards the heads of the patients, and light floods their bodies.

"Thank you." Noah turns and pauses.

Jillian holds Wesley's hand, she lets go and moves to the other bench, placing her hand on his raised arm.

"How is he? How's his temperature?" He crawls along the bench, placing the urine bag by his hip, then stands, turns around and gets down on his knees by Wesley's waist. He opens the blankets enough to expose his shorts. He puts on latex gloves on his hands and prepares the kits for use, connecting all the pieces together for the cleanest transition.

"He seems agitated. His temperature is the best we've had. His pulse races then turn slumberous. I've panicked a few times waiting on the next beat. His breathing acts like his heartbeat, erratic. Or I should say they match; when he's breathing heavily, his heart races. When breathing slows, so does his heartbeat." Jillian smiles sadly. "I can't imagine being isolated in your body like this." She laughs. "Well, yes, I can but I wasn't really aware of me, more like a cold floating feeling, between awake and asleep. Aware but not physically."

"Yes, I understand." He touches Wesley's leg and is pleased by the warmth. "How about his toes?"

"Amazing, really. Only the very tips show dark. They will shed skin, but not much. Nothing needs to be removed."

"That's good." Toby pats Wesley's leg. "Wesley, I'm going to set your body up with a urine bag and an I.V., then the same for Rick. Once those are completed, I will finish building the bridge to your inner mind. We will be transmitting you over the radio so your fans know you both are doing okay. Then, some specialists will come and take you away and try to put you back the way you were. It won't take much longer. Hang in there." He pats Wesley's leg again. "I'm starting now on your urine bag. There will be discomfort, but I'll make it quick."

He pulls down Wesley's underwear and gets to work feeding the thin tube up his urethra to his bladder. The warm fluid flows through the tubing and pools in the bag. He pulls up his briefs. "That should help your body's comfort level. Now the I.V." He strips off the old gloves and puts on new ones. Places the rubber tourniquet on his arm, swabs, and inserts the needle, tapping it down. Loop, tape, connects it to the hose then the hose to the bag. Adjusts the flow, checks for leaks and nods, handing the saline bag to Jillian. "Good, now you have fluids. I'm off to do the same with Rick. I'll be back. Dr. Paulson will check you out before we hook you up and sound out on the radio. He will check you after also." He turns to Jillian. "You are doing beautifully. Keep it up." He steps over the back of the bench. "Phillip, could you please bring me those two kits?" Toby asks.

Phillip brushes off the hair on Rick's face and neck. "Sure, no problem. I just got done. Dr. Paulson went to get something from the ambulance. He said he was almost completed with the assessments."

"Good evening, Rick. I want you to know what I'm about to do. I'm going to be inserting a small catheter tub up the urethra to empty your bladder. I will also install an I.V. to give you fluids. Once Dr.

177

Paulson finishes, we will be bridging into you so you can talk on the radio. I will be hooking you up to that nifty, expensive amplifier and company laptop. Later, we have some specialists coming for you and Wesley. To take you away, to help you gain control of your body and put you back the way you were. So here we go. Thank you, Phillip."

Amethyst sits quietly, holding Rick's hand.

Toby gets to work. Strips off the gloves used on Wesley. Snaps on new gloves, opens the colostomy kit and assembles the parts. When the only thing left is to connect to Rick, Toby opens the blankets and pulls down his underwear. "Slight discomfort." He feeds the hose up the urethra. He stops when warm fluid flows through the tube and ends in the catheter bag. Toby checks the line for leaks, seeing none he pulls his underwear back up and recovers him. He strips off his gloves and pulls on a new pair.

Amethyst moves to the other side to touch Rick's arm.

He takes the I.V. kit and opens it, setting out the parts and tools he needs. He tourniquets his arm inserts the needle, tapes it down, connects the hose, loops it and tapes it down. Then connects to the bag. Hands the saline bag to Amethyst after he checks for leaks. "You are doing a great job. Keep it up. Human contact is a powerful thing." He checks over Rick. "How's he doing? Temperature evened out, right? Breathing and heartbeat erratic?"

Amethyst nods. "Yes. Jillian and I are comparing and noticing the same things. His toes are the best that only some skin will peel off. Otherwise, whole with mental communication possibly handy. You're doing great. Jillian and I have been telling these boys what you're up to; very entertaining. We especially like when you ask without looking up, and poof. Your answers materialize. The light was funny, but out done by the tarp roof to these benches that are retractable. How cool are you?"

Toby snorts. "Super."

Amethyst laughs.

Jillian giggles.

Toby shakes his head. "I still have work to do, don't distract me." He sighs. "Later."

Amethyst laughs.

Muffled sounds come from the next booth.

"On to stage two." Toby crawls out of the booth.

CHAPTER TWENTY-FOUR

"Dr. Paulson, how is John?"

"I think he is showing signs of the flu and depression, plus we don't know what the daze added to the mix. I'll order hydration and see how he is doing tomorrow."

"Good. I hope he comes through this okay. He had me a little worried." Toby looks back at Rick and Wesley. "What about these two?"

"Yes, Rick and Wesley. You were right to heat the bodies, though this wasn't frostbite per se, but showed the same symptoms."

"Couldn't their minds create the conditions for true frostbite?" Toby looks at the doctor. "What I mean is the mind receives signals from the outside world. If they couldn't interpret those signals, couldn't their minds alter their perception of reality? Instead of summertime here, couldn't their minds interpret the initial coldness of their bodies as the onset of a harsh winter storm? Thereby stuck in the storm as snow piles up, their bodies start to freeze, and frostbite takes hold." He looks to Amethyst. "Is his arm flexible?"

She nods. "Yes, since we got their body temperature up." She moves the free hand she holds, lifting and bending his arm for him, showing his flexibility. "When they pant and their heart race, we've noticed a sheen of sweat on their brows." She looks at Rick. "I travelled through a desert once, it was summer, and we were hiking through a national park and during the afternoon, we all panted like that to cool our overheated bodies. I remember I thought my heart was going to pound out of my chest."

Toby's head pops up. "Do these episodes happen right after you change their bottles?" He doesn't wait for an answer, snatches the Doc's stethoscope and leans over Rick, whips off the first blanket. "How long ago did you change these?" His fingers touch a bottle still too hot to touch comfortably. Rick's heart races, panting in short breaths.

180

Toby uses the blanket and moves the bottles a foot away from Rick's body, all around, and takes the bottles out of the saddle of his legs. He whips open the blanket and touches Rick's damp belly and upper thighs.

Rick sighs.

Toby listens to his heart again. It slows and grows stronger. "Jillian, move Wesley's bottles to surround a foot away, loose the top blanket and open the bottom two." Toby shakes his head, disgusted. "We were the cause of distress. We were cooking them." He shakes his head at what he missed.

"Toby, are you a god?" Dr. Paulson asks seriously.

"What?" Toby's head snaps to the doctor in surprise. "No."

"Well, only a god is all-knowing. The rest of us mortals have to stumble along and figure things out with the clues we are given. Sometimes the clues morph after a time, no longer giving us the same hint, but a different one." He pats Toby's hunched shoulder. "I can honestly say I never would have put these clues together and come up with a solution that makes half as much sense as yours. Which given the daze and tonight, I believe you understand more than I of what's going on internally with these boys." He squeezes Toby's shoulder. "Don't beat yourself up. They are alive and doing better now. What distress you put them through, unknowingly of course, but you know now and can ensure their body comfort." He looks at the two prone men. "You are doing very well, and you made the right calls when the information was presented to you. Don't doubt yourself now. If they are trapped in a reality created by their minds, you think you have the means to bridge them back to us. Don't you think they would do anything to touch something familiar? Weren't you questioning your own reality earlier tonight? How did you feel isolated, but everyone was still, surrounding you but unable to communicate? How did you feel when I walked into the ring?"

"So relieved I wanted to laugh and cry. Very emotional, regardless. Thank you, Dr. Paulson. I seem to be on an emotional rollercoaster tonight."

Dr. Paulson chuckles. "You are holding up well. I would be crouched babbling in a corner, smacking my head on the wall."

Toby snorts. "Don't think I didn't consider it."

Dr. Paulson laughs. "We are very grateful that you chose other actions." He looks at all the electronic equipment. "Do you need some help hooking these boys up?"

Toby nods. "Yes, I know I need to connect them at the same time. If you could help, that would be great. Does the ambulance have two defibrillators? When we plug them in, their hearts may stop and having two would ease my mind. Some adrenaline on hand might be good, too."

"Good to have thought all sides and possibilities. You're welcome on my team any time." Dr. Paulson slips through the canvas. "Zack, get the two defibrillators and double the adrenaline on the double. Bring another bottle of conductive gel and bring Charles. Tell Becky to hold tight with John." Dr. Paulson slips back into the walled-off section of the pub. "Okay, run me through what my part is and how you want it done."

"Thank you, sir. You are an excellent doctor." Toby smiles, then turns all business. Explaining the overall procedure, then the specifics down to the placement of the electrode pads and how to connect the wires to the nipple on the pads. "I think for a better array, we should coat their skulls with the conductive gel, which means we need to prop up their necks." Toby looks around, thinking and sees the round O'Malley's coasters. He nods. "Fin, can I get two sleeves of coasters?" Toby turned to the flap when it was pulled aside.

Charles and Zack come in, each outfitted with their med kits.

"Set up on their side." He turns to the two booths. "Ladies, cover them up and let's clear out the bottles. Fin, bring the cart crates empty. Phillip, if we have to use the defibrillator, then I want Fin to pull those earphone jacks, and you clip this wire carefully." He points inside the amplifier. "Very carefully solder it quickly when we get a pulse. Fin will plug the jacks back in at the same time. Everything must be synchronized. Ladies, when we make a connection, you will be out in the van being extra hands to Irving and me who is probably at the station. We will conference a call between us. Fin, can you give speaker phone for the call?"

Fin hands one sleeve of coasters to Toby and the other to Dr. Paulson.

They move to their patients, lift a head and slip it under their necks. Their heads suspend off the surface about three inches. He grabs a pair of gloves, snaps them on, and then grabs the bottle of conductive gel. Squirting all on Wesley's head and smearing it around to coat it evenly, being careful of the headphones adhered to the skull."

"Yes, to the conference call. Yes, to the bottle removal; almost complete. Yes, to pulling the jacks and reconnect; synchronized."

"Good. Dr. Paulson, we wrap the wire on the pad as I showed you then we place them same spot same time. Our left and right. He pulls off his gloves and tosses them in a bag for bio waste hanging from the coat hook between the booths. Under the bag hangs the I.V. bag. He nods. "You guys are a great team." He turns to the stripped Ethernet cables. He quickly separated and twisted groupings of wires at one end, leaving the long exposed wires for the probe pads. "We need another soldering iron." He looks to Phillip. "Once they are probed, we are going to solder these in this order." He tags the groupings with numbers. "In these positions, 1, 2, 3, 4." He points out the spots.

A soldering iron and stand move hand to hand to arrive in his. He snorts. "Thank you." He hands it to Phillip. "Plug it in and break off some solder. Remember to heat the wires and contact simultaneously, adding solder slowly, no flooding. We can't screw this up. One chance. And I don't have a plan B." He watches Phillip. "We can do this, right?"

Phillip smiles. "Right, you will do fine." Phillip's confidence makes everyone chuckle.

Toby snorts. "I'm glad you think so." He said dryly.

The door to the pub jingles. "Mr. Toby, the phone in the van is ringing and won't stop." A voice floats over the canvas walls.

"Tell One or Two to answer and let the man calling know I will be there directly."

"Right, sir." The door jingles.

"We are getting down to the wire..." Toby snorts. "I'll take the ladies out to the van. This gives anyone here the opportunity to take a drink, a leak, or a break. Once I get back, we are headed for the finish line and no stopping. Keep someone talking to these two while I'm gone." He looks to the ladies. "Are you ready? Do you need a moment?"

Amethyst and Jillian both shake their heads.

"Okay, let's go. Rick, Wesley, I'll be right back. We are doing the finishing touches to broadcast you from your inner mind." He escorts the ladies from the canvas enclosure. Three and four stand at the end at the side of the structure, standing watch.

Noah nods to them.

They tip their heads.

"Doing great."

They nod.

"Ladies." Noah holds out his arm to the door. He slumps behind.

They step out to a larger crowd.

O'Malley steps over and walks with them to the van. "Word got out that we are reopening the doors tonight. Well, a lot of words are flying all over the place." He laughs. "We have representatives from our neighbor states."

Toby snorts. "We're getting closer. O'Malley, within the next thirty minutes, you will be slammed behind the bar as the thirsty horde floods the pub."

O'Malley laughs. "No, lad, controlled entrance is the key; only four every five minutes."

Noah snorts. "Glad you already have that worked out. I'll send you Fin and Phillip once we are up and running."

"Sounds good. I'll let you go."

184

The three of them approach the van. One and Two stand in front of the doors. They step in and follow closely. He closes one door and looks back at One and Two. "Doing great. Now you guard the van and these two women."

They nod silently, step back into place, and go back to the van.

"Excellent." He turns to the console with the two seats. "Ladies, take a seat, please." He picks up the receiver sitting on the desk. "Irving, I have Jillian and Amethyst here to man the van controls. I'll have you on speakerphone in a moment." He reaches over and pushes a button. "Go ahead."

"Hello, darlings. Are you ready for me?" Stevens' smooth, deep bedroom voice slides around the inside of the van.

Jillian giggles.

Amethyst flushes. "Yeah, baby, I'm ready."

Jillian laughs. "I'm ready to do this in the van." She flushes at what her words imply.

Stevens laughs. "Only business for now, but we can meet in the van later, my lovely doves."

Noah growls.

Toby coughs. "Enough of that, Irving, we have work to do."

Stevens laughs. "Toby, go take five minutes under a tree or find a patch of grass. We need to be focused. It's been a stressful night. You need to decompress before you blow. I'll call the pub in six minutes. Go, I got these doves in hand. We'll be fine."

Toby rubs the back of his neck. "Six minutes." He turns to the door and steps out. He asks One. "Where's the closest big tree or a nice patch of grass?"

"Downtown park, across the street, both."

The girls' laughter ripples out of the van.

Noah rounds the van and crosses the deserted street. Off to the left, a large old oak stands majestic over the large park. Once he enters the deserted park, hidden by the tall hedge, he straightens his back and runs to the tree as fast as he can. He stops and flops on the

185

thick, lush grass under the old tree. He sets his internal alarm for five minutes and closes his eyes. Relaxing every muscle in his body, taking only seconds, then he feels himself melting into the rich soil to rest in the loving fingers of the roots of the oak. He feels the fingers of roots slip into his veins and arteries, feeding and nourishing him.

The spirit of the grand old dame wraps around his spirit and soul, giving comfort and assurance. Just before his five minutes, the spirit released him, leaving a warm glow. The fingers of roots retract and push him up, full of energy and in complete control. The blades of grass freshened and swept clean all negative energy. When the five minutes are up, his eyes open, he springs to his feet and runs to the entrance to the park.

He slips into Toby when he crosses the entrance to the park. He crosses the street and enters the pub. He ducks into the canvas structure.

All stand present.

He looks at Fin. "Irving's call in thirty seconds." He looks at Phillip. "Ready?"

Phillip nods, eyes wide in surprise. Toby turns to the doctor. "Ready?"

Dr. Paulson wears a similar expression as Phillip and Fin. "Yes."

His eyes move from Charles to Zack. "Ready?"

Their expressions mirror the others, and they nod stiffly.

"You all are participating, so you cannot fall into the Daze," Toby says forcefully, an order.

"Yes." They say in unison.

Toby snorts with a goofy grin. "We will get to the end of this day without anyone dying. I'm buying the first round for the pub when we pull this off."

CHAPTER TWENTY-FIVE

The phone rings.

Fin answers. "Yes, different." He nods, watching Toby move to the chair at Wesley's head and sits down.

"Doctor, have a seat and let's get started."

"Yes, Toby." Dr. Paulson shakes his head and sits down, taking a deep breath.

"Phillip, is there another discharge band for the doctor?" Toby asks, handing over an Ethernet cable to the doctor.

Phillip appears at the doctor's side, removes his watch and places the band. "Your watch will be in your right coat pocket that hangs on the chair."

Dr. Paulson nods. "Ready."

Noah looks over at Rick and Wesley. Then pulls out his blue marker and inks. He spots where the probes go, eight in all. He gets up and marks Rick's head to match, then sits down. "Separate the red and blue wires and feed them under the headphone harness. Red right, blue left. Correct. Wrap the right clockwise and the left counterclockwise. Hint: to start the wind, hold the end of the wire against the nipple and use your finger to band the wire to the arc. After your second rotation, you can grip the wire like a string of a yo-yo. We are coiling the wire, so we can't be sloppy. Each rotation of the wire needs to be snug up. When the nipple starts to flare at the top we wrap down, laying the wire in the saddle of the two below. We should reach the casing at the bottom next to the end. We need it tight. Make Tesla proud."

Phillip coughs.

Noah wraps the red wire to the probe and looks at Dr. Paulson.

When he completes it, he holds it out for inspection.

"Good." Noah nods. "Right temple."

They place it.

"Blue wire, pinch the end round and round." Noah hums a round-and-round tune, with one upbeat for placing the probe.

They work through the other six, picking up speed but not losing precision.

Noah sits back and holds out his hand.

Phillip places the amp/ohm meter in his hand.

He clicks the dial and pulls the probes, then turns it on. He checks each probe pad nipple to the wire, each nipple twisted end of the Ethernet cable. Then moves to Rick and checks the doctor's work. Check each connection.

Toby stands. "Stand by, doc. Remove the chairs. If their hearts stop we need to jump in and pump for them until we know we have a charge to the paddles. I'd rather not zap them. Too many reasons." He turns to the radio table. "Fin, get into position. Phillip, ready?"

"Yes." Phillip stands with the soldering iron in hand, at the ready, wires lined up, taped to the table, ready to connect.

"Ladies, ready?"

"Yes, Toby." Jillian answers calmly.

"Irving?" Toby smirks.

"Yes, Toby," Stevens says dryly.

"You're buying if this doesn't work."

"I'm not worried. I know you are buying. When have you failed?" Stevens laughs.

"Never. Right. Wesley, Rick, buckle up, boys, and hold on tight. You're going on a ride for life." Noah nods to Phillip.

They both pick up one wire and solder it into the amplifier. Quickly, they work as one. Two go in, Three go in, Four go in.

Wesley and Rick jerk.

"Check him, doc." Noah puts the stethoscope to Wesley's heart. Nothing.

188

He climbs up and starts pumping. "Count 'em out, doc. Charge the paddles. Adrenaline to the heart on a breath."

Both EMS techs use a manual resuscitator mask on their man and nod.

Straddling over Rick, Dr. Paulson calls. "1, 2, 3, 4, 5, 6, 7, breathe."

"Adrenaline." Charles stabs both syringes into Wesley's heart and hits the plungers.

Dr. Paulson calls. "1, 2, 3, 4, 5, 6, 7, Breathe."

As Dr. Paulson calls, Noah starts to sing a song to call the boys back. The same rhythm as a good, strong heartbeat.

On the fourth cycle, Dr. Paulson says. "Toby." Instead of breathing.

Charles and Zack breathe anyway for the patients.

"Paddles. Doc, call it heavy on the charge." He stands on both benches. "Clip and pull."

"Ready." Fin and Phillip say in unison.

Charles hands the paddles and stands at the controls.

Noah rubs the paddles together. The song still runs in his head. He starts to sing again.

Dr. Paulson calls the charge.

"Ready." Charles and Zack reply.

"Clear." Dr. Paulson calls. "Now." At the second mark.

Noah keeps singing while the paddles discharge into Wesley. When the paddles clear Wesley, Charles presses his fingers to his neck artery. He breathes for him at the appropriate time. He shakes his head.

Dr. Paulson calls the charge.

Noah keeps singing, his voice rich and warm, calling the men back to their bodies.

"Ready." From Charles and Zack.

189

"Clear." Dr. Paulson calls. "Now." On the second beat.

Paddles discharge.

Charles places his fingers on Wesley's neck and shakes his head, then breathes for him.

Dr. Paulson calls the charge.

Noah keeps singing. Imagining, he reaches out to Wesley and Rick, drawing them closer and pulling them back.

"Ready." Charles and Zack call.

"Clear." Dr. Paulson calls. "Now." On the second beat.

Noah imagines slamming them back into their bodies when the paddles discharge, sealing them in. He continues singing to ensure them, they made it.

Charles looks up hopefully with his finger on Wesley's neck. The breathing mask descends towards his face when both Wesley and Rick gasp for a breath on their own.

Noah nods to Fin and Phillip.

"Reconnecting," Phillip calls. "Now."

Noah continues singing, imagining that Wesley and Rick's voices from their heads travel down the wires through the amplifier, along the cables, through the program.

"Computing," Phillip calls.

As Noah sings, he pictures their voices running along the cables to the van.

"Got them." Jillian calls excitedly.

"Sending," Amethyst says happily.

Noah sings, his thoughts travel with their voices as they shoot out to a satellite and bounce back to the station.

"Hot damn! Man, you never fail." Stevens hoots.

Noah continues to sing, staring down at Wesley, unseeing. His mind focused on their voices travelling from the station, out across the county, finding any radio to receive their voices. He comes to the end of his song and falls silent, breathless, waiting.

"That was Toby "Super Geek" Robins, singing The Long Road Home. Brought to you by the fine folks of O'Malley's Pub." Wesley's voice has an ethereal quality. "This is Wesley with Rick on location tonight only here in South County at O'Malley's Pub in the downtown area, on Main St. Rick, can you believe the night we've had?"

Noah blinks and sees Wesley's eyes blink and focus on him. He smiles.

Wesley smiles back.

"Wesley, I don't even know where to begin to describe what we experienced."

Noah looks over at Rick.

His mouth moves as his words come over the radio. They match.

"No delay?" Noah says to Stevens.

"Hey, we are speaking at the speed of sound." He laughs. "I don't like stilted conversations."

Noah looks down at Wesley and Rick. "Welcome back, boys." Noah laughs with joy at the impossibility of the feat they pulled off. "Drinks are on me. Open the doors." He looks at Wesley and Rick. "You're public awaits." Joy ripples through him, only finding release with his laughter.

"Wesley, I think our "Super Geek" is pleased with his results on the impossible task he assigned himself." Rick smiles and winks at Noah.

Noah laughs harder.

"Yes, Rick, well pleased. We have exceeded his expectations."

"Far exceeded, beyond all measures." Noah laughs again. "Gentlemen, before we go on, let me introduce those who had an instrumental part in bringing you out of your mind and onto the radio." Still standing over Wesley, he points to the doctor. "Dr.

Paulson, who did all the heavy work on Rick, and our on-call doctor for tonight's events."

"Hello, Wesley and Rick. Glad we got you back this far. We'll be rooting for a full recovery."

"Thank you, doctor, for getting me this far." Rick's ethereal voice comes across the radio.

"Dr. Paulson, you may not realize how much you have helped Toby through this difficult night," Wesley says warmly. "You always had the right words for him when he needed them most. As did Fin and Phillip."

Noah nods. "They seem to have been aware the entire night."

Rick comments. "Yes and no."

"What Rick means is that we had two realities playing simultaneously. Like watching TV and sweating on your sofa cause your air conditioner is broken. You experience and pay attention to the movie to ignore sweating your ass off. Oops! Sorry, Ed. I'll try to keep it clean since you can't bleep out the words, no delay." Wesley laughs.

"So, what Wesley was explaining was similar to what we experienced. Imagine a big picture frame where our reality plays on without us. Just the observers now. It happened sometime during the fight. There was a slight shift in perspectives. At first, we didn't recognize the difference. We were still commentating about the events to each other, but nobody else really responded."

"It was after the Flesh-eating Zombie and Jackson almost mangling himself that Toby noticed lost time, lost reality, and Jackson's lost voice. In our shared reality, Rick and mine, I could turn to him and talk to him, still sitting at the table, and he responded. That wasn't unusual. We tried to talk to Toby to reassure him that we were right there with him. That's when we realized we weren't there." Wesley explains.

"Very disconcerting, really. You have this idea the world will cease to exist if you aren't playing your role. Bzzz! You are wrong. It just flows around and fills in the cracks like water. So, we watch our reality while our shared reality shifts around us. You were very close to what we experienced before Amethyst brought our condition to your attention. Hanging before us was our old reality, a little hazy at the outer edges. Around us turned to the wilderness with us sitting in our chairs behind the table. The weather turned cold, and snow started to fall, piling up around us. We couldn't get up, only look at each other. We were thinking our numbers were up when that beauty, Amethyst, found us."

"We did have hope, though, especially when Phillip started that ping-pong chain reaction. That was hilarious. And our man Toby laughed so hard all the dolls dazed swarmed, and that tigress jumped him. It was an Indian summer; snow still packed around us, but the heat seeped bone deep. We knew that Toby would get us out like he got the others out. Later, we came to understand we have an extra influence on our situation. So we challenged our "Super Geek" to find a solution to bring us back."

"Wesley, that Tigress is Jillian, I believe."

"Yes, Rick, I know her name. She did sit with me, holding my hand, her sweet voice whispering in my ear." Wesley chuckles. "She told me all sorts of things, but you never reveal a lady's confidence, do you, Toby?"

"Never, it's not gentlemanly," Toby responds gravely.

"Never disrespect a Lady in Toby's presence. Otherwise, you'll end up a Flesh Eating Zombie."

"Or if you have to watch the confrontation, doll dazed. Have you ever seen anything like that, Rick?"

"Wesley, I have never seen anything like what I saw tonight. First, the fight that wasn't. But it was somehow so funny it made, what…200 people, amazed, stupid…mindless. Then I saw all two hundred people frozen in their daze, watching Toby. The eyes creeped me out, always following his movements. However, it was pretty funny when he was working on Jackson and those awake slipped back to mindless. When he looked up and they were all around him, closer, even I felt the urge to run and say the hell with it. Sorry, Ed.

Or could you be referring to when he started moving the people around like dolls? A touch here, walk. A touch there, stop. A touch here, squat.

Or when Toby laughed and those Dazed animated themselves and swarmed while on the other side of the pub bumper, people ran riot.

Or getting attacked by the Tigress, then jumping up twelve to fifteen feet and working the bar like an Olympian with the Tigress latched on like a tic and executing a perfect landing; ten!

Or could you mean Toby as the pied piper, well, whistler, calling the dazed to awaken?

Or would it perhaps be that since we can't use our vocal cords at the moment, this amazing combination of science allows our thoughts, or as Toby says, our inside voice, to be heard in our reality, which thankfully is our only one?"

"Yes." Wesley's voice was highly amused.

"Then, no, never have I seen anything like tonight. Folks, if you thought about coming to O'Malley's tonight and didn't, you missed a rollercoaster of reality experience. If you were here, wow, what a ride!"

On the other side of the canvas walls, the room rocks with the crowd's agreement.

"Could it be that the once dazed are back in the house?"

The crowd cheers, whooping and hollering.

"They snuck right in. I didn't even realize."

Someone from the crowd calls out. "Toby warned us."

Toby snorts, shaking his head. "I warned them not to breach the boundaries."

Many laugh in the crowd, one calls out. "Like we'd take the chance of pissing Toby off. We saw what happened to Jackson and that over insulting a Lady. He wasn't pissed, just doing his good deed."

From the crowd. "A lady in need is his good deed."

194

Toby snorts, giving a goofy grin. "Let's get back to introductions. Also instrumental in the continuance of your lives were Charles and Zack, our EMS techs of the night."

"Thank you, Charles, for stabbing me in the heart twice and giving me breath. What's with the purple spot between your eyes?" Wesley asks curiously as Charles leans into his line of sight.

Charles laughs. "The mark of the Dazed. You two have a different look since you're special."

"Really?" Rick asks curiously. "What's our look?"

Zack leans to look him in the eyes, mimicking the hand on the earphone. "Besides the fact that your earphones are melted to your head and one hand, your bald except under the band of your headphones, head slimed with gel with electrode pads wired, all highlighted by Toby's blue marker. He's very precise, you know."

"Does anyone have a mirror? I'd love to see this." Wesley chuckles.

"Put your mirrors away, ladies," Toby says. "In good time, gentlemen."

"Did you hear that, Wesley, the gasps of the crowd? He called it, didn't he? Can he see them?"

"No, he can't." Phillip laughs. "He's been calling for items, and they appear. He just expects they will, and they do. Amazing, really."

"Isn't it, though? Amazing as dying and coming back to life. Which we truly appreciate, Zack, thank you for your part." Rick says earnestly.

"We would be remiss if we didn't mention that death/life experience. Don't you think, Rick?"

"Yes, Wesley, we would. We must, once more, comment on the amazing Toby "The Super Geek" Robin's actions."

"Not just on the physical plane, which was monumental and we are grateful for all your efforts. We must speak of the spiritual plane, not a pray to Jesus act but a spiritual rescue."

"If Toby hadn't sung that song over and over, calling to us, we would have floated away. When we got close enough, that song, and I suspect Toby's spiritual form or soul, reached out and grabbed us tight, slamming us back into our bodies right when the voltage hit. That song told us to breathe and our hearts to beat. Somehow, we followed that song, and now we are able to communicate with our reality once again."

"Many will not believe what we know as truth, but they weren't here. You, The Awakened Dazed, know what we speak of, don't you?"

The crowd shouts as one. "Yes!"

"Tonight wasn't just a step out of our own perceived reality, but an experience of unknown possibilities realized."

"It showed us, Rick, that possibilities are infinite. Anything can happen under the right circumstances with specific elements involved. And our limitations are those we place on our own minds. Before tonight, Rick, did you believe you controlled your limitations?"

"Absolutely not. My abilities were assigned. Like classes for school, I had no input. That's what I got, so adapt and live with it. Now, I know better. If I'm weak in an area, I just need practice and guidance to improve. When more agile mentally, we can think better. When we think better, different solutions show themselves for the same problem."

"It was an enlightening evening listening in to reality here while experiencing our joined reality in the wilderness of our minds. Though our bodies were stressed, at no fault to anyone. I would rather be hot than cold."

"Cold was a real bitch. Sorry, Ed... Can you find brain waves?"

"We got the exquisite privilege of watching, or listening, to the honed mind of Toby as problem after problem appeared. Not once did he say I can't, just how can I? Trial and error, few though they were, none life-threatening. He always held the lives in his charge respectfully and sacred. He erred on the side of caution. He also paid attention to everything. Every detail meant something. Just a puzzle to piece together."

"Wesley, we also noticed that the emotional aspects were different. The emotions we witnessed were varied and expansive, once expressed back to calm confidence with a heavy dose of humor."

"It was either laughter or tears. Laughter is more productive and lifts the spirits." Toby offers.

Noah is seriously uncomfortable with this dissertation. This looks into the internal man.

"That's it exactly, isn't it, Rick? That attitude of productive realism."

"Productive realism; the attitude that won the day. I think your attitude, your state of mind, can really define your situation. If Toby was prone to a bad attitude, he would have walked away and left a bar full of psych ward patients; lights on, but nobody home. Then where would we be?"

Wesley watches Toby. "Not here, Rick, enjoying interacting with our reality. I think Toby needs a drink. He looks embarrassed about our extolling on his fine qualities. Wow, he needs something, and it appears. Did you see that, Rick? He reached over the canvas, and now he's drinking that down like water."

"He deserves it, especially now that he doesn't have to worry about us."

"You're right. He is a worrier, though he hides it well. A bit hard on himself at times, but he shakes it off. Can't hinder the mind with problems to solve."

"Enough about me, gentlemen. You saw Phillip in action as the catalyst of chaos. He was also my electronics assistant. Fin was my girl Friday. Sorry, Fin."

The crowd laughs.

"Excuse me, I misspoke, Fin is my sidekick, Girl Friday. How's that sidekick's name? Is it as cool as Flesh Eating Zombie?"

Fin, along with everyone else, laughs. "Good to start, but I bet you, before the doors lock, it will be Fin Friday."

"I don't know. Flesh Eating Zombie is so good because it is funny. Are we going for sounds good or funny?"

The Once Dazed yell. "Funny!"

Everyone laughs.

CHAPTER TWENTY-SIX

"There you go, Fin, The Once Dazed has spoken. You will forever be known as Toby "Super Geek" Robins' sidekick, Girl Friday."

The bar patrons cheer. "Girl Friday! Girl Friday! Girl Friday! Yah! Woo!"

"Quite the atmosphere you've created here, Toby." Stevens' voice comes over the radio.

"Yes, isn't it, Irving?" Toby snickers.

"I did warn you, remember. I'm counting."

"Keep Counting, Irving. It only matters if you catch me." Toby taunts, his whine heavy.

"Rick, Wesley, meet my friend Irving, who was also instrumental in your return. Actually, without Irving, I don't know what other solution there could have been. Irving likes puzzles, too. He wrote the astounding program that your brain waves travel through translating into words to travel out to Jillian and Amethyst sitting in your van, sending the translated word out to a satellite circling the globe to bounce back to earth and arrive at your radio station, and shot out in all directions to your listening audience. Say hello, Irving, Ladies."

"Hey, guys, you were a rare, glorious puzzle, as puzzles go. Most very predictable, not you two. Varied and unusual combination of science and mysticism with a dash of medicine, psychology and physiology, and physics. Quite lovely, as puzzles go, but I hear you're not much to look at."

The crowd laughs.

"We are very pleased to encounter fellow puzzlers when we find ourselves trapped in our own minds, unable to get a message out. Here's to keen, finely honed, puzzling minds. I'm holding up my glass."

The crowd cheers.

"Ladies, thank you for being a comfort for us, explaining what was going on and what was coming. For being considerate and respectful of our bodies, your touch was gentle, soothing, and reassuring, linking us with our reality."

"Here. Here." Wesley agrees heartily.

"It was our pleasure to help you. We had a small idea of what was happening to you." Jillian replies.

"Like grains of sand on the beach, we understood, but even at that grain level, we would have wanted someone to be there for us, so we needed to be there for you and us. I'm glad you're this far on your journey back. When you reach the body destination come and visit us at O'Malley's." Amethyst says. "Only then will all the dazed be returned to normal. Toby was very adamant about that. He mistakenly believes he's the cause of the Doll Daze. Didn't you say something to the effect that the right combinations of elements could create any possibility? We just saw that mysterious combination tonight. Take out any one of them, and we wouldn't have experienced the unreality of our minds."

"That's right, Amethyst. If Jackson had listened to me earlier, we wouldn't have had the same kind of night at the pub. Who knows what it would have been, but I can guarantee it wouldn't have been the Doll Daze." Jillian explains. "So, Toby, with that keen, sharply honed mind, know you alone cannot mesmerize the masses to mindlessness."

Stevens laughs. "I wouldn't bet on that."

Jillian laughs. "Okay, how about he wasn't solely responsible for tonight. The jury is still out that he can purposely daze 200 people at once."

Stevens laughs. "That I can agree with. And just so the jury knows, he would never purposely Daze a crowd unless someone important to him was in danger." Stevens clears his throat. "Why hasn't anyone mentioned Noah?" He dangles that bait, waiting for a bite. He doesn't have to wait long.

"Who's Noah?" Jillian jumps on the question.

"Noah is the reason Toby is in town. Noah is the man behind the man. Toby is okay and somewhat impressive. You could say the tip of the iceberg. Noah is the one everybody should praise because of him. Could Toby do what he did tonight? Am I right, Toby?" Steven taunts.

"You know you are. I will admit Noah is my everything." Toby says dryly. "Without Noah's cunning, imagination, and business acumen, Toby would not be here. Satisfied?"

"Yes." Stevens laughs. "Give credit where credit is due. Nicely done, by the way."

Toby snorts. "Thank you. Irving puts up with me, but is the best friend to Noah."

"Man, you just don't stop." Stevens laughs.

"Where's the fun in that?" Toby smiles. "Come on over. I'll make an exception and daze you on purpose so you can really fit in with this crowd. We're family now, aren't we?"

The crowd responds as expected. "Yeah!"

"Irving should be a member, right?"

The Dazed love it. "Yea!"

"See you soon, Irving. Did I mention O'Malley's has a regulation ring here?"

"I'll be right over. I got a date with those two in the van anyway. See ya, Toby." Stevens laughs. "Rick, Wesley, I'll see you in person soon. Your people here will let you have the air time for now. When your ride shows up, they will transfer your signal. Keep in touch. Toby and I would really like to stay up to speed with you two. If you find how things are going down with them, we can always beat the crap out of them and take your bodies somewhere better. I'm telling you this so you know you both have options, the right to your decisions and the muscle to back them if need be. We brought you out. Nobody messes with what's ours. Our science bridged the gap. Remind them if they need it. Mostly, I bet they will be drooling all over you, especially because you have all your marbles."

"Hey, Irving, are the ladies done working the controls in the van?"

"Yeah, the van should have knockouts to slip those cables through, then lock it up. If not, a couple of guards will do."

"I'll check. One and Two have been guarding for a while. One of them answered the phone."

Wesley says. "Three and four."

"Yes?" They call from the other side of the canvas.

Rick and Wesley laugh so hard that their breathing becomes labored, and tears run down their temples.

Toby snorts.

Stevens hoots.

Toby coughs, then clears his throat. "I was getting to them. My miscellaneous hands. Four right, four left, four pairs. 1, 2, 3, and 4. I didn't have the mental capacity to remember names with faces while doing deep science. So, number I remember, so number them I did. And never have I had such excellent miscellaneous hands. Three and four have been very handy, as any miscellaneous hand should, but exceedingly so. In fact, how would you like to see your public before the men in white coats take you away?"

"Toby, you know your word choice is a touch edgy at times. But I think we would love to see all the once Dazed reanimated to their glory." Wesley says, pleased.

"I couldn't agree more about everything. But I may refuse to go if they arrive in white coats. But we do have Irving's reassurance they'll watch our backs. So we'll have to see. What does the O.D.D. s think?"

"Rick, who are the O.D.D.'s?"

"Are you sure you left with all your marbles? Toby's men in white coats will want to know. Once Doll Dazed; the O.D.D."

"Well, Rick, that's really odd."

"Yes, Wesley, Yes, it is. It fits, doesn't it?"

The laughter roils around the pub.

"Now for the question: is the O.D.D. ready to see you? You may send them right back. Then they would be FUDDAS, Fell Under Doll Daze Again. Are you or they ready?" Toby asks.

Everyone shouts. "Yes!"

"Your call. 3 and 4, please enter. I have another job. Phillip will oversee to help protect Wesley and Rick and their equipment. Dr. Paulson, do you have to go or are you to stay to pass the buck?"

"Definitely, pass the buck, Toby." Dr. Paulson laughs.

"Fantastic, always good to have a doctor in the house, especially this hose. Charles, Zack, you have a patient to transport. Tune-in, it may cheer him. After you've delivered John, are you going home for your well-deserved rest, or should we expect you?"

Charles and Zack say. "Expect us."

"Gladly, we will be pleased to see you. Sooner gone, sooner returned." Toby turns to the doctor. "Dr. Paulson, could I trouble you once more? Could you assist Phillip in protecting all this that is Wesley and Rick?"

"Yes." Dr. Paulson agrees.

"Amazing, blind acceptance." Toby shakes his head.

"It could be some of that odd business. But I know you have other duties to see to and want to ensure everyone's safety. I, too, like to ensure people's safety, so I'm more than happy to help."

"Thank you. Now, 3 and 4, this is what I want." Toby pulls a paper from the bottom of the legal pad he had used. He lays it on the work table in front of the group. "Do you think it will work?"

3 and 4 put their heads together.

3 picks up a pen. "May I?"

Toby smiles. "Please."

3 changes a few details that make more sense than the original.

Toby nods. "Can you get the supplies this late, and will it be sturdy enough? Will they be safe?"

"Rick, my guess would be something to help us see our public, but what, I have no idea. I'm giddy with curiosity."

"So am I. I don't think I've had this feeling since being a young child."

"Yes, exactly, Rick, the wrapped box with your name on it, the promised trip to somewhere wonderful, the wonderful surprise around the corner. Toby's joyful laughter."

"Oh, please, laying it on thick, aren't we, gentleman?" Toby snorts, amused.

"Let's ask those that mobbed you when said joyful laughter was in play. Odd Mob, are we laying it on thick?"

"NO!" They shout seriously, then break down laughing.

"You see, you don't see what we see. You haven't experienced what we experienced. You are the Dazer. We the Dazed. You care for us when we can't. Now we care for you always."

The Odd Mob applauds those words.

Noah, moved beyond understanding, bows respectfully and says softly in his regular voice. "I stand corrected, gentlemen. Please continue, but without me, I have a task to complete." He turns and nods to the four men by the table and slips out the canvas walls and out the doors.

CHAPTER TWENTY-SEVEN

Fin, a step behind, follows silently to the park across the street.

Noah slumps to the oak and flops on the grass.

Fin sits behind him and leans back against the fine old oak, breathing deeply.

After five minutes of silence, Toby whispers. "I don't understand them."

Fin nods. "Intense emotion can be overwhelming, especially magnified by hundreds, exponential in its power. There's so much it's pouring out the door and flooding the town." Fin thinks about it for a moment. "What's to understand? They have unconditional love for you."

"But why? How can that happen?"

"Let me ask you something. Have you ever been completely hopeless, the bottom of the barrel, I'm dead hopeless, and an honest hand is extended to you in unconditional aid, nothing owed, nothing expected? Just help freely given when you needed it most?"

"Yes." He says softly.

"How did you feel about the person attached to that honest hand?" Fin asks softly.

"Adoration, respect, love, every good emotion. I would do any and everything to show my gratitude. I was obsessed with evening the balance, but it would never happen since death came calling and I was cheated. I never did enough. That obsession scares me, I don't want the Odd Mob thinking they have to work beyond reason to even a non-account."

"Ah, if you were given more time with your helping hand, you would have naturally come to realize that most people understand that situation is a non-account, but you, the helping hand, get a reward for your selfless deed, whether you acknowledge it or not, a special love. A hero's love. Like the kid who stands up to the bully, that kid is adored by all right after it happens. After some time, it turns to friendly acquaintance and, with more time less intense emotions but always associated with good feelings. So, a couple of minutes or hours in Wesley and Rick's case, after the hopelessness of complete isolation, the cold certainty of death was crawling up your spine as your warmth disappeared, the shocking realization of no control. The knowing that even if you could decide you didn't want this, there was no action to take for one, you couldn't and another, who could think? With Wesley and Rick in a terrifying situation still, their hopelessness was manifesting in their physical bodies. They had death perched on their shoulders and were pulling their souls from their bodies. Your honest helping hands denied death and gave them hope and the means of expression so they are no longer isolated in the void.

There is no amount to assign to a life you said is so priceless. Saving hundreds of priceless lives in hours in one community is undying love. For you not only saved their life, you saved friends, loved ones, mothers, sons, fathers, daughters, and other family members. You brought back the minds of two loved local celebrities and important members of the community: judges, doctors, police, and the mayor's son in the crowd. My friend, this town can only love you, because your honestly helping hand selflessly brought everyone back. They can see the care you have for them especially by that incident with John. Everyone outside knew John was going through grief. You and I didn't, as new to town as we are, understandable, so we sent John into the bosom of the community still not right. No fault. They were warned he wasn't in the best condition. When John snapped in his fevered mind, you showed care for everyone. Because you believe you caused the Daze, you had everyone turn away so they didn't FUDDA. Had Becky close her eyes so she didn't FUDDA. I didn't turn away. I peeked. You used your damn blue marker to disarm a man, save the girl, and render the attacker unconscious so he couldn't hurt himself or anyone else. All to keep the Odd safe. I know you're not ready, but you love us, the Odd. Something happened here tonight: a strong, thick bond, and it's unlike any relationship in your life. Your Girl Friday knows what he's talking about because, honestly, this rapport we have is an individual expression of the whole. I'm your friend, a true friend, always here to listen when you need an ear. I'll give you my thoughts and ideas, no expectations, no demands, and freely give an honest helping hand when you need it. Oh, as a friend, I can tell you when you're being stupid, but I will let you continue if that is your wish.

So, stupid, do you understand you are loved by hundreds of people tonight? Can't guarantee tomorrow, probably concur with the other hundreds. Enjoy it while it lasts. We found out there are no guarantees in this life or this reality. What a mind twister."

"Thank you, Fin. You do have a way of putting things in perspective for me. This town is unlike any I have been. It doesn't follow the rules the rest of the world does. Many times, I have felt like Alice in Wonderland. And yes, I was overwhelmed again. I believe I'm suffering from responsibility overload. So, I guess it's time to set it aside and not worry. Well, to a point, until we pass the buck of Wesley and Rick. The no responsibility, so make sure Jillian is either rendered harmless or keeps us separated. That, Girl Friday, the sidekick of the Dazer's responsibility."

"Deal. I'm going for harmless, not as much trouble. And, Dazer, Girl Friday? Seriously?" He laughs, climbing to his feet.

Noah can't help the joyful belly laugh.

Out of the corner of his eye, he sees red and black stripes streaking towards him.

Pouncing, she knocks him over,

He can't stop laughing.

Jillian is all over him, nuzzling his neck and chest, licking his face.

Laughter just rolls out, unstoppable.

She stills and sits on his chest, watching him. Smiles big, then giggles, which causes him to laugh harder.

He gently pitches her to the ground and takes off running.

Giggling, she's up in a flash and takes off after him.

Around the park, they cavort, and the laughter ripples through the night.

Noah races by a laughing Fin. "You're not helping."

Fin laughs harder. "When she's like this, I'm no fool. I'd be torn to shreds. Head for the pub. I'll lock up the van. Keys?" They fly to him. "Thanks."

Noah laughs. "Chicken."

"Damn smart." Fin laughs, heading to the van. "Wear her out chasing you, then you won't have to fight her so hard." He crosses the street with their laughter echoing in the night like music.

Fin steps into the van.

Amethyst talks with an unfamiliar mountain of a man.

The man turns before Amethyst notices him.

The man looks him over carefully. His eyes were a friendly blue, his hair dark, but his face was harsh and intimidating. He could easily scare children, but not him. His face had a lot of character. And then he hears Toby and Jillian's laughter, his face transforms before Fin's eyes. He is beautiful and intimidating. His eyes grow bluer and sparkle like the sun on the water. Almost too much to witness, almost, especially tonight, but not quite enough.

Fin holds out his hand. "I'm guessing, Irving?"

The beauty vanishes instantly, replaced with a mulish scowl. "That little pipsqueak is getting the count every time for everyone." He mutters under his breath.

Fin howls. "What's the count too?"

Irving smirks evilly. "31." He says happily.

"Really, why? Irving is a beautiful, distinguished name, very fine." Amethyst says sweetly, without an ounce of guile.

Irving looks at her as if she has lost her mind.

Which she had, but now part of the Odd Mob, she must protect Toby "The Dazer" Robins. Confused and worried, her fingers brush her cheek. "Is there something on my face? What's wrong?" She looks horrified. "Is it blood? There was a fight tonight. Ooh, it was ghastly. I had never seen such destruction to one body." Amethyst shudders now panicked, she demands. "It's blood, isn't it? Oh, how do I get it off?" She starts wiping her cheek repeatedly, eyes wide with distress or suppressed laughter.

Fin has to look away, down was the only safe direction. He sees the knockout next to the door. He bends down and tucks the wires. When he has control of his voice, he says. "Geeze, woman, it wasn't that much blood. It's not like zombie blood that eats flesh off the bone."

Amethyst's horrified gasp nearly doubled him over. She starts panting and wiping faster. "Please, sir, tell me where it is. I can't have it eat my beautiful skin away, please, sir." She's almost in tears of laughter, sounding remarkably like real sorrow.

Toby and Jillian's musical laughter is a creepy counterpoint to the whole episode.

"Irving, I need to lock up," Fin says straight-faced.

Irving whispers a hard. "32." He was looking at Amethyst's chin.

"Oh, god, there too?" She whines, her face turning a lovely shade of crimson. She rubs and rubs, rocking and rocking. She starts keening, tears flowing unrestrained. She shudders. "Wh... Wha...What, a...a...am....I...I..tt...to...d...d...do?" She keens again.

Irving stares at her, seriously worried. Every time he tried to tell her she was mistaken, she cut him off.

Toby and Jillian's laughter still echoes playfully in the park, a weird counterpoint to the theatrics Amethyst was playing.

Fin says, exasperated, the only way to mask the laughter boiling within. "Woman, have your hysterics elsewhere. I have to lock up. Now."

"Bbuuttt...Ir...Irv....Irving...ssaiddd...II'mmm...c...cov...cover...co vered...innn...BBBLooooodddd!" Amethyst wails and hops up and races out of the van, heading straight to the pub, crying in laughter, gasping, wheezing, and trying to breathe. Dashes through the open door.

Toby and Jillian still carry on. Their laughter rolls around the park inviting all to join the play. The joy is tangible, wrapping around all the hearts of those close enough to hear.

"Come on, Irving. I got to get back to work."

He whispers darkly. "33"

Fin coughs. "Say, did you hear about those radio guys? This is their van. Did you hear them on the radio? They were covering a fight, oh yeah, the one that woman was hysterical about. Hard to believe a woman experiences blood every month most of their life, and yet one little fight and get all teary. The guy who won freaked cause the other guy bled on him. The guys were squeamish. And he mostly just touched him with his marker. You know a touch was worth a point. Oh, you know the guy who lost tripped on that marker and landed on the cap." Fin waves his hand to get Irving moving.

Finally, he unfolds from the seat, steps down and stands up and up. He is huge, at least 6'8", with broad, thick shoulders, a massive chest, and arms the size of Fin's legs. This was Toby's friend. A Mountain.

Fin snorts, closing and locking the doors and checking the others. Then ambles to the open pub door and continues. "That cap was top-down, and that loser somehow landed just right and cut a circle in his ass through two layers of denim. I never knew a marker cap was sharp, and they give those to kids. You can't ride a bike without a helmet, but here, take this sharp bit of plastic and cut out circles of your flesh. Unbelievable. So, the winner apologized for dropping his marker and causing the loser to fall. But the loser was speechless with anger, of course, he could have been angry that the winner warned him to watch his step. He went down like a tree, well, on his ass, actually. So the loser's bleeding out his back pocket. Did I mention it cut his drawers, too? Ass in the air marker cap punched in his ass. You know the winner was happy to get that cover back. He had to wipe the blood off, and got it on the marker too. So out comes the hanky to wipe away the blood and then the hand sanitizer to wipe the blood germs. The winner is a bit particular about germs. Doesn't like them at all. So he offers to shove his hanky down the loser's pants to bandage the wound or maybe stop that germy blood from getting on him. That looser knocked that hanky away, and the winner snatched it back out of the air like he was worried about all the germs on the ring floor. Wouldn't you know that loser's lip got in the way of that hanky and split it? Need a few stitches, but he will. Then, the blood started pouring. It was impressive since hankies don't have any sharp edges. Here, my darling child, hold onto your hanky. You can make the bully bleed. What mother says that to a young boy, Irving?"

He growls. "34."

Fin steps in the pub and turns a few feet inside the door allowing Irving in but halting his progress.

The room quiets instantly as Irving scans the pub.

Fin decides to show Toby what he is telling him. "So, Irving..." He says loudly.

"35." The sound of crushing rocks is more pleasant.

"...what exactly do you plan to do? What was it, 35 times?" Fin asks innocently, and he has an idea.

"Pound that little pipsqueak." He growls loudly.

"I thought you were friends." Fin stirs the pot.

"Noah's my best friend, so I put up with that pipsqueak and the others." A raging thunderhead.

"You're saying Noah has more like Toby?" Fascinated, he decides to dig.

Irving laughs disgustedly. "More than is wise. More than I know. I have never seen that pipsqueak. I never wanted to. Now I have to, to pay him what he so richly deserves." He growls with relish, rubbing his fists the size of a baked ham.

"Aren't you worried Noah won't like it?" Fin continues to grill him for information.

"Noah won't mind, he'll think it's funny."

"Are you sure you can? You have never seen Toby, so how can you be sure?"

"The only one who can beat me is Noah."

"So, it's been a while since you lost a fight?"

"Yeah, you could say that." Irving looks around. "Where are you hiding, pipsqueak? It's time to pay!" He growls and finally notices the unfriendly atmosphere, very chilly.

Laughter, rich and warm, washes into the pub, and every face gentles with a sweet smile. A pure, sweet, innocent giggle follows, triggering laughs and chuckles. They continue to trade off washing in the waves of joy crashing on the shores of humanity.

Even Irving is affected, he smiles beautifully, eyes softening.

Fin decides to step in further, knowing that Toby and Jillian are moments away. Gauging by the sound of their laughter.

Irving follows him in, caught by the joy the laughter expresses.

"You know, Irving, the loser, had that same attitude and lost badly. Worse yet, not a punch was thrown. All was damage self-inflicted."

"Pssh, like I would have anything to be worried about. Stop wasting my time. I'm here to pound some sense into that pipsqueak 36 times." He growls, agitated.

"Why does the number keep growing so fast, Irving? Is it minutes to see him?" Fin couldn't help it.

"It's none of your damn business, he'll know. The little coward didn't run off, did he?"

Silence greets him, the laughter outside wars with the tension in the pub.

"Why did I think he would be waiting to get his ass kicked?" He looks up, growling. "Noah, you're not getting away with this behavior. You control this." His eyes close.

The deep laughter swells, light giggles trilling after.

His attention shifts to the laughter, and his beautiful smile returns. He starts to turn, but he's too late. They are no longer at the door.

Every face glows with love and joy.

Two bodies dodge around the crowd. One hunched in a weird slumping accordion stride while speedy looks like slow motion. The other was a graceful female in a black and red dress that gave the appearance of stripes like a tiger, her stride feline in nature, hunting her prey.

They circled to the bar, and glasses were lined up. The deformed man grabs the first two he comes to and, still on the move, empties them and gently places them on the bar further down. Picks up three this time and keeps moving. The woman mimics the man's movements, downs those two, placing them next to his glasses. Then takes three and a harder time drinking one and handing off the glass to one of the adoring crowd. They get closer to Stevens.

He watches, entranced by the man's movements. He couldn't look away. The woman tracks the man. He keeps just out of her clutches. They get closer, wending their way through the unmoving crowd. Everyone watches, chuckling at the antics.

The hunched man now only had two glasses. The woman is the same. When one drinks, the other drinks also.

Stevens continues to watch the man.

His movement is awkward but somehow graceful. No matter how he moves, it is beautiful to watch. He dodges left, she follows, and he spins right. Then he was behind him. The woman giggles and lunges one way. The man laughs and moves smoothly, unhurried, but moves fast in slow motion, and before he knew it, they were circling him, the laughter and giggles bombarding him senseless. Then the man stops suddenly right in front of him and hands a glass to him.

He takes it without thinking, then he is gone, and the woman slaps a glass into his other hand as she goes by.

She screams in frustration at missing her prey, slinking after him.

Stevens shivers at the sound, feeling the jungle closing in. His eyes track the pair circling back to the bar, collecting glasses, draining them and collecting more.

Working back to him, they each had two glasses, drank one each and passed their reaming glasses to him, circling back around him once more. The man stops in his tracks, almost suspended between steps. Very unnerving, that pause.

His huge green eyes pool, magnified by large, ugly, thick-framed glasses. His dark hair parts sharply down the center, and his scalp glows brilliant white. Just long enough to tuck behind his ears. He wears a short-sleeved dress shirt of poor quality with a plastic pocket protector stuffed full dragging his shirt off center so it bangs on his concave chest. The ugliest tie known to man in polyester hangs around his tight collar, his Adam's apple and head movement reminiscent of a vulture.

His eyes are drawn to the pants adjustment that are worse polyester and too wide around the waist his pockets flap under the material. His voluminous shirt is cinched up with a cheap belt with the fake plating peeling away.

Unable to stop, his eyes travel down to the three-inch high waters white socks blinding with black orthopedic clodhoppers that a blind man would never wear.

A stain catches his eye on the ultra-white sock, blood? Blood. Blood! BLOOD! Stevens' head snaps up, and stares. "No....ah." He breathes, his mouth hanging open.

CHAPTER TWENTY-EIGHT

Before his eyes could really reconcile this oddity with Noah, it smiles huge and goofy and snorts.

Speechless, he watches him gracefully dodge the clutches of Jillian. The Tigress was the one? Does that laughter come from Noah? The man who was so sober nothing phased him?

He can't help watching, fascinated. He had never witnessed one of Noah's disguises. He was even told the events of the day, but somehow seemed as farfetched as talking trash.

It all happened...It all happened? It all happened! And without embellishments. Just the facts, Noah said. And ran through those events in his head, but somehow, they slipped away.

Stevens' eyes could only watch Noah. He was a joke, a beautiful joke. He knew it and was happy to share the joy with anyone who opened their perceptions and let the preconceived ideas go.

He was threatening in his confidence, recognizing the cunning that was masked by the idea of meekness. It was an illusion. There isn't anything meek about Noah.

This creature flitting around the room was the antithesis of the Noah he knew, and yet somehow, it was all still there with cunning bits to distract the eye. You really don't realize Noah is about 6'4" and almost as big as he was. His eyes were distracting, like watching an accident happen, horrified but unable to look away.

His goofy grin was both pleasure and horror to those to witness, depending on your perception.

Good grin if good heart, run for your life if bad.

They circle by again, rounding him again and again. Jillian's dress tiger stripes every movement except never the same, always on the move.

The conversation started around him and movement, people no longer recognizing the threat that he was. He was now a piece of furniture, a shelf for drinks. He tries to drink one, but his arms don't move.

Noah pauses, tilts his head and watches him a moment too long. Jillian reaches out her hand to grab him, but he sidesteps barely and catches her hand and spins her expertly, pecks her lips, spins her away and lets her spin away. He takes a glass and takes a thoughtful sip in a horrible voice that makes Stevens want to punch him. "So, what do you think of me now?" He takes another unhurried sip, then replaces his drink and slips away, travelling back by the bar.

Stevens tries to move, really, with everything he has, but nothing happens. He can only observe. He notices everybody in the bar has a purple bruise on their heads between their brows. Though he has a hard time focusing, his eyes keep straying to Noah and Jillian.

He noticed Jillian didn't have the purple mark.

The bar quiets when a bell rings by an older man similar to the one in the van. "I just got a call from the mayor in light of the events of tonight and in honor of "The Dazer." He has given dispensation for tonight, so we're open until you leave."

The room rocks with the vibration of celebration.

The man rings the bell, and the room quiets down. "The Mayor will be arriving at some point to give an announcement."

Polite applause acknowledges the announcement.

"Toby's friend, Irving, is in the Doll Daze. So, please remember. I'm sure Toby will release him after he has calmed enough. We all heard the threats by Toby wouldn't appreciate cruelty on the helpless."

What?

"We also have a grand surprise for everyone. Toby designed, with the help of 3 and 4, something we will all appreciate. It's for Wesley and Rick, our two not quite back but working on the path of Odd. To complete their journey, they will have to leave us for a time, but they believe they will fully recover the use of their bodies. We all heard their story and understood that what we experienced was a small percentage of what they went through. I'll not lie to you. They look rough. Death had them in hand, but Toby wouldn't allow it and brought them back as far as he could. Please remember Irving had an instrumental role in their journey back here. He wrote the translation program that allows us to understand them. Without his help, we would have lost these two. For now, let us set aside whatever issue Irving has with Toby and enjoy the evening. On the other hand, we could always let them settle it in the ring. However, if you decide to watch FUDDA, Toby won't do anything about it tonight. So remember, if you start feeling fuzzy around the edges, stop watching, laugh, talk, and move. Without further ado, please welcome back Wesley and Rick and their new mode of travel and a way to see their reality as they know it."

The applause is deafening.

Out of the corner of his eye, Stevens sees the canvas move. But he can't quite understand what little he sees.

A gentle touch on his shoulder turns him so he faces the canvas enclosure. With a light touch to his lower back, Stevens moves forward. When he gets a few feet away, a hand gently touches his chest.

He stops.

The sight before him horrifies him.

Two men on slabs of wood, at the top of each slab of wood Wesley and Rick's names carved in. Both men lay upright on the tilted slabs. The upholstered footboard keeps them from sliding off. Where their bodies rest were also thickly upholstered in very fine material. Their legs were in very fine cotton pants that snap up both sides. Their shirts were of the same material in the same style, back snaps to front. Both men have a hand up on one side of the earphone muff. They were bald except for the thin strips of hair under the headphone band and around the earphone muff, though trimmed short. Electrode pads wrapped in wire dot their suspended heads; a thick liquid sheen makes their heads glow, with wires sprouting out of the probes snaking down and back behind their slabs. Their eyes sparkle with life, and a small smile wreathes their lips. Otherwise, their bodies appeared dead. The bleached-out skin doesn't help. A series of sheepskin padded leather straps anchor them to the boards. Two quilted roll straps to either side of their bodies.

The hysterical woman steps up next to Rick, and Jillian steps up next to Wesley.

"We would like to share with you what your contributions have created." Jillian starts. "These fine oak slabs were the tables that Toby broke in our dire need for warming chambers to combat the frostbite of their hopeless despair.

Beside Stevens, Noah whispers. "Literally, blackened toes were frozen stiff, freezing to the touch while a dangerously high fever ravaged their heads, 105-106 degrees."

Jillian continues. "Thank you, O'Malley."

The other woman points at the clothes. "I donated all the raw materials and design. My seamstresses, Mary, Sue, Jacky, and Billy, worked furiously for the last few hours. Thank you for your time and skills. They each have a set of three. The fabric is a fine Egyptian cotton, breathable but will protect their bodies."

"That's Amethyst James, an amazing woman," Noah whispers.

Amethyst looks over and winks with a cheeky grin then panicky, switching quickly to horror. She laughs, sounding strangely like she is crying, and then she laughs again naturally. "Sorry, folks. I know I look like I lost it. I played a little trick on Irving before he Doll Dazed. But in my defense, I didn't start until he started in on counting the beating for Toby. I was just priming the pump."

Jillian giggles.

"Ah, isn't she glorious?" Noah whispers.

Jillian looks over at Stevens. "You should work on your attitude. That kind of bad attitude Jackson had, and look where that got him. The hospital is speechless." Her eyes turn to Noah and she smiles as sweetly as her giggle. It makes one want to return it. "Toby, you should go give him the dose. I'm pretty sure he won't bother me and how can he apologize without a voice?"

In Toby's voice, Noah responds. "If that is your wish, we will go tomorrow so he can apologize. Amethyst? You know it would be much too dangerous for us to go without you."

"Yes. I shall enjoy his apology after running him off for what fifteen years, give or take."

"Thank you," Toby whines. "Back to Wesley and Rick, please. They are being very patient."

They both wink at Noah.

Toby snorts, tipping his head.

Jillian turns back to Wesley. "The beautiful carved oak trim was donated by South County Police Dept. Please extend to all that they are sending are boys in style."

Amethyst runs her hand along the rolled quilts. "Since Rick and Wesley can't control their body temperatures yet, we have outfitted their conveyance with temperature controlled warming pads in the upholstery their bodies and feet rest on. These rolled quilts are attached to cocoon their bodies if need be. Let us demonstrate."

Jillian steps over to assist.

They pull elastic straps from Velcro. They unroll their quilt half to lay on Rick's snog up to the neck and snug over the footrest.

"Thank you, The Quilting Club, for donating the quilts and the labor to make them custom to Wesley and Rick's needs."

Jillian rolls her side up and Velcro's them back in place.

She steps back to Wesley. "These bolster cushions are heated and also very firm to ensure their heads stay suspended. Another feature is the gentle massage to stimulate brain function, and it feels incredible. I tried it earlier. I donated those. The outer covers are washable. We have three sets. Each of the covers is made of flannel, nice and thick."

"Now, we get to the real workmanship. Don't get me wrong, the window dressing is just as important as the window, but without a window, why dress?"

The crowd laughs heartily.

219

Amethyst shakes her head and turns Rick carefully, holding his hand. "It's still unnerving for them to not be able to control their bodies let alone balance or equilibrium. We hold their hands so they can feel our warmth and care. Let me show you a side view of the ingenious engineering that Toby provided with 3 and 4, adjusting for comfort and convenience. This is the result. Jillian, would you please go to horizontal?"

Jillian holds Wesley's hand and pushes a button on the frame below the slab. The slow, controlled descent of the head and the raising of the feet. "Now, all the way down for transport." She pushes a button and the slab lowers to the floor slowly. "Back up, please." She flips a lever, and it rises slowly. Then, the lever was locked back. "Let's raise the feet or lower the head." Another button. "Back up and then to an original upright position, which can be stopped along the way."

Jillian still holds his hand and pats his arm with the other, rubbing up and down.

Noah whispers. "Can you imagine being trapped in your body without any way to change your circumstances? Because of the amp, they ended up way deeper than you are now. They watched our reality like a mobile playing on the TV, but their combined reality was based on their body condition they could no longer change. Plus, the added horror of their helplessness and hopelessness created a winter storm frozen in imagined chairs at an imagined table with the imagined winter storm manifesting in their physical form. Blackened toes here, in summer. Thank you, my friend, for helping me save them. Neither of us will truly understand the horror of dual reality, knowing our bodies are lost to us forever. We did a truly great and amazing thing today. You and I, with their help, of course, built a bridge to the inner mind to give voice to the inner voice. Your translation program is so very beautiful, elegant and to the point, a work of art you should be proud of. I am truly honored to call you my friend.

As your friend, I am telling you I will not tolerate your bad attitude here. We can have a great time tonight. I will even fight you in the ring, but these people are now mine, and I will protect them to my dying breath and beyond, for I will figure out how to keep my spirit alive and torment any that mess with them. They feel the same about me. I'm theirs, and if you insist on this childish hatred of your name. We will have a problem. I love you like I would love a brother. Let go of the anger about your name. It has caused you most of your problems.

In the place you are now, is a name important? Does it change your situation at all? Yes, our name helped shape the man you are today. Are you still the little twerp on the playground that's all arms and legs? Or are you a man who protects those weaker than you? The one to stand by the underdog and encourage and teach that pup until he doesn't have to take abuse? You are a superior man with a stupendous mind, but our social skills need work. Okay, they suck. But I'm your friend because I see that great huge heart that wants only to care for and love.

That's one of the reasons we are friends, because we have the same condition. AN unending supply of love but no one to share with because few understand what we are or the damage and abuse we have survived. Most would consider us freaks because our brains work so well, and we have a great understanding of everything. Because we don't limit our possibilities, anything is possible. Like me, mesmerizing 200 people tonight in under a minute, so deep that they cannot escape and soon turn hopeless. I didn't do it on purpose with them. It just happened. I turned to the silent crowd, and they just stared like you are now. As long as I was in their field of vision, their eyes followed me." He chuckles softly. "It honestly freaked me out. Wondering if I had stepped out of time. Everybody was frozen as if time stopped. It was very disconcerting. I figured out how to wake the Dazed, and they would slip back in. I finally separated them from me or told them not to look at me because I didn't know it would amaze their minds into a Daze state. My team here isn't as prone now that they have spent time with me.

Stevens, man, I want you to be a part of this family. That's another reason I dazed you, so they will accept you.

Somehow, I know I belong here in this unreal town. It doesn't even have a proper name. I'm sure Jillian is a lot of it, but I know she's really the reason I'm here. Please, my friend, my brother, take a chance towards happiness, acceptance, and a better life. Warm companionship of people who just like you."

"Toby! Get over here and bring Irving with you. We are taking a picture with Wesley and Rick before anything else happens." Amethyst smiles warmly at them.

"I guess I get a reprieve. Let's go. Picture time." Noah places his hand on Steven's lower back and, with a gentle touch, positions him in the center between Wesley and Rick.

CHAPTER TWENTY-NINE

"Toby, can you get him to smile?" A man asks, holding a camera.

Toby laughs. "I don't know. Fin, when I was laughing, did they smile while mobbing me and Jillian?"

"No," Fin says, laughing.

"Why don't you try positioning it? You positioned Charles, Zack, and O'Malley. Didn't Phillip get it, too?" Amethyst asks, laughing.

"No, Phillip caused the ping-pong problem, which caused Toby to completely lose it and laugh so hard that Jillian jumped him and kissed him, but the mob was already on the move, and they were surrounded. He was laughing so hard," Fin explains.

The crowd sighs in pleasure.

Toby snorts. "If we want to place blame it was you who caused it all. You were guiding Amethyst and Phillip at the same time and only paid attention to Amethyst. When I noticed it was too late, Phillip was on a collision course, and that started the ball rolling, so to speak. He hit then went backward, I think you were second, ma'am. What's your name?"

"Carol." A plump woman says sweetly.

"Carol, he sent you right towards that group of young Ben closest to your table, then you sent all in every direction, and you went backward, slightly turned. You travelled on.

After the initial horror of such chaos, the terror of any of you getting hurt, I stood there wondering how I ended up witnessing such an absurd event.

It was chaos in nature, all started by my Girl Friday. So unlike my regular life, so outside my regular expectations of a day in my life. It was insanely funny. I don't think I have ever laughed like that before. The people of South County tickle my funny bone constantly." Noah laughs and turns to Stevens.

He places a finger in the corner of Stevens' lip, pushes up, and lets go quickly. "It stayed nifty." He laughs, pleased with his discovery. He places his other finger on the other side of Stevens' lip, pushes up, and let's go.

He steps back and laughs. "It's uneven. This is harder than I thought it would be." Noah rubs his hands up Stevens' face up into his hairline.

Amethyst steps up behind Noah's left shoulder. She tilts her head to the side. "Now he looks like he's been flung from a catapult, and the wall is closing in fast." She reaches around Noah's shoulder and smooths her hand down the side of his face from forehead down.

Jillian steps up behind Noah's right shoulder, "Now it looks like he had a stroke before impact." Jillian rests her bent arm on Noah's hunched back, dropping her chin on her arm. Her hand reaches around Noah's shoulder and wipes down the other side of his face from fore head down.

Noah smiles, touching his face to understand all the muscles in action.

Fin stands directly behind Noah, standing a little taller. He reaches both arms over and moves his hands across Stevens' face, pushing here and pulling there. He pulls his hands away with a pleased expression. "There! It's done."

A flash of light over from the left.

The crowd laughs, calling suggestions.

"Move up on the left."

"Ridge the brow."

"Curl the lip."

"Flare the nostrils."

"Squint the eyes."

At every suggestion, Fin makes adjustments. He steps back and tips his head from side to side, then rubs Stevens' brows backward. He reaches up and puts his fingers into Stevens' black hair, pulling here and smoothing it out. He steps back again. "How's that? The before."

A flash of light from off to the left was accompanied by the crowd's approval.

Fin reaches over again and pulls down on certain areas. "The Dumb Daze." He reaches out again.

Noah slaps his hands away. "Go Daze your own. Then you can play with their face." He laughs.

Fin laughs. "Unfair, I don't know how."

Noah laughs harder. "Well, I guess you're out of luck. This is mine to sculpt. He is my friend. He may not appreciate those you did." He wipes his hands down Stevens' face repeatedly. Then wipes up and back gently, over and over, brushed up the sides by his eyes, up by his brows. Then pressed his here and there. Leans back and looks

"No, there's something missing." A woman from the back of the crowd calls. "He heard you and Jillian laughing. We saw him smile. He was being all pissy. "34, 35, 36, I'm beating him...blah, blah, blah." Then he heard you two laughing up a storm and transformed before our eyes. A beautiful Angel stands were a demon ranted, a dark cloud around him. The beautiful angel with the god light in his eyes. Those eyes shimmered, and sunshine on the water sparkled. They almost glowed and the love was so strong, I nearly fainted."

Laughing, Noah looks into Stevens' eyes. His eyes dance, so magnified. The image starts to swirl one way and then the other.

Stevens feels his insides swirl, one way then the other, back and forth, the swirling continues. He can't look away, feeling his insides swirling one way and then the other. That knot in his chest loosens, he breathes easier, and he feels more comfortable in his big body. He is no longer crammed in a small body. He has a big spirit, but his body is big enough because he isn't confined. He can be bigger than the body, like a shadow on a wall. It's bigger than the body; it depends on how close to the light the body stands on how big the shadow is. The shadow is his spirit; it is attached to this body, but it isn't confined to it. It can overlay it, bigger than the physical body.

He wasn't confined to fit his body.

He had it wrong, and his body fit in his spirit. The possibilities are only limited to your limited mind. But his mind wasn't limited.

Noah said he limited himself by his childish obsession with a name.

Does a name define you?

No, a name is a label, and you define it.

How have I been defining it?

With anger, not love. It's the emotion.

What is anger?

Anger is fear. He's afraid that he's not worthy of love.

But he is because Noah loves him; Noah is the best person he knows. And Noah thinks he's worthy. Why call him when he has a really serious problem, life and death?

Noah loves these two, Wesley and Rick, because he brought them back from the clutches of death.

Noah loves him so much he wants him to be a part of this family.

A family.

They would be brothers, and tiny little Jillian would be his sister, and he could love her. She will love him like a brother, and when Noah makes her mad, she will come to him and cry, and he will beat Noah. He will care for her because Noah loves her and wants to marry her.

He will have a family.

He will love and be loved.

That woman said she could feel the love in him. She thought he was beautiful as an angel with the god light in his eyes.

That guy, Fin, from the van, a friend of Noah's. Fin wasn't scared of him. He liked Stevens or Irving. Did the name really matter?

Amethyst, a beautiful woman, wasn't afraid of him. She played a trick on him. She played with him. She was Noah's friend. She could be his friend, and she was friends with Jillian.

Phillip was friends with Noah. He could be friends with everyone here.

The possibilities were only limited by a limited mind.

My body fits my spirit; my mind has no limits, so anything is possible. He and Noah can call this town home. Home is not just a place to live but a place where people know you and accept you. They say hello on the street. Hug you because you make them feel good.

He can be at ease with Noah. Noah likes him. Noah wants him around. Noah wants him here with him. Noah wants to share a family with him. He was wanted by the best man he knows.

The possibilities are endless, and the Daze takes hope from the hopeful. He was hopeless, and Noah gave him the hope he hadn't had since he was a very small boy.

The possibilities with hope far exceed anything he conceived previously.

Noah set this up to give him hope. Noah, as Toby called him, Irving, to get him here. He knew what he was doing. He drew him in because he truly loves him and truly cares about him. Wants him to find the inner peace he has found, the joy he has found, the life he has found. He is now one of Noah's Doll Dazed. Noah wants Stevens' part of this special bond. Noah Dazed him so he was forced to consider everything.

Noah was always true to him. Never demanded or expected, just offered the hand of friendship with undying loyalty.

Especially in the dark days, Noah has always been his reason for continuing life.

Nothing ventured, nothing gained.

Did he want to go back?

Or did he want to see where this new opportunity leads? He knew what that was: depressing and hopeless.

With Noah, he can be his true self.

He can start here being what he wanted, not what someone told him to do, say, or be.

Noah thought his social skills needed work. An unlimited mind always learns. Just another subject to learn. Not a difficult subject like merging physics and physiology, Noah's hobby.

How do I want to live my life? That is true to me.

How do I want to be?

Noah is whoever he wants to be whenever the mood strikes him, but he is always him. He is true to himself.

What is my true self? Who is it?

Noah will help me figure it out.

Yes, I want this. I want to travel this road with Noah, my brother, my friend, and my family.

Stevens focuses his mind. The shadows disappear from his soul. He no longer needs to hide. He is his beautiful spirit, not this hulking lump of flesh. That body is just the interface for his soul to communicate with others. He came up with another layer, shedding all his fears since they didn't apply to these new variables.

Those were the fears of the old Irving, not the Great Spirit where his body rests now, endless possibilities spin out around him. No longer restricted by unreasonable fears. He now knew that he had restricted himself in any number of ways.

He is free! He expands his spirit, stretching it out around him and focuses on Noah.

Noah stands in front of him, glowing golden, his spirit larger than his body. It was so warm, and he was so warm. Noah was holding Stevens' face, staring deep into his eyes. Noah's spirit expands and folds around Stevens' body and spirit, warming them both.

Stevens can feel the love, the warmth holding him close. Noah's warmth, his love, charged his soul, he can feel the difference.

Noah smiles and pulls his hands away. "Is this better?" He asks the people behind.

228

The woman from the back whispers. "Yes, that's it. My god, would you look at him? He almost glows. Can you feel the love?"

Noah looks at Stevens and smiles. Satisfied with the results, he turns to the left and nods.

A light flashes off to the left.

He walks over to his place in the group. "Smile, The Oddities of South County, Smile."

Everyone smiles bigger as flashes of light and clicks come from the crowd.

Wesley laughs. "The oddities of South County. I like it."

"We should have a charter. And a roster because everyone will want to join after tonight, but if you aren't sporting a distinctive purple badge, you can't."

"Yes, Toby should be president since he's the Dazer. That should be the official title of the chair, "The Dazer.""

"What do you say, Oddities? Should we have an official club?"

The crowd cheers boisterously.

Noah laughs. "Phillip, would you assist me with this organization? Remember, I'm being irresponsible at the moment."

Phillip chuckles. "Ah, Toby, that's very responsible of you to assign the work to someone. And, yes, I would be pleased to assist."

"While I have everyone's attention, I'd like to thank everyone. You of South County have opened your arms and brought me into the fold. You have no way of understanding how much this means to me. I will say I have always been adrift in the world, but I have finally run aground on the shores of South County, and I feel like I found my lost home. So thank you." Toby bows formally to all in the pub.

They cheer with such force the room buzzes from the vibrations.

Noah holds up his hand.

The room quiets.

"I'm hoping that my friend, Irving Stevenson, will join me here. I hope you all will ignore his behavior when he first arrived. He was upset because I was purposely making him mad. Like myself, Stevens hasn't known what a home is or has ever had one. We've had places to sleep but never a home with neighbors who look out for each other. Please be patient with us, we haven't really fit in anywhere. So, again, thank you for your warm hearts and open arms. We have finally found a home."

The crowd cheers wildly.

"The last thing I have to say officially tonight. Well, right now, is that 1, 2, 3, and 4 will accompany Wesley and Rick to their destination and assist them for the time being, at least the first week. We'll know more later. "The Hands" are taking a leave of absence from their jobs at short notice, so if we can help them cover their missed work, that would be great. I'm seeding a fund for the six of them for expenses. If you care to water those seeds, please see Fin at the bar. Jillian told me that the winnings from the bet on the books for the Super Geek vs. Flesh Eating Zombie fight will be added to the fund. Jillian, Amethyst, and Phillip bet together, so their combined winnings will all go together."

The crowd cheers and chants. "1, 2, 3, 4!"

The four men step up, two between Rick and Wesley and one on each side.

A flash of light comes from the left.

"Enough of this formality. We want to talk to the people before we have to go."

"Right, you are, Wesley. Step forward, oddities. We can't bite."

The crowd laughs.

A hand lays gently on Stevens' back.

He steps forward, moving away from Rick and Wesley.

From behind him, Noah says. "One and Two, please put the rope up. Folks, don't step over the rope. Touch them. Human contact warms more than their bodies. Keep it clean."

230

Stevens continues across the bar, back to where he started and stops when Noah's hand rests on his chest.

Noah steps in front of him and smiles up at him. He leans close and whispers. "I think you have discovered a thing or two in the Daze. I hope you forgive me for putting you in the Daze. I took a calculated risk with our friendship. By the light in your eyes, it paid off. Most coming out of the Daze are disoriented and have a hazy memory. With time, all memory returns." He looks over his shoulder. "Are you ready, Fin?"

"Yeah. What if he's not happy? He looks like he could crush my head in one of those fists." Fin steps up next to Noah.

Noah/Toby laughs. "He could. Remember, there's a short time of disorientation. If my Girl Friday is that faint-hearted, run. Anyway, he probably won't bother with you. He'll go after me first, then you after he's done with me."

"Not faint-hearted, cautious." Fin laughs. "Remember, big guy, it's him you're after." Laughing still, he points to Toby, his eyes glowing with mirth. In his other hand is a large stainless steel bucket, its sides moist with condensation. He plunges his hand into the bucket and nods.

Noah reaches up and flicks him really hard between the eyes just above the bridge of his nose.

CHAPTER THIRTY

An exploding star of pain blinds him. He blinks repeatedly as tears moisten his eyes.

Icy water descends from his brow and wraps around his neck. Little rivulets track down his torso. His hand slowly rises and rubs between his eyes, just above the bridge of his nose. He rubs his eyes, sight comes back fuzzy at first, then sharpening.

A man stands before him, smiling a big, goofy grin full of joy. He looks vaguely familiar, but he can't remember where he's seen him.

"Come along, Stevens. Let's get you moving. It helps get the marbles rolling again. Now, you are an official member of the Oddities of South County. An exclusive group membership has just closed. You are the last member. This exclusive group is just for the oddities of this night. We are a special group of people who share the bond of a unique event, The Doll Daze. In this exclusive crowd, there are four categories of experience. The Dazer, me. The hopeless, the majority. The double hopeless, Wesley and Rick. The hopeful, you." The hunched man leads him around the bar.

People reach out and touch him. Some hug him. Some pat his shoulder, and some squeeze his hand, some rub his arm, chest, back, and cheek. Every person he passes smiles at him.

Confused, he doesn't know anyone, yet they all greet him warmly. He starts nodding at those who greet him. Then he smiles at any smile offered. He touches those who touch him. Mirroring their actions.

A lone woman looks at him and smiles.

He smiles back.

She reaches up and strokes his cheek.

He mirrors the action, and carefully, his large hand strokes her cheek.

She laughs.

He laughs spontaneously and stops, surprised by the sound and the feelings. It was a very strange good feeling.

She laughs again.

He laughs and isn't surprised, and the warmth floods his body, and energy showers down his body. He feels great and laughs again, deeply.

The woman giggles, steps closer and hugs his waist.

His arms come out, unsure what to do. He turns his head to the man next to him.

He nods and pushes one of his arms around the little woman.

Tentatively, his other arm crosses her back, barely touching her.

She rewraps her arms and squeezes him.

He copies her and squeezes lightly.

She laughs and squeezes tighter and tighter.

He laughs and squeezes until she squeaks. He snatches his arms away, afraid.

She giggles and takes his arms, puts them back, and squeezes him again.

He laughs and hugs her firmly, then releases her.

Smiling, she steps back and curls her finger at him.

He leans down so his face is level with hers.

She kisses his cheek and hugs his neck.

He was stunned. She kissed him.

She was holding him. She was comforting him.

She squeezes tighter, pushing both shoulders forward.

The man next to him smiles and takes Stevens' arms and puts them across the woman's black and red back.

She pushes on his shoulders again and squeezes his neck, her cheek on his.

He wraps his arms around her and stands.

She hangs from his neck. She giggles, pulls her face away, looks him in the eyes and smiles. "I'm Jillian, and now I'm your friend. Okay?"

Blankly, he stares in awe. Slowly, a smile grows, blinding in its brilliance. "Okay." He whispers and reverently kisses her cheek. He draws her close, buries his face in her neck, and shudders, overwhelmed by unfamiliar feelings. He wants to cry.

She rubs his back and strokes his hair. She starts humming a soothing song, unhurried. At the end of her song, he bends down and puts her on her feet.

She squeezes his neck tight and pulls back, kisses his cheek again, and steps back, smiling up at him.

He bends down and kisses her cheek, then stares into her eyes, smiles gently and strokes her cheek with the back of his finger.

She takes his big hand in her two small ones and squeezes his hand, staring into his eyes earnestly and nods reassuringly. She steps away with an impish grin and a wink.

He laughs and winks back.

She giggles and waves and walks away.

The man next to him chuckles.

Stevens turns to him and looks. There was something in the back of his brain prodding him when he looked at this weird, hunched little man.

The man notices him watching and turns to face him, smiling up at him confidently.

There was something strange about the man. He was dressed in ugly clothes that didn't fit. But he had a confident carriage, except his body was all hunched and awkward, though graceful. He was a mass of contradictions.

In a blinding flash, the answers burst into his conscious mind. What he was looking at was one of Noah's disguises. His eyes travel from the top of Noah's head and slowly descend to his horrible orthopedic shoes and back up.

Noah just stands there still, with huge eyes full of mirth, waiting for Stevens' reaction.

Stevens stares at an unfamiliar Noah, speechless. He was used to seeing Noah in excellent clothes that fit, with no eyewear, posture straight and proud, powerful, strong, intimidating, handsome, commanding, dangerous, and even mean. This, before him, wasn't any of those things. His lips twitch. He coughs. He snorts.

Noah grins at him and winks.

Stevens loses his ability to control the laugh building up from his belly. It bursts out, rumbling and rolling around them.

Noah starts laughing.

Stevens laughs harder, his stomach contracting, his chest heaving, his eyes tearing. He holds his sides, laughing at the Noah before him. He never would have guessed. Noah had to flash little hints at him to recognize him. He laughs and laughs, and he can't stop. Gasping for breath, shaking his head. "No…ah!"

Noah laughs harder, shaking his head and putting a finger to his lips.

Stevens remembers. Toby stands before him. He gasps and lightning-fast grabs for Toby.

Noah laughs tauntingly and unhurriedly pivots out of reach.

Stevens lunges and comes up empty-handed. He growls.

Noah, just out of reach, laughing, holds up his hands and waves them taunting.

Stevens laughs and leaps to grab him.

Noah slips away in no hurry and ducks into the crowd, navigating through the table.

Stevens follows, trying to cut him off.

Every time, Noah just barely gets away.

The crowd cheers and groans.

Wesley and Rick commentating on the near misses.

Stevens, about a foot away from him, notices Jillian sneaking up. Steven's smile turns gleeful. It looks like he has a partner. Stevens moves fast, going for the kill.

Noah steps aside and then ducks back, twisting around, barely avoiding Jillian's clutches. He laughs gleefully, ambling away.

Jillian ends up in Stevens' grasp.

He laughs, pecks her cheek and sets her aside. Leaning down, he whispers in her ear.

She nods, her eyes glowing. Giggling, she dashes off into the crowd.

Stevens calls after Noah. "Hey, man, why are you running away?"

Noah snorts. "You are back, and your memory is probably restored. You did vow to pound me, Irving, in front of all these nice people."

"Yes, but that was before. Before, you made me odd. What does that mean?" he follows Noah.

The crowd answer. "Once Doll Dazed."

"That is odd, and it was an odd experience."

"Yes. So, was I right? Hopeful?" Noah slumps Toby's walk along the bar, picking up two glasses. He knocks one back and returns it to the bar.

"Yes, fascinating, really, the Daze. For me, it separated the ID from the programs. It allowed me the chance to see the programs for what they are: limitations." Stevens lengthens his stride along the skirt of the regulation-sized boxing ring.

Noah, a few feet ahead, heads for his corner.

Jillian pops up at the corner, giggling; their trap is almost closed.

Stevens jumps from behind.

Noah hops up on the skirt, clutching the corner post, and swings his body over Jillian's head and over the ropes to land in the corner of the ring. Whistling, he turns and walks away.

The crowd cheers, stamping their hands and feet.

Noah stops when he feels Stevens roll into the ring under the ropes. He turns smiling. "I know you want to pound on me, and I did promise you the opportunity. But they have rules here." He chuckles and waves his arm around the pub. "It is only right that we follow them." He steps to the side so Jillian stumbles into Stevens. "Now, is this very sporting?"

Jillian giggles.

Stevens sets her on her feet, laughing. "She seems to want to play too."

Jillian rushes Noah, her arms out.

He grabs a hand, spins her to him, and steps them to the side just as Stevens grabs for him.

Music comes over the speaker system, playing a fast-tempo, lively song.

Noah spins Jillian towards Stevens. When he stretches out a hand, Noah spins her back. He brings her close to whirl them out of Stevens' reach.

Stevens changes his tactics and direction continually. He corners Noah and goes for the capture.

Noah has another idea. He spins Jillian off along the ropes, then dives out, grabbing the top rope to slingshot back and land in front of Jillian to dance away.

Stevens holds up his arms, laughing as the crowd goes wild over that stunt. He bows to the dancers and the four sides of the room.

They cheer him on.

The song comes to an end, and with a flourish, Noah dips Jillian. They laugh, breathing heavily. They stare at each other, caught, they move towards each other.

Outside their awareness, Amethyst, slaps the man, going ignored, she slaps the mat and calls. "Irving, now's your chance. Get him!" she laughs.

Big hands grab Noah's upper arms. And lifts them up, twisting them around to standing. Stevens releases one hand on Noah and puts a finger under Jillian's chin, turning her face to his. He laughs. "Thank you, Jilli girl, we caught him. Now, go see Amethyst." He tips his head in Amethyst's direction.

Jillian's big, smoky grey eyes forlornly look back at Noah, who looks hungry for her. At Steven's urging, she steps back, and that's as far as they get. Noah wasn't letting go. So Jillian starts moving back to him.

"No! Jillian, no!" Amethyst calls exasperated, laughing. "Separate them, man. We don't have much time now. Fin, where are you?"

"Huh? Not much time, what do you mean?" He pulls Noah back, but he's pulling Jillian closer, faster. "What happens?"

"Nothing good because we have to stop it. Don't let them kiss. It's so much harder after they do that." Fin says on the run.

The Oddities all laugh and hoot.

"Irving, stop that and just separate them." Amethyst directs from the floor.

CHAPTER THIRTY-ONE

Noah and Jillian stare into each other eyes. The connection is almost tangible, drawn to each other, the pull unstoppable. Closer and closer, ecstasy only a breath away.

Noah is pulled but resists, and he has to get to Jillian.

Jillian is pulled on, but Toby's grip is stronger, drawing her to him, right where she wants to be.

Only a breath, then something covers Toby's lower face. Confused, she pulls back and sees a huge hand grip Toby's jaw from ear to ear. She screams in frustration and grabs the wrist covering her conquest, pulling and pushing, enraged.

Nothing happens.

Toby's eyes focus, and he look up at Stevens, who grins sheepishly and shrugs his shoulders. He points to the side of the ring, where Amethyst stands slapping the mat.

"Toby! Focus, man." Amethyst barks her command.

Toby's foggy eyes turn and see a mad Jillian clawing Stevens' wrist. He sees Fin step over and hands a bottle to him.

"You better give it to her. She's getting meaner." Fin laughs. "Toby, give her the bottle."

Noah reaches out, takes her hand and puts the bottle in it; then the other hand, he wraps her fingers around the neck. He guides it to her lips and tips it.

She takes over and chugs it down.

Stevens swears. "Holy shit, that's whiskey, isn't it?"

Fin laughs. "Yeah, they are putting it away like desert dwellers drink water. It's the fever. If they are tanked, the fever is at bay, but if either or both starts to sober up, watch out. They start to smolder with a raging inferno just a spark away. Come to think of it, if we did set a spark next to them, they could literally go up in flames with how much whiskey is in them."

"Funny, Fin, get her over here. Nice move, Irving. I never thought of that. But Toby's not looking real happy." Snickering, Amethyst takes charge of the bottle-sucking Tigress, Jillian.

Stevens looks at the huge, stormy green eyes staring at him over his hand clamped to his jaw. Stevens looks at Fin. "So, what do you do with him?"

"Well, normally, he has been very responsible, but I talked him into putting that aside for the rest of the night as long as I kept her juiced up. I guess all that exercise sobered them up. Feeding him seems to help. He sucked down a sub plater for twelve in about two seconds. Weird how he can move so fast when he's taking his own sweet time." Fin smiles. "You could just stay that way."

Noah tenses, his eyes darken.

Stevens notices the changes immediately. "Get out, Fin, now! No time for rules. No time for formalities. I'm about to get my ass kicked if I don't let go. Go, man, so I can let go. He's getting mad."

Noah's eyes continue to darken, muscles loosen, and weight shifts to balance.

Fin laughs, backing up cautiously, feeling the danger. "I'll leave him in your care then."

Stevens barks. "Run!"

Fin turns and runs for the ropes, sliding under and ends up standing a few feet away. He takes off for the bar. "O'Malley, whatever you do, do not get involved in that. Ring the bell and tell them something but to stay out of it. This is a Toby we don't know, but Irving seems to. This Toby is very dangerous." He turns to the ring just in time to see Irving land on his back and roll to his feet in a lightning move hardly moving.

On the other side of the ring, Amethyst wrestles with Jillian, who screams her Tigress' expression of frustration. "I'm helping Amethyst." He runs off.

O'Malley gets up and rings the bell. "Listen, folks, the fever runs hot, and the lad is working off some frustration with his friend. This is not a dispute that follows the regular rules. This is between them, but since we will be watching, I'll open the books for five minutes starting now. If it's over before then, we'll call it a draw. Do not get in the ring or piss off the lad. For a line at the book."

In the ring, Noah gives Stevens a nasty smile, taking his pocket protector out and tossing it over his shoulder. It hits the wall of the booth the women sit and land on the table. Quickly, more items land next to the pocket protector. His wallet is last.

At the table, Jillian grabs the wallet and pocket protector.

Fin arrives, blocking the end of the booth.

Jillian calms, picking up a full glass, and drinks the whiskey down.

Stevens takes out his keys and wallet, tossing them to Noah's pile. He keeps his eyes on Noah the entire time, and he knows Noah is about to blow. If he wasn't watching, it would be painful.

Then Noah moves.

He keeps in character with Toby's slumping, hunched, springing actions, difficult to extract tells of movement. So every action will surprise. It has taken a lot of time to develop each character's fighting style. Each one has special moves and distinctive abilities.

Jarvis, the exterminator, uses the tools of his trade as weapons. He can poison, stab, trap, and know all the hidden places. His fighting style is down and dirty, just like he is, mean in a fight. He knows the moves of the animals but is taunting and crude. He likes pissing people off.

Larson, the contractor's style is pounding power, like a sledgehammer. He can fight with a knife but hammers closer to hand, also screwdrivers and rake handles are used like a staff. Wickedly accurate with a nail gun. But he most likes the feeling of flesh hitting flesh. Stupid as a bag of cotton, but piss him off, and you're getting your ass kicked.

Gramps was wicked with a cane and solid as a rock. Normally, Gramps doesn't get into a fight. He's slow except for his cane arm, very fast. Crusty old goat doesn't take shit from anyone and says what's on his mind, regardless of the company or subject.

Toby, the office geek is distinctive because of his posture that had to be maintained. Not just his posture but also his accordion gait and slow-motion speed. Toby can use anything and accidentally cause injury, like the hanky, the marker and the cap. He can disguise his actions with blinding speed. Toby doesn't use a knife or gun. He uses office supplies or what's on his body. He is unholy with a ruler and stapler; done right, a ruler edge can cut.

Toby doesn't have office supplies right now. Tonight Noah bleeds through Toby, giving him a dangerous reputation, which might be okay since he doesn't have the look of danger. Most people only see the outside package.

Frustrated, he's a ball of unexpressed emotion. His outlet just tossed his keys and wallet to the table. Without waiting, Noah moves at Toby's speed. He slumps up to Stevens and slaps him across the face to get his attention. Ducks the ham hock fist aimed for his head and stiff-fingered jabs up to Stevens' inner arm to that nerve cluster.

Stevens twists his arms and only gets a stinging glancing blow. He steps away and shifts to only defensive.

Noah follows, hitting him in the solar plexus with the heel of his hand, winding Stevens.

Gasping for air, moving back, Stevens has never seen fighting like this, not telegraphing the moves. It was more like the South American dance fighting, Capuera, a type of martial arts, but nothing like it. He has to really focus so he doesn't get hit anymore.

Noah follows and catches sight of Jillian hugging his pocket protector and wallet to her chest. A vision of Jillian flashes in his mind. Her in the ring, jumping into his arms. He holds her up by the waist and licks up her leg. At the last moment, he ducks the punch for his head and automatically jabs up stiff thumb for that inner arm. He dodges the left that comes in quick, grabs the wrist, keeps moving, kicks the back of his knee and steps on his calf, launching himself up to straddle Stevens' shoulders. Adding extra weight throws Stevens off balance.

Stevens stumbles to the left, then stomps, bending down and jerking his shoulder to shift Noah down. Stepping back, he whips around to the left, straightening his arm to fling Noah off his arm.

Noah slides down his arm, grabbing his wrist at the last moment. Facing the floor, he jack knifes his body. He swings down, pushing Steven's arm back and up before him past the peak of the arc, arching away and releasing Steven's wrist to land six feet away.

Stevens flips and lands on his back. He rolls to his feet, shaking his big body.

Noah grins goofy and slumps towards Stevens. "What's wrong, Irving, out of practice?" He scrapes his hair behind his ears and pushes up his glasses.

Stevens laughs. "I've never fought with a monkey before. Are these your monkey moves?"

Noah laughs. "Hey, that was just opportunity knocking, so I answered. I was pleased with the results."

Stevens rolls his shoulders. "I'm sure you are. This is an unusual style of fighting, very fluid in a jerky way. You do this with each one, customize?" He twists his neck and shifts his spine, repositioning after the jarring flips.

"Of course, customizing is a must since each is distinctly different. Would you care to meet some? It can be arranged." Noah slumps closer, circling.

"Before you turned me odd, I would have said, hell no. You know the whole idea freaks me out." Stevens shifts his weight onto the balls of his feet.

"Oh, yes, I fully comprehended your feelings and the reasons, actually. But that was before meeting me here and the Daze. Now?" Noah slumps down, extending his leg sideways and swooping up under Stevens' arm, chopping him under his knee, causing his leg to kick out over balancing him. He pushes sharply down on his shoulder on the unbalanced side.

Stevens tucks and rolls to his feet. Turns, stepping back to face Noah again. "Now? Hell, yes. You must know you are an artist."

"Yes...Robin Vauhn." Noah says straight faced, slumping by Stevens unconcerned. He spins when he reaches his side extending his leg chopping across he backs of his thighs.

The blow stings and pushes Stevens forward and folds his legs, a fake descending stairs. "Robin Vauhn?" He ends up sitting on the mat and looks over his shoulder, amazed. "You mean, The Robin Vauhn, the painter?"

Noah laughs. "Yes, a recluse, you know. Not many have that privilege, though he is in constant demand. He's tiresome, always bitching about the establishment and the deteriorating society. He is a snob, really, and a hypocrite since the establishment and that deteriorating society pays his outrageous fees for crappy paintings. Did you see that one, Harvest Moon, got awards and was featured in Time Magazine as one of the year's greatest achievements? What a joke. The thinner soup can was sitting on an unframed blank canvas when Chester the Cat knocked over unsealed paint cans, lost his footing and slid across the canvas. He was a mess covered in red, blue, and black. Chester is pure white, well, was. Can't remove the pigment. Tried everything except shaving. Did you know that it sold for 1.5M? Yes, you heard right. It is most noted for its superior brushwork." Noah shakes his head. "You know, sometimes you have to scratch your head and go; "Huh?""

Stevens just stares at him, shocked.

Oh, crap! He didn't fall back into the Daze, did he? "Ah, Irving?" He steps closer, concerned.

Stevens curls up and falls over, quivering.

Seriously concerned, Noah kneels down beside him, rolling him over.

Tears pour out of his eyes, and holding his stomach. Stevens' laughter explodes out. Taking a great gasping breath, he laughs and laughs.

Noah starts laughing.

They laugh so hard, rolling on the mat.

Every time Stevens looks at Toby and thinks about the serious, almost dour Noah, he laughs harder. Then Robin Vauhn, the superstar in the art world. 1.5M for a mess made by a cat, Chester. He can't stop laughing, it's too damn funny. He's known Noah forever, and he never knew Robin Vauhn was Noah in one of his disguises.

He knew that each identity had "a life," but he had no idea these characters were so established. He has to know all now, and the curiosity is killing him. Sucking in great gulps of air, he asks. "Who else?" Breathing heavily, he watches Toby fascinated.

CHAPTER THIRTY-TWO

Noah looks around at all the smiling faces and whispers. "Skylar Robinso."

Stevens gapes. "The musician?"

Noah nods. "Dr. N. R. Skylar."

Stevens' jaw drops. "The physicist?"

Sheepishly, Noah looks around. "Maxwell Christopher Hastings the IV"

Stevens' eyes get bigger, he croaks. "The millionaire?"

Noah twists his lips and peeks at Stevens. "Larson E. Wilson." He looks away.

Stevens chokes. "Lars Wilson, the architect? When do you have time for your business?"

Noah shrugs, looking embarrassed. "I pick what interests me. It's all by word of mouth. I pick a job when I feel like it or am convinced it's dire. Then I step into the snarl. Out west, there was a bit of shifty business on the rodeo circuit and so D. W. Tanner decided he wanted to ride. So he did."

Stevens sucks in and coughs. "Dusty Wind Tanner? Good God, No…Toby, how does this happen?"

Toby barks a laugh. "You're asking Toby "The Dazer" Robins how infamy happens? How in the hell do I know? Maybe we should ask Chester the damn cat."

Stevens howls with laughter. "I just may. Where is he?"

"At the studio, of course. When not in residence, there is a woman, an old woman, who gathers mail and sends it on, takes care of Chester, and cleans a little. Robin is not concerned with dust. "Life has grit, so does his art, so the art critic praises."

Stevens sits back, trying to reconcile all these with Noah, and has a real problem. "Are there more?"

"How many jobs have I taken over the last eight years? Don't know the exact number, I guess we could count, but I'm sure I will miss somebody. Once a type is established, it gets used again. This one is the top dog, but maybe not anymore. Today has put him on shaky ground, partly the bleed-through and partly the Dazer." Noah shrugs.

"You really are amazing. And to think all this time I didn't want to know. You do realize that tonight is like breaking through the ice and then stepping onto the beach of a south tropical island."

"Good analogy; cold barren lifeless, the plunge, then warm lush life. I like it. I've been writing a bit. And before you ask, Lambert Wellington, stuffy pompous, award-winning."

Stevens laughs. "I don't know how you do it. My mind is boggled. Who else?" He can't help but ask.

Noah chuckles. "Dr. N. S. Robinson, Victor Johnna/policeman, Rocket Masters/biker-daredevil, Burt Lam/homeless bum, Ed Duncan/drunk, Chris Majors/all services military, Michael Donovan/office executive and family man, Gramps, Chip Brewster/Frat boy, Jarvis Shitz/exterminator. He and Lars are in town. Jillian ran into them as well as me, Toby. One week apart to the day. Right after the dream."

"The dream?" Stevens searches his mind.

"The dream I think Jillian and I share. Each time worse than the last. I wake with the taste of Danger from the dream. So hyper-alert than the lust. Nothing works to relieve the tension; the normal method makes it worse. Saltwater at sea. I'm getting a good workout, about a gazillion pushups. And still not enough. I'm dreading next Friday."

"What's the dream?" Stevens looks over at Jillian hugging Noah's wallet and pocket protector. He smiles.

"I swim out of a large lake or sea and run up the beach. Jillian jumps up in fear and runs away. I run past, grabbing her hand and dragging her behind me. Danger breathing down my neck. We get

247

to deep shadow, and I stop and swing her around and kiss her. She climbs up and latches on, and we spin and hit the ground. On impact I vault up in my bed alone, ready for a fight or feed on Jillian."

"What's this fever business?" Stevens watches him closely.

"This insane lust that is haunting us, I believe." He looks over at Jillian.

She smiles sweetly and waves.

He snorts and waves back, smiling, then turns back to Stevens. "O'Malley told Amethyst and Jillian that she's suffering from the fever, I assume fever of the blood, in heat. She hunted me down at the county offices today and sniffed me out. A heightened sense of smell led her to me. And if I wasn't so keyed up horny, I'd think it hilarious. There's Toby working diligently at his desk when Jillian, in that red and black dress, pounces on him. He shrieks like a girl. She's crawling all over his lap, running her nose everywhere. He grips the armrests, shaking badly, fighting himself to not touch her. Amethyst shows up laughing. That is all I can say. "Get her off me."

Jillian started licking my face. I only had two choices: throw her on the desk and mount her or get away. Phillip is the HR manager there. He walked in, and somehow, I got away until she ran up and jumped on my back. I think I was about to shatter.

I ended up giving her a taste so intense that kiss, she fainted in my arms or passed out. The only thing that saved us. Of course, Toby had an audience on both occasions.

Amethyst asked me to carry Jillian here, and the rest goes into the annals. And I mean that literally. O'Malley the ancient started a running account of history in the bar and town the day he opened the doors.

So now Toby is not only a serious ladies' man, "Ladies in need, my good deed." But also a funny, badass fighter. I won't even go into his skills, mind-blowing. Oh, yes, I blew away 200-odd people's minds right out of their bodies. I'm not sure if the Dazer will survive the current job." He shakes his head. "I like Toby."

Stevens chuckled. "I like Toby, too. Maybe Toby could only make limited appearances elsewhere. He has decided that his own interests take precedence for the time being." Stevens looks around. "Though he will be missed here. Are you going to let anyone know?"

"I'm trying to figure that out, though I suspect a very select few might be catching some clues. Jillian will know at some point. I won't live a life of lies with the ones I love. And even though it's been almost no time with her, I know. Thus, I must protect her, even from myself. I would greatly appreciate it if you could sign on for that task. Amethyst understands that I won't hurt her, so she stands between Toby and Jillian to protect us both." Noah rubs the back of his neck. "But she doesn't know about the others. she is collecting clues, smart she is, and observant. Fin, too. He's a good man.

"Dr. Paulson knows my body isn't that of this form. I catch him watching me, eyes speculating. Jillian is probably closest to knowing. She's very observant, plus she ran into three, physically. The fever clouds her mind, so realization will come as a flash."

Stevens laughs. "You can't be simple, can you? I understand a little. I think I may have dropped a whole box of clues when I first arrived, and Fin and Amethyst were present." He shakes his head. "You know that the Odd will accept it, completely and without reservations. At some point, you should come out of the closet." He laughs harder. "Literally, and stand in the light, un-shrouded. They may request visits from time to time, but how fun would that be?"

Noah nods and climbs to his feet. "I'm considering it, at least with Toby. Maybe more, we'll see. No decisions tonight and no actions until after the jobs are complete." He holds his hand out to Stevens.

Stevens takes it and is launched to his feet. "Are you going to clue me in on the job? Since I'm sticking around, you may as well put me to work." He adjusts his clothes.

"I'll put you to work, but I will wait until tomorrow and when we are alone to get into the details of the job. Let's just say something fishy is going down in South County. Possibly trying to dig in feet to establish a firm foundation for future ventures. Nothing good so far as I've found." Noah turns, slips through the ropes and hops down.

Stevens hops down beside him. "I'm you, man. What now?"

Noah heads to the table with the women and Fin. "Now, we drink and wait for your doctor to take Wesley and Rick, hear what the Mayor has to say, and keep Jillian and me apart when we are sober and allow us to play when we are juiced. Then leave and sleep it off. I still have to work tomorrow. I want the job over so I can figure out the rest. By that, I mean Jillian and our future."

"Even when you set aside responsibility, you have a massive agenda." Stevens claps Toby on the shoulder.

"My life is a bit complicated." Toby whines

Stevens laughs. "A bit?"

"Okay, that was an understatement. But it's not as complicated as, say, thermodynamics. That's tricky." He chuckled.

Stevens gaped at Toby, shaking his head. "Yeah, thermodynamics, tricky." He chuckled.

Noah slides into the end seat on the bench with the two women. "Fin, my good man, I'm feeling a bit peckish. Could you help me out? Whatever you have will be great." Noah looks at Stevens. "Are you hungry?"

Stevens nods. "Yes, I can eat."

Fin laughs and slides out of the booth. "No problem, Toby." he hands Noah a full glass of whiskey. "Drink up before I go. I'll return with enough to feed thirty. I'm sure between the two of you, there won't be a crumb left." Fin saunters away after Noah empties his glass.

Stevens slides onto the open bench, moving to the corner, his back to the wall, extending his legs along the seat. "What's that about?"

Amethyst laughs, picking up the open bottle, and fills the six glasses on the table. She slides one over to Stevens. "Toby "The Hoover" Robins has been noted to make food vanish in large quantities."

Jillian leans forward, sliding Toby's items to him, everything except his wallet. She slides Stevens' keys and wallet towards him and smiles.

Amethyst nudges a glass closer to Jillian. "So, do you feel better, Toby?" She chuckles. "You didn't look so happy up there." she turns to Stevens. "But you walked out on your own."

Stevens smiles. "He wasn't trying to hurt me; even mad, he knew I was helping him."

"Yes, Stevens helped take the edge off." Noah picks up the glass and knocks it back. "Stevens has agreed to stick around and add a helping hand with fever control."

"Lovely, I'm glad, my friend. Will you go with us tomorrow to the hospital?" Jillian reaches over and rubs Stevens' arm. "We are to see the Flesh-Eating Zombie Andrews and give him his voice back." She looks at Amethyst. "Not that I believe he will use it well. He's a bit thick."

Stevens nods. "I'd be pleased to go."

"Good." Amethyst smiles. "I need all the help I can get with these two. Maybe a leash for her and a muzzle for him."

"What do you mean? I'm harmless," Jillian says, offended.

Everyone laughs uproariously.

"Yeah, harmless," Fin says, putting a large serving tray on the table, covered in food. Two sub platers, two cold platers, and two pies. "One apple and one blueberry." he laughs. "Enjoy." He unloads his tray as Stevens turns in the booth. Fin steps away with a flourish.

Noah looks at Stevens and laughs at his expression. The only way to describe it was aghast. He positions the subplatter in front of himself, catches Stevens' eye, and winks. He reaches for his napkin and whips it out to place it gently on his lap.

Fin returns and places four pitchers of ice water on the table with two large glasses. He bows and steps away.

Noah takes a deep breath and unhurriedly picks up a sub section and takes a bite. He mows through the two platers with pauses for glasses of water. Half of each pie appears on a platter, and he continues unhurriedly shoveling food into his mouth. His water glass remains full, except when he drains it. When the last crumb vanishes, he picks up his water glass and drains it. Takes his napkin and pats his mouth, folds it, then places it on top of the stacked platers. He sits back with a sigh.

"Done!" A voice yells from the crowd.

Numbers are shouted out.

Noah looks over at his companions and shrugs. "6.3" He reaches for his whiskey glass.

Stevens laughs.

Noah looks over at him.

Stevens still has plenty of food in front of him.

"Are you going to finish that?" Toby asks. "I'm unusually hungry today."

Stevens laughs, waving at the food. He nudges it to the center of the table. "Please, help yourselves, Ladies. Please, you'll starve if you eat your meals with that. your food will vanish before you have a chance to smell it." He laughs. "Haven't lost any of your speed. Has any of that hit your stomach yet?" he watches, amazed as Noah leisurely nibbles on a sub, purposely trying to slow down. It was gone unnaturally fast.

"I think this need to feed is related to the fever." Toby shrugs. "I wasn't like this yesterday, three square, and I was good."

"Wow! Really?" Jillian asks, fascinated. "You didn't eat super fast?"

Stevens laughs. "He's always been fast, not that fast."

Toby smiles. "Fast, yes; warp drive fast, no. A bottomless pit is a new development. I imagine witnessing the combination startling."

Amethyst choked on her drink. "I'm getting the feeling you understate everything."

Stevens chuckles, tapping the end of his nose. He picks up his glass and takes a drink, looking elsewhere.

Toby looks away. "Not everything."

Amethyst laughs. "Okay, I guess I can judge for myself as time goes on."

Toby snorts. "There are t..."

A commotion at the door of the pub interrupted him. He turns to the center of the pub.

A man in a three-piece suit walks to the bar.

A young man moves towards him from the far side.

Wesley announces the new arrival. "The Mayor of South County has arrived. Welcome, Mayor Sheffield."

The Mayor turns around. "Thank you..."

The young man steps up and leans in, talking rapidly.

"Good God, boy, seriously?"

The younger man continues speaking quickly, arms twitching here and there.

"My, my, extraordinary."

The young man points to the ring, to a table from the direction he came. He points out here and there, then at Toby and keeps pointing, emphasizing a point. Everywhere the young man points, the Mayor looks. Now, he watches Toby. His head turns sharply to the man, startled shock, slowly, his head turns and takes in all the people in the pub. He did a double take on Wesley and Rick, horrified by them.

"Yes, quite horrifying, isn't it?" Wesley observes, his lips still. "We looked regular but hours ago."

Rick jumps in. "You really have no idea a few hours can impact a life so drastically. We are pleased we can rejoin this reality, limited as it is right now." He, too, doesn't move his lips.

The mayor realizes the sound wasn't coming from the men on display, framed by canvas structure with the floodlights backlighting the pair. Their heads glow weirdly. He looks around, searching, until the young man says something that catches his whole attention. He turns and focuses solely on the young man. He leans back sharply at a blow of shocking information, then leans forward, ready for more.

"I believe that young man is the Mayor's son," Wesley comments, watching the men.

253

"I believe you are right. What was his name? Mat Sheffield. Yes, that's it." Rick says confidently.

"Wasn't there a Mathew Sheffield a couple of years ago that took our football team to the finals?"

"Yes, there he is. He's been off at the University. He came home for summer break. He has one more year, I believe."

"My, Rick, you do keep the pulse of the community, don't you?"

"I hear things and remember. There was a conversation before the Daze. I don't know if it's factual. It's just what I heard."

"Well, we of South County are not known as rumor mongers. Just the opposite."

"Thanks to O'Malley, the Original. It's amazing how one man can shape a community with only an idea, without the benefit of a powerful position. Just an average working man."

"We have witnessed tonight how one man shaped the community with only and idea. And the power of two men sharing the same idea accomplished what was once thought impossible."

"We have indeed, Wesley. A most memorable night, as the Oddities will attest."

The crowd yells a resounding "Yes!"

The Mayor is startled by the response. His head comes up and he stares in wonder.

Mat Sheffield didn't stop talking, pointed over to Rick and Wesley, then back to Toby and now Irving. He points up, then wound down to point down, coming to the end. He stands there breathing heavily, and waits.

The Mayor looks around, sees someone and waves him over. He sees another and waves at him. He turns to O'Malley.

O'Malley nods and waves him to the back door.

The Mayor and the three others head to the back door.

O'Malley joins them after a word with Fin.

Smirking, Fin takes his post behind the bar.

Before the Mayor crosses the back threshold, the front door opens.

In walks a stylish woman and four men in white coats.

CHAPTER THIRTY-THREE

The crowd of Oddities laughs gleefully at the sight of the new arrivals.

It stops four white Lab-coated men in their tracks a few feet passed the doors, appearing confused. The woman with them steps past, looking around scared. They spot Wesley and Rick. Gasping in shock, all five take a step back in horror.

"Rick, you know, I thought he was speaking figuratively, not literally. How did he know?" Wesley's lips remain still.

"I think by now you would accept his words at face value and then figure out all the layers of hidden meaning. All factual if you have the wits to decipher it. A keener mind I haven't witnessed, this comes from one detached mind to another." Rick's lips remain as still as Wesley's.

The crowd laughs and cheers.

"I love the Odd, they so understand us."

"Those five don't look so understanding. I'm now glad the four will be with us."

"Yes, if nothing else, the four can interpret for us."

Rick laughs. "The hands were interpreting the mind; it's called art."

Wesley chuckles. "Very amusing. I wonder if we get the label of Dazer; they look a little lost. But it is the night for it."

"Toby, could you please greet our guests?" Rick asks, amused.

"Our Guests, might I give a friendly bit of advice? Don't look directly at Toby for long periods of time."

Rick chimes in. "Unless, of course, you would like a new perspective on your work."

Wesley continues smoothly around his partner. "Miss, seriously, you may want to have your white coats face the door."

Rick flows in. "It's for their benefit and yours. It's time-consuming coming back from the Daze. Yes, you will need plenty to get through the information dealing with us."

"Are you willing to risk all five of you?

Toby gets up, shaking his head and waves at Stevens to follow. "Dr. Paulson?" Toby's grating nasal whine calls out. "Time to pass the buck."

The smiling crowd separates for Toby and Stevens, followed closely by Amethyst and Jillian, closing smoothly after their passage.

All watch.

Toby slumps to the woman and stops with Stevens beside him.

Unable to look away watching Toby's approach she tilts her head.

Toby extends his hand.

She tentatively extends her hand.

Toby gently clasps her hand, raising it to his lips while bowing. "Toby Robins, Lady, a pleasure to make your acquaintance."

Eyes wide, she tips her head the other way, her hand forgotten. "Ingrid, Ingrid..." She whispers.

Stevens laughs and shakes his head.

Toby pats her hand. "A lovely name, Lady Ingrid. Might I be so bold to direct your attention to my associate who contacted you? Let me introduce you..." Toby raises his brow at Stevens.

Stevens shrugs, grinning.

Noah nods with a snort. "Irving Stevenson, who goes by Stevens often. Stevens, this is the lovely Lady Ingrid." He turns back to Ingrid.

She just stares.

"Looks like we may have lost her," Wesley notes, amused. "Irving, break the connection before it's too late."

"Good call." Rick chimes in. "Step in front of Toby, the roster is closed, no new members."

Stevens laughs and does as he's told, stepping in front of Toby and taking her hand.

Behind him, Toby suppresses the laughter.

Stevens throws back an elbow but makes no contact. He looks into Ingrid's eyes, a nice rich brown. He slaps her hand briskly and calls loudly. "Ingrid!"

She blinks and looks up, startled, shakes her head, blinking again.

Stevens chuckles. "Ingrid!"

Her attention snaps to him, snatching her hand away, confused.

Stevens smiles.

She openly gapes, breathing hard, her hand holding her heart.

Toby snickers. "Stop smiling, beauty."

Wesley says, amused. "Look, it's the Dazing Duo: Beauty and the Beast."

The Oddities howl with laughter, clapping and stomping to show their approval.

Rick chuckles. "But who is who?"

"Does that matter? Like Toby, layers on layers."

The crowd responds with whooping and hollering.

Stevens chokes out. "Wiser words were never spoken."

Toby jabs Stevens in the lower nerve cluster and has Stevens on his knees, laughing between him and Ingrid. "Lady Ingrid, I seem to have an effect on...well, most everyone. Suppose I could get you to not look directly at me for...well, while you are here. We have pressing business to care for, and they are Wesley and Rick. Please, dear lady Ingrid, focus on them. We must have our wits with us to discuss this pressing issue."

Ingrid's eyes started to fog.

"We can't have this. Oddities distract the white four, please. Back to me. Get them alert. Dr. Paulson, please snap her out. It's not too late. I'll stand behind her. Stevens, get up. Watch that smile. I never had to worry about its effects before, but now..." He snorts. "Beauty and the Beast." He snorts again. "I like it, Wesley, very witty and full of twists and turns. Nicely done." Toby steps behind Ingrid and Dr. Paulson.

A group swarms the white four turning them to the door, patting and questioning to get a response. At first, it was slow and stilted, but soon, conversations flowed between all parties.

"Thank you, Toby," Wesley says, amused. "It seemed fitting. You two are an interesting pair."

Rick replies. "We would love to hear your story."

Noah looks them in the eyes earnestly. "I will tell the Oddities all when you two come back to us whole and hardy."

Stevens stops and stares agape. "Really?"

"It will be worth everything to me to see these two back in complete control. And if my offer is a positive catalyst to their benefit, I willingly give it freely. This telling will be only for the oddities ears. We are family, and we shouldn't keep secrets from family."

The Oddities cheered their approval.

"Well, my curiosity will certainly be a driving force in our recovery. What say you, Rick?"

"I'd hop back in the captain's chair now if I knew how, just for that little carrot."

Stevens laughs. "Tip of the iceberg would better symbolize what we are discussing. And I'm not referring to that puny one that took out the Titanic. Let that idea buzz around the hive."

Toby snots. "Let's move onto the important business of the road to recovery."

The Oddities cheer.

Toby and Stevens follow behind Dr. Paulson and Ingrid.

Doc has her responsive quickly, guiding her to Wesley and Rick, not speaking about anything important, just sharpening her mind.

Amethyst and Jillian take their positions beside Rick and Wesley, holding their hands and rubbing up and down on their arm. Both pairs are guarded by 1, 2, 3, and 4, evenly spaced behind the rope.

Dr. Paulson stops in front of the two men at the rope.

Ingrid comes to a halt beside him.

From behind the pair, Toby speaks. "Lady Ingrid, may I present our local radio celebrities? On the left is Wesley, and on the right is Rick. They had a DOA-TX hooked into their equipment and were broadcasting when the event happened and were adversely affected. Wesley, Rick, I present the Lady Ingrid to whom we will be ensuring your care and eventual recovery."

"Hello, Ingrid. A pleasure to meet you."

"Hey, Ingrid, we are really pleased to communicate with you here. The alternative is just too undesirable. Death, you know, pulled from its clutches, we were. Thanks to Toby. Assisted by Dr. Paulson, of course."

Ingrid clears her throat and turns to the doctor. "Excuse my lack of professionalism, but what?"

Dr. Paulson nodded, unfazed. "Yes, I understand completely. You're at a loss. Quite natural, really. A fish out of water, floundering on the shore, hoping to find something familiar." He turns his head to look behind them. "Toby, how would you like to clarify? No, dear, it's just best if you don't look." He stops her in her turn. "I know it seems strange to hold a conversation turned away, but much easier to focus and think, which you need to do."

"Thank you, Doctor, for your concern, but I need to understand what is going on." She started to turn again.

Toby placed a finger on her shoulder to pause her actions. "Lady Ingrid, you do not need to watch me to get the information you need. But if you insist, I will give you a first-hand understanding of what is going on here. One that will change your life and perceptions and undoubtedly improve your practice beyond all comprehension. For those reasons alone, I'm tempted, but it has been a trying day, and I'm more concerned about getting these two back to full control of their bodies and giving into temptation. I will leave an open invitation for a time after they are returned to us as a reward for a job well done." Toby speaks precisely in his grating nasal whine.

"Okay, I don't understand why I have to not look at you. I have seen all types of people. You won't offend me."

Toby snorts and says dryly. "I am glad to hear I do not offend a lady of your caliber, Lady Ingrid."

Stevens laughs. "You're missing the point, Ingrid. Think back on when you first saw my friend, Toby here. Could you look away? Was your logical mind still firing? Could you process any observations and hold them or did they drift in a fuzzy feeling stealing over your body?"

Ingrid closed her eyes for a moment. Slowly, they opened and looked at Dr. Paulson. "What exactly would have happened if I continued to watch Mr. Robbins?"

Dr. Paulson considers his words. "Well… How can I explain?"

Toby snorts. "You could lose contact with your conscious mind and become trapped in your body, unable to think or do anything, except witness the outside world. As time goes by, your body cools to possible dangerous temperatures, indirect manifestation representing your hopelessness and realized helplessness." Toby turns to Stevens. "How is that explanation?"

Stevens coughs, holding back the laughter. "Succinct and to the point, no extra unnecessary information."

Toby snorts. "Something I failed to mention, that Irving has so kindly pointed out, is that while you have no control of your body anyone else could, though I wouldn't allow anyone else control you. We learned our lesson, didn't we, Fin?"

From across the bar, Fin laughs. "Yes, indeed."

"I… See." Ingrid says hesitantly.

Toby snorts. "No, you don't. Nor do you believe it's possible by just looking at me. Well, take a look around and know that almost everyone here had that experience and was trapped for an hour and more. Wesley and Rick had an amplified experience because of that DOA-TX they were hooked up to. The actual fall into mindlessness happens for all within the first minute. Go and ask. Or talk to Stevens here. He was an individual case. I wanted him to truly understand what we accomplished here tonight. I succeeded once again, on a whim, just to see what would happen. After seeing your reaction to me and watching you slide into the daze, I know that I am the catalyst. I pulled all these people out of the daze, that mindlessness, and restored them to full control of their bodies. Only two are not restored because of that added element of DOA – TX. We brought them out as far as we can, and it was risky and difficult."

Dr. Paulson huffs. "Understatement, near impossible."

"Okay, let's focus on these two right now." Ingrid nods towards Wesley and Rick.

"Lady Ingrid, please remember the awareness is not gone, nor has the recording of outside events or memory. These two, as you put it, can hear and understand that you just relegated them to things. They are individuals with names and feelings, trapped and terrified that they can't get back to what was. I would guess every patient you have had that was unresponsive to the outside world was trapped in a daze, unable to communicate with the outside world. With Wesley and Rick, we figured out a way to allow communication with the outside world. They hear everything. Now, they can contact us and tell us if they are cold, lonely, or hopeless. We have bridged to the inner mind so they could at least talk out to us, though they are going for the effect. They can move their lips some and have control of their eyes. They breathe on their own, but their body temperature is controlled more by their state of mind than internal functions. We were alerted to their unique circumstances when we noticed their temperature was vastly different within their bodies. Raging fevers on the head of 105 to signs of frostbite on the toes. Muscles were literally frozen in position. Once we made contact, they told us that their reality and their combined mind was a winter storm, the symbol of their hopelessness. A physical manifestation of their main mind state."

Ingrid raised her hand, rubbed her face, and started to turn, then caught herself. "Listen, Mr. Robins, I'm still having a problem here."

"Yes. Ask your questions." Toby states kindly. "To me, the doctor, Wesley, Rick, or anyone else. We need Wesley and Rick back in control."

"How is it possible? How did you manage it? How…"

"First question first, anything is possible."

The oddities call out. "Possibilities are only limited by a limited mind."

Toby snorts. "Onto the second question. We managed well enough. But perhaps you are looking for the specific steps, yes?"

Ingrid sighed and nodded. "Yes."

"Now, please open your mind to endless possibilities. You don't have to throw out your beliefs right now; just set them aside for the moment. Ready?"

She nods. "Yes."

Toby sighed and shook his head. "We should've let her slide into the daze. Then, it would have been easier to explain all this with that basic experience to relate to, and Wesley and Rick would get better care. Should we vote or push on?" Toby looks at Wesley and Rick. "I put the question to you two."

"I will concede to your decision."

"I will agree with Wesley. There are pros and cons to both sides. Ingrid should also have some input. You didn't purposely daze the odd 200. It happened. The one you did was only for his own good. We can see the difference, and he is your friend. So you took some liberty. But he was hopeless and found the hope, not lose it. The experience building not destroying like all the odd 200." He smiles. "Ingrid, what do you say?"

"After all the warnings, I'm hesitant to willingly subject myself to the experience." Ingrid states.

Toby nods. "Yes, wise words, Lady Ingrid. We shall wait for a later time. My impatience is showing. I do apologize, Lady. We can

263

cover the nuts and bolts of the bridge we built and see where we can fill in any holes in your understanding. I will give an abridged explanation and then a detailed report. This explanation encompasses many blends of science. A bridge is not just a hunk of steel reaching from one shore to the other. If I may, Lady Ingrid, might I know which discipline you practice?"

"What? Oh... Professional... Dah..." She shakes her head.

Toby chuckles. "Please, Lady, we understand the mindless state. That's why I asked."

She chuckles. "I really am feeling like that landed fish." She pulls a card out of her pocket and hands it over her shoulder. "I'm a Dr. of psychology and a Dr. of psychotherapy. I've been the only one to repair the damage to the mind from the DOA – TX." She states confidently.

"Could you please give us an overview of the damaging effects the DOA – TX has on the mind and what you do to repair it. How successful by individual and by group ratios?" Toby decides to strengthen her mind before bombarding it with the science he and Stevens performed. They would blow her back on the shore.

"The effects, in a nutshell, are the synapse over fire or misfire. A command is given. In the brain, a little bolt of electricity passes from one stem to the other, and the command is followed. In the DOA – TX patients, a command is given to open the mouth, the little bolt of electricity overshoots or doesn't fire consistently, or the bolt is 10 times as large and fries the receptor. If overshot, the eyes close or an arm lifts. It just depends on where that command went. The inconsistency is hit or miss, and over-fires burn out the receptor. In most cases repeating action strengthens it or reroutes the process to a different neighborhood. If you live in a new, safe neighborhood, your TV will be there where you left it the last time you were home."

"And the success ratio, individual and group?" Toby asked avidly.

"As I stated before, I am the only one in the psychotherapy field to have any success."

"Bravo. Let's hear the depressing numbers. We can take it. Wesley and Rick will have a full recovery. Won't you boys?"

"Indubitably. "Without a doubt, curiosity may kill the cat, but it's feeding us life. Besides Toby, I have a feeling your mind isn't done chewing on this problem."

"You know, Rick, I had that exact same feeling."

Toby snorts. "I will grant you, there has been a nibble or two, but I am tired, drunk, and overextended. So chewing will not happen tonight."

"Did you hear what I heard, Wesley?"

"Yes, indeed I did. You may chew at your leisure. We know you have an attribute Dr. Ingrid does not yet possess."

"The unlimited mind. Give us the numbers, Doctor. We'll improve your average."

She shakes her head. "Individuals 65% average. The group 40%. The group average is affected by death rates."

"Well, not as bad as I expected. Let me ask you something I hope you won't take offense and answer honestly, Lady Ingrid." Toby states.

She nods. "All right, ask."

"On those that died, were they isolated, denied human contact, and treated as a scientific problem?"

She was quiet for a moment. Reluctantly, she nods.

"I would give you a way to increase your overall numbers. Make sure none of those things happen anymore. Human contact is a must. Please direct your eyes to Wesley and Rick. Ladies Jillian and Amethyst have been touching them on and off since we became aware of their special circumstances. Gentlemen, would you please tell her what that human contact and attention did for you?"

"Dr. Ingrid, it has given me comfort, warmth, bolstered hope, and the knowledge of the care of my existence."

"I might also add a distraction of the endless void. I can't do anything except think, oh, blink my eyes, and move my lips a little, but other than that, nada. And when fear and loneliness take hold, hopelessness is not far. These lovely women were describing what

265

was going on in our world we were robbed of. They told us funny stories, and they explained every move Toby was making in preparation for that wonderful bridge. We were glad they recognized we, Wesley and Rick, were still human and aware. There really is no way to express properly the huge positive effect these ladies had on our continued existence. They talk to us, not at us. Therein lies a huge difference. Toby, too, was constantly telling us what to expect. Even how he was feeling. He knew we were still in these bodies, though far, far away. His faith in our return gave us the faith to believe him. In believing him, the fear vanished for the most part. The loneliness was set aside because they involved us, and the hope was cemented in. Do you see that human contact is mandatory for conditions such as these?" Rick asks kindly.

"You mean to tell me that, before this bridge, you were aware and understood what was going on around you?" She whispers.

"Yes, our eyes are the windows into our souls or, if you'd rather, our spirits. That is the basis of life, what animates the bodies. From our place, the reverse is true. Our eyes are the windows into this reality. Before the bridge, our awareness created an environment and alternate reality. Like a window on the wall, we see the other reality, our original reality. If you can imagine one moment sitting at the table here in this pub hours ago, interacting with the people here, the next moment, Rick and I are still sitting in our chairs behind the table with our mics, but we are sitting in the wilderness. Specifically, a glen surrounded by forest. Out in front of us is a rectangular, though hazy at the edges, window to our reality. We watched all the action in our combined field of vision, like a TV. We had sound and full living color. We could not interact, and this realization of our situation bloomed in our minds or spirit. A winter storm raged, and we just sat there, unable to change even the circumstances of a second reality. Snow piled up, and we watched Toby figure out the dazed and how to extract those people from it. He worked nonstop until Amethyst came to us for our turn. But we were different, she could feel it and brought Toby back. He looked this over. Talked to us and found our bodies were temperature-challenged. As he moved down our bodies, they got colder. He pulled off a shoe and sock, and we were suffering from the onset of frostbite.

266

That's the first clue he had with us. Another was our light sensitivity. When he asked a question, we tried to answer. We somehow alerted him that someone was home. He noted every small thing and came to the conclusion that we were trapped together and that the amplifier was a part of the prison. His priority was to keep the body alive. Then got the idea of how to communicate while taking the others out. He contacted Irving to help. He wrote a computer program to translate our thoughts into words. Our thoughts are traveling a huge journey for you to hear them. As I understand it, we are sending our thoughts out to a satellite to bounce back to the radio station and they kindly are sending it out so any receiver can pick it up in range. We are speaking to you through the radio. We hear you through the mics. We are unsure because of the earphones. I was told they are melted to our heads, as is the one hand. We should tell you these amplifiers are not safe, among other reasons."

"I... Wh..." Ingrid started and stopped and started and paused.

"Okay, overload. Dr. Paulson, please escort the lovely lady to the bar get her something to drink and have a moment to process. It's a lot to take in on so many levels and many different ways." Toby watched the doctors move to the bar.

267

CHAPTER THIRTY-FOUR

"One, two, three, four, I'm glad you decided to accompany Wesley and Rick, thank you. You heard about human contact. I expect you to remember to touch Wesley and Rick. Please bear with my repetition. It's to put my mind at ease. Did you guys get the van ready? Are we positive Wesley and Rick will fit and ride safely? I need a guarantee, gentlemen."

Three smiles and looks at the others. "Worse than my mother. Yes Mother, we modified the van so both can ride safely and reasonably comfortably."

"Wesley and Rick's heads mustn't be touched by anything except the way I told you earlier. And only when reapplying the conductive gel. If they get a doctor to remove the headphones, you must impress upon him the importance of not disrupting the array field. Ah, hell! Excuse me, ladies."

Jillian and Amethyst laugh.

Fin hands him a glass full of amber liquid. "The mayor wants to meet you."

Toby takes the glass of whiskey and pours it down his throat. "Of course he does." He sighs big "I'm having second thoughts about letting Wesley and Rick go." He hands the glass back to Fin. Turned and put his head down, slumping away, turned and slumped back. He looked up at three. "Did you get the batteries and other items I requested?"

Three nods patiently. "Yes, as requested. No substitutions."

Toby nodded, slumped off, turned and came back. "You know, I just realized I never flicked either Wesley or Rick."

Fin nods. "True, you shocked their system with a lot more energy than your very hard flicks." He rubs his brow and sets off a chain reaction.

Everyone who watched the movie mimics it, and everyone else soon follows.

Toby snorts and slumps off, turns, and comes back. "What about a receiver for the signal coming from the satellite?"

Three smiles gently. "Toby, the radio station will send it on when it comes in. The rush order went out the moment we requested. They're going to broadcast Wesley and Rick through the computer website until they ensure Rick and Wesley are good. Their audience might cause a ruckus when they can't hear them."

"You see how he worries for just the two of us? This isn't about responsibility."

"No, much deeper. It would hurt him a lot if we slipped the way, especially when not in his care."

Toby stopped his slumping pace, a hard look in his eye. "Don't talk like that, you won't die." He paces away, slumping hard.

Stevens turned to Rick and Wesley and watched them. "You'd better not. I expect you will get a visit with a doctor Toby sends to fiddle with your headphones. If Toby sent him, you don't need to worry. If anyone else comes and there is no mention of Toby, have one of the four call. Remember, the four are your hands and helpers and guards. We are your muscles, don't forget. Do one of you have a cell phone?"

Three smiles. "Yes, all four of us do now, and the fifth one is on Toby. Four numbers are in the memory: one, two, three, four. Mother made sure of it. We had to show him."

"Good, did he give you my number also?" Stevens asks as he pulls out. His phone rings he looks at the screen. One was calling. Stevens laughs. "Was this done during my daze?"

"Yes, of course." Answers one.

"Would you show me your modifications on the van? It might help Toby, though I doubt it, but it will ease my reservations."

"Yes, Father, we would like to show you our work so you may be proud of us." Two says.

The rest snicker.

269

"Then lead the way, the second son." Stevens follows the two out the door.

Toby paces agitated.

Fin steps in his path. "Take a minute and see the mayor. Distract that brain for a moment and get the mayor done. Okay?"

"I'm really not in the mood. When does that matter? Lead the way. Keep watch on his eyes. If he starts fogging up, step in his line of sight. If he falls into the daze, I may leave him there until tomorrow."

Fin chuckles. "Not a lot of confidence in Dr. Ingrid?"

Toby snorts. "No human contact except on procedures. I'm sure she's horrified by all her dead. I know I'm being harsh. The code of the doctor is to do no harm. That doesn't just mean I don't beat your patience. Okay, I'm on the cusp of causing a scene. Must be getting sober. Are you still watering Jillian, or should I get ready to run?"

Fin laughs. "Fully watered, working on flooding. We understand you can't handle the Tigris right now."

"Thank you, Fin, for everything."

"Yes, yes. I know you mean it. I know your emotions are charged. I know I'm a release valve for you. I also know you have to express this. If only we could figure out a way to express your feelings without me having to hear it all the time. You're welcome forever and always. My parts are done. What about yours?"

"My thanks, forever and always." Toby laughs.

"Good. I accept, so you will never say it again. We are friends. I'm grateful for you. You are grateful to me. We are friends, period." Fin turns to the man in the three-piece suit. "Mayor Sheffield, this is Toby Robbins. Toby, this is the Mayor of South County, Roger Sheffield."

"Ah, it's a pleasure to make your acquaintance, your Eminence. A finer city I haven't found since I am well-traveled, I am a good judge."

"Thank you, Toby, not everyone recognizes this gem."

270

"Yes, well, I have a refined eye."

"I'm sure they see a lot."

"Yes, your Eminence, I see you have your son with you. It's Matthew Sheffield, isn't it?"

The mayor's son smiles at him, warm and friendly. "Yes, sir, thank you for pulling me out."

"Fin, I'm starting to see." He focuses on Matt. "Matt, no thanks necessary. We are here for each other. In the future, at some point, you will need some help. I will help you as you need tonight. No thanks needed." He smiles and pats him on the shoulder. "And it's Toby. Just think of me as a good brother."

"Okay, Toby. But I'm hoping I'll be able to fix my problems with an unlimited mind."

Toby chuckles. "Ah, you are already reducing the problem to a question. Just keep your head, and it will work itself out fine. But sometimes we need help. The wise man realizes this and acts quickly to get the help he needs to solve the problem."

"Like Wesley and Rick?"

"Yes, exactly; I'm not as handy with a computer as Stevens. He's a key player in bringing Wesley and Rick out as far as we did. Without his help, I have no way of knowing where Rick and Wesley would be. Possibly dead since it was touch and go. I knew I needed help, so I asked and received exactly what I was looking for."

"You are a very fascinating man."

"That is kind of kind of you, Matt." Toby looks at the mayor. "You have a fine son, your Eminence. You should be proud." Toby looks closer at him. Not quite gone, but sliding. "Fin, you aren't watching. Step in front of me and sting the skin. Stevens slapped Dr. Ingrid's hand. Well, not a good example; he smiled at her, and she almost had a heart attack. Where is Dr. Ingrid? She should witness this." Toby looked around and saw her at the bar.

Fin steps in front of Toby and slaps mayor's hand.

Toby slumps off, stopping behind the doctors. "If you want to witness the slide into the daze, look to the mayor, back and to your left."

Dr. Paulson looked over and saw Fin slapping the mayor's hand. "What is Fin doing?"

"Trying to stop the slide." Toby shakes his head. "This is really tiresome, doc. I'm just plain tired. All I did was say hello and have a nice conversation with his son." Toby looks back and sees the stillness of the son. "Crap. Matt slid back. I warned them. Go, Dr. Ingrid, whisper a secret into that young man standing next to the suit, the mayor. It will give you irrefutable proof that, yes, they hear. Please don't look at me. I need a short break. I will be back. Dr. Paulson, please go see if we lost the mayor, too. Finn is going to damage him if he continues." Toby turns and slumps away towards the door.

Outside was quiet and peaceful. He sees Stevens by the van. He waves at him, crossing into the park. He heads to the oak and lies down in the fragrant lush grass. He closes his eyes, setting his internal alarm for 10 minutes. He needs this respite and recharge.

He melts through the soil to rest in the fingers of the roots. The plug-in and he is one with this beautiful oak.

While floating, he wonders if he, Noah, was a Mesmer or if it was just Toby. Did Toby need a vacation? He did. Would this night never end?

He needs a break from the weird reaction to him. Could it be just this town? Magnifying some attribute he had in abundance to overwhelm the masses? This made no sense. He wasn't doing anything special, just talking.

Oh, wise oak, can you clue me in on what I'm doing that affects all these people?

He drifted, keeping his mind clear. Hoping for an answer but not expecting one, open to receive but not disappointed when he did not.

Life was.

He drifted up through the rich soil. And laid there, awake and aware. After a few minutes, he says, "So, you were saying it's not me. I said it was. You came, I dazed you, you saw. I only talked to the doctor for a moment, and she was headed down, but we got her back. The mayor wanted to speak with me. I told Fin, I'm not in the mood. I said only a few words with him, a stilted conversation. I talk to Matt, the mayor's son, and an odd. I turned to the mayor, and there he was sliding down. I go tell Ingrid, go look. I look back and see the son slide back full daze. I talked to him not five minutes. So, you tell me it's not me."

Stevens laughs. "It's definitely you."

"Jeez, thanks for that. What's starting to freak me out? Is it Toby or Noah? If I'm doing it, how? Can I control it? When will this night end? Is it all this night only? Or..."

"Or have a drink." Stevens holds out a bottle over his mouth.

Noah opens his mouth and keeps gulping down as Stevens pours.

"Planning on taking it all?" He stops pouring. He lifts it to his lips and takes a deep swallow. "Fascinating really, it could be the paradox."

"How?"

"Toby is very similar to Noah in many ways. Maybe your illusion is fading. I noticed how graceful you are all hunched. Your body movements, effortless fluid control. Your voice is annoying and obnoxious, but your words flow beautifully and earnestly; lyrically. Of course, those magnified eyes may have a strong running. When we were about to take the picture, you stared at me. Your eyes sort of swirled one way and then the other, back and forth. My insides started untwisting, unknotting; it forced me deeper, for deeper realizations, deeper understanding. For me, it was all good. But with those eyes, wow, a real show-stopper. I've been wondering: how can you see?"

Noah snorts. "Contacts. I usually take Toby off right after whatever temp job I take. I'm really a mess right now. My back is killing me, my eyes burn, drunk but not drunk. I put away enough food tonight to feed the local football team with boosters. I've consumed close to a case of whiskey, and I'm horny. Other than that, I'm great."

"Yeah, I get that, except for the people falling into the daze any time you get near."

"Yeah, except for that."

"And except for the two, you couldn't get back and feel heaping amounts of responsibility for because if you weren't here, they wouldn't have died because the success rate was pitiful."

"Yeah, except for that."

"And except that you are going to send those two men with Ingrid because we give her a chance."

"Yeah, except for that."

"And except you will go back in there and awaken the mayor and his son because you can't leave them there."

"Yeah, except for that."

"And except for feeling like you're spinning out of control and about to implode, or worse, shatter. Then the people will say look at all the pretty pieces."

"Yeah, except for that. Is it showing that much?"

"Only for those with the eyes to see. Not many do. My guess would be Finn, Amethyst, and Jillian. The inner circle, so to speak."

"Yes, well, I guess I should go back and wake up the mayor and son. I warned the odd, maybe I should leave them for tomorrow."

"You won't. You just made son and father closer, and possibly a good example for Dr. Ingrid at something to think about."

"She has plenty to think about, but I do hope she will rethink her medicine. I am very concerned for Wesley and Rick."

"Yes, we all realize that. As are the rest of us. So, is Dr. N.S. Robinson going to take an interest in this case?"

Noah laughs. "I don't know if telling you was a good idea or not. Yes, Toby will be sending Dr. Robinson for a consult. Not that he doesn't trust Dr. Ingrid, but..."

274

"Toby is not very trusting."

"No, not so much." Noah springs to his feet and stretches his entire body. He walks upright until the deep shadow at the entrance to the park, then hunches and slumps across the street to the pub.

Stevens sighs. "I just watched Noah turn into Toby before my eyes." He shakes his head. "Wow, my friend, it is truly a wondrous thing you can do."

Toby snorts. "My doing that doesn't bother you? You really did find many things in the daze."

"Yes, I'll tell you one day of my experience, very different from the average odd."

"I noticed your eyes were different. I will look forward to the telling."

"Good. Now get in there champ; release those two plus odd, get Dr. Ingrid to pay attention to the important information, load Wesley and Rick and the four into the van. Then we can call it a night. I'm crashing at your place."

"I didn't expect anything else." Toby opens the door. "The list is shorter, at least."

"That's right, look on the bright side." Stevens steps in. "Nice reset on the van, your design?"

"No, Lars Wilson, he's not just good for houses." He holds the door for Stevens.

"Yes, give credit where it's due." Stevens snorts. "I sure hope Wesley and Rick recover quickly so you can step out." He steps in, looking back at Toby.

"I hear you, my friend. Dr. Robinson will work towards that end. Maybe I will warn the good Dr. Ingrid to expect him." Toby follows, stepping into the pub.

"Tell her now and less complications later," Stevens says over his shoulder and stops short. "Now, this can't be good." He steps aside so Toby can see.

A crowd forms around the center grouping. The mood is not entirely friendly.

CHAPTER THIRTY-FIVE

"What's going on?" Toby whines, stepping closer.

From the outer edge, a man turns to him. "One of those white coats, he started getting nasty, running off at the mouth. The oddities took exception to the abuse, so they subdued him. The other three decided they didn't like that, then a brawl, really. The oddities hold the floor. Ms. Doctor is fit to be tied. Mad as a hornet. Mad at everyone. You, especially."

"Me? What did I do?" Toby whines in shock.

"Those white coats bad-mouthing you, that's what started it."

Toby sighs. "List just got longer." He taps the next man on the shoulder, which starts a chain reaction. A path leads to the center, where Dr. Ingrid paces back and forth. Toby sighs and then takes a bracing breath. "Bring it on; I think I'm ready for a fight. Let's see what happens. No more warnings." Toby clears his throat. "Would you care to explain to me, Lady Ingrid, why the good people of South County thought it necessary to subdue your orderlies?"

Dr. Ingrid turned sharply to him. "You!"

"Yes, me, Lady Ingrid, what about me do you wish to discuss?" Toby slumps up to her and looks deeply into her eyes.

"You caused this!" She points behind her and they see behind her all four orderlies twisted in the ropes of the ring, their jackets twined around their arms.

"How did I cause this? I stepped out for only 13 minutes. I didn't know there was trouble until I returned. Could you please explain the events leading up to this situation, Lady Ingrid? You have me at a disadvantage since you were present during this societal breakdown." Calmly, Toby looks at her agitation. Could this be caused by fear? "Please, Lady Ingrid, let us calmly discuss what happened."

"You did something to these people. All of them." She accuses.

"Yes, we discussed this when you arrived. I warned you that you shouldn't watch me. I told your orderlies to face the door to ensure they, too, would not be caught in the daze. That doesn't tell me what transpired to end with your orderlies bound, and these good folk felt it necessary to restrain them." He looks around the surrounding crowd, definitely unfriendly. "Please, lady, tell me." He looks back at her.

"They threatened us." She grudgingly exclaims.

"Why? These people are unique in that they take their confrontations to the ring. You see, they even put your men in the ring. Something was said or done to start this downward slide to anarchy. We cannot put things to right until we discover the cause." Toby watches her fidget. "Do you know and don't want to say, or are you in the dark as to the cause of this?"

She turned defiantly and stared at him, confronting her fear. "Honestly, I don't want to say." She looks away quickly.

"Are you afraid of my reaction?" Toby asks Ingrid, amazed. "Do you see me as some tyrant?"

The crowd chuckles.

She twitches. "This is unnerving." She confronts him again. "I don't know what to think of you, but you have a strong influence here. These people could do serious damage to us because you wish it or to protect you."

Toby slumps unthreateningly up to the ropes, noting none were injured and all had blindfolds. "I imagine it is unnerving, stepping into unfamiliar territory and not finding what you expect. Every time you think you now have your feet under you solid, your balance is questioned and you stumble a bit to regain your feet. With the only real desire to stride out the door and keep walking briskly, yes? Stepping through the rabbit hole? The Twilight Zone? Do any of these accurately express your state of mind?"

She deflates with a sigh. "Yes, exactly."

Toby nods gently, smiling. "You know what I did this morning?" He waits for her response.

278

"No, what?" She asked softly

"I went to work at the county offices. I'm a Professional Temp. That man over there was my boss today. Give a wave, Philip. I didn't know a soul in this town prior to this morning. I met some wonderful people today. But it was a job. I meet wonderful people all the time in different cities and different jobs. That's all, job done, clock out, and head to where I stay while in town. In all the years I've worked as a temp that never changed, until today, here in this town." He looked out at the crowd and smiled gently. "Lady Ingrid, take a quick look at me. Then ask yourself if a temp, looking like me, came and worked at your place of work for a day, would you ask me to join you after work for a drink and conversation?"

Her head pops up. She looks sadly and shakes her head. "No, I wouldn't."

"Thank you for your honesty. That really shows your quality, to be honest, regardless of the consequences." Toby smiles proudly at her. "Well, it did happen to me today, in this town, at this pub when I walked in the door. They cheered and greeted me warmly, accepting me instantly. Their response to me was to enfold me in a warm embrace of family returned. That was my first impression of this group of wonderful people.

I had moments of the unreality of the situation, but the fun and communion with people I liked, who returned the sentiment, overshadowed that approach to the deep dark rabbit hole." Toby paces in front of the men in white coats wrapped in the ropes of the ring. "From the moment I stepped through that door, what, at 5:15 PM on Friday, until 3 ½ hours later, I felt like an actor in a play. We had an audience, and they were involved with us at our table. I wasn't offended, flattered, really, and unnerved because of so many eyes on me. They were betting on my actions honestly, it was all in good humor. No nastiness until a man confronted one of the ladies from my table. I stepped in, as I believe right, especially since I brought her in, my right and responsibility as a gentleman. He offered a challenge. I accepted. Here in South County, I learned that they take a dispute and turn it into an event. There are judges…" Toby waves in one direction.

The crowd separates to show Dr. Ingrid the three judges.

279

"… An official timekeeper…" Again, he waves, and he is shown. "… Live radio coverage with the two favorite local celebrities…" He waves again.

The group opens to frame Wesley and Rick.

"… A doctor on hand…"

Dr. Paulson steps out of the crowd.

"… EMS on standby…"

Charles and Zach step out of the crowd to either side of Dr. Paulson.

"… And a referee in the ring, to keep the rules and to stop the match if it became life-threatening." He waves to O'Malley behind the bar.

O'Malley waves as the crowd opens to highlight him.

At each introduction, Dr. Ingrid nods her head and follows Toby's directions.

"The ring was lowered and secured. A nifty bit of engineering, absolutely marvelous. The proper people were called and arrived for a regular occurrence here. They are very straightforward; no rumors are allowed to hold here in South County. They are an above-average community. If a fight is going to happen, let it be witnessed and judged by the community. That is another unique quality not found in many places in the world. So the stage was set, the contenders signed legal waivers, and the rules were explained. For each confrontation, I found out, to ensure everyone is playing by the same rules." Toby pauses, slumping, and looks at the ring. "It was time to enter; I caught my foot on the rope and stumbled in. I will admit now it was on purpose. Misdirection and your opponent's ego are your best weapons in your arsenal." Toby snorts, remembering Jackson's reaction.

The crowd chuckles and snickers as they, too, remember.

Toby smiles. "Then we waited and waited. The doctor and a judge were caught in traffic, but finally, they arrived. The bell rang, and the match started. Jackson, the other fighter…" Toby notices that she is looking around. "… who is currently residing in the hospital, jumped up and ran to the middle. One of the rules of the ring is that we must fight with everything the same as at the time of the challenge, minus keys, knives, guns, etc. I was told a touch constitutes a point. So I got out my Big Blue marker and proceeded to touch Jackson, leaving a record of my passage. That enraged him, of course, as intended, and came at me. I slapped him as I spun around, back hand, open hand, and caught myself by planting my foot on his.

He went to walk it off. I warned him I dropped my marker and cap, and to watch his step. He was too mad to listen and fell. He found my marker. The cap was still missing until he rolled over; it was embedded in his bottom. He had landed on it; his weight drove it into his flesh, cutting through two layers of denim and one of cotton." Toby looked at all the smiling faces and smiled back. "That was the first hint I was deep in Wonderland. The referee didn't do anything. The crowd was unusually quiet. Wesley and Rick were silent. The rounds were set at five minutes, but no bell.

At that point, we were past. This being my first time in this type of venue, I shrugged it off and picked Jackson up." Toby turns to Dr. Ingrid.

She's watching him avidly.

"I'm telling you this so you know what is happening is not normal for anyone here. We shared an impossible event." He turns away and moves off at his slumping pace. "When I had enough, Jackson was seriously hurt, caused by his own actions. More than 15 minutes of the entire match passed. I really took stock of my surroundings.

Everywhere I looked, these people watched me, still as statues. No restless crowd sounds and no sound except Jackson's heavy breathing in dealing with his pain. I was virtually alone, surrounded by staring people." He turns and looks directly into her eyes. "You think this is unnerving?" He steps closer to her. "Try 200 people you have good feelings for turn from laughing, animated, warm humans to silent and lifeless cold dolls except for the eyes. The eyes were truly creepy. It was like watching someone trapped and dying. I couldn't help seeing a small image of themselves pressed up onto

281

the lens of their eyes, pounding to get out and seeing the rising waters of hopelessness creep higher and higher." Toby rubs his neck.

"So there I was, standing in the ring. The referee was a frozen, lifeless wild-eyed man I enjoyed talking with. There was Jackson, silent in pain, bleeding on the mat. Nothing life-threatening, but it needed to be seen too. And all the rest was watching; hungry, desperate, wild.

I seriously questioned my reality, time, and alternate realities. I talked. No one responded. Finally, I paged Dr. Paulson quite loudly, firmly and insistent. Over and over, and there he walks into the ring. You can't understand the scope of my relief that someone was active with me in this experience. It was overwhelming. But it also told me that by calling the good doctor, he woke up.

Hope at last, I went to get the medical kits so the doctor could help Jackson.

I passed O'Malley, flicking him hard between the eyes, and he woke up. He followed me to the EMS techs. I repeated the action to both of them and watched them wake. I took their kits, told O'Malley to follow up with the EMS techs, and huffed it back to the doctor and Jackson. Dr. Paulson was sitting next to Jackson, staring at him. I opened the kits to get to work, having temp jobs with a hospital; I knew what needed to be done. I noticed the doctor was moving slowly but I really didn't understand what that meant. I was seriously startled when I looked up, and there they were, all back in the daze, staring but moved.

O'Malley, Charles, and Zach were standing over us, the doctor sitting, all staring. Flashes of horror scenes played in my head. It really unsettled me, but I was doing a job, so I finished it. I decided I would deal with those four after I had settled Jackson. That was unnerving, having them standing over me, my back to them, and not knowing what they would or could do." Toby turns and sees a glass traveling from hand to hand to his. He drinks deeply and returns it to the hand that gave it with the nod. "So I went to the doctor and attempted to talk to him, no response. I paged him againand got through. He moved. He talked. He was sluggish and slow.

I needed to shock them back awake. I went to get ice water, saw Fin and tested my theory on him. It was a success. And he hasn't slid back. That sealed it for me, so with Fin's help and a lot of paranoia, I got both EMS techs out to the ambulance, woke them, had Fin get them thinking, questioning, and reasoning again, and got Jackson to the ambulance. Unfortunately, I lost the doctor again en route, and I had to give him the treatment. I had Fin talk to them to make absolutely sure that all were fit to drive away." Toby turns and slumps up to her and looks deeply into her eyes.

She leans back and blinks.

He nods. "Please, don't take offense; I'm just checking your condition. You can't take much more exposure." He turns away, slumping along. Toby looks at the crowd. "Check your neighbors. If anyone else has FUDDA, line them up with the mayor's son. I'll wake them, as you probably knew I would."

The oddities laugh with a couple of "yes" thrown out.

Toby snorts and shakes his head. "I later realized that the doctor was not fully extracted from the daze until he was about to leave. That's why he kept falling back in, same with the others. We have been FUDDA-free for a few hours." Toby turns and accepts another glass. He takes a deep swallow and slumps on, taking it with him.

"Now it's just me and Fin and most of 200 people. I had to wake them. If their experience was as nerve-racking as mine, I had to if I was able. I could not leave a soul in that tenuous void of loneliness with hope draining away every moment. But I also needed to get some personal support. I was still in a dangerous state. Fin actually inadvertently shifted my attitude by setting in motion the ping-pong problem which gave me the medicine I really needed. Laughter, deep, rich belly laughs came from my soul at this utterly ridiculous situation I found myself in.

That laughter animated half of this crowd and mobbed me, which, at the time, I found extremely funny. I later found out that all these people were chilling in relation to their state of mind; their hopeless state. My laughter warmed them to the bone. I didn't know laughter was so powerful to give hope to the hopeless. But after I figured it out, I told everyone to laugh. It helps them come back into themselves faster.

I got my support group to assist me in waking those you see here. We were two-thirds done when, as we told you earlier, Wesley and Rick's condition came to light." He turns, finishes his drink, handing it off looking at Wesley and Rick. "I will be sending a Dr. Robinson to you for a consult on Rick and Wesley. Honestly, I trust Dr. Robinson with the delicate work around their heads. No one else would I trust." Toby had stopped in front of Dr. Ingrid and waited, staring at her until she looked away.

"Alright, I'll tell my staff to expect him." Dr. Ingrid says.

"Good. You will also be taking the four hands. They will ensure the safety and comfort of Wesley and Rick. One of them will be on hand at all times. Please assist them in finding lodging as close as possible to your facility. They know what can and cannot happen with Rick and Wesley. If any of these cannot happen, you will get a visit from Stevens and our friend Noah. He is about as big, though not nearly as friendly, especially when friends are abused. This is not a threat but a guarantee, cause and effect. Rick and Wesley were promised muscle if needed. The hands will ensure all parties are happy. We all want Wesley and Rick fully back in control of their bodies, so we work together towards that goal. If anyone tries to hinder that goal through negligence, stupidity, or ignorance, we'll have a problem. The muscles will be sent. We will have a tense time on our hands. They ruffle easy, and the only way to smooth them is through confrontation." Toby looked over at Rick and Wesley. "We will have them mobile shortly; I'm going to work on that next.

I was waiting for you to come to grips with your situation, but you've had all the time I can spare. Their satellite van is at the curb, now refurbished for their current needs. The hands will transport them on all legs of your journey. You can stay in contact with Rick and Wesley with your radio and a call to the radio station. If you travel outside their range, the radio station is broadcasting them on the Internet. The hands have the information. They will stay on-air until you come up with their route to recovery. We have a receiver on order and will arrive at some point, then they will free up the station and be totally mobile and enclosed broadcasting. When the receiver arrives, I will arrive." Toby turns and looks at Dr. Ingrid. "Do you understand why I told you our experience?" Toby waited and watched.

Dr. Ingrid fidgets and looks around, "I guess you wanted to impress the point of power you wield."

Toby shakes his head.

The oddities groan.

"You missed the entire point with your fear. Wake up!" He claps his hands together in front of her face. It cracks like lightning.

Ingrid jumps.

"I did not do anything in particular. I did not chant an incantation. I did not have strobe lights. I stood in a ring and interacted with another man. I was unaware of their condition until later. I'm trying to impress you that I, and this group experienced a seriously strong bonding; they, on the road to death, witnessed and rescuer. I saved every wonderful beautiful soul in this room, so they continue their experience of this life. I am their Savior. They are my rescue. Now bonded, we protect each other.

My entire tale was to impress on you; I do not wield the power here. They do. I am one man, they are 200. I hold a special position with them, but I am not their leader. If anyone is the leader of this group, it's O'Malley. It's his pub.

What you may have mistakenly labeled leader was director or manager. In this situation, I know the most because I did the work. I need help, and help arrives because we, the 200, are working towards one goal: to get all back hail and hardy." Toby turns away, annoyed. Dense woman, Ugh! He paces away, hands patted his shoulder consolingly. Some rub his back. A few fists hammer down without much power. That heartens him. He turns back to her. "Did you see that, Dr. Ingrid? I'm frustrated by your denseness and they console me with human touch. I interpreted their emotions by their actions; there was a: Buck up, Hang in there, We know you're trying, We know your heart, You're a good boy."

As he calls them out, chuckles and gasps follow the line of touches. Then, all laugh together.

"What just happened is me being me. I pay attention to everything; each touch is like a whisper in my ear. When someone shouts at you and grabs your wrist tight, are they conveying anything caring or gentle?"

"No, aggressive, hostile, hurtful." Dr. Ingrid answers competently.

"Good, you understand that." Toby winks at the oddities. "When the confrontation happened, how were your men handled?"

They smiled back.

"Carefully, five people to a man, four on the limbs, one holding the waist. Along the way, blindfolds were tied on." She says grudgingly.

"As a doctor of human behavior, by their actions, what would you label their intentions?"

"Restraint, containment, no harm intended."

"Why do you suppose the blindfolds were used?"

"Light deprivation, a control mechanism."

"An answer like that says a lot about you and your practice. I will contact you to review your therapy schedule for Rick and Wesley." Toby turns to the group. "Would anyone like to tell the doctor and orderlies why blindfolds were used?"

An older woman, grandmother probably, steps out of the group. "We're protecting them so they do not fall into the daze. It's a slippery slope. You don't realize you're on the slope until it's too late. Now panic has jumped on you. The panic shows you're powerless to do anything but witness your world. Powerless, you only have flitting thoughts because panic still rides you. Those thoughts are focused on your powerless panic. Round and round it goes, draining away hope. Then you have your powerless, hopeless, panic and thoughts of being trapped forever or trapped to death. We don't want anyone else to experience it without some warning. We didn't realize we were trapped until Toby started to look around with a concerned expression. Then he started in about lost time and reality, which really didn't make much sense to me, but I could tell he was very upset. I remember focusing on a friend facing me and thinking she looked wrong, too, still. And with that thought, the slide started, very terrifying." She shakes her head. "No, we don't want that for anyone. If you want to experience it, go for it. Not knowing, no. Irving is the only one who had a good experience in the daze, but Toby said it was because he was hopeless to begin with. I will say this: I'm glad I went through it. It taught me many things about myself that I never even considered. I'm a better person for having the experience, but the plunge into cold hopelessness is a real eye-opener."

"Thank you for that explanation,..." Toby looks at her curiously.

"Margaret." She smiles and pats his cheek.

"Margaret." He leaned down and gently enfolded her in his arms. "You are precious, Margaret, more than you realize." He released her, smiling softly.

She smiles back wiping her eyes, slipping back into the crowd, enfolding her in its warm embrace. Margaret receives many soft, gentle caresses.

Toby turns back to Dr. Ingrid and watches.

She watches Margaret get lost in the crowd. She had a thoughtful look. "One of them made a derogatory remark about you." She admits.

"Was it only about me?" He asked seriously.

"Primarily." She answers helplessly.

"Which one? In this town, it's out in the open and head-on. It's only right I hear what came from his own lips, what he said about me." He looks over at the crowd. "It seems that it was the group goal. The other three were only trying to defend one of their own. I believe they are restrained so they won't cause problems, not understanding the customs." He turns to the group. "Could whoever packaged the three release them, please? Be kind. You unknowingly terrified them. Orderlies from a psych hospital fear being restrained and deprived of sensory experience because they are expected to do it to others. Dr. Ingrid, I would beseech you to reevaluate such practices. As a rule, it's cruel. Or at least experience it yourself personally, so you know exactly what you prescribe others. I do believe the Hippocratic Oath mentions do no harm. By your own reaction to what these orderlies experienced, you took it as harm. No harm was intended, as I'm sure when you or others prescribed the practice, you meant only to help. But intentions are not in direct relation to the experience. States of mind, like attitude, colors every experience. Your state of mind and attitude since you walked in has been challenging. I imagine walking into a crowded pub with everyone pointing and laughing puts you on your guard, and you make snap decisions and judgments. Would you hear why everyone was laughing when you entered and then tell me if it matched with your snap judgment?"

"Yes, all right." She watches Toby curiously.

"Earlier, I had told Wesley and Rick that men in white coats would come that take them away. Everyone heard. They laughed because men in white coats showed up to take them away." Toby smiled and nodded.

"Not a match, completely off the board." She shakes her head.

"Let me caution you when dealing with people, learn to read their actions, not by your definitions, but theirs. Each action is like a word. A series of words strung together, a sentence. A series of sentences strung together, a paragraph. Each action has context, like each word used in the English language. Words change meanings depending on the context or the words around them. If you pay attention and learn the definitions and contexts, you will get a story unfolding before your eyes without a word passing the lips. Once you are able to define other people, you will become more effective.

You will be able to note, for instance, that man…" He points to the white coat on the left. "… stopped smoking about three days ago, doesn't like crowds of people enclosed, and has an old improperly treated right knee injury. The man in the middle has an infant in the house, working two jobs, and his feet are killing him. But what should you expect wearing a half size too small. The man on the right is seriously afraid of me, though I intend him no harm. His left shoulder was recently dislocated, but he has refused to wear the sling. Probably because he has to work, his fear of being poor won't let him rest, even at the cost of his health. He has a bug bite on his left thigh." He turns back to Dr. Ingrid.

Looking amazed, she turns to the white coats. "Well?"

They nod down the row. "Exactly." The one afraid of him had to express.

She turns back to Toby. "How… did you do that?"

"I just told you." Toby shrugs. "All actions originate in the brain as a command. Each command has a destination; it's fired to the receptor. You told me that. That bit of electricity zips down the line to its final destination at the end of the line, the command turns into action. There are two types of action: conscious, and unconscious. Conscious is short-term or worrisome. Unconscious is established; a habit, or clinical phobia." Toby looks over his shoulder at the man still on the ropes. "That one is a bully to the weak, physically abusive as well as verbally. He's abusing prescription drugs; my guess would be the psychotropic. And he's wanted by the police in this state."

"What?" An off-duty policeman asks for the crowd. He starts moving toward the ring.

"How could you know that?" Dr. Ingrid stares in shock.

"Well, look at him." Toby steps over beside Ingrid, holding out his hand, indicating what he's seeing. Even with the blindfold on you can see his eyes are all over the place; paranoia, or of course, he could be tripping. Look at his hands: old scars, fresh scabs and old. Suppose I don't miss my guess, different scratch marks and at least two different bites that look like women's teeth. I'd check your patience, and see if he's been taking liberties. You can't ask the women because bullies threaten pain for talking. He has extremely low self-esteem but is a wanted man."

She shakes her head. "How could you know that by looking at him?"

Toby snorts. "His picture is on a wanted poster at the county offices. How else would you expect me to identify a wanted man if I didn't look?"

The crowd laughs.

289

Toby feels Ingrid tense up beside him. "Dear lady, please don't get upset. I'm trying to help you understand and deal with this unusual set of circumstances. I mean no disrespect to you, your practice, your profession, or your integrity. I am trying to ensure the best possible care for my two friends, Wesley and Rick. If what I tell you sink in to consider later, wonderful. You will be the best in your field over all the others. If you can take away only some, then so be it. I am trying to share with you what I have observed to be factual. It's hard to take such information from me, a professional temp. But I believe once you leave, your guard is down, and you are seeing your patience, you will see the truth I am speaking of. I am not looking for accolades or special notes. I have enough on my plate. I want the best caregiver to assist Rick and Wesley back from the inner void." Toby turns away to the off-duty police officer. "I believe his name was listed as Art Franks."

Dr. Ingrid gasps, looking over at the other three.

They were shaking their head and shrugging their shoulders.

The police officer steps over to Dr. Ingrid and asks, "Is that his name, ma'am?"

She wipes her face. "Yes." She looks over at Toby. "Seriously? How is this possible?"

Toby snorts, watching the officer pull the Art Franks from the ropes of the ring. "Two questions I've asked myself repeatedly tonight. You're making progress. Let's move out of the good officer's way." Toby places a hand on her lower back and leads her away.

A few snickers from the oddities that note the significance of his hand placement: working the Doll in a Daze.

"Now, would you like a moment or jump right in?" Toby asked the doctor. "Fin, is it prepared?" He stopped by four people lined up. "You take a moment and watch. I'll jump right in. First, look at their eyes. Look deep and open yourself to feel the impressions you get. Remember, the brain is both transmitter and receiver. Signals are always flying around. Tune in if you can. Let's start with the man in the three-piece suit. This is his first experience, though he had foreknowledge. That doesn't really help. You forget before you realize you're caught."

She steps over and looks into the mayor's eyes. She pulls back quickly and shudders, looking away.

"He's been in about 35 minutes. In the Daze and the void, time ceases to be except in relation to your hopelessness." Toby moves down the line. "I'll be right with you, Mayor. Don't fret, you'll be out soon." He touches his hands to his skin and turns him with this light touch to his shoulder. "Matt, this is Dr. Ingrid. She's going to take Wesley and Rick away. Will you listen to her and remember, then tell her what she said before she goes? Thank you, Matt." Toby rubs Matt's arms, skin to skin. "Look in his eyes. Can you see the difference?"

She looked but wasn't repelled by anything. "They look alive, calm, confident."

Toby nods. "I'll be back, Matt. I want to show her two more. Then I'll pull you out. You're doing great." He turns him to face his father's back.

The last two were also calm, confident, and alive.

He turns them to form the end of the line.

"Why is the first one so different?" She asked.

"Because he hasn't experienced it before. When you don't panic, you can have a wonderful experience. Talk to Stevens, his experience made his eyes glow more than when he smiles. Okay, folks, here we go. Fin, are you ready?"

Fin laughed, stepping up next to Toby. "Sidekicks are always ready."

Toby snorts. "All right, G. Friday. Here you go." He walked to stand next to the head of the line." "Dr. Ingrid, please stand behind me all the way. Once one has been in the daze, it's harder to extract them. The mayor will be the easiest. The others will need a little more force. Oddities, we need four escorts ready to take charge of the odd ones." Toby smiles out at the crowd, who watched avidly smiling back. Four people step out and line up, ready to guide their charges. Fin stands across from him a few steps ahead, a bucket of ice water in one hand, dripping wet rag in the other.

Toby scans the area and nods; all are ready. He takes the mayor's hand and squeezes it. "All is ready, your Eminence. I do apologize for the wait, sir, other problems needed my attention. Now, here's what's going to happen: you will feel a sharp sting between your eyes, your eyes will water, and you will have a small pain in that region. You will be disoriented and foggy-headed. Nothing to worry about. Your Eminence and disorientation will fade, your head will clear, and your memory will return. It's time, sir." Toby flicked the mayor between the eyes hard and started to whistle a moderately paced tune. With a slight pressure on the mayor's back, the line starts forward.

The mayor's eyes blink when Finn sloshes his face and neck with the icy cold soaking bar rag. His hand comes up and steps forward, rubbing between his eyes. One of the judges takes his arm and guides him into the group. Hands reach out, touching and stroking as he passes.

Toby flicks Matt harder between his eyes and sends him on to flick the last two. He watches and whistles until the last one gets enfolded into the group. Toby turns to Dr. Ingrid. "Now, are you ready to see the science behind the bridge to the inner mind?"

Dr. Ingrid stares at the crowd an amazed expression on her face, a stillness to her body.

Toby steps closer and looks into her eyes. She seems a bit hazy but not gone. He reaches over and takes the rag from Finn's hand and squeezes it out, then places it on her face.

Dr. Ingrid's head suddenly jerks back, unconsciously taking a step back.

Toby tosses the rag to Fin and looks deep into her eyes. "Good, fully conscious. You were sinking into the daze. Glad we caught it before you fully submerged. It really is a bother watching everyone closer than ever before, devising ways to counteract the descent into the daze. But as Margaret stated, I, too, wouldn't wish anyone to experience it without their consent. Since you haven't consented, I couldn't, in good conscience, allow it to happen." Toby turns away, looking at the room at large and all within. "Even now, I think you would benefit greatly from the experience, but that's not my call. So, vigilantly, I watch you because you refuse to follow wise advice for your own safety. Even boldly, you watched me, a countermeasure for the fear you cling to. A fear I don't rightly understand." Toby stands silently and waits for her to fill the silence.

"I fear you." She says softly.

"Why? Have I done anything threatening to you or to your orderlies?"

"No, you haven't done anything threatening per se. It's more of an impression, a feeling of great power, of the overwhelming will of character."

"You fear me because I have self-confidence?" Toby snorts and shakes his head, shocked. "Really?"

"Your self-confidence is more overwhelming than anything else. It highlights what others lack, a yardstick that measures how far below the mark we stand." She says carefully.

"You do yourself a disservice, Lady Ingrid. Self-confidence is all internal. You fear me because you doubt yourself. I know my strengths and weaknesses and I work with an honest heart. I am no better than anyone else. We all start with the same potential. It's what we choose to do or be that defines us from others." Toby rubs his neck, bone weary.

"We don't always get to choose what happens to us." She says defensively.

"You are correct, but we choose our actions or reactions and our attitude." He turns and looks at her. "Listen, Lady Ingrid. I understand terrible things happen to innocent, unsuspecting good people. Things that should never be allowed to happen all the time. That's life.

We are members of the animal kingdom, and we live in the wilds of a society of animals. If you expect animals to be sedated all the time, you are delusional. You lie to yourself to keep that pretty sedate picture in your mind as the definition of society and proper human behavior."

She looks mulish. "Why is it wrong to expect people to behave properly?"

"It's not wrong, only naïve. Besides, who are you to define the way an animal behaves? What's proper?" Toby turns to the listening crowd. "Do you tell your cat not to jump, pounce, or slink? Will your cat care or change its behavior because you want it?" He looked back at her. "When zoologists study a type of animal, do they step up and say whether a behavior is right or wrong, proper or improper?"

"No, they just record events and responses, social order, individual and group behavior. But we are not animals in the wild jungle; we are human beings with awareness and a conscious."

"We are animals, warm-blooded mammals, a bipedal primate, a hominid. We have been classified and recorded in the books. We are no better or worse than any other animal. We are arrogant, I grant you, thinking we are better; a delusional fallacy, of course, as is that we are the only ones with awareness and consciousness. Look at the family dog. He is aware and consciously defends his pack, the family." Toby looks away. "Many cities are known as concrete jungles and more dangerous than the green variety. But, we, as beings or spirits, have free will. We have a choice. You choose to do or not do. You choose your attitude. Attitude is the feelings associated with the action." Toby turns and accepts a glass of whiskey, drinks it down, then hands it back. Another was placed in his hand. He took a sip.

"We can't always choose, when someone's will is stronger than another, they have to submit." She looks scared, defeated.

"No, they choose to submit. Will is determination. Determination is a firm or fixed purpose." Toby takes a sip

"What about a life or death situation?" She says that desperately.

"What about a life or death situation? I choose life, my purpose fixed, absolute." Toby takes another sip and looks at her.

"What if a man held a knife to a woman's throat and told you to do a thing against your will?"

Taking a sip, Toby chokes and looks at her.

The crowd chuckles.

She looks pleased to challenge his position.

Toby takes a breath and shakes his head. "Unreal." He snorts. "Funny, you should use that example. I threw my big blue marker at his hand, he dropped the knife, I snatched the girl away, and rendered the man unconscious for a short time."

"What?"

"Yes, quite a coincidence, really, that happened tonight. Isn't that curious? Regardless, I choose life for all parties involved. I had recently retrieved them both from the road to death. I wasn't going to allow either them or me to revisit that path. So, I chose to act. My actions were nonthreatening to keep my adversary ignorant of my intentions. I moved in quickly to throw off his balance and his will. In the end, all parties were unharmed and safe. I choose to act for the good of all and am pleased by my success and actions. My overall attitude to that episode is it happened, but we diffused it. So, no harm, no foul. Life happens."

"What? No harm, no foul? What happened to the man? You let him go?" Highly offended, she grits out. "How could you?"

"Quite easily, actually, he wasn't really dangerous. He was sick and grief stricken from the recent sudden death of his lady before the daze. When first awakened, disorientation and hazy thoughts are common, as well as a spotty memory. John was in the grips of a fever, grief, disorientation, hazy thoughts, and spotty memory. When he woke up after reducing his fever, he was horrified by his actions. The woman involved, Becky, was best friends with John's lady. She, too, was grief-stricken by her loss. She understood John wasn't in his right mind because he wasn't previously a violent person. He requested the opportunity to apologize. We asked her, and she accepted. We escorted her to him, and they talked. As a fact, she accompanied him to the hospital so neither would be alone. In the end, I choose the right actions for the situation and am satisfied with the results."

"But... But... How can you let it go?"

"What would you have had to happen? I chose, knowing he was running a fever, to release him to the care of the group. My hands were busy trying to reverse the frostbite on Wesley and Rick while reducing the dangerously high fever and keeping them alive long enough to figure out how they were different than the other dazed. Then have to pull them out even partially from the effects of the DOA–TX amplifier until you can come save them.

Finish waking the dazed as fast as I could because I realized that as more time passed, these people were cooling. I assume that Wesley and Rick were further along the same path. I had taken one from the group and sequestered him in the men's room. He was my control subject. Now, I know it was cruel and unfeeling, but I was sailing in uncharted waters of a different world. I didn't know what I didn't know, nor what I did know for sure. Remember, I just got to town and didn't know anybody well. I only knew the names of six people out of 200. That man I picked because he was closest to the John was John, fever-ridden, grief-stricken.

After we found Wesley and Rick and administered emergency aid, we looked at John, who also had a fever, and his lower extremities were very cool. Everyone else out in the general group was chilled further down, warmer up top.

My facts at the time, but my actions were not. Given all the same information, I would choose as I did. My attitude is good.

When we found John's condition was worse, he went to the head of the line and awakened. I chose to send him out, with a warning to watch him and give him an aspirin to reduce his fever. If anything odd or unusual went on with him, let me know. I felt doubly responsible, but I couldn't spare any more attention if I could help it. So, I sent him out to his friends and neighbors to care for him. I was still unaware of his history. In fact, I thought we were calling him John because I put him there, in the John."

The crowd chuckles.

"Now, knowing all sides of the situation, what would you have done in my shoes? What would you have done to John after diffusing the situation? You successfully used your marker; the knife is on the ground, the girl is safe, and the man is unconscious. What now?"

296

Toby finishes off his whiskey and passes the glass on, only to be handed another full one. He snorts, nods his head and raises his glass. "My pardon, Lady Ingrid, would you care for a libation?"

"No, thank you." She huffs. "I would send him to jail."

"Why?" Toby takes a drink.

"What do you mean, why?" She looks confused.

"Why would you send John to jail?"

"He was a threat. He was threatening that woman. He could have stabbed or cut her."

"Could have, but didn't. He wasn't really threatening her, and she was his tool. He was threatening the group first. The group wisely chose not to act or acknowledge the threat, thereby neutralizing the situation temporarily, a stalemate. He couldn't act if they didn't acknowledge him. If he chose to act, he would have lost his position of power. He instead waited for one to acknowledge him. That was me. He was threatening me. Fortunately for him, I don't recognize threats. I recognize actions. I knew he had no intention of actually hurting her."

She jumps right in. "How? How could you possibly know what his intentions were?"

"For one thing, he was holding a knife with the arm holding her. Another, it wasn't even pointed at her. If anything, he would stab or cut himself. If his intention was to cause her harm, he would have used both arms, one to hold and restrain her, the other pressing a knife to flesh. Reading his body language told me he was defeated already and in pain, physical and emotional. Since I didn't recognize a threat, and he had no real intention of harm. I don't see the point of wasting time and money on sending a sick man to jail for not committing harm. That seems backward to me, sending a man to jail for not committing a crime." Toby took a sip.

"But he's a threat." Clenching her fist, she accuses.

"To whom?"

"To society." She declares resolutely.

"How?"

"What do you mean, how? He held a knife to a woman and threatened harm."

"And…"

"What do you mean, and?"

"And, what does that situation of not committing a crime have to do with him threatening society? By the way, how does one threaten society?"

"He could do it again because he did it once. He threatens the unity of society, so that could break down."

"Could, could, you could pull a knife out of your pocket and plunge it into my heart because I don't agree with your backward thinking. Should we send you to jail for a possibility?" Toby looked out at the crowd. "You, the oddities, are John's society. Will you disband and go your own ways when John is released from the hospital? Do you believe John's a threat? Do you think John will hold a knife to Becky or any other woman's neck again? Are you satisfied with my actions by sending John to the hospital and not jail? Does anyone think John should go to jail?"

Margaret steps out in front of the crowd. "I guess I'm the odd spokeswoman." She chuckles. "We discussed all this right after it happened while you carried John away. So what I say now is the consensus of the group. But I also agree personally. We believe Toby acted in the best interest of our society. We know John, personally, everyone. We know John won't hurt anyone. We know John's actions tonight were due to the extenuating circumstances. And if he had harmed Becky by accident or intent, we would stand by Becky's decision. She would have been the injured party. If she chose to send him to jail, then we would wait to see what her actions were after he got out. If she was afraid of him, we would ostracize him, pushing him out of our society. No one person can destroy our society here in South County. If one goes bad, we call them out to be replaced by a heartier good one, like Toby, good and hearty, an asset to any society."

"Kind words, Margaret. I accept." Toby grinned, raising his glass in tribute to the group. "I'm glad you thought so since I had already decided this is where I belong."

Oddities cheer.

"Society has spoken, Lady Ingrid." Toby turns to look at her. "Are you satisfied, or are you going to think you know what's best for a society you don't belong to?"

"I believe it's for the good of all societies."

"For the good of all societies, you would send a man to jail for not committing a crime?"

"He threatened her."

"That's not a crime."

"It should be. It's not right what he did."

"It's not wrong either."

"How can you say that? He imposed his will on her." She says impassioned.

"I disagree. She chose to stand there. She could have gotten away easily." Toby rubs his chin, watching her. "What happened here or this society's position, isn't really the issue, is it? This dogged stance is personal. A man threatened you, and you unwillingly chose to submit, destroying your self-esteem and making you feel powerless. Now, instead of confronting your own personal issues, you decide to reshape society at large by ramming your ideas in anyone who will listen and ignore anyone with a different position."

"I didn't choose to submit. I wasn't given a choice." She whispers.

"There are different forms of submission." He watched her closely and saw the shutter and rubbing of her lips. "You were raped." He says it baldly.

Her head shoots up, she stares at him warily and whispers. "How could you even guess that?"

Toby shrugs, sipping from his glass. "Body language, your beliefs, your positions, your emotions; it all boils down to rape when you were young. You shut down during her teen years when everything is black or white, good or bad, up or down. You hadn't reached diagonal thinking. No gray colors your thought process. I

299

think it wasn't a singular event, but reoccurring and abusive by a man in his early 30s, close to the family, and unassuming. I remind you of him, don't I?"

She looks away ashamed and whispers, "Yes."

"It was emotional blackmail with physical pain to hold you silent for continued submission. You probably don't want to hear this, but submit you did, the lesser of the choices offered." Toby looks off in the distance, processing information. "Ah, a younger sister, yes, the younger sister gets it if you don't submit. Your choices are unpalatable: the younger sister, you, or death. With those choices, I believe you made the correct one, though after the fact, I imagine you thought death would have been preferable. But if you chose death, what you endured would have been visited on your younger sister. And that twists in your mind. The guilt for such thoughts, the resentment that you had to endure what she did not, the knowledge that you would revisit that hell for her again willingly to keep her safe, the frustration of accepting her foolhardy actions, the doubt of her love for you because you feel you're damaged."

Finn steps up with a bucket of ice water, dips the rag, rung it out, and hands it to Toby with a nod at the doctor.

Toby turns quickly to Dr. Ingrid.

Her eyes were wide, almost popping out, a sea of emotion. Tears stream down her quivering cheeks. Her skin leached of color, mouth open, lips quivering. She hugs herself, shivers rack her body.

Gently, Toby dabs her sweating brow. "Oh, dear lady, I thoughtlessly disseminated the information my mind collected with no thought to your sensibilities. Lady, please forgive my brutish behavior. I never wanted to cause you harm." Toby hands back the rag and hands her his glass. "Drink this, Lady Ingrid, it will help." He helps her take it to her mouth and tips it, pouring the fiery whiskey in.

She swallows it, then gasps and starts coughing.

"Well, I'm making a muddle of this." He pats her back and than rubs soothingly. "Lady, please breathe. Take a deep breath, and then let it out slowly."

She takes a deep breath and bursts into tears. She lunges at Toby, collapsing against him, her head tucks into her arms, choking his neck.

Toby's arms flung out in surprise. His face is a mask of shock, turns his head to the crowd looking for help.

Staring, their expression matched his.

Fin had his hand over his mouth, convulsing with laughter until the enraged scream of the she-cat echoed the room. Intense fear replaces Fin's humor.

Toby twisted his head in Jillian's direction, staring Fin in the eyes.

Fin shakes his head.

Toby went squinty-eyed and jerked his head in Jillian's direction, then jerked again to prod Finn to move.

Head bowed and mumbling. Fin trudges off to confront the angry she-cat in the grips of the fever.

The oddity split, half turn to watch Fin approach Jillian, the other wait for Toby's next move.

Toby bends and scoops Ingrid up walks into the crowd, and finds an empty chair.

Someone pulls it out for him.

He nods his thanks and sits down with her in his lap, rubbing her back to ease her tears.

Wracking sobs compete with Jillian's angry screams of frustration.

Toby holds Ingrid close, rocking her back and forth. Not able to take much more, he does the only thing he can think of to quiet the two women. He starts to sing in his normal voice, a hauntingly sweet melody.

CHAPTER THIRTY-SIX

The first humming bars catch everyone's attention, the pub quiets and absolute stillness reigns for the first words to pass his lips

Impossible life choice love sacrificing new law in girl innocence lost torment, anger, despair love enduring good spirit survival twisted mind love presenting frustrated danger to damage doubt guilty notions love accepting unreality, oddity, surprise silence broken love healing mortifying thought idea communion love resurrecting choice acceptance will fixed love living possible life choice

Noah's strong, rich voice caresses the ears, warms the hearts, and eases the minds from the troubles of life. The haunting melody swirls ethereal through the sound system. Every soul expands, touched by the journey of life and the acceptance of the impossible choices. When the last word passes his lips, he eases into humming the last few bars. The haunting melody swirls in the air after he stops, like an afterimage. No one breaks the silence to play on in the minds of his audience.

Ingrid just rested against Toby, exhausted.

Toby tentatively peaks at the oddities worried he crossed the awesome line and dazed the room again. The first person he sees is Jillian, tears streaking her cheeks.

She smiles gently, caresses his cheek, leaning in, and rewards him with the innocent kiss of love. So soft and gentle, fleeting, and it was gone.

His heart thunders, and emotion flushes his body. He, Noah, dropped all illusions and let his heart's emotions for her shine through. Love pure glowed from his huge eyes, innocent sweetness of first love wreathed his lips. He held out his hand.

She accepted it.

He pulls her close, and puts her hand on his chest, clasping it over his thundering heart. He closes his eyes and just enjoys the feeling of her acceptance and love.

Jillian stood next to Toby, stunned. Her heart thunders from the emotions exploding between them. When she heard him singing, the image of her sea God flashed in her head. She flashed by an unaware Fin, Amethyst, and Irving, all enraptured by the ethereal song haunting in its melody.

Under normal circumstances, she would have been caught with everyone else. But this wasn't normal somehow. She knew Toby was her sea God, but not totally. It didn't make any sense to her fuddled mind. She watched him sing to the distraught doctor sitting on his lap as he rocked her, soothing her damaged heart, mind, and spirit. Jillian realizes the love of her heart was this man, whoever he really was. She thought about all the inconsistencies of this man and was mentally blown away. He seemed to know everything in detail.

Thinking back through the night, she was amazed by the varied topics: medicine, electronics, structural engineering, physics, philosophy, music, wordsmith, and physiology. Those were the only ones that he touched on tonight. O'Malley turned that parabolic mic for his conversation with the unreasonable Dr. Ingrid. It was fascinating how he took random bits of opinion, comments, questions, body language, and feelings, tie them all together to get childhood rape.

He was so caring of others, disregarding his own comfort. He's been on the go since early this morning. This morning, when she ran into him on the street, the rich, deep voice yelled at her about her safety. The same deep, rich voice for singing this song. The same deep, rich voice with wolfish comments. Oh, my God, oh my sea God. Yippie!

That cinched it for her, the same voice of the dream. She looks down at the Emerald on her ring finger, the same color as his eyes, the one that appeared after she ran into him, the one he looked at and smiled pleased.

The song was coming to a close; so lovely and uplifting. The impossible life choices become accepted and, hence, possible life choices.

She realized he just made that up. It was too close to the conversation. The end of the song, pointed to now, gave her goosebumps. Unreality oddity surprise, if that wasn't this night, she didn't know what was.

Jillian's heart went out to the woman, to live silent with all that bottled up. She loves her sea God even more to ferret out the truth and release her from her personal self-inflicted light daze, scared, hopeless fear crippling her growth and development. Jillian saw Ingrid as a small girl who finally found safety from the harsh, cruel, careless world. And she had, Toby surrounded her, around him were the oddities, around them was the pub, around the pub South County, many insular layers to protect the wounded spirit.

Toby hums the last bar to gently ease out of the glorious song created only to heal that damaged girl who made the impossible choice for love.

The melody hangs in the air in the silence.

She could still hear it in her head, wrapping around her heart, mind, and spirit, expanding her soul.

The room seems to shimmer with the unified emotions of the oddities like their souls were called to heal. The energy focused down to Toby and Ingrid, in a vortex of almost seen energy that centered on Ingrid.

Toby stops rocking, takes a breath, lifts his head slightly peeks, afraid of what he'll find.

Jillian's heart swells even more for this mystery, so much so that a pure smile from her heart greets him.

His head rises as soon as he sees her, happy to see him.

Jillian had to express her floating heart. She leans in and gives him a kiss of her first love, an innocent, pure token of her bursting heart. When she withdraws, she watches him transform from Toby into a closer image of her sea God.

His eyes glow with sheer innocent love that makes her heart thump really hard, and then he smiles. It's glorious.

Her heart pauses, then races, thumping so hard she might faint.

He holds out his hand, and she places hers in his beautiful, gentle hand. He draws it to his chest and clasps it to his thundering heart, and she knows he feels exactly the same way. Her heart thunders in time to his. He closes his eyes, that glorious smile still on his lips. He bows his head to keep this between them, not wanting to share this first knowledge with anyone.

She steps behind him, her arm stretching from his heart up over his shoulder. She steps up close so their bodies touch, and he lays his head on her breasts. With her other hand, she reaches around and class the side of his head, holding him in place, his ear against her heart, his head tucked up under her chin. Jillian closes her eyes and just enjoys this moment of theirs and theirs alone. Her fingers gently stroked his sable soft hair around behind his ear.

Noah, holding her hand against his thundering heart, gently strokes her wrist, top and bottom with his thumb. Slowly, sound comes alive around them. It doesn't intrude, it doesn't distract, it just is. Even the hands of the odd that needed to touch in tribute and love didn't displace their solid unity.

It takes an act of Fin and Amethysts, six glasses and two bottles of whiskey thunking down on the table, loudly and repeatedly.

A lot of chair scraping and adjustment, and the table dragged here and there.

Toby pressed her hand to his chest, and she cupped his head and stepped back. Slowly, her eyes opened, she felt drugged, she was sort of drunk on love. She tried to move further away. Toby still had her hand and wasn't giving it back yet. She tugs again, and nothing happens. She tugs harder, but nothing. She giggles.

Toby didn't look up or acknowledge her. He sits in his chair with a sleeping Ingrid in his lap.

She still had that damaged young girl look.

Jillian strokes her hair gently, and her head nozzles Jillian's hand. Neither of them wanted her to move, so she stepped back to where she had been with her free hand stroking Ingrid's head. She looks over at the table and sees the searching looks from Fin and Amethyst.

"So…" Amethyst breaks the silence. "That was some song."

Toby snorts. "Yes."

Fin watches Toby strangely, thoughtful. "I've heard something like that once. I can't quite remember where. It's driving me crazy. Where did you hear it?"

"I don't know, here and there perhaps, I don't pay much attention to what's on the charts."

Irving steps up, pulls out a chair and sits down on Toby's left. "I'm having the same problem. I feel like I know the artist. If only recall was allowed."

Toby reaches for a drink.

Jillian's radar quivers. "Yes, Toby's voice reminds me of someone I've heard before. I wish I had a name."

Amethyst watched them carefully. "I've heard a musician that has a similar sound. His name is…" Her head turns when she hears her name called out, and she nods to someone across the pub. "Excuse me." She hopped up and raced to the bar.

Jillian looks around at the bar.

Amethyst chats fast with their old music teacher from high school, Margaret, who listens only to good music. Toby's music was good. She swings her head, looks at Irving, and watches him closely. "I wonder who Amethyst was going to say."

Irving licks his lips.

He knows something.

Jillian turns to watch Fin, who is lost in thought.

He doesn't know.

She leans down and looks at the side of Toby's face. "Who do you think she was talking about?" She asked softly, close to his ear. Her fingers on his chest start exploring and finding cut muscles and defined pectorals.

Toby closes his eyes, and his breathing elevates. He grabs her hand and squeezes it, then shakes his head and tilts it towards Ingrid.

Jillian mentally kicks herself, insensitive. She pats his chest, then relaxes against him.

Toby hugs her arm. What a woman. He continues stroking her wrist, a gentle, constant tempo, top bottom top.

Amethyst plops in her chair. "Sorry about that, Margaret had a question. Toby, did you know that she was our high school music teacher? Back in her early days, she had a nice gig, put out some songs."

Toby's tempo changes slightly, hardly noticeable, but Jillian does, curious.

"Really, I didn't know. I like her. She has been helpful to me." Toby says easily.

"Yes, she's great, always liked her. She's always had the best musical library in town." She watched Toby closely. "When we were talking she said that you remind her of someone, but couldn't recall who it was."

"I'll be interested to hear. I hope it is someone famous and good. I wouldn't want to be a hack."

Amethyst laughs. "Who would? I have a…"

Jillian jumps impatiently. "Will you spit it out this time, or are you going to run off again?"

Toby lightly pats her hand, soothing her agitation.

"My, my, aren't we impatient for a name?" Amethyst watches everyone.

"Amethyst, don't toy with me tonight… this morning." Jillian stares at Amethyst with meaning.

307

Amethyst laughs. "It's good, so good to see you as human and talking, Kitty."

Jillian vibrates her throat, remarkably, it sounds like a cat growl, a big cat, one that can eat you.

Everyone laughs except Ingrid exhausted from her ordeal.

Fin's head pops, and he stares at Toby.

Toby stares back.

Fin shakes his head, then tilts it, then looks off in thought.

Jillian saw Irving pick up a glass and take a sip, trying to hide a smile, which is impossible for him since he glows like an angel. He knows something. She catches his eye. She raises a questioning brow.

Irving's smile vanishes, and he looks away. Can't say; secret.

Jillian cleared her throat. "I've been meaning to ask this again, Irving, and now you're here, and we're in a calm spell; you mentioned someone on the phone during our last phone call, and you never answered my question. I asked Toby, but I never got an answer because the fever struck..." Jillian is distracted by Toby's heart pounding hard. "... But it was Toby..." getting stronger and faster. "... Who was in its grip first? So my question then and now is..." Toby's heart thunders again. "... Who is..." Toby's heart suspends. "... No...ah?" On each syllable, it slams against her hand. She looks over at Irving, raises her brow, her eyes rolled down, indicating Toby, and then she looks directly at him.

His big, beautiful smile appears, and his eyes glow. "Yes. Noah. My best friend, Noah Robinson Skyler, is a very unusual fellow; you could say he's a juggler with a lot of different balls flying. Or you could say he's a pie maker with his fingers in a lot of pies."

Amethyst jumps in. "You said, before you were dazed, that he's the man behind the man and that there were more like Toby."

Jillian watches a smiling Irving, now positive who the man is: Noah Robinson Skyler.

Toby's head turned slowly to Irving. "Oh, really."

308

Amethysts offer. "And that he sent you here."

Jillian decides now is not the time for this here. "Amethyst, you were going to call out a name, a musician?"

Toby's fingers lightly tighten convulsively, and then continue as they were, holding her hand to his heart and stroking her wrist.

Jillian wants to play with Noah. She had to figure out how to innocently play with him, especially with Ingrid on his lap. Between his strokes, she tugs locks of hair from the back of his head so no one would know.

Noah nudges his head back to get her to stop. A mistake, his head pushes into the pillow of her breasts and feels the hard nub. His head jerked forward with a gasp, tipping his head and closing his eyes. He brutally focuses on Wesley and Rick's last building project. His hand clamps her wrists.

Jillian puts her hand back on Ingrid's head.

That was a bad idea. Once his head pressed into her breasts, she instantly peaked; heat flushed her body, and moisture flowed. His fist was wrapped around her wrist. Head bowed, she closed her eyes with her breathing increasing.

On each breath, their bodies shift slightly.

She couldn't help sighing deeply.

He leans forward an inch to stop the slight friction. His breathing increases to match hers. Her breath brushes the fine hairs on the back of his neck. He can't force himself to release her. His heart kicks up. He was having trouble thinking of anything but the warmth behind him. He breathed in deep through his nose and regretted it instantly. He could smell her musk, the moisture and the special scent. He started sweating.

Jillian breathed in deeply and smelled him. He smelled divine. She leaned forward, her nose an inch from his hair, and breathed him in. He smelled delicious. She leaned down further, an inch away from his neck, and smelled him. Oh, God! She opens her eyes and sees a small bead of moisture traveling down his neck, heading for his collar. She reached with her tongue and stopped. Her finger reached for the little bead before it soaked into his tight collar. Carefully, her fingertip brushed his skin to capture the little treasure.

Noah felt like he received an electrical shock. Shivers rippled down his spine at light speed to pool in his groin.

"Toby." A voice called.

He concentrated on breathing and math.

"Toby." A soft voice, off to his left.

He opened his eyes and looked in that direction. "Ah, Lady Ingrid, you are awake." His voice was a hoarse, grating nasal whine. He clears his throat. "Do you feel better, Lady?" He doesn't sound any better. He blinks his eyes and tries to focus on her.

Ingrid still has the look of a child. "Thank you, Toby." She smiles tentatively at him. "That was a lovely song. Where did you learn it?"

"Here and there, I picked it up somewhere." He tried to catch his breath, but every time, Jillian invaded his body. "Could I get you something, water or a drink?" If he went somewhere, Jillian was coming with him, which could cause problems, not for public display.

Amethyst and Fin had their heads together, looking over at him and presumably Jillian. Their eyes looked scheming.

"I would like a juice if I could, cranberry, please." She stood up and moved to the right. "Thank you." She sat in the chair and smiled sweetly.

"You're welcome, Lady Ingrid, rest easy," Toby whines out nasally.

Noah stands, clasping Jillian's wrist in his fist. His heart pounds furiously under her hand.

Toby bows his head. "We will return shortly." He turns and drags Jillian behind him to the bar. "O'Malley, my good man, one Cranberry and as much whiskey you can fit in your largest container, two please." He strokes her hand with his free hand, unable to stop himself from the intense pleasure.

O'Malley leans over the bar to look at Jillian.

Jillian breathes heavily, color high, her eyes dark smoky grey with flashes of fire.

He eases back and takes a closer look at Toby.

His eyes glow green, his color high, his breathing heavy, almost a pant.

"I would not look at Jilli at the moment if I were you. I see the fever grips you both."

Noah nodded, and he felt her lean her body against his.

It feels heavenly. He could feel her heart violently beating like his. His eyes closed to feel her better. All her soft spots pressed all along his back.

Her free hand slides from his waist around to his abdomen, pulling herself up tight. Her breathy, soft gasp nearly brings him to his knees. He grips the bar with his one free hand. The fingers on his abdomen barely flexed, pressing into his hard muscles, sending showers of tingles cascading down both his legs.

O'Malley plunks down a very large mug full of amber liquid in front of Toby. He plunks down the other one closer to his left side, in reach of the hand working its excruciatingly slow way up his front.

Noah clamps down his upper arm, trapping her arm. He reaches for the mug with his free hand and pours. He turns to the side so Jillian can reach her mug of fever reducer. He releases her arms, but they stay clasping him to her lush body.

Jillian was lost in his scent, holding him close to her body. Everywhere she touches, he's covered with hard, thick muscles. She's drooling, her nose buried along his spine, her cheeks cushioned on the ridge muscle on either side of his spine, her nose in the Valley.

"Jilli, come on, lass, look at O'Malley." O'Malley says as he watches her nuzzle Toby's bent spine.

Jillian focuses on O'Malley, standing across the bar, holding out a mug of amber liquid. He nods at the glass, stretching his arm further. Her free hand didn't want to stop its slow exploration, but

O'Malley was an expert. Her hand releases Noah and reaches for the mug compulsively. Once in her hand it goes automatically to her mouth. Gulping down the fiery liquid continues with O'Malley's finger assisting from the bottom. At halfway, he removes his finger. She put it down on the bar, still clenched in her hand. She leans her head against Noah's back and breathes deep. Her body was no longer pressed up to his. Her hand was in his possession, still pressed to his strong chest, valiant heart, calming from its frantic pace, as was hers, her wrist still in his fist, he squeezed gently.

"Better, Jillian?" Toby's nasal whine was still hoarse.

Jillian nods her head where it rests on his back, remaining silent. She lifts the mug to her lips to drain another good portion. She sighs, tightens her captured arm hugging him quickly and then raises her head and finishes her mug. Once done, she puts it on the bar next to Noah's empty mug. "Thanks, O'Malley. I'm glad we have you to watch out for us." Her voice was husky and smooth.

Noah hears her smooth huskiness, and his mind flashes to a vision of them wrestling in twisted sheets. He groaned softly, rubbing his forehead. He picks up a glass of cranberry juice and drags her back to the table. He whispers over his shoulder. "Please, Jillian, no talking for a little while." His voice is thick and rough, and he feels her arm quiver. It looks like he had to remain silent for a time until his voice returned to normal. He breathes carefully, trying not to notice her scent rising from her arm clamped to his chest.

He just wants to drag her away, put an end to this torment, if only he could. That wouldn't happen until the job was done. She knew about him and his organization until they had a chance to know each other and decided together to join for life. He was ready, but he needed to make double sure that she really and truly wanted him forever. It would almost kill him to walk away, but he could do it if that's what she wanted, as long as they didn't jump the gun and hop into bed the first one they saw. With his reaction to her, there is no way he would ever leave. If they stepped that far over the line, it would be a life commitment. He would not live a casual life. He had waited this long, he could wait a bit more. During the dark years of his youth, he witnessed how casual sex screwed everything up. He wasn't going to make the same mistake he witnessed affect his life.

When he finally allowed himself to become intimate with a woman, it would be a celebration of their commitment to each other. He had put up with a lot of ribbing through the service years because he hadn't ever allowed himself the pleasures of the flesh.

Instead, he had learned, any and everything he could get his hands on. All of his degrees were originally in his name. He made up fake documents and gone into school records to make a bogus file to match the names. They were attached in a clever way to his original file, so he felt it was legally okay. He was just practicing these different professions under a different name. He couldn't imagine what anyone would say if it ever got out that he was noteworthy in multiple fields. Right now he was working on electrical engineering. He knew most of the information and concepts he have known for a long time. Now, he was getting the document that confirmed he understood the entire required curriculum.

He was also into mechanical engineering. That one was just in the beginning stages, though time-consuming, not terribly difficult. He would complete the electrical within the month and the mechanical in six months unless he was distracted from his regular study time. Jillian in the picture now he would have to reorganize to ensure he had time to spend with her.

It will alter his life drastically. For these 30-odd years, he had no one; no one to fill his time, no one to share with, no one to love. He hoped he didn't mess this up because he really wanted her in his life and needed to have someone to love. He hugged her arm, circling his torso.

She returned the feelings, pressing her hand to his chest.

They arrived at the table.

Everyone was chatting amiably.

Toby places his glass gently on the table in front of Dr. Ingrid. "Here you go, Lady Ingrid."

"Thank you, Toby." She smiled shyly up at him. Then she notices a woman's hand clasped to his chest. Her smile dims a little. She looks back at the table. The only two chairs open were on either side of Stevens. She looked back at Toby and the woman who just stood there next to the table. She picks up her glass and walks around the table to the open chair between the two men. "Please, take that seat." She takes a sip of her juice, trying not to feel awkward and disappointed.

Toby haltingly sits down, Jillian still caught in his grip.

Jillian smiles. It really was too much. She tugs at her arm, but nothing. She giggles and tugs again, no, not an inch. She leans down next to his ear and whispers softly, "I'd like to sit down. I will give you my other hand in exchange." She tugs her own, but nothing. Time to pull out the big guns, softer still she whispers against his ear, her lips barely brushing his skin. "Let go, Noah." She pulls, and her arm comes free easily. She slips her other hand in through his open fist to rest on his thundering heart. Smirking, she pulled the chair closer to him and sat, and was uncomfortable with her arm at a weird angle. She pulls her arm away, Noah's limp hand moving along with it. She places her hand over his and slides her arm out of his slack fist until her hand grips his. She looks up at him.

CHAPTER THIRTY-SEVEN

His expression is comical, shock being the most prevalent emotion on display. Somehow, he displays a plethora of emotions simultaneously: pride, joy, amazement, curiosity, impatience, and desire. His head starts to turn to her.

Noah is floored. Emotions tumbling around inside him, he feels set adrift in the raging sea. His mind is in turmoil. He can't hold a thought. He realizes her hand is no longer on his chest. She was sitting next to him, close. He feels her hands on his. He feels her grasp his hand, stroking the back. Wow! She figured it out. How? He starts to turn his head.

"I dream of you, Noah." She whispers in his ear, squeezes his hand, and turns to the table with a shaky hand, reaching for her glass.

Noah is having trouble catching his breath. His heart is beating too fast, and he feels lightheaded. He looks at her and watches her shaky hand reach for her glass and picks it up. Amber sloshes in the glass.

Amethyst was moving to help.

Noah brushes his lips against her ear when he whispers in his voice. "I dream of you, Jillian." He presses his lips gently against her ear and sits up, reaching for the closest full glass. The one in Stephen's hand and sucks it down. The

Stevens raised a brow at Noah and watched his whiskey drain into Toby's mouth. He looks at Jillian in just as bad condition. The glass in her hand slipped her grip and was caught by Amethyst, who was watching Jillian closely, her expression curious. He looks back at Noah; the shock, pride, and amazement are still easily seen on his face. He thinks about Jillian's silent question to him. She figured out who he was. What a clever girl. Well, it looked like she called him by his true name. "Toby, is Noah due anytime soon?"

Jillian's head turns to Stevens and smiles gratefully, seeing she had a supporter with Irving. "I would love to meet him, Toby. Do you think that would be possible?" She looked over at him and smiled sweetly.

Noah clears his throat carefully. "That can be arranged," Toby says forcefully and clears his throat again. "I have an errand to run late in the afternoon. I'll see after that." He squeezed her hand.

"Lovely, I'm so looking forward to meeting the man behind the man. You are very impressive, Toby, but somehow, I know he is much more. I hope you won't mind if I want to spend time with him." She smirked at him.

"It's entirely your choice, Lady Jillian, who you favor. I will always be grateful for the time you spend with me. A precious jewel of memory held close and enjoyed when parted from your excellent company." He grinned goofy, and he could tell he was going to love playing with her.

"What of the other men? Would you be just as accommodating?" Jillian can't help herself. She had an idea she had run into Noah previously and the idea was startling. He would be the construction guy and the exterminator, which is really mind-blowing, since all three were physically different. Noah was a very intriguing mystery, and she loves mystery.

"I certainly would try to be, there are many who wouldn't be as concerned for your well-being as I. But I do know many who would be, you know, birds of a feather flock together." He looks at her directly, smiling carefully showing enough teeth hopefully to get her to get his point across. "My concerns would be for you, your happiness and safety. Someone like Jackson is not of the caliber I speak. I would be fine with Irving or others of his ilk to play escort. I'm sure he will introduce some. "He squeezes her hand.

Jillian squeezes back. "That's nice. Of course, I will stay clear of those like Jackson. I always have." She winks at him. "But since I haven't dated much, it would be nice to meet new people."

Amethyst snorts. "Try, never date; I've been after her for years to go out there and take a dip in the dating pool. But she won't have it, says it's just shark-filled waters ready to devour the flesh foolish enough to enter. She says she's looking for more, something superior. I don't know how she's going to find superior sitting home night after night." Amethyst sips to drink.

"She ran into me on the street in the bright morning." Toby smiles proudly.

"No offense, Toby, but you aren't superior," Amethyst says gently. "You're great, even amazing, but not superior."

"None taken. I'm comfortable with being great and amazing. Many haven't seen me as such." Noah squeezes Jillian's hand. "I can only think of one to see the true man within."

Jillian squeezed back. "It's not necessarily the words spoken as the actions taken that reveal the heart within." She strokes his hand, trailing her fingers up his arm and back down. "My superior will be of the heart, not the outer packaging. An appealing outer wrapping would be nice but not required. A must is a healthy system all parts working properly. When I find my superior of healthy body and mind with a good, strong, caring heart, I'm keeping him all to myself. No sharing with other women, mine and mine alone." She takes her fingers away from his arm and grabs her glass, takes a deep swallow, and puts it down.

Fin laughs. "Are you planning on locking him away in your tower and only letting him out when you want?"

Jillian chuckles deep in her throat. "No, the bedroom."

Amethyst hoots. "Her personal bedroom boy."

Noah chokes. He picks up a full glass in front of him.

Jillian giggles. "That will be nice, I'm sure, but what I meant was that Mr. Superior may interact with others freely except intimately. I don't want to hinder him in the life he created, just as I expect not to be hindered in mine. Optimally will be a blending so we may share our lives together."

Noah breathes deeply and carefully. "That's very thoughtful to consider his interests as well as your own. You, Lady Jillian, seem to match your heart's desire, superior. And might I be so bold and say your packaging is very beautiful, to my eye as the beholder." He winks at her.

Jillian blushes with a pleased smile. "What a lovely thing to say, Toby. I'm pleased to hear I rate a superior. Your close, Toby, don't believe Amethyst. She swims easily in those dangerous waters, so her eyes may be a little blurry. But I think, once she focuses, she will see as I do." Her fingers find his arm once again skating across his skin.

"It is great to be seen for who and what you are." He says softly with unmasked pleasure. "It will do my heart good to have two ladies of quality accept me, quirks and all."

Amethyst laughs. "Toby, even with blurry eyes, I accept you, quirks and all. Jillian, with her clear sight, obviously sees something I missed, which leads me to believe when my sight clears, you will only be more intriguing."

Stevens coughs, shaking his head. "You can say that again." He says quietly.

Jillian snickers in her glass.

Noah kicks Stevens and redirects the conversation. "Very silent, Lady Ingrid. Are you doing okay?" Toby looks closely at the woman.

She smiles shyly. "I'm fine. I'm not used to this, not very social. I spend most of my time working."

Stephen chuckles. "Don't worry, Ingrid, you're not alone in that. This has been the longest time I've been with this many people ever. I'm a bit of a loner."

Toby snorts. "A bit?"

Stevens chuckles. "Okay, more than a bit."

"Well, Irving, prepare yourself. Now you are an oddity and will be more social." Fin laughs. "I still have some business with you per our conversation on the phone. But that will wait for another day. Besides, when Toby is off temping, we'll need you to fill his spot. Won't we, girls?"

Jillian giggles. "Oh, yes, Irving, don't think you're a placeholder. We want you for yourself. You are still very much a mystery to us."

Amethyst laughs. "You don't yet realize how we love a mystery."

318

Stevens looked a little hunted. "I'll try to socialize more, but no guarantees. After a time, I started to feel claustrophobic. Then I'm gone. But so far, so good, tonight, all the weirdness is fascinating."

They all laugh

Toby slaps his shoulder. "Where were you during the onset of the daze? Standing up there with me would have riveted you from that amount of weirdness." He shakes his head. "Do you think we will ever be able to leave the Pub without anymore?"

"God, I hope so." Fin chuckles. "If we get lucky enough, besides the doors open again at 10 AM, a new day is filled with possibilities."

Toby groans. "I don't know if I can handle another day of the same quality of weirdness, especially back to back."

Amethyst laughs. "Then let's hope for a slow day tomorrow, well, today."

"Speaking of that, let's finish up with Wesley and Rick and get Lady Ingrid loaded up and on her way. We need to close this day. I'm bushed." Toby whines

Jillian stands, placing her glass on the table. "It sounds like you need to finish your work, and I need to visit the restroom." She tugs on her hand, but nothing. "Toby, you can't go in with me." She laughs. She tugs on her hand and gets nothing. "I'll go and hold Wesley's hand after I'm done. Yours will be busy. Once you are done and Wesley's on his way, you may hold it again." She tugs her hand, but again, nothing. She leans down and whispers softly in his ear, "I'll even let you walk me home, Noah." She presses her lips to his ear lightly and steps away, withdrawing her hand easily.

Noah places his warm hand on his chest as he watches her walk away. What a woman. Yowza! He drained his glass, placed it on the table and stood. "Stevens, Dr. Ingrid, breaks over. Time to run down the procedure we did. And then make Wesley and Rick mobile and rechargeable. Pack you off and send you on your way." He extends his arm towards Wesley and Rick. "Fin, Amethyst, please spend your last minutes with Rick. We don't want him to get jealous, do we?" They walk away.

319

Amethyst laughs. "Wouldn't dream of it; I'll go make a pit stop and be right there." She stands and puts her hand on Fin's shoulder. "We'll continue after RW leaves. I think I like the idea. It would definitely free us up."

"I'm not sure what will happen if we can get them together. They have fire, yikes! They will combust if we don't do something." Fin grumbles.

"Jillian was hesitant earlier about Toby. And that business about going out with other men doesn't bode well. But if nature takes a hand, who are we to intrude on those conditions, right?"

"Right, we'll all walk Jillian home. How are we to keep him there?"

"We need to step up the booze, get them both so tanked we can pour them through the keyhole. We need a way to make opening the door too difficult to bother, just in case."

Fin looks over at Stevens. He seems resourceful. "We could get Stevens to help. I get the feeling he would like to see those two together."

"Yeah, I got that feeling, too. The way he kept smiling at them was a big clue. We are missing something that those three know."

"I saw the looks, heard the inflections. I just can't make sense of it all. It could be the mass amount of alcohol diluting my blood. Well, we'll figure it out." Fin stands, collecting the glasses and bottles. "I'll drop these. Go pump, Jillian. See what you can get out of her. When I have time I'll get Stevens agreement to help." He turns to the booth and looks over his shoulder and winks at her.

"Sounds good." She winks back and heads to the lady's room. She enters to find Jillian washing her hands. "Wait for me."

"All right." She turned off the taps to grab some paper towels. "I never would have guessed what this night would hold."

Amethyst enters a stall. "Right, welcome to the twilight zone here in South County."

Julian laughs. "I think we are starting the ride, tonight was the big incline with the freefall zooming us down."

"Sweet, I love roller coasters. The wilder the ride, the more I love them."

Jillian nodded, staring at the Emerald. "I really love this one. I hope it never ends." She turns to a watchful Amethyst. "Look at how many fascinating people we have met. Good quality people, now friends."

"Yes, good friends, three great guys." Amethyst keeps her eye on Jillian. "That's Toby is a one-of-a-kind, amazing what he knows, how he figures stuff out. He's quite a guy."

Jillian smiles secretly. "Yes, he is, one of a kind." Her face flushes rosy. "I wonder what Noah is like."

Amethyst looks confused. "Noah?"

"Yeah, Noah. You said Toby wasn't superior, so the man behind the man, more than Toby, wouldn't you agree? If Toby isn't superior but close, it stands to reason Noah is superior." She looked at Amethyst, her eyes a light silvery gray. "I can't wait to meet Noah. I'm all a flutter just thinking about him. I hope I don't embarrass myself when I finally get to see him."

Amethyst scratches her head. "Ah, Jillian? You've been all over Toby tonight; I thought he was the one."

"Oh, he's one, but I want to see what tomorrow or today brings. You heard Toby, and he's okay with me spending time with other quality men if that's what makes me happy." She holds in a laugh seeing Amethyst's shocked expression, a complete reversal of previously held beliefs for her.

"I never would have expected to hear this from you." Amethyst laughs. "Going to be stepping out with many a man. I sure hope Toby was serious." She washes her hands and grabs a few towels.

"I'm sure he will let me know if I step out with an undesirable." She turns to the door. "Ready?"

"Ready. Let's cuddle up to Wesley and Rick before they go." She follows her out.

They travel across the pub quickly. Most everyone stilllls present, all waiting for Wesley and Rick's departure. Toby, Stevens, and Dr.

Ingrid stand behind Rick and Wesley next to the electronics on the table. O'Malley and Fin are behind the bar doing a hopping business. Philip stands in front of Rick and Wesley, talking. O'Malley or Finn adjusted the speakers to allow Rick and Wesley's radio transmission in the areas around them. They could hear everything pretty much, but they had their mics turned away from the open room, so they only picked up some of the noise.

Noah watches Jillian and Amethyst cross the room. Jillian's dress flashes tiger stripes, hugging her ripe, tight body perfectly. Smooth and confident, she slinks gracefully, muscles flashing. She greets Phillip and goes directly to Wesley, Amethyst to Rick. The five of them lively in their conversation, he had to fight the desire to snatch up Jillian. Now, was not the time, so he focuses back to what he was saying: "You understand why no one can just touch their heads? The way I set up the antenna array, everywhere you see the gel is part of the field, and we needed as much amplification as we could get to send it along its path. Our current radio equipment isn't sensitive enough to pick up the signals emitting from the brain. I've seen studies where two men were separated by thousands of miles and easily transferred thoughts. So, it's possible. Our brains are sensitive to receiving and then sending. Our equipment is not. We are working on getting better equipment for these two."

"This is amazing, Toby." Dr. Ingrid inspects the men's heads from a distance. "Is it possible you could replicate it in a more manageable way, like a cap form or hood? I would love to use this on some of my patients and let the inside voice be heard outside. I imagine those silent ones would benefit from a way to communicate."

Noah looks to Stephen. "You'd have to do all the heavy lifting for a project like that. I'm too busy as it is, but I could help where I can. Certainly, work on the design and teach the wiring. It's very precise. We screw up the wires, we could potentially screw up the patient even more."

Ingrid grips Steven's arm. "Oh, please say you'll do it. I always feel bad after spending time with them with no progress. Now I've seen what you've done here, I know we can open communication. Did you say, Toby, that they have a lot more hope now that they can

322

communicate? Just think how much hope you'll be giving, Irving." She looks up at him, beseeching with her big, soft brown eyes.

Stevens was caught. He couldn't look away. He can't deny her request. She looks too hopeful, an expression they hadn't seen. He couldn't take her hope either and sighed. "Yes, all right. But I'm warning you, we can't rush this. It has to be done carefully. Not like this with toothpicks and twine."

Noah snorts.

"Yes amazing piece of work, Toby, with the tools at hand. But what Ingrid wants is something that can be put on or taken off. Right?"

Ingrid nods, "Yes, something anyone can wear."

Toby chuckles. "I wasn't offended, more amused that it worked. I agree with your assessment. It will take considerable time to get a working prototype. The largest hurdle has already been crossed. We got it to work twice, with little time and almost no proper equipment. Yours will be based on this design, but nothing like it. We also have to understand what part that nasty amplifier really plays. That being the case, we have to tiptoe around it if we don't want to end up in your office professionally."

Stevens laughs. "I'll get you a foil helmet to protect your precious noodle."

Noah snorts. "Oh, thank you." Toby smiles. "I have plans, and a broken noodle would hinder them."

Stephen chuckles. "I have no doubt." He turns to Ingrid. "I'll let you know when we get closer, and if I need any information from you, I'll call."

Toby smiles. "I'm sure you'll be talking regularly. When I can't be reached, you can talk to Stevens about Wesley and Rick. I want regular updates. Daily to start, after we get some good results, we can cut back. I would greatly appreciate your willingness to humor me. I'm already unsettled letting you take them. Believe me when I say it's not you personally. I would have this problem with whoever stepped through that door." He shrugs his humped shoulders.

"He's not very comfortable handing the reigns over. He's the beginning, middle, and end kind of worker. Not for the assembly line, our Toby." Stephen laughs. "Not unless he's building it from the land up."

Dr. Ingrid looks confused. "How does he do temp work?"

Toby snorts and shrugs. "Since I didn't start the project, I get by but I end up doing a lot of the extra steps. Philip was thrilled I completed all the work that's been lingering in the county offices for the last five years. And I know that for a fact, I filed a document dated five years ago."

Philip steps up. "True. It's not an errant paper floating in any inboxes. In my time there, this is the first. I might have to have Toby come once a year to keep things orderly."

"I told you, I'm not coming back, Philip, much too dangerous."

"Walked out with the danger in your arms and came here."

"Yes, see how dangerously things got out of hand? I was just trying to restore the office to the state before my arrival and extract the danger from your halls."

"You mean you were running for your life but baiting her out?" Philip sputters.

"It worked, didn't it? Your halls are danger-free. I'm sure Mary is very grateful. I heard she almost got mauled."

"You mean you got caught." Philip laughs. "And Mary's fine. That was our best day in years. So you're welcome anytime." He snickers. "You know Jillian drops by all the time. It was only in reaction to you she turned into a dangerous she-cat."

"Yes, well, the ladies do like me."

Stevens snorts.

Dr. Ingrid smiled shyly. "I like you, Toby."

"See?" Toby smirked at Stevens. "A lady of quality."

Phillip laughs.

Stevens laughs. "Yes, but she spends all her time with loose screws. You fit right in."

Noah laughs, and Toby whines. "Yes, but I fit in everywhere."

"I'd give money to see you fit in at a midget convention." Stevens chuckled.

"How much?" Noah asked dryly.

"Big money, man, big money." Steven gasped.

"Deal." Noah is challenging himself lately, maybe because he is restless, lonely, or bored. He had an idea of how to pull it off. To that end, he had been exercising to that end, along with his regular regime.

"I don't see the challenge," Philip says. "He's very personable, charming even. I'm sure he can win over anyone. If he has difficulty, he can always daze them." Phillip laughs.

Stevens chuckles. "Don't remind him."

CHAPTER THIRTY-EIGHT

Toby snorts. "I hope that never happens again. And now I wonder if I've been doing that for a while and just left, leaving countless DD in my wake. Now I have to call previous employers and see if any odd happenings exist." He shakes his head.

Stevens pats Toby's hunchback. "I think you would have heard. This is the place where your new skills manifested."

Dr. Ingrid looks thoughtful. "You know that throughout history, there have been mesmerists. From what I understand and hear, your ability is much stronger than those of history. I'll look into it, Toby. I realize now you really are concerned for those unsuspecting falling under your spell. I thought that you were really ridiculing my profession."

"I understand and would appreciate any help in understanding this bit of weirdness."

"Gladly. Now, you've gone over everything, and I need to get started. We have the drive back to the estate." Dr. Ingrid turns. "I'll get my men ready to leave. How much time do you need?"

"About 10 minutes will work, then a careful loading of Wesley and Rick, and off you go."

"We'll be ready." She walks off.

"Philip, would you please tell O'Malley, Wesley and Rick will be loading up in 10 minutes," Toby asked as he started moving equipment.

"Sure, Toby, I'll tell Wesley and Rick, too."

"Thanks," Toby whines, his head bowed, adjusting the brackets.

"This is a clever idea," Stevens says, watching Noah lock the bracket holding the amplifier on the bottom of the board.

"We had to come up with a way to move these two simultaneously and equipment. Ideally, they should each have the electronics, but I don't know if it would separate them. Might as well have company then be eternally alone. From what they said, they can still speak to each other without broadcasting and have internal personal dialogue."

"Have you asked whether they can manipulate their terrain?" Stevens bends down and holds in place the large bracket to hold the rechargeable power source.

"No, didn't think of that, though a wonderful question. When I go visit, I'll have a more focused mind and less whiskey in me. That's been bugging me too. Between the two of us, Jillian and I really aren't slobbering drunk. We should be. Probably at least a case, unless they are watering it down, which is still an extreme amount. It doesn't taste like it's watered. Strong and fiery, I'm drinking it like water."

"Maybe all that sexual desire is burning it away, or neither of you can afford to slobber right now. Maybe when you get home, the slobbering will begin." Stevens chuckles, assisting smoothly, knowing from experience when to do what. It was like old times.

When they were boys on the street, Noah, being really smart, was in charge. He always knew what to say to get the best handouts. He knew who would give them a job for a meal or a place to sleep.

They moved around a lot so they wouldn't wear out a welcome. Always on the go, like the strays, they were, half wild, always ready for a fight, careful of a kick, and took affection were given but never expected.

On the streets, Noah was a legend. Nowhere-everywhere was the name he got stuck with. Nowhere could vanish before your eyes and reappear right next to you. He could be in a clown suit, a really loud one, and vanish from one spot and appear before you, pressing that red nose into yours. You go to catch him, and like smoke, he would drift away untouched.

Stevens only knew about Noah since they teamed up, not before. He knew it was bad. Noah used to have horrible night terrors, which were much worse than a regular nightmare. When he had one, he wouldn't sleep again until he was so exhausted he just stopped and slept. He remembered the first time that happened. It scared him so badly. He was about eight, Noah seven; they were traveling through a particularly dangerous section of the city. Running through an alley, Noah just stopped and collapsed.

He tried everything to wake him up but with no success. Footsteps and loud talking from this street warned him he didn't have much time.

Everyone wanted to press Nowhere into their gang. But Noah knew it was better to be a free agent. So, with little time, Stevens searched for a hiding place. The only thing he could find was the dumpster. He picked Noah up and silently went to the crevice behind the dumpster. He had just reached his goal when the pack of bragging thugs entered the alley not that far away. Stevens had held his breath and crouched down tiny and became still inside as well as outside the way Noah taught him. They had passed by none the wiser. It was a long, harrowing night. The alley was a favorite shortcut for everyone except the scared. They took a long way.

Sixteen hours later, Noah's eyes popped open, and all he said about it was, "How long?"

Later, Noah told him that he was keeping track so they would be in a safe place when sleep came. He never went out when sleep was due. It left you dangerously vulnerable. If you wanted to live, you learn quickly what left you vulnerable and avoid it at all costs.

If you had to be vulnerable, you did it in the safe havens littered throughout the city. There were only a few that you could let your guard down completely, though that really didn't happen because you never knew when life decided to surprise you.

They had run wild on the streets when one day Noah decided it was time to go to school, and the only way to do that was to go to an orphanage. Noah had researched the different organizations and picked the best one. They were an asset to the home because they worked for food and board. Noah wouldn't enter until the director agreed to the terms. Noah had negotiated a small wage for both of them for the extra work that they completed in addition to the negotiated chores.

Soon, other children requested jobs and were paid for extra work they wanted to be like Noah and Stevens.

Noah was always his own man, even at seven when Stevens was rescued by him. Some huge, mean brute caught Stevens when he ran by. Stevens hadn't done anything to him and didn't know at that time, but Rigor liked to beat boys to test their mettle. If they died, he had a good time. If they survived, he watched them grow. If he liked what he saw, in later years, they would get another beating. If they survived, then they were taken to Rigor's den to heal and were forever after one of Rigor's Mortise.

The Mortise were a vile bunch. They enjoyed handing out pain to anyone foolish enough to get close.

Nowhere was on their most wanted list, and let it be known that the one to bring Rigor Nowhere would inherit his kingdom and had an extensive organization. Nowhere was still wanted. Rigor foamed at the mouth any time Nowhere was mentioned, so rumor stated.

That day when Noah crossed Steven's path was the best day of his young life, and one of the worst. The worst was getting calm by Rigor. When the best part showed up, he was close to giving up and asking death to step in.

Noah came walking up, whistling a merry tune. Not a care in the world, a scrawny seven-year-old in ratty old clothes sauntered up just out of reach. Close enough to talk but too far away for a lunge. "Whatch ya doin'?" Nowhere asks, looking curiously at the bloodied boy in a heap on the ground.

"I'm beatin' him. What it look like?" Rigor looks at him as if he were nuts.

"Why?" Nowhere pulls out a candy bar and unwraps it, nonchalantly takes a bite

"Cause I feel like it." Rigor turns fully to Nowhere. "Aren't you afraid of me?" He asked curiously.

Nowhere laughs and slaps his knee. "Afraid of you? Why?" He took another bite and watched Rigor intently, like he'd turn into a duck or something.

"I'm Rigor." He states it so matter-of-factly that it should explain the why.

"I know. Why should I be afraid?" He takes another bite of his candy bar and munches, waiting.

"Cause I like doing this." He points down at the bloodied boy.

"Yes, I know, but why?" Nowhere looks Rigor up and down, shrugs his shoulders. "I just don't see anything to be afraid of. That's why I keep asking. Maybe it's something that can't be seen." He popped the last bite into his mouth folded his wrapper, and tucked it into his pocket.

"Because when I catch you, I beat you," Rigor said manically.

"What happens when you want to catch someone to beat but can't?"

"That never happens."

"Really? You really don't look like much." He folded his skinny arms across his small chest and shifted his weight to one leg, one hand raised to his chin. "Go on, I didn't mean to interrupt your work. I'll just watch and look for what you have that should make me afraid." He started tapping his foot impatiently and then started to hum in time with his tapping.

Rigor just stared at him, then lunged and came up short.

Nowhere raised a brow and stepped back. "If you aren't going to continue, I'll come back when you have someone to beat. I'm very curious." He turns and saunters away, whistling the same tune as when he came.

Rigor screams enraged a little punk would dismiss him. He goes after him, but every time he almost has his hands on the annoying little bastard, he is just out of reach. The entire time he chased him, he kept whistling that tune, the type that stuck in your head.

At one point of almost capture, Nowhere turned and snickered, "No, not much." His sighed. "You know what I call that tune? Rigor Mortise Reel. What do you think?" He turns and saunters away, looking over his shoulder. "Is it catchy enough, do you think?" And vanishes before his eyes, though he was still whistling.

Rigor roared, turned, and stomped back to where he left that kid. He was gone. That was worse.

Nowhere slips up behind Rigor. "What happened to that kid? You were coming back to beat him more, weren't you?" He was back out of range by the time Rigor spun around, startled. He lunged, he was so mad, he wasn't even close.

"See? I don't understand." He shrugs. "Well, since you have no one to beat, I'll mosey along." Whistling the Rigor Mortis Reel Nowhere saunters off following the blood trail.

He really needed to teach that kid some basic survival skills. First, how not to get caught. Second, when injured, don't leave a trail. He would learn.

He appeared beside Stevens as he stumbles down the alley. "You really need to learn some things, kid." Nowhere says.

He scared Stevens so bad he fell "No… ah!" Falling hurt badly.

Nowhere squats down beside Steve. "Did you just call me Noah? I like it. Nowhere-everywhere isn't a proper name, and I don't know if I have one, so thank you for the fine name, friend. Now I really have to teach you everything I can. You have given me what no one else has. Do you have a name?" Noah stuck out his hand and helped him to his feet.

"Irving Stevenson," Stevens whispers.

"Wow, two names. You are so fortunate." Noah puts his arm around Stevens and helps him limp along

"Actually, I have three." Stevens stumbles then catches his balance with help from Noah. "Steve Irving Stevenson."

"Steve Stevenson?"

"My mother called me Irving."

"Wow, you had a mother? Richer and richer." Noah leans over and looks at Irving's face. "I'm pleased to meet you, Steven Irving Stevenson. We shall be best friends forever." Noah states the facts or premonition.

"Alright. Great meeting you, Noah. Thank you for distracting Rigor."

"Noah, my, that sounds nice." He looks around the corner, holding Stevens in place. "No problem. Rigor needed to see that not everyone feared him. But you're welcome." He leads Stevens around the corner.

"What were you whistling? I liked it. I can still hear it in my head." Stevens tried to hum some but he soon lost his breath.

Noah laughs. "Rigor Mortis Reel. Rigor wasn't too happy with the name." he shrugged. "It seemed fitting since I started whistling when I saw him, and that's what came out."

"You mean you just made that up?" Stevens stops, amazed, swaying on his feet.

Noah shrugs, "Yeah, it happens."

"Really? That's cool." Stevens starts walking again. "Can you teach me the Rigor Mortise Reel?"

"Sure, it is not difficult." Noah looks around. "Where are we going?"

"To where I sleep." He points to a rooftop of the brick building.

"Is it safe? Does anyone know you sleep here?"

"No. I just got here." He says sadly. "It's better than where I was. Anywhere is better than there." He shudders.

"You want to talk about it?"

"Not really."

"Okay, let's get you settled. Do you have food? What about water? We need to clean your so they don't get infected. That would make you vulnerable. If you want to survive, you can't be vulnerable."

"Ever?"

"No, never."

Stevens watched Noah as Toby expertly put together the automatic power switch so the equipment never lost any power when the plugs were pulled. When it was plugged in, it would switch back and any excess energy would recharge the batteries. It was ingenious. This entire rig was so over-the-top advanced it blew his mind. To think about his seven-year-old Savior and then to see what that boy was capable of years later. Rigor was so below what Noah was it was laughable.

"Can you pack up these things here? They belong in the van." Noah checked his work. He was so exacting, checking and rechecking, then again before he put power to a test. When he was satisfied, he installed it, wiring it into both the laptop and the amplifier.

Every piece of equipment now had a place on either or both boards that held Wesley and Rick. The whole production, from start to finish, is beyond anything he suspected. When Noah called him and told him what he needed, he thought it was a shot in the dark. It had taken little time to find the information he needed to write the program. But once he had then maybe 20 minutes and he had done his part.

He didn't feel like he had done enough to fly out and take care of the radio station. That wasn't hard, a quick explanation of what happened and why, well part of why, the amplifier the radio station is trying out for the first time. Than carte blanche, they were very accommodating. One reason Wesley and Rick were well-loved around here and the radio station would lose advertising dollars if they were permanently out of commission and would broadcast third. So get them back to full health, and until then, broadcast their experience; win, win.

A crowd of people were saying their last goodbyes before the guys got loaded up.

It was odd to see such a close community.

Everywhere he's been only family showed this kind of closeness. Noah said they welcomed them as a family when he walked in the door. He probably would've gotten the same treatment if he hadn't been such an ass. But that was before the daze. Noah saved him again. He felt wonderful. Not angry, not lonely, not depressed. Fit and hall. He felt right. He felt hope.

Somewhere, he had lost it, maybe during the service. They chewed up young men and then tossed them aside to deal with all the repercussions of what they were told to do, the stuff of nightmares, but all in the name of patriotism and justice. He hadn't seen any justice, and the patriotism was programmed in the new recruits while exhausted. So you really didn't have a chance since they stacked the deck in favor of the house, the White House.

Noah had, of course, been the exception, as he always was. He excelled in everything. He never failed. They kept sending him on missions that seemed doomed from the start and always came through untouched.

CHAPTER THIRTY-NINE

They were sending him on missions to get him killed. They reasoned he would be too dangerous out on his own. Especially if he decided he didn't appreciate them anymore. They failed; he didn't even get scratched in all those death missions. As soon as they stepped off base, Noah disappeared. Somehow, he was given the nickname of nowhere. At first, Noah thought he was behind it after a while, he realized that he got that name because he was nowhere anyone thought he should be.

When Noah disappeared, no one could find him. Leaving the service left them at loose ends. What did they do now? Noah's answer: to school. So they went to university. Stevens had studied computers because he liked them. Noah went into medicine and became a doctor. He said because he took so many now he had to save as many. And he did, maybe more. He worked as a doctor for as long as they were in the service. As soon as that time was up, he quit the hospital. He went back to school, this time for architecture structural engineering. Because in the service, he had destroyed houses and office buildings and since he was at the school anyway, he got his doctorate in physics.

Stevens was positive Noah was learning something, as he always was. He picked up the crate he packed and moved to the door.

Fin stopped him before he reached the door, looking around. "Say, Stevens, could I have a moment of your time?"

"Walk with me. I have to get this to the van before they do." He continued to walk. "What's on your mind?"

Fin stepped ahead and opened the door. "Well, you see, Amethyst and I had this idea, and I thought I should run it by you and see what you think." He let the door close after Stevens.

"What's this idea?" Stevens wasn't as smart as Noah, but he wasn't dumb, either. He knew it was about Noah; why ask him otherwise. Amethyst was involved, so he guessed it had to do with

Jillian, too. The only reason Noah and Jillian would rate an idea was the fever. So they wanted to ease the urgency. The only way would be if they got together, so they wanted them to work it out in private so it wouldn't be so dangerous for everyone else. He knew Noah wanted her. He thought that Jillian wanted Noah. In fact, he knew she figured out he was Noah and still wanted him. If the looks and possessiveness were any indication, they were almost there. He wanted Noah to find someone he could share his life. He also knew that if he loved Jillian, which he suspected, he did put a ring on her finger, then it was just down to timing, and if he knew Noah, there would be a lot of time yammering. What both of them really wanted was to get naked with each other. He knew Noah was adamant about no sex until he knew they would be forever.

He never understood it. Since it came up first when they were running the streets he figured it was from the dark days. He thought Noah was past due to lose his virginity, but Noah had asked for help. Well, he figured he was helping them by moving the ball faster. And sometimes friends do things to other friends without asking, like the daze. A good experience and one he was grateful to have had. So, didn't it stand to reason that he owed Noah an equally life-changing experience? Yes. "Never mind, I have an idea as to what it is. You just need to go over the plan; I'm in."

Fin stopped and stared. "Uhmm...Right friend of Toby. I should've known. What was I thinking? You have to have a very agile mind to keep up with him." Fin started walking again. "Okay, we get them really hammered and leave them alone, let nature take its course. Amethyst said we have to figure a way so he can't leave. She suggested Jillian's place, but I don't know how we can stop him from leaving." Fin opened the side door of the van

Stevens stowed the plastic crate and turned to face him. "That is a problem. If he doesn't want to stay, he can't be kept." Stevens thought about all the angles. "I can only see one way to get him to stay in that as if Jillian asked it. So my advice is to work on going to Jillian and get her to ask him to stay. Ask him to take her home, and she asks him to stay and see if nature is stronger. He has an amazing strength of will. But we know nature's pretty durable and can't be subdued. If we don't get lucky, excuse me, if they don't get lucky then we work on a subtle campaign."

"Okay, we definitely don't want to be obvious but throw them together as often as possible where things can escalate without prying eyes. I'm guessing when they blow, it's going to rock the county. Did you see them at the table? Toby wouldn't let go of Jillian. I wonder what she said to get him to release her. It was definitely shocking. I know that one, the other expressions all jumbled together and I was confused." Fin walked beside Stevens as they headed back to the pub.

Stevens laughed. "That was quite the display of emotion, wasn't it? I'll try to figure them out and get back to you. I wonder what she said. She keeps amazing me."

"I've been getting stories of Amethyst and Jillian since we were in high school. We were in the same grade, not the same school, town, county, state, or even country." Fin laughed and opened the door. "O'Malley would call weekly, and the highlight of each call was the adventures of Ame and Jilli. At first, I thought O'Malley was making it all up, then one of the girls made the paper, and they were photographed together. He sent it to me. And then I knew I had to come and meet them and finally I have and they don't disappoint. This day is one for the books. I can't wait to read all the different accounts." He laughed. "I'll tell you a secret not many know." He looked around.

"What?" Stevens smiled. He liked Fin

"I recorded the day. I have cameras planted all over the place, so I would get every angle. I told Jillian earlier in the day, Friday afternoon, that I would explain why everybody reacted the way they did during her confrontation with Jackson. I was going to play it after the fight, but well, we were all dazed and then things got hairy. So, that's what I was going to show you: Toby in the fight, Jillian the Tigris, and Philip and the ping-pong problem. Just thinking about all that footage…I can't wait to see it all."

Stevens stared in shock. "You filmed it all?"

Fin laughed. "Yes, full sound too. We have parabolic speakers and microphones. That song, holy bat wings… Oh, when the dazed attack Toby…Oooh, the gymnastics." Fin's eyes glazed over at the treasury he had.

337

"I would love to see it, but I don't know if Toby will thank you if this gets out to the public," Stephen says carefully.

"What do you mean?" Tin focused on Stevens.

"I don't know if Toby would enjoy the notoriety, and the dazing is his fault. He knows it was him and doesn't like it. What if the power the dazed everyone projects through the camera? You could easily daze the nation if what you're saying is as good as you think."

"I didn't think about that. Toby would call that his fault, too." Fin frowned. "He's very responsible."

Stevens laughed. "You have no idea how responsible you are, so have fun editing your film. Tell O'Malley so that when you're working on it and become dazed, he knows to get Toby." He rubbed his neck. "You may want to let Toby know you have this. He might want to see it; he might want no one to see it." He rubbed his head. "It's your film, your footage, he'll recognize that, but a lot of the footage is Toby doing amazing things. It's your call, but I would rather be upfront with Toby than groveling because you didn't. Do you understand what I'm trying to tell you?"

"Yeah, tell Toby first before even watching any." Fin sighs deeply. "Yes, wise counsel. I'm glad I said something. My excitement was leading down a selfish path." Fin nodded. "Maybe only the oddities could watch it since we all participated," Fin said hopefully.

Stevens chuckled. "Tell him tonight. If he says yes, you can jump right in. If he says no, beg and plead for the oddities. That's how I play it."

"Thank you, man. You want to see it real bad, don't you?"

"Oh, yes, I would love to see the fight and, well, all of it." Stephen nodded and smiled. "If he says absolutely no, beg for private viewing for a very selected few. I better be one."

"I'll see what I can do," Fin says dryly.

"Good, see that you do." He slapped Fin's shoulder.

Fin stumbled ahead a couple of steps. "Careful, big guy. Damage me, you won't see anything." Fin laughed.

"Is it my fault you're like dandelion fluff? I barely touched you."

"Dandelion fluff?" Fin laughed. "Girl Friday." He shook his head. "I think I need to work on my image." Then laughed. "But my confidence is rock solid."

"Good. At least you have a strong mind." Stevens laughed and patted Finn on the head. "There's hope for you yet."

"I'm glad you see it. Maybe you could polish me up some and make me shine." Fin turned towards the room and saw that everyone was moving their way. "It's time. Get the other door, would you?"

They turned back to the door.

Fin steppe through holding one open.

Stevens quickly unlocked the other door and held it open wide for the entire procession of oddities led by Phillip. The next were the four hands moving Wesley and Rick, who were head-to-head, wires stretching between them. Following next to each radio announcer were their female attendants, and finally, Toby with O'Malley at his side.

In their wake, the entire pub full of oddities followed to see off their two fellows of the doll daze. The only two didn't make it completely back. The mood was hopeful, encouraging, and positive. These people knew that they would return to them restored. Their faith was absolute.

The head of the procession reached the back of the van. Phillip opened the doors wide and stepped aside. The hands activated the mechanism to lower their charges, then carefully, with two on each, lifted the man and slid them into the channels installed on the inner walls of the van.

Once in place, the hands dropped large cotter pins in all four channels to contain the board snugly.

Toby hopped up on the back of the van and leaned over each man to look into their eyes.

Philip had started the van and turned on the radio loud so everyone could hear.

Toby squeezed Wesley's shoulder. "Work hard, keep in touch. If you need me, tell your listeners to get a message to O'Malley or tell the hands. I'll be by to visit, look for me. Dr. Robinson will be your physician. He'll fully understand what's going on and the only one to trust. Please give your support to Dr. Ingrid, but if you have misgivings, stick to your position. You may refuse treatment if you don't think it's to your benefit. Remember, you're not alone, all of the rest of us are here rooting you on. If you need anything, just ask. You aren't in a position to make do." He squeezed his shoulders, rubbing down his arms. "Safe travel."

He hopped down and leaned over Rick, took his shoulders and squeezed. "I'm sure you heard all that. But I want to stress to you both that we are in unchartered waters. There are no guarantees in life but infinite possibilities. You choose what to believe; if you believe you will have a full recovery, then the way will be shown how to get there. We believe you will. Make sure both of you do also. I'm sure the oddities will be by to visit. Make the best of your time and share your experiences with everyone. They do not have a clear understanding of the mind or the void beyond. You two are in an exciting position to alter the minds of science through your experience. Be wise, happy, and positive." Toby squeezed Rick's shoulders again and rubbed down his arms. "Safe travel." Toby stepped away.

Dr. Ingrid stepped over to Toby. "Thank you, Toby, for everything." She held out her hand.

Toby shook it.

"I'll take good care of them. I now understand how much they mean to everyone." She looked over at the crowd arcing on the sidewalk. "I understand so much more now and will be thinking a lot. You have done something amazing for me. You saw the tormented little girl and helped her realize she was valiant and worthy. That shift in perspective has made a world of difference in just a short time since it happened. Since there isn't the time or the words, I'll just say again, thank you." She reached out and hugged him.

Noah was touched.

Toby wrapped his arms around her and hugged her back. "You're welcome, but there is no need. I know you are bursting with goodwill. Spend it on those in need. I just extended a hand to you when you needed it. When you see someone going under, extend that valiant, worthy hand, and you will understand no thanks are necessary." He stepped back and bowed formally. "It was a pleasure, Lady Ingrid. Safe travels on your journey. We will be in touch, just because distance separates us does not mean the hand has retracted." Toby stepped up on the sidewalk.

Dr. Ingrid nodded, waved and climbed into her own extended van and took the lead, pulling away.

The hands climbed into the van.

From the radio, they heard Wesley and Rick.

"Thank you, the oddities of South County. We may be on location, but our hearts stay with you." Wesley says cheerily.

Rick broke in. "We decided to take calls from our fans in a regular time slot. We will let you know tomorrow after we are settled when those timeslots will occur."

Wesley stepped in smoothly. "We give special thanks to our super geek, Toby "The Dazer" Robins and his flock of angels."

"You noticed that too? Every one of them was beautiful in their distinctive way."

"Yes, but their true beauty came from the hearts and minds, and all shined bright."

"Only fitting since The Dazer shined brighter than all. We'll be seeing you, Toby. Keep the oddities safe."

Toby called. "Get going, and they can continue without you waiting. Call when you get there." He slapped the van twice. "Bye, boys, don't get too crazy."

Rick and Wesley laughed, and said together. "On location is supposed to be crazy."

The oddities cheered them from the sidewalk, whistling, whooping, screaming, and yelling.

The hand behind the wheel honked twice and pulled away.

The oddities lingered on the sidewalk, chatting and mingling.

Toby turned to O'Malley. "I believe I need a drink and relax. The last serious hurdle of the night has been cleared."

O'Malley slapped Toby on the shoulder. "You did good, lad, real good. I'm proud to know you."

"Thanks for that. It's been a challenging night. I wish it could have got them back, too."

"We all do, lad. Take heart, one man brought out almost 200, and two partials with a way to communicate with us. 95.5% recovery is respectable, lad, and that .5% is on the road to recovery. In time, you will have your hundred percent. Have faith and patience. Same as you told those lads. It's in the heart of belief. The way will be shown." He nudged him towards the door. "Let's get you that drink."

"O'Malley, you and Fin are very similar. You both say exactly what I need to hear."

O'Malley chuckled. "Of course, lad, we come from a long line of pub owners. Bar psychology is used more and wiser. No hang-ups here. We get to call it as it is: the harsh truths. More impact for being harsh, we get better feedback too."

Toby laughed. "You shoot from the hip and watch them fall. That's why I like you both so much. No airs, you're you, I'm me; just the same, but unique in our own ways."

"You get it, lad, could tell right away."

They made it through the door and paused in the empty pub.

O'Malley shook his head. "This is going to be a doozy of an entry in the book. I already have a stack of accounts."

"At a later time, I would love to read your book. I find the entire practice impressive especially the effect on the citizenry. South County is one of a kind. No better place exists the planet-wide."

"I'm glad you recognize it, lad. We welcome you home." O'Malley stepped behind the bar, pulled a bottle off the top shelf, and lined glasses on the bar. As he placed the glasses, the intended appeared.

Toby got the first glass. To his left, Stevens stepped up. On his right, Fin. Next to Stevens, Jillian stood. Next to Fin, Amethyst. Philip was next to her, and on his other side, Zach stood. Dr. Paulson stepped up next to Jillian with Charles beside him. O'Malley placed the last glass in front of himself. Carefully, he poured two fingers into each glass. When he was done, he set the bottle aside and raised his glass. "To The Dazer and his flock of angels." He raised his glass.

The crowd of oddities had silently followed them in. On hearing the toast, they roared their approval, all hands raised with or without a drink.

O'Malley drank and slammed it to the bar.

Dazer and his angels followed as one, and the concussion of glass on wood exploded in the pub, sealing the moment.

Noah felt a tingling and shivering engulf his body. He gasped in surprise, as did everyone else. It had a magical feel, a bonding of great power It left behind sweet pleasure.

A series of flashing lights came from behind O'Malley.

O'Malley poured out another drink in the line of glasses. He raised his. "To choices." Then he drank and slammed his glass down. "I'm glad you made the ones you did."

Noah lifted his glass and drank, slamming it down.

Perfectly timed, each pair successively repeated his action. Hammering along, they impress the importance of the toast choices.

The sound echoed in and around the pub, being caught up in the sound system and mic, repeating back into itself. The highlighted choices were unending, circling back so you can choose again.

The experience left Noah a little lightheaded. He shook his head to clear it, then blinked at a smiling O'Malley.

O'Malley placed a new bottle on the bar in front of Toby. "Here, drink this with your flock before you go." He turned away to the crowd.

Toby picked up his glass and bottle turning to the room to see tables had been pushed together to seat nine.

A man stepped up behind the chair at the head and pulled it out for him. He sat and saw the others were treated with the same courtesy. He opened the bottle, poured two fingers exactly, and passed the bottle to his left. It went around the table to return to his right hand. He raised his glass. "To the flock of angels." He drank and slammed his glass on the table.

The other eight at the table responded as one copying his actions.

The tables vibrated from the combined assault.

Toby poured it again and passed it on. When the bottle returned, he raised his glass. "To the Oddities of South County." He drank and slammed his heavy tumbler down at the same time as his angels. The tables quivered like they were wire strummed.

Toby poured more and passed it on. He raised his glass when the empty bottle arrived back to him. He looked at every face with a glass held up, all equal. "To love of life." Toby tossed it back and slammed his glass on the table.

They all moved as one.

The vibrations of the table increased.

Everyone picked up the glass at the same time, just as the tables turned to fiber. Laps, legs, and feet were covered with wood debris.

Shocked silence echoed around the room.

Toby looked up to all eyes on him. "It wasn't me." He said defensively and pointed. "It was the Angels."

Everyone in the pub exploded with laughter.

Noah shook his head. Unreal! How is this possible? He looked over the shocked faces of his flock. He snorted, leaned over and picked up the unbroken bottle. He stood; wood fiber and dust cascaded down to the floor. He tapped each toe to the floor, knocking off the majority. Shrugged and walked to the bar. "O'Malley, you have a most unusual establishment." He placed the bottle on the bar more sharply than he intended, and it imploded to a pile of sand on the bar. "Okay, that was me." He turned and walked to the booth and slid in picking up a bottle and pouring out a glass to the top. He knocked it back and refilled it.

Jillian giggled, stood and walked over. Wood fiber and dust clouded out at each step. She slid in next to him and took his hand. She accepted the glass he filled, placing the one in her hand on the table. He filled one for himself and tapped it to hers carefully. They drank and slammed down defiantly.

The boom released the rest of the people in the room, who then howled with laughter.

Noah snorted, then great deep belly laughs.

Jillian joined in with a melodious counterpoint. Their laughter was so charming that the rest of the angels joined in and moved to the booth. The clouds of dust and wood fiber mark their passage. Stevens slipped in next to Jillian, with Phillip, Amethyst, and Fin sliding in the other. Charles and Zach brought another table with chairs upside down on top. They butted up to the booth table and took their seat. The doctor was the last to arrive with another bottle and his glass and took his place at the head. "Well, that was something." He observed and set off another round of laughter.

Stevens recovered first and asked. "So, do these kinds of things happen around here often?"

That set the locals off.

Noah, Stevens, and Fin looked at each other.

Fin smiled. "From what little I've heard, this is not a sedate little town."

Stevens gaped at him. "So weird stuff like tonight happens here all the time?"

Toby snorted. "Not to this extreme, would be my guess."

Stevens looked at Toby. "But the fact that it happens is in question, not to what extent."

Gasping, Amethyst held up her hand. "Nothing like that has ever happened in the living memory of South County." She pointed to the nine chairs sitting around wood fiber and dust. "That is way outside our reality. But remember, you convinced us all that possibilities are limitless." She snorted. "The look on your face was priceless, Toby, more so when you brought O'Malley the bottle."

Phillip coughed. "He was so nonchalant, picked up the bottle, tapped his toes, walked over with clouds of dust trailing, and slammed the bottle down, and it turned to dust. Maybe we should call Toby "The Duster.""

Everyone chuckled.

Toby shook his head. "This has been the weirdest night of my life. Are you sure that South County isn't really named Twilight?"

Fin laughed. "It would fit."

"It used to be called something else," Jillian said carefully. She tucked her chin, picked up her glass and drank. She looked at everyone at the table, waiting expectantly.

Stevens clears his throat. "What was it called?"

"Dusk." She said matter-of-factly.

"No way!" Charles and Zach said together, aghast.

"Didn't you tell me that a few years ago?" Amethyst looked off thoughtfully.

"Wait, that sign in the square. It says Dusk was founded in 1623."

Fin stared. "It's true?"

Jillian looked at him, offended. "I wouldn't lie."

"Not lie, play a joke, which I know you and Amethyst love doing," Fin said, amused.

"No, it's true. The name was changed in..." She looked up thoughtfully. "... 19... 26..." She looks at everyone. "I think the date is right, but I will confirm."

Noah looked over Jillian's head and at Stevens. "Well, it looks like I brought you to not the Twilight Zone but the Dusk Zone. No longer will your life be dull and predictable. Welcome."

"I've only changed for the better since arriving." Stevens laughed, unable to hide his smile.

Dr. Paulson chuckled, watching Stevens smile. "Now we'll have angels walking the streets and flesh-eating zombies ensconced in the hospital."

Everyone laughed.

"Angels and zombies in the same town, very dusky." Fin laughed. "I could make a fortune from the film."

"What?" Everyone said, except Stevens and Toby.

Fin looked at a still Toby. "You see, I placed cameras all around the bar Friday morning. I have a passion for it, went to film school, graduated with top marks. So I thought I might make a documentary in my free time. I thought about all the interesting interactions people had in a pub, different than a bar, because it's more a family. I got O'Malley's okay and had to get everyone's permission if they ended up in the documentary.

I was overjoyed at the possibilities for a day in the life of a small town pub. By late morning I thought I hit gold with Jillian and Amethyst coming in so early, then their appearance later with the new tigress dress and Jackson. When you walked in with Jillian draped over your arms, I just about passed out. As the night progressed and the lively crowd performed beautifully, I thought I was in film heaven. Then Jackson approached Jillian, and you stepped in. I thought good continuity. Then the fight, action, flesh-eating zombie, comedy; I was going to have it all." Fin's eyes glazed over for a moment. "All I could see in my mind was an amazing film based on the amazing night. My first night here was like a reflection of the future. Then I talked to Stevens to remind him about our phone conversation and my promise to show him something amazing. I told him about the cameras and the footage. He brought me the reason I had left behind in my excitement. So here I sit in front of The Dazer and his flock of angels. What should be done with the recordings?" Fin picked up his glass and drank deeply, remaining silent.

Noah was floored, knocked out, and laid on the floor. He shook his head. "Of course." And snorted and burst out laughing.

Every face was that of shock. They, too, melted to amusement, laughing at the insanity of it all.

347

Stevens chuckled. "I, for one, want to see what Fin would do with it. But what do you do after viewing isn't my call so much as others."

Phillip cleared his throat. "I guess everyone would like to see it, but since the flock of angels is in support of The Dazer, may we hear what your opinion is on the matter of the creation and first viewing. We should table all else for later."

Dr. Paulson nodded. "Level-headed thinking, Phillip. Focus on the two important pivotal topics, leaving the rest pending."

Noah looked at each face focused on him.

Everyone looked hopeful.

Fin sat with his head bowed waiting; he had made his case now he waited for the decision, respectfully leaving the choice Noah's to make first.

He had mixed feelings about the documentary since he played a major role. But it wasn't his project. It was Fin's. He wouldn't allow another to dictate to him about a project, though the end product would be a different matter. How would he know without a viewing? Since all other possibilities for the Film are pending, the only choices to make are if Fin edits the footage and if a viewing. He could view both. He nodded and made. "Yes, and yes." He watched Fin's head pop up, a huge smile on his face. "Let me warn you, if the daze comes through, we can't allow that. Let someone know when you work on it to check on you. But as to working with the footage to shape it, that is your call, your project. I would never allow anyone to tell me what I could or couldn't do. That you ask my opinion shows what a great man you are. You honor me, my friend. That my opinion matters to you warms my heart. You're a very fine man, Fin." He raised his glass to Fin, and the others followed in tribute. Fin picked up his glass, and they all drank without slamming the table. All glasses hung an inch from the tabletop.

They all laughed.

Toby looked around the table. "As to the viewing, provided Fin doesn't daze out, I think it should be O'Malley, me, and the flock.

After, we should vote on viewings for oddities, South County residents, county, state, and nation. I can already tell you my feelings range from yes, of course, to hell no, consecutively. I think South County residents who were not present may need a visual aid explaining the happenings here tonight. I am neutral on County viewing because it was all broadcast throughout the countryside, so pictures to go with the events on the radio may clarify and possibly ease some War of the World panic. As to the state, I lean to no, no need to bait the bear. If you toss out a film at these events, every vulture and snake will defile the streets of South County. The nation will be considerably worse, beyond all understanding." Toby picked up his glass and took a sip. "I guess what I'm saying is I look forward to experiencing your work, Fin."

"Oh, God." Fin closed his eyes to contain his joy.

Stevens held up his glass. "Here's to a day in the life of the pub O'Malley's: The Dazer and the Flock of Angels."

Every glass rose.

Fin opened his eyes and looked around, a huge smile on his face and raised his glass.

As one they drank slammed them on the table defiantly.

The oddities cheered.

Everyone at their table laughed and simultaneously said, "O'Malley." They all knew the parabolic mic was directed at their table.

Noah shook his head, repressing a smile. "O'Malley certainly knows his audience. If I didn't know better, I'd say today was orchestrated by the man himself. His reign in this kingdom will always be known, especially if a movie is made. You'll have your work cut out for you, Fin, to top this."

Fin laughed. "What do you mean? This is the beginning of mine. It's my first night here, my movie. I think I'm starting off with a bang."

Everyone laughed.

349

Dr. Paulson stood. "Well, Angels, Dazer, I'm beat. I need to get to my bed. I've had all the excitement and weirdness I can handle in one year, let alone in a day. It was my pleasure meeting and working with you. I look forward to the movie Fin. And if anyone needs a doctor, give me a call. Until next time, good night."

"Good night, Dr. Paulson, we'll see you later." Toby smiled at the man.

Everyone said their parting words, and the doctor left

Phillip nodded. "I should head out, too. I am exhausted and drunk. Luckily, I don't live far. The walk will do me good." He nudged Amethyst.

Amethyst nodded and poked Fin.

Fin smiled. "It looks like this party is breaking up." He rose to his feet. "Later, my friends, I'm off to review footage." He walked off distracted, his mind already piecing together the basic storyboard.

Charles and Zach stood. "Were off, too. We have a shift tomorrow evening. Stay out of trouble, but if trouble finds you, we may show up." They laughed and waved, walking off.

Noah looked out at the pub. It seemed everyone was ready to call it a night, and people were streaming out. Noah sighed. The end was near.

Amethyst slid along the bench and rose. "Irving, would you walk me home? I live in the opposite direction of Jillian. That way, we can get better acquainted since we'll be chaperoning those two tomorrow." She weaved on her feet and grabbed the table. "Wow, standing puts a spin on things." She laughed.

Stevens chuckled at her wink at him. "Where Is Your Place, Toby?" He asked, climbing to his feet.

"Two blocks north on Main, turn west two blocks, Havens Hollow apartment 123." He dug in his pocket, pulled out his keys and tossed them to him. "Let yourself in, you remember. No need for you to wait outside. Make yourself at home." He looked down at

Jillian, resting her head against his shoulder, half-asleep. "I'll see Jillian home." He said softly.

"Okay, works for me." Stevens drains his glass and extends his arm for Amethyst. "You may want to hold on." He winked at her.

She laughs. "Good idea. We need to stop by the bar and get my purse." She looks over her shoulder at Jillian and then Toby. "Her purse is with O'Malley. You'll need to get it to get her in and to bed when she's like that. She needs help. You should get her in bed." She snickers and weaves out of the bar with Stevens.

Stevens whispers into her ear. "Really? Not subtle at all." He chuckled.

Sounding more sober, she whispers back. "Just planting ideas, all true, I might add. She's very difficult when she's reached this stage. Normally, with me, it's; "don't go," "help me," "I don't feel so well," "rub my tummy." She snickers.

Stevens laughed. Noah was doomed. "What a mind you have."

"Me?" She chuckled. "You said the only way he would stay was if Jillian asked. She'll be asking. He'll be staying. Job done. We'll see who's stronger, nature or Toby." She looked pleased. She turned to O'Malley at the bar. "O'Malley, may I have my purse, please? Let's settle the tab tomorrow. My head is swimming." She smiled sweetly at him.

"No problem, lass." He reached under the bar, pulled out Amethyst's purse, and put it on the bar. "We'll be seeing you tomorrow. Get some sleep, lass. If you need the remedy, stop by, opening at 10 AM as usual."

On the bar to the left of them was a pile of glass dust with the labels still standing, covered by a glass cake cover.

Stevens laughed. "Are you going to sell tickets?" He nodded at the pile and on the bar.

O'Malley laughed. "Not a bad idea, maybe a cover charge for those not odd." He rubbed between his eyes. "Easy enough to tell."

Amethyst and Stevens rubbed their purple bruise compulsively.

351

That set off a chain reaction with the remaining odd. Just the motion triggered the others to mirror the move, rubbing the deep burgundy bruise that spotted them all between the eyes, which now started to darken.

"Jillian will be leaving soon. Make sure her purse goes with her." Amethyst snickered

O'Malley chuckled. "Giving nature a hand, are you?"

"Can't hurt, the way I see it." Amethyst reached over and squeezed O'Malley's hand. "Another memorable night at O'Malley's."

"More so than others. Night, lass. Keep her safe, Stevens. Good meeting you, lad."

Stevens held out his hand. "Good to meet you too, O'Malley. She'll stay safe. Good night, sir." He turned Amethyst to the door. He noticed only a couple dozen people remained, most of whom were preparing to leave. He glanced back at Noah and Jillian.

Toby's head was tipped back on the padded bench, his eyes snapped open, and he raised his head in parting.

Stevens turned back, raised his hand, and opened the door for a tipsy Amethyst. "Point the way."

She laughed and pointed down the street, "That way."

They turned and walked off.

Noah sighed, watching Stevens walk off with Amethyst out the door. He was beat, bone weary. But he had to get Jillian home first. He leaned down and bumped his shoulder. "Jillian, let's get you home."

No response.

"Jillian." He was never going to leave if he waited for her to wake up. He slid them both along the bench. When she was at the very end, he pushed the table away. It cleared enough room for him to squeeze by and clear the booth while holding Jillian up. He turned her on the bench, turned his back to her, crouched, took her arms over his shoulders and stood. He leaned forward and jounced her up

352

his back for a better position. He reached back with both arms, clasping his wrists to form a seat.

She draped him limply but mumbled in his ear, her lips brushing his neck. Her arms came to life and encircled his neck loosely. Her face nuzzled his neck.

He sighed, straightened some, and went on to the bar. "O'Malley, could you tell me where Jillian lives so I can take her home?"

O'Malley chuckled. "Sure, lad. It's not difficult. Out the door, take a right go to the traffic light, right one block, a left, then follow it until you get to the only three-story house on the right. Hers is the next one across the street on the corner. A little white house with green and beige trim. A classy look to it. Nice lawn and garden with a few excellent trees. You can't miss it." He put Jillian's little purse on the bar. It was black with red trim.

Toby leaned forward and shifted his hip, exposing his back pocket. He let go of Jillian and pulled out his wallet. He extracted a card and handed it to O'Malley. "I'll leave this with you now. Put the lady's tab on it as well as mine and the rest of the Angels, add any property damage you see fit and a gratuity of 25% I know the costs, O'Malley. Do it right, no skimping. I will be disappointed if it's a small number. That's to cover The Dazer and his flock. I know I alone put a huge dent in your food stores. So please, money, I have plenty of, goodwill of others is more important, yours specifically. I did damage here." He chuckled, shaking his head. "Your inventory of furniture is seriously depleted."

O'Malley laughed. "Alright, lad, don't get worked up. If it will make you happy, I'll even add a cleaning crew and carpenter."

Toby laughed. "Yes, it would. I happen to know a carpenter. Would you like me to send him? He's reasonably good." He was having a hard time holding in his laughter. Charge Toby for the repairs done by Lars, all of him. It was one way to move money. Crazy here in Dusk. He repressed a laugh.

"Send him by; I would be happy to put him to work. There's a few other things that need to be done that I won't charge you for." O'Malley looked adamant.

Toby put his wallet away. "I won't fight you on that." Chuckled and readjusted Jillian.

She hummed in his ear.

"Good night, O'Malley. I'll stop by later for the card."

"Night, lad." O'Malley opened the register, pulled up the cash tray, and dropped in Toby's credit card.

Toby turned to the door.

The last customers leaving, they held the door for Toby with well wishes.

He nodded and headed down the street following O'Malley's directions and realized that the three story was the one he worked on and ran into Jillian. He approached it on the sidewalk. It was a great house, if a little rough. When he saw it, he decided to work on it while in town. He bought it on the second day in the area with cash. It was a bargain. It had sat idle for many years; it had some problems, but for the most part, it had good bones and a great skeleton. There is some water damage from a leaky roof, but nothing too extensive. He called a good roofing firm to redo it entirely. They had started on that next Monday.

He passed his new house and walked across the street. How crazy was this? He was neighbors with his intended, literally the girl next door. Noah chuckled normally.

Jillian stirred. "Noah." She said softly.

He almost dropped her. Her saying his name so naturally made him weak in the knees. In his natural, deep, rich voice, he said, "Yes, Jillian."

She hugged him. "When do I get to see you, Noah?"

"Soon," Noah said confidently.

"Will you tell me something about Toby and the others?" She asked curiously, without pressure.

"Yes, I will tell you everything." He said forcefully.

"That's nice. You know, I've not officially met Noah, but I love him." She said simply in earnest. No games, no competition, nothing with but truth.

He stopped in his tracks. "He hasn't officially met you either, but he loves you too." He whispered roughly. "I love you." He pulled her around his body and held her close.

Her arms adjusted so she could hug him, chest to chest, heart to heart, which were both beating wildly.

Noah was a mass of emotions. He never thought he would find anyone to love or that it would be returned. His voice, harsh with bottled emotion, whispered, "Thank you for this great gift." His voice caught. "I never believed it was possible for me. Oh, Jillian, is it real?" He asked worried.

Jillian heard the worry and desperate longing. She also heard the loneliness. It broke her heart that this amazing, confident man was still a lost, lonely boy who was afraid the love offered was really an illusion.

She slowly pulled her head back and framed his face in her hands, looking deeply into his eyes. "Yes, Noah, it is real love I feel for you, deep and abiding, from my heart to yours, forever and always. It is too new yet, to have confidence in it, so we will take the time you need. I need no time. I can feel your heart because it echoes mine. I recognize my superior mate in you. You can't change my mind; you may choose you don't want what I offer, but my heart, mind, and spirit are all united in loving you. My choice made; now or later, the choice is yours." She leaned in and kissed him gently, allowing all her heart's feelings to pass from her lips to his.

He groaned, clutching her tight, as a shower of warm, rich emotion flooded his senses. He felt like he was being drowned, clutching her and letting go to get a better grip. Grasping, he tried to contain the expanding emotions bursting within. "Oh, Jillian!" He whispered his heart's desire.

She leaned back and smiled. "Easy, Noah." She wiped the tears from his cheeks. She understood this man. These tears were his emotions that overflowed his system and ability to deal with not a breakdown of blubbering. Woe is me. She leaned in and held him, hugging him to her heart, somehow knowing instinctively that this was what he needed more than words. "Let's go in." She whispered.

Haltingly, he moved them to her door. He turned the knob and pushed a slight resistance, and her door opened. He stepped in and closed it behind him.

She was about to tell him her key was in her purse. "Noah, my door was locked." She giggled.

He stopped, turned and looked at her closed door. Her door jam and molding hung shattered around her door. "Oh, why do you bother?"

She giggled, hugging him tight. "You will fix that."

He chuckled. "Yes, of course, I did that."

She giggled harder. "Yes, you did." She brushed her fingers through his sable hair. "Go straight up the stairs and straight to the door at the top on the landing." She poked him in the side. "Go."

He didn't react except to walk down the dark hallway, up the stairs, through the door at the top. They stepped into her large bedroom, and he stopped in his tracks, suddenly unsure.

"Walk to the bed and sit." She commanded.

"Jillian, I don't think that's a very good idea." He stared at the inviting cloud of comfort longingly.

"Did I ask for your opinion, Noah?" She asked sweetly.

"Freely given." He croaked. "Seriously, Jillian, I think it a very bad idea for me even being in your bedroom." He clutched her tight to his chest as if the floor was going to collapse.

"Yes, I did understand that." She smiled. He was as timid as a virgin. She thought it amusing since she was a virgin. "Walk." She said, amused.

He took halting steps in case she changed her mind or hoped she would. He was completely unprepared for anything in a woman's bedroom unless it had to be repaired. That he could handle. He was at a loss. What would be okay to do? What wasn't he to do?

"Noah?" She asked carefully.

356

He was startled. He shook his head and croaked. "What?" He had to get a hold of himself. He fell half wild.

"Why is it a bad idea to sit on a bed with me?"

"Because I'm afraid." He whispered hoarsely.

She barely heard him, but she did hear the fear loud and clear. "What are you afraid of?" She whispered, stroking his hair soothingly.

"Everything." Softer still, he whispered hoarsely.

"Are you afraid because I love you?" She whispered.

"Yes, no, yes… No." Confused, he stopped halfway to the bed, quivering with great emotion.

"Noah, tell me. It will be all right, I promise." She whispered. "Would you feel more comfortable sitting on the sofa?"

"Yes." His relief was palpable, he spun on his heel and was downstairs before she could say anything. He found the living room, walked to the sofa, and sat with her in his lap. He was breathing heavily like he'd run for 20 miles. He sunk down on the sofa so his head rested on the back. He felt lightheaded and nauseous.

"Wow, you take my breath away and make my head spin." She laid her head on his shoulder, wrapping her arms around his chest.

He snorted in disgust. "Yeah, I know how you feel. I feel that way too."

"Really? You desire yourself as much as I desire you?" She asked innocently.

A surprised laugh escaped his lips. "Well, no." He took a deep breath and let it out, and felt a little better. "I do desire you a lot." He admitted softly.

"Was that part of the problem?" She asked just as softly, stroking his chest.

"Yes, part." He sighed. He needed to confess and see what happened. "I don't know what to do. I'm afraid I will hurt you." He clutched her closer, shutting his eyes.

357

"Why?" She stroked along his neck and down his chest.

"I'm feeling wild, unsettled, and out of control." He admitted gruffly. "Vulnerable." He whispered.

"Vulnerable?" She whispered gently. "Do you think something bad is going to happen?"

"If I hurt you, it would be very bad. That would hurt me." He whispered harshly. "I have to protect you, even from me."

"From you?" She asked doubtfully. "Do you normally hurt women?"

"No, never." He said adamantly. "They have to be protected."

"Then there's nothing to worry about." She said matter-of-factly. "I'm a woman, you know."

A surprised bark of laughter escaped him. "Yes, I know." He said dryly and sat up straight, looking down at her curled up in his lap. "But I want to do things I've never done with anyone else." He released his grip, on one hand, reached up, and cupped her cheek. Looking deep into her eyes, he whispered, "I want you with every cell of my body."

"Well, that's good." She stroked along his back and chest. "It's good to be wanted. But what do you want to do you've done with no one else?" She asked, confused.

He shook his head and chuckled. "Sex, Jillian. I've never had sex before." There it was out in the open.

She sat up, surprised. "Really? Me neither." She melted back against him. "I guess we're both in the same boat, getting tossed around on the raging sea of desire. I'm happy you're in my boat; it's not so lonely, and you can do all the rowing." She nodded. "Besides everything and all that, I haven't met Noah yet, and I'm not having sex with Toby the night I met him. So put those worries away until after three dates with Noah. Then you can worry. I'd be more worried that I'm going to hurt you." She snuggled closer into him, pushing him back to where he was. "I never claimed I wouldn't hurt a man."

Stunned, he fell back, holding her close. "Then what's with going up to your room?" He asked, confused and unsure.

"I wanted to sleep, and since that's where it normally happens, I thought it would be the best place to go." She kicked off her shoes and yawned. "But if you think you will be comfortable on the sofa…" She shrugged. "… Then the sofa it is. I'm comfortable where I am, and I'm sleeping here. I really haven't been getting good sleep for the last three weeks. Now with all that whiskey, it being so late, I'm surprised to be able to talk. So, kick off your shoes, stretch out and sleep with me." She faded to a mumble. "I love you, Noah. I also trust you." Then she dropped off into sleep.

Noah chuckled, looking down at her. She wanted him to do all the rowing. She was so accepting and confident in her choice. She was amazing. She accepted Toby saw the real man. She wanted him forever without knowing anything about him, except he pretended to be Toby and probably Lars and Jarvis.

She was firm in her decisions and beliefs. Not having sex on the first night. He chuckled, he wondered if she would like unwrapping the disguises to find Noah. Would she kiss any of them? She kissed Toby. What was he doing to her reputation? Nobody knew who he was. He shook his head. Now wasn't the time to worry about that.

He kicked off his shoes and climbed to his feet, holding Jillian in his arms. He straightened fully and felt wonderful. He carried Jillian straight back up the stairs and into her bedroom.

It smelled like her.

The large room was minimally filled, making it appear bigger. Her large bed dominated the longest wall; it had a long rectangular window stretching across the wall about shoulder height, and it was undressed. The view of treetops gave the feel of the house surrounded by woods. She had a lounger in the corner with a small table, lamp, and a book next to it. There were two dressers and a bench at the end of the bed.

The bed was a large, white, fluffy cloud. The frame was a four-poster wrought iron with sheer white drapes that glowed in the dim light pulled back and tied off with red courding. A swirling Squiggle crawled across the down comforter in a different shade of white from the white background. Plump white pillows piled haphazardly against the curved headboard, and at the foot of the bed draped a thick white fleece blanket.

Her bed was so inviting, just as she was: pure, soft, comforting, and inviting.

He walked over slowly. He was so tired; maybe he could just lie down with her for a few minutes. He would then get up and fix her door, then head for his apartment. He sat down and groaned, with one hand reaching for the throw to wrap around her.

On the bedside table, he placed his pocket protector, then emptied his pockets, juggling her around though she remained asleep. He pulled off his tie and unbuttoned the top three. He pulled off his uncomfortable belt and laid it with the tie and his pile of miscellaneous items Toby carried. He finally took Toby's magnifying glasses off. He wished he had the contact case to stop his eyes burning. They were extended wear contacts so just closing his eyes for a while would help relieve the burn.

Positioning Jillian in his arms, he shifted onto the bed, laid back and groaned. It was like you imagined as a kid what laying on those puffy clouds floating across the sky felt like. He sighed as his head sunk into the pillows. Slowly, his body released tense muscles, and he started feeling boneless.

Jillian shifted and stretched out on top of him, turning into her stomach, her head on his chest. Her blanket draped over him, her legs mingling with his. She mumbled and poked at his chest. After a minute, her hand explored for her discomfort. A button was digging into her cheek. She mumbled grumpily and unbuttoned the ones she found. She sighed when her cheek rested on his bare chest. Her arms stole into his shirt to wrap around his torso. She hugged him close and rubbed her cheek against his bare chest. Her lips kissed his heart and she smiled. She was happy he was with her, finally.

Noah was shocked. In her sleep Jillian had opened his shirt then burrowed in. They were flush, front to front. He was no longer boneless, now tense throughout his body. He worked at relaxing his muscles, one by one. He finally got himself to a floating relaxation, his arms wrapped around Jillian. He was content. Before he had another thought, he slipped into sleep, deep and still.

His dreams were peaceful and sweet, a rarity.

Made in the USA
Columbia, SC
22 July 2024